PENGUIN  CLASSICS

EFFI BRIEST

THEODOR FONTANE, born in Neuruppin in 1819, was descended from French Huguenot settlers in Brandenburg, and was brought up on the Baltic Sea coast of Prussia before spending most of his life in Berlin. He trained as a pharmacist but in 1849 decided to earn his living as a writer. He spent several years as a foreign correspondent in London and his prolific non-fiction output includes journalism, poetry, theatre reviews, local travelogues of Berlin's hinterland, unpartisan accounts of Bismarck's wars and two autobiographical works. He published his first novel, *Before the Storm* (1878), at the age of 58 and this was followed by sixteen further novels which established his reputation in the twentieth century as Germany's finest realist novelist. Fontane's sensitive portrayals of women's lives in late nineteenth-century society are unsurpassed in European literature. *The Woman taken in Adultery* (1882), *Cécile* (1886), *Delusions, Confusions* (1888), *Jenny Treibel* (1892) and *Effi Briest* (1895) focus on problems of love and marriage, while the late works *The Poggenpuhl Family* (1896) and *The Stechlin* (1898) provide humorous family portraits of Prussian society in decline. He died in 1898.

HUGH RORRISON was educated at Ayr Academy and the universities of Glasgow and Vienna. He has published extensively on modern German theatre. Among his translations are Wedekind's *Lulu Plays* (performed at the Almeida Theatre), Pavel Kohout's *Maple Tree Game* (West Yorkshire Playhouse), Heiner Müller's *Road to Volokolamsk* (BBC Radio 3), Brecht's *Berlin Stories* and *Journals 1934–55* and Piscator's *The Political Theatre*. He lives in Edinburgh and works freelance for radio.

HELEN CHAMBERS was educated at Hutchesons' Grammar School, Glasgow, and the University of Glasgow. She has taught at the universities of Leeds and Melbourne. Her publications include *Supernatural and Irrational Elements in the Works of Theodor Fontane* and *The Changing Image of Theodor Fontane*, and, as editor, a study of Joseph Roth. She is Professor of German at the University of St Andrews.

THEODOR FONTANE

Effi Briest

Translated from the German by
HUGH RORRISON and HELEN CHAMBERS

Introduction and notes by Helen Chambers

PENGUIN BOOKS

PENGUIN BOOKS

Published by the Penguin Group
Penguin Books Ltd, 80 Strand, London WC2R 0RL, England
Penguin Putnam Inc., 375 Hudson Street, New York, New York 10014, USA
Penguin Books Australia Ltd, 250 Camberwell Road, Camberwell, Victoria 3124, Australia
Penguin Books Canada Ltd, 10 Alcorn Avenue, Toronto, Ontario, Canada M4V 3B2
Penguin Books India (P) Ltd, 11 Community Centre, Panchsheel Park, New Delhi – 110 017, India
Penguin Books (NZ) Ltd, Cnr Rosedale and Airborne Roads, Albany, Auckland, New Zealand
Penguin Books (South Africa) (Pty) Ltd, 24 Sturdee Avenue, Rosebank 2196, South Africa

Penguin Books Ltd, Registered Offices: 80 Strand, London WC2R 0RL, England

www.penguin.com

This translation first published by Angel Books 1995
Published in Penguin Books 2000

10

Translation copyright © Hugh Rorrison and Helen Chambers, 1995
Introduction and notes copyright © Helen Chambers, 1995
All rights reserved

The moral right of the translators has been asserted

Printed in England by Clays Ltd, St Ives plc

ISBN-13: 978-0-140-44766-8

Contents

Introduction

Thomas Mann in 1919 said of *Effi Briest* that it belonged among the six most significant novels ever written.[1] By that time the Wilhelmine Empire evoked in Fontane's major novels had already become history, and it is Fontane's achievement to have captured that world on the eve of its dissolution. Its centre was Prussia, much maligned since, but dear to Fontane's heart, and he has left us, in the voices and lives of a representative few, his diagnosis of the aspirations and ills of a society whose unspectacular decline he saw with the disabused clarity of old age.[2]

When *Effi Briest* was published as a book in 1895, after being serialized in the *Deutsche Rundschau*, its seventy-five-year-old author experienced his first real literary success. Recognition had been slow in coming to the man who was later to be seen as the greatest German novelist between Goethe and Thomas Mann. The reasons were both personal and political. He was born in 1819 in Neuruppin, thirty miles north-west of Berlin, son of the pharmacist Louis Henri and his wife Emilie Fontane, both descendants of the French Huguenot community in Berlin. His most vivid childhood memories are of the Baltic port Swinemünde (today Świnoujście in Poland) where his father took over a chemist's shop when Fontane was seven. Swinemünde, a strange combination of stuffily provincial resort and cosmopolitan seaport, was the model for Kessin in *Effi Briest*. After haphazard schooling Fontane was apprenticed to his father's trade and qualified as a pharmacist in 1847. There was no capital to set him up in his own business. He decided in 1849 to become a writer and years of struggle followed.

Fontane was steeped in English literature, in particular Shakespeare, Scottish and English ballads, Scott and Thackeray, and his literary experience was quickened in 1844, 1852 and 1855-59 by visits to England and Scotland, on the last occasion as London press agent for the Prussian government. His work as foreign correspondent involved close scrutiny of *The Times* which became a source for many of his own pieces. He admired especially the polished style of the leaders which were, surprisingly for a German, devoid of any whiff of dry officialese. Charlotte Jolles sees his own sovereign and stylish prose as in part the product of those years of reading *The Times*.[3] The year of revolutions in Europe, 1848, saw him writing political polemics at home on the future of Prussia and Germany for the *Dresdner Zeitung*, some of them censored by the editor. He produced translations of Chartist poems, of *Hamlet* (c.1843), and of Catherine Gore's novel *The Moneylender* (c.1850), as well as an essay on the worker poet John Prince (1842). Fontane's experience of English life and literature was decisive. It focused his thoughts and feelings about his homeland. Victorian London was his first experience of a modern metropolis, and the seething centre of the Empire gave him a liberating sense of the wideness and diversity of the world, of infinite energy and possibilities, but at the same time he could see the power of history and tradition in Britain, which unlike politically fragmented Germany with its scores of sovereign states had no identity problems and could devote itself wholeheartedly to the serious business of making money.

Back in Berlin Fontane spent the next twenty years writing non-fiction for a living. Between 1862 and 1882 he published four volumes of local travelogues dealing with the towns and villages, the buildings and people, the history and anecdotes of Berlin's hinterland, *Rambles in Brandenburg* (*Wanderungen durch die Mark Brandenburg*). These were the years when Bismarck embarked on the wars that unified Germany and saw the King of Prussia proclaimed Kaiser of a new German Reich at Versailles in 1871, so at the same time Fontane found himself chronicling Bismarck's military campaigns, in books on the war in Schleswig-Holstein against Denmark, then the Austro-Prussian and Franco-Prussian wars. In 1870 he was appointed theatre critic on the liberal *Vossische Zeitung* for which he wrote regular notices for the next twenty years. He published volumes of ballads and poems in 1851, 1861 and 1875. All this was excellent preparation and made him better informed than any other writer of his time, but it left little time for fiction, and though he started his first novel, *Before the Storm (Vor dem Sturm)* in 1862, he took until 1878 to finish it. So it was at the age of fifty-eight that Fontane launched his career as a novelist with a historical narrative that views a community from multiple perspectives while Napoleon retreats from Russia somewhere offstage. He wrote sixteen more works of fiction before his death in 1898. *Before the Storm* was followed by a series of social and psychological novels, often subterraneously political, which put Berlin on the literary map for the first time. Of these *Delusions, Confusions (Irrungen, Wirrungen)*, *Cécile* and *Frau Jenny Treibel* stand out as close-ups of characteristic segments of Berlin life - not as genre-paintings in words but as portrayals of individual lives that point beyond themselves to wider truths about society and humanity.

In choosing plots for his novels Fontane preferred to start from fact. In this respect the genesis of *Effi Briest* is typical. Fontane described his novel as 'a story of adultery no different from a hundred others'.[4] He had heard of the scandal in 1888 or 1889 from a friend, and the lady involved, Elisabeth Baroness von Plotho, was still alive so he was understandably concerned that she might recognize herself when the novel appeared. Unlike Effi she survived to the age of ninety-nine, dying in 1952, having divorced her husband in 1887 and devoted herself to a career in nursing. Her husband Armand Léon von Ardenne was an officer and aristocrat from an estate near Rathenow. He was only five years older than her and frequented her parents' house. The seventeen-year-old Else, as she was known, was often prevailed upon to come indoors and listen to him playing the piano, and the detail of her red-haired playmates calling 'Else, come back' in the open window was, according to Fontane, decisive in his conception of the novel. After marrying Ardenne Else led a not uninteresting life and presided over a lively salon in Benrath Castle on the Rhine, where she met and fell in love with Emil Hartwich, an unhappily married district judge and amateur painter. In 1886 they planned to marry, but Ardenne forced open Else's box of letters from Hartwich, challenged his rival and killed him in a duel. The divorce went through the next year and in old age Else still wrote of Hartwich, the lost love of her youth, with vivid recollection and strong feeling. Ardenne was, in accordance with Prussian law, awarded custody of the children, spent a token period in prison for the illegal duel, but was soon pardoned by the Kaiser and pursued a distinguished military career, dying in 1919.

There are crucial differences, some of them surprising, between the facts of the case and Fontane's fictional treatment of them. The age gap between Effi and her husband becomes twenty-one years. In the social context of the novel this allows Innstetten to have achieved an elevated position in society, albeit at a relatively early age. As Landrat in Kessin he is a senior civil servant with responsibility for a large rural district and so requires a wife as fitting social appendage. Effi with her blue blood suits the job description admirably, and it takes no effort of imagination on Innstetten's part to find her. He simply returns to his home ground and seeks out the family of the sweetheart of his youth – Effi's mother. For her part Effi at seventeen is already so conditioned by the expectations of her social sphere that it never crosses her mind to object to this marriage of convenience which mirrors her own parents' union. In contrast to most English novels of the period money plays no part in the arrangement. The prerequisites are status and background.

There are psychological, sexual and political dimensions to the age difference too, and the mismatch between Effi and Innstetten is partly a function of the wide gap in their educational experience. Their relationship can be seen as symbolizing the conflict between nature and culture. Effi is associated from the outset with fresh air, plants and water, playing games in the garden. Her own associations with the classroom are of exotic tales of fallen women and other improper anecdotes from the geography lesson, and much later she tells her studious daughter that mythology was her favourite subject. This is all a world apart from her husband with his law degree, plodding pedantically through the churches and art galleries of Italy on their honeymoon and taking notes for conjugal culture sessions during the long winter evenings in Kessin. Major Crampas to whom, ironically, Effi turns in her anguished attempts to comprehend what she instinctively perceives as threatening in her marriage, deliberately undermines her loyalty to her husband by calling Innstetten a 'born pedagogue'. This contrast between them is a modified reprise of a motif in the earlier Berlin novels *Cécile* and *Delusions, Confusions*: Cécile in constant danger of making gaffes in cultivated company and Lene's spelling not passing muster. This is more than just a symptom of the couples' incompatibility, it is part of the sexual politics of relationships where the inexperienced child-wife is manipulated by her knowledgeable husband. Education was, and still is, a cardinal aspect of German cultural identity. The subtext of *Effi Briest* – and even more strikingly so in *Frau Jenny Treibel* – is subversive with regard to education. The narrative stance favours nature and questions culture – not in any extreme polarizing way, but it does urge a critical adjustment of currently cherished values. In this as in so many areas Fontane is drawing attention less to the 'what' than the 'how'. Education and culture are all very well, he is saying, if pursued with an appropriately human and flexible emphasis. They fail in their function if they become instruments of repression which eliminate freedom of thought and scope for imagination, instead of facilitating them.

The sexual dimensions to the age gap remain beneath the surface in this discreet and allusive novel. They are suggested, as is much that is vital in the inner action, by the symbolic texture of the narrative. Effi's sexual inexperience at the beginning of the novel is beyond question, and the premature loss of her virginity is prefigured by the twins calling her back to the garden through a window framed by Virginia creeper. The allusion becomes less subtle in English for the plant in German has two names. Fontane chooses '*wilder Wein*', literally 'wild wine' suggesting both freedom and Dionysian pleasures, but it is also known as '*Jungfernrebe*', 'virgin's vine' (after the botanical name *parthenozissus*) which adds a further layer of meaning to the scene. Effi's apprehension at her introduction to sexual relations is reflected by her unease at the strange, exotic creatures in the Kessin house: the stuffed shark and crocodile, and the Chinaman's ghost which is associated with problematic sexual experience.[5] Innstetten, however, perhaps because of his early exclusion from sexual fulfilment with Effi's mother, proves to be dysfunctional here. Through years of bachelorhood he has become accustomed to a variety of displacement activities. His career has first claim on his energies and his young wife is left with 'one or two tired if well-intended caresses' at the end of the day or, as she points out, on their way back from the dull round of duty visits to local gentry, he has constant recourse to his cigar and sits there beside her in the carriage 'frosty as a snowman'. It seems that after years of self-discipline and mortification of the flesh Innstetten has regulated his natural urges into a state of atrophy. That Effi then seeks sexual experience with another, admittedly also older, but not previously celibate man, is presented less as the fulfilment of overwhelming unsatisfied sexual desire than as the need for natural human warmth and freedom from the constraints of artificially acquired self-denial and rigour.

The political dimension to the age difference, like the sexual one, is less close to the surface than its more obvious social and psychological aspects. Throughout his life, which spanned the greater part of the nineteenth century, Fontane closely followed the political developments of the age. In March 1848 joining the radicals he briefly manned the Berlin barricades with a theatrical-prop musket. In 1860 he joined the editorial staff of the conservative 'Kreuzzeitung'. By the end of his life his attitude to Prussia and the Prussian establishment, always ambivalent, had become increasingly critical. The question of Fontane's shifting political position is currently a matter of perhaps over-zealous scrutiny by Fontane specialists. Christian Grawe's clear overview of his attitude to Prussia concludes, 'Prussianness thus represented to Fontane's contemporaries a mixture of militarism, Lutheranism, loyalty to state and king, order, ambition and obedience, the Kantian ethic of doing one's duty and Hegelian apotheosis of the state - a combination of elements which Fontane regarded highly critically and to which he attributes the essential reponsibility for Effi's destruction'.[6] By placing Effi and Innstetten in different generations Fontane is showing a society in the process of change, where the old, atrophying values have lost their ethical validity but are still in place to the extent that they can vitiate the life of the up-and-coming generation in a way that is fundamentally questioned by the narrative point of view. The age difference is at the heart of an undercurrent of political commentary which questions the hold of the old age over the new. Innstetten's final, impotent recognition of the hollowness of his establishment principles coupled with the dying out of his family name prefigures the inevitable demise of an antiquated social and political construct. Fontane agrees with Charlotte Brontë: 'conventionality is not morality'.[7]

The role of Bismarck on the periphery of the narrative – mentioned and visited but not seen – is a central aspect of Fontane's critique. It has even been suggested that the Chinaman's ghost, which in Fontane's celebrated and in terms of subsequent critical enquiry uniquely stimulating words is 'a pivot for the whole story', represents Bismarck.[8] Bismarck stands for much that threatens Effi and the literal dividing of the ways in Chapter 6: right to Kessin and domestic life, left to Varzin, Bismarck's residence and official duty, like all the geographical details in the novel has more than literal significance. However, it would be misleading simply to equate Innstetten with Bismarck and see him as the representative of Prussian orthodoxy. As with so much in Fontane's fictional world the opposite is also true. In his last, great novel *Der Stechlin* the aging Junker Dubslav von Stechlin says, 'There are no such things as incontrovertible truths, and if there are, they're boring.' This paradoxically self-invalidating statement encapsulates the quintessential Fontane: humorous, self-reflexive, distrustful of absolutes. He functionalizes Bismarck in a characteristically shifting set of constellations of characters, on the one hand – parallel to Innstetten – as the correlative of duty, absolute obedience, career-conscious striving, and also as inimical to women and family life for Effi is excluded from the invitations to Varzin; but also as parallel to Crampas, for Fontane saw and despised in Bismarck the opportunist who disregarded principle in favour of expediency, that is the opposite of Innstetten the 'stickler for principle', incidentally a label Fontane also applied disparagingly to Gladstone.

Fontane chose his title and the name of his heroine with care. In early drafts he called her Betty von Ottersund, making pointed reference to her elemental, aquatic affinities, but in the end he chose Effi Briest for its sound, 'because of all the "e's" and "i's"; those two are the fine vowels.'[9] Effi is not a common name in German and it has been speculated that he may, as a keen reader of Scott, have taken it from Effie Deans in *The Heart of Midlothian*. The echo of 'Eve' with implications of the fall from grace is surely intended too. Many of Fontane's characters' names are invested with symbolic overtones. Innstetten's first name 'Geert' not only means 'a tall slender stem' as old Briest remarks, but also a 'switch', an instrument of punishment and control. Innstetten is cast in the role of trainer and tamer of the spontaneous inclinations of his young wife. The titles of over a third of Fontane's novels are women's names, bearing out Ebba Rosenberg's dictum in *Beyond Recall* (*Unwiederbringlich*): 'Women's stories are usually far more interesting.' Of course Fontane is not alone among nineteenth-century novelists in choosing such titles, but the preponderance of women protagonists is striking, and a comparison with the often-invoked sister novels of adultery is instructive.[10]

Flaubert's title *Madame Bovary* suggests that the problem, the central concern is the marriage, the turning of Emma into the wife of someone whose bovine name proclaims his character. The marriage fails to satisfy her, but equally she fails to assert a separate valid identity as Emma. Tolstoy's *Anna Karenina* articulates the conflict inherent in the simultaneous existence of the private individual Anna, who experiences true love and passion, and the social role as Karenin's wife. *Effi Briest* is quite another matter. Effi's problem is that she cannot complete the socially required metamorphosis from Fräulein von Briest to Frau von Innstetten, for this would entail a denial of her self, her natural, playful exuberance, the self-confident magnetic personality we see in the games in the garden on the one hand, and on the other her risk-loving nature, her propensity to let herself be carried away, her desire for the out of the ordinary, her unpredictability. As her mother says, she is 'altogether a very odd mixture'. Ironically, although Innstetten is attracted by her natural, youthful charms it is precisely those sides of her that he then sets about stifling. That she remains Effi Briest at the end of the novel, a fact explicitly asserted by her instructions for the wording on her gravestone, is a sign that although she has succumbed physically in the draining conflict with the rigid forms of society she has managed to hold on to her own inner integrity, she has not lost her self. She has not been sacrificed like Anna to a grand passion. Her affair with Crampas was not a crucial emotional experience, it was merely a symptom of her need to preserve some area of freedom and spontaneity; nor has she been sacrificed like Emma to romantic notions and an egocentric personality. She has been sacrificed – and the motif of sacrifice runs through the narrative from the gooseberry skins' watery grave at the beginning to the sacrificial stones by Lake Hertha and beyond (Chapter 24) – to a set of conventions which Wüllersdorf and Innstetten recognize as empty: 'this cult of honour of ours is idolatry', without being able to extricate themselves from the power of 'that social something which tyrannizes us' (Chapter 27), but she has not relinquished her irreducible sense of her own independent identity. That she finds her way back to being Effi Briest – a unique, beautiful name free of its aristocratic 'von', its social indicator, in her chosen, natural setting in the garden of her youth is an assertion of a triumph of a kind. It is an ambiguous one, for she has not survived to grow into mature adulthood, but the fact of her death constitutes an accusation levelled at a society whose warped logic it has exposed.

This reading requires qualification to the extent that the assertion of Effi as herself at the end, only in death, equally implies that the individual cannot survive independent of a particular social and historical context. Even if society's values are wrong the only possible existence is social existence, and you either conform or go under. Going back to the garden – Hohen-Cremmen has frequently been seen as a paradise from which Effi is expelled – is not a viable option. On the other hand Innstetten's option is only viable in very reduced terms. The career to which he sacrifices Effi, Crampas, home life and happiness brings him no joy in the end for he comes to see the price he has paid for shoddy goods.

The central question of a theory of time-limits raised by Fontane's placing the discovery of the adultery at a remove of almost seven years from the act is a further aspect of the way in which he used an individual case as representative of wider social and political questions. That the loyal servant of the state should agonize over this matter of form and convention and decide in favour of a traditional code which demands the meaningless sacrifice of human beings and human values signals that the society portrayed is a society in decline. It is an age of transition and Fontane spotlights this transition and illuminates the unease, diagnoses the illness without being able to help the patient, except by the bracing and sympathetic clarity of his vision. The cult of honour, which derives from the military code, a male construct, is shown to lack moral foundation and be unequal to the dilemmas of real life in the social and domestic sphere, and indeed politically irrelevant too in the age of Bismarck's *Realpolitik*, where pragmatism and opportunism have determined the very shape of the contemporary state. The inflexibility of the code is radically at odds with 'the re-evaluation of all values' – to use a phrase from Fontane's contemporary Nietzsche – that was going on in Germany, above all in the young metropolis Berlin in the years of industrial expansion that followed unification.

The novel is set in the 1880s and Fontane was working on it during the first half of the '90s. He claims to have written it 'as in a dream and almost as if I were using a psychograph'.[11] In fact the birth of the novel was prolonged and difficult and this comment can only apply to the initial draft written in 1890. In 1892, the year in which he returned to it, Fontane suffered a severe physical and nervous breakdown from which he recoverd by following his doctor's advice and writing down memories of his childhood (*Meine Kinderjahre*, 1893). The main work of revising and correcting, always a laborious process for Fontane, took place in winter and spring 1893-94. Comparison of the final result with earlier versions reveals the extent to which the finished text is the product of constant refinement, reduction and paring away of redundant material.

Fontane's particular brand of realism with its subterranean dynamic, not unlike Jane Austen's, is based not on the naming or describing of an abundance of people and things. It works rather through glimpses and allusions. There is a strictly limited circle of characters whom we encounter in small groups. Large social occasions such as Effi's wedding tend to be referred back to. The most striking example of this deliberately oblique, retrospective technique is Fontane's treatment of Effi's adultery. Only when we read the letters over Innstetten's shoulder seven years after the event do we become sure that it actually took place, and we may then examine earlier chapters to find what we missed. Fontane was well aware of this aspect of his artistry. He wrote in a letter to Ernst Heilborn in 1895:

> I'm glad to see that you're in agreement with my leaving a lot to the reader's imagination; I would find it quite impossible to do otherwise, and for me complete obscurity would always be preferable to the gas-light illumination of certain things whose depiction, even if it's skilful (which is very seldom the case) still doesn't really work.[12]

Such deliberate avoidance of dramatic scenes is rare in nineteenth-century literature. When Fontane does portray significant occasions directly in the present of the novel, as is the case with Ring's New Year party and Annie's christening, then we are given access to a series of dialogues which expose attitudes and interrelationships, not decisive turning points in the development of the plot. They are reflective rather than active and the reality of the characters is created in terms of their discourse, of what they say, rather than what they do or how they look. Dress and external appearance have little role to play in creating an authentic sense of location and period. Such details as there are point to the underlying concerns of the novel. Effi's loose tunic at the beginning, authentic and realistic in the sense that in it Fontane replicated the dress and demeanour of a fifteen-year-old English girl he saw on a hotel balcony in the Harz, symbolizes her natural, childlike state, just as Johanna's corseted 'shapely bosom' in Chapter 35 is a detail used to epitomize the opposite: correct but artificial restraint and denial of natural impulse.

Fontane's narrative technique is very different from the leisurely, discursive style of many more familiar nineteenth-century English novelists. It is different in kind in its concentration and density of symbolic pattern and reference. In this respect it is closer in form and intention to the dominant genre of German realism, the Novelle, whose symbolism and taut structure Fontane reproduces in *Effi Briest*. The Novelle form has been defined as a circular line drawn around a central point, so that every detail refers back to that centre. This description fits *Effi Briest*, although readers cannot immediately see the connections, and it would spoil the cumulative effect if they could. They can nonetheless sense that the references are there to be unravelled in retrospect.

The connections take many forms. The light-hearted discussion of Crampas's death by drowning at the end of Chapter 15 is characteristic of Fontane's use of ironic patterning. The reader senses that in this conversation about death on a sunny day late in the year, with Crampas's prediction that he will die a proper and, he hopes, an honourable soldier's death, there is more going on than meets the ear. It is only later that we comprehend the full irony of this exchange; that it has been a central concern of the novel to show that what is 'proper and honourable' in this society, and perhaps in every society, is at best relative and at worst fatal. The opening paragraph of the novel too, typically for Fontane, is a classic example of the way in which his symbolic charging of the text is achieved unobtrusively before the reader's eyes, while its full impact can only be appreciated in the light of the narrative as a whole. When we put the book down at the end with the sense that what has happened had to happen, it is worth going back, to find the signs that pointed the way from the beginning, before the characters themselves ever appeared on the scene. Looking again at the opening, we can more readily pick up what is so clearly signalled in the Prussian manor-house: its social and historical place, the deceptive idyll which is a combination of nature and civilization, park and garden, the enclosed space with the boat moored in the pond suggesting but denying the possibility of escape, while the only real ways out are either into the house, or through the gate into the churchyard. Looking again at the rickety swing which at intervals in the novel allows Effi to experience danger and exhilaration, to fly in the air, we recognize it as a highly ironic symbol of the inadequacy of the spirited heroine's wings of desire. Above all, in the very first sentence of the novel our attention is drawn to the roundel, the circular flowerbed – in the beautiful and apparently salubrious environment which both nurtured and trapped her – whose ultimate function is seen in the final passage.

Writing of *Confusions, Delusions* Fontane referred to the '*tausend Finessen*', the thousand subtleties in the novel. The apparently straightforward, restrained and undemanding realism of the surface conceals a web of cross-reference at a virtually inexhaustible variety of levels. Some critics, like Karl S. Guthke, have asked the question 'art or artifice?'[13] about Fontane's style, finding his use of symbolic allusion and techniques of suggestion and anticipation overdone. The broad consensus however finds the finely woven texture an unfailing source of new discovery and delight in the novels.[14] The range of possible points of entry into the interior of *Effi Briest* may be exemplified by Klaus-Peter Schuster's study which approaches the text via references to paintings, especially those of the Pre-Raphaelites, developing an elaborate theory whereby Hohen-Cremmen is both the *hortus conclusus* of the Annunciation and the Garden of Eden, and Karla Bindokat's analysis which approaches *Effi Briest* via the history of traditional literary motifs, examining Fontane's borrowings from folk legend, myth and saga all of which feed into the social criticism in the novel.[15] Numerous examinations of individual details in the novel, ranging from the heliotrope in the garden as a symbol of divine and earthly love and of Effi's need for light and warmth to Cousin Dagobert's Christmas card with its huddled bird in a snowy landscape with a telegraph pole as metaphor for her emotional deprivation and isolation, have progressively cast more light on the work's intricacy.[16]

One effect of this all-pervasive allusiveness in a work of realism is the active involvement of the reader to an extent that is belied by the unassuming surface of the novel. In the space between the relatively few characters and their uncluttered milieu Fontane has left room for readers to interpret events and bring their own experience and observation to bear on what has been offered. This is quite deliberate on Fontane's part; as we have seen, he was always in favour of too little rather than too much. He maintained that if there was anything superfluous at all, then it was a flaw.[17] The realistic detail in *Effi Briest* all serves a wider scheme or structure, that of the historically and socially determined world in which the characters live.

The framework in which Fontane operates, as recent studies have shown, is one which points firmly forward to twentieth-century preoccupations. Patricia Howe sees this modern tendency in terms of the overriding of the conventional moral design of nineteenth-century realism. When Effi reads *David Copperfield*, a novel of wickedness punished and virtue rewarded, she has chosen a fiction that does not correspond to her own world. At the end of *Effi Briest*, Howe argues that neither Effi's death nor that of her seducer restores order, but signals its disintegration, and that the final 'injunction against further questioning' must be seen as ironically undermining the apparent closure of the text.[18] Walter Müller-Seidel in his authoritative study of Fontane's novels sees the modernity of *Effi Briest* in terms of its 'missing or reduced tragedy'.[19] He attributes this to the almost ridiculous seriousness with which Innstetten reacts to an offence so far in the past, and to the fact that the fatal repercussions derive from an unintended sliding into a state of guilt. The serious consequences arise out of a combination of the everyday, the trivial, and the ridiculous. He sees in this disillusioned view of the novel which is no longer tragic but founded on half-comic absurdity, evidence of a tendency towards a modern consciousness. One of the problems in the earlier reception of *Effi Briest* by academic commentators accustomed to tragedy and passion in the novel was precisely this perceived lack, this shift in awareness that was then negatively judged against the high seriousness and emotional intensity of say *Anna Karenina* or *Middlemarch*. The scene that follows Innstetten's fateful discovery of the letters is indeed remarkable for its comedy. It is a game of nicely observed one-upmanship between the servants, which may owe something to the Shakespearean tradition of comic relief, but which equally serves as an instant corrective to any more serious or indeed sentimental interpretation of events. The prosaic age of relativism and pragmatism has laid claim to the idealistic preserves of love, honour and loyalty.

Fontane's realism has a characteristic flavour of its own which derives from a compound of refined irony, restraint and perspectivism. He created an ironic narrative tradition in German literature which was to be followed by Thomas Mann, Heinrich Böll and others. Like most great modern novels *Effi Briest* is a self-reflective narrative, a fact which can be seen more clearly in the original in the recurrence of the word *Geschichte*, 'story', which for reasons of idiom has sometimes been rendered by 'affair' in the translation.[20] In the first chapter, two of Effi's comments both anticipate and call into question the entire narrative to come. She says, 'A tale of renunciation is never bad' and, 'What happened was what was bound to happen, what always happens.' The reader's response in accepting these propositions at the end is proof of the aesthetic truth, coherence if you like, of the novel and in rejecting them of its moral force and coherence. That these responses can be harboured simultaneously demonstrates the sophistication of a work that evokes assent at one level and rebellion at another.

Effi Briest is the finest of Fontane's portrayals of women living in a male-dominated society and, as the title of one Fontane study, *The Woman as Paradigm of Humane Values*,[21] suggests, it is the female values that are vindicated against the male ones. In *Effi Briest* there is a warmth of human understanding and a non-judgmental attitude to human weakness which affords the reader a critical view of reality without destroying a sense of coherence and order. The intimate sphere of a broken marriage is a barometer of the health of the state and society as a whole, but in Effi Fontane has equally created a warm, attractive personality who, whatever she represents, is above all a vital, convincing character whose life and world we come to know and understand, and in knowing and understanding them we may know ourselves and our own world better too.

Notes

1   In a review of Conrad Wandrey, *Theodor Fontane*, 1919, the first major study of Fontane's novels, Mann observes: 'A set of novels selected according to the most rigorous criteria, even if it were restricted to a dozen volumes, or ten, or six, could not possibly dispense

with *Effi Briest.*' Reprinted under the title 'Anzeige eines Fontane-Buches' in Thomas Mann, *Das essayistische Werk*, Frankfurt am Main 1968, pp. 106f.

2   William L. Zwiebel, *Theodor Fontane* (Twayne's World Authors Series), New York 1992, Chapter 4, has interesting commentary on the Prussian dimension in Fontane's novels.

3   Charlotte Jolles, 'Fontanes Studien über England' in *Fontanes Realismus. Wissenschaftliche Konferenz zum 150. Geburtstag Theodor Fontanes in Potsdam*, ed. Hans-Erich Teitge and Joachim Schobess, Berlin 1972, p. 104.

4   Letter to Friedrich Spielhagen, February 21st, 1896, in Theodor Fontane, *Briefe*, ed. Gotthard Erler, vol. 2, Berlin and Weimar 1980, p. 395.

5   See Helen Elizabeth Chambers, *Supernatural and Irrational Elements in the Works of Theodor Fontane*, Stuttgart 1980, pp. 185-214, on the role of the Chinaman's ghost.

6   Christian Grawe, *Theodor Fontane: Effi Briest*, 4th ed., Frankfurt am Main 1992, p. 13 (my translation - H.C.).

7   Charlotte Brontë, Preface to *Jane Eyre*.

8   Gudrun Loster-Schneider, *Der Erzähler Fontane. Seine politischen Positionen in den Jahren 1864-1898 und ihre ästhetische Vermittlung*, Tübingen 1986.

9   Letter to Julius Rodenberg, November 1st, 1893, in *Theodor Fontane: Briefe an Julius Rodenberg. Eine Dokumentation*, ed. Hans-Heinrich Reuter, Berlin and Weimar 1969.

10 See also J.P. Stern, *Re-interpretations*, London 1964, pp. 315-47.

11 Letter to Hans Hertz, March 2nd, 1895 in *Briefe an Wilhelm und Hans Hertz 1859-1898*, ed. Kurt Schreinert, Stuttgart 1972.

12 Letter to Ernst Heilborn, November 24th, 1895, in Theodor Fontane, *Briefe*, ed. Gotthard Erler, vol.2, Berlin and Weimar 1980, p. 387.

13 Karl S. Guthke, 'Fontanes Finessen: "Kunst" oder "Künstelei?"' in *Jahrbuch der deutschen Schillergesellschaft* 26, 1982, pp. 235-61, also as 'Fontane's craft of fiction: art or artifice?' in *Essays in Honor of James Edward Walsh*, Cambridge, Mass. 1983, pp. 67-94.

14 See for example Alan Bance, *Theodor Fontane: the major novels*, Cambridge 1982; Henry Garland, *The Berlin novels of Theodor Fontane*, Oxford 1980.

15 Peter-Klaus Schuster, *Effi Briest - Ein Leben nach christlichen Bildern*, Tübingen 1978; Karla Bindokat, *"Effi Briest": Erzählstoff und Erzählinhalt*, Frankfurt am Main 1984.

16 Klaus Dieter Post, '"Das eigentümliche Parfum des Wortes". Zum Doppelbild des Heliotrop in Theodor Fontanes Roman *Effi Briest*' in *Fontane-Blätter* 49, 1990, pp. 32-39; Christian Grawe, '*Effi Briest*. Geducktes Vögelchen in Schneelandschaft: Effi von Innstetten, geboren von Briest', in *Fontanes Novellen und Romane*, ed. Christian Grawe, Stuttgart 1991, p.229.

17 Letter to Spielhagen, February 15th, 1896.

18 Patricia Howe, 'Realism and Moral Design' in *Perspectives on German Realism. Eight Essays*, ed. Mark G. Ward, Lampeter 1995, p. 60.

19 Walter Müller-Seidel, *Theodor Fontane. Soziale Romankunst in Deutschland*, Stuttgart 1975.

20 For example in Chapter 5: 'Were you happy about Effi? Were you happy about the whole affair?'

21 Norbert Frei, *Theodor Fontane. Die Frau als Paradigma des Humanen*, Königstein/ Taunus 1980.

Translators' Note

This new translation of *Effi Briest* was produced in response to a widespread
feeling that existing translations, two abridged and out of print, the other fail-
ing to render vital aspects, denied the English-speaking reader adequate access
to the greatest realist novel in German literature. Much has been written about
the difficulties of translating a writer as subtle as Fontane, and there is no doubt
that he presents particular problems. We have tried to get as close as possible to
the effect of the original by rendering the natural feel of the conversation while
still retaining the more poetic aspects of the text. Without, we hope, being
anachronistic, we have avoided old-fashioned expressions, for the effect the
novel had on Fontane's contemporaries was anything but old-fashioned.

Despite the novel's simple, at times colloquial diction, its underlying
artistic qualities, which reside partly in the rhythm of the sentences and the
creation of verbal and symbolic echoes and patterns, require careful attention. Wherever we could we have retained these echoes and patterns. This
was not always possible because of the divergence between German and
English idiomatic usage. One has to be alive, for example, to gender-specific
usage, with adjectives in German that may apply equally well to men and
women, but don't in English. Because of differences between normal German and English sentence structure it is impossible to replicate the rhythm
of the German faithfully without doing violence to the idiom of English. We
have done our best to produce a version that has a rhythmical flow and
dynamic of its own.

Titles and forms of address posed particular problems, especially the
polite form *gnädige* or *gnädigste Frau*. Oscar Wilde's *Lady Windermere's Fan*,
which was written at the same time as *Effi Briest*, suggested 'my lady' and 'my
dear lady', with 'your/her ladyship' as the form used in place of 'you' and
'she'. Titles such as *Landrat* generally remain untranslated, but are explained
in the end-notes. The number of German words now current in English is
increasing, and it seemed undesirable to impose a set of approximate equi-
valents deriving from the British Empire and civil service on the Prussian system. The German titles better preserve the geographical and historical context. Similarly street names have been left to speak with their own German
voice, with annotation where appropriate.

This translation is designed above all to be readable, but also to fulfil the more stringent requirements of the reader who seeks a reliable rendering of the original. We have kept faith with the text as closely as possible, both by preserving echoes and by avoiding repetition where there is none – this proved a significant problem as Fontane often places different expressions with similar meanings close to each other. Some deviation was inevitable and in particular the puns in Chapters 17 and 23 were untranslatable. Introducing the word 'slug' as the correct English expression for the red-hot metal put in a box-iron also caused us discomfort, as the term for 'slug' does not occur in Fontane's fiction. The alternative English term would have been 'weasel'. There are no weasels in Fontane either. German miles have been converted to British miles throughout, so that the distances are rendered accurately. We have paid attention to plant names, for Fontane, the pharmacist, had a detailed knowledge of the subject and chose his flowers carefully.

In translating *Effi Briest* we have had the pleasure of gaining new insights into the fine detail of how the text works; and even compiling the end-notes has thrown fresh sidelights on its hidden subtleties, particularly on Innstetten's allusions. Our translation is offered in the hope that it may help to find Fontane, belatedly, a wider English readership and facilitate a more informed assessment of his place in world literature.

Effi Briest

1

To the front of Hohen-Cremmen, country seat of the von Briest family since the time of Elector Georg Wilhelm, bright sunshine fell on the midday silence in the village street, while on the side facing the park and gardens a wing built on at right angles cast its broad shadow first on a white and green flagstone path, then out over a large roundel of flowers with a sundial at its centre and a border of canna lilies and rhubarb round the edge. Some twenty paces further on, corresponding exactly in line and length to the new wing and broken only by a single white-painted iron gate, was a churchyard wall entirely covered in small-leaved ivy, behind which rose Hohen-Cremmen's shingled tower, its weather-cock glittering from recent regilding. Main house, wing and churchyard wall formed a horseshoe, enclosing a small ornamental garden at whose open end a pond and a jetty with a moored boat could be seen, and close by a swing, its horizontal seat-board hanging at head and foot on two ropes from posts that were slightly out of true. Between the roundel and the pond, partially concealing the swing, stood some mighty plane trees.

The front of the house too – a sloping terrace with aloes in tubs and some garden chairs – offered a place to linger and indulge in all manner of amusements if the sky was cloudy; but on days when the sun beat down there was a clear preference for the garden side, especially on the part of the lady of the house and her daughter, who on this particular day were sitting out in the full shade on the flagstone path, with windows wreathed in Virginia creeper at their backs, and beside them a short projecting flight of steps whose four stone treads led up from the garden to the upper ground floor of the wing. Both mother and daughter were busily at work on an altar-cloth that was to be made out of several squares; countless strands of wool and skeins of silk lay jumbled on a large round table, and between them, left over from lunch, were some dessert plates and a large majolica bowl filled with fine large gooseberries. The ladies' wool-needles went back and forth, swift and sure, but while the mother never took her eye off her work, the daughter, Effi as everybody called her, laid down her needle from time to time and stood up to stretch and bend her way stylishly through a full sequence of health-promoting home gymnastics. It was obvious that these exercises were a labour of quite special love, even if she deliberately added a comic touch, and as she stood there slowly raising her arms and bringing her palms together high above her head, her mother too would raise her eyes from her

5

work, but only for a surreptitious, fleeting glance, for she had no wish to show what delight she took in her own child, fully justified though such a stirring of maternal pride was. Effi was wearing a blue and white striped linen dress that would have been a straight tunic had it not been drawn in at the waist by a tight, bronze-coloured leather belt; the neck was open and a broad sailor's collar went over her shoulders and down her back. Grace and careless abandon were combined in everything she did, while her laughing brown eyes revealed much good sense, a great zest for life and kindness of heart. They called her 'the little one', but she tolerated that only because her beautiful, slender mamma was a hand's breadth taller.

Effi had just stood up again to do a few gymnastic turns to right and left when her mother, looking up from her embroidery again, called to her, 'Effi, maybe you should have been a bareback-rider after all. Always on the trapeze, a daughter of the air. You know I almost think that's what you would like to be.'

'Perhaps Mamma, but supposing I would, whose fault would that be? Who do I get it from? It can only be you. Or do you think from Papa? There, you can't help laughing. And then, why have you got me in this shift – this boy's overall? Sometimes I think I'm going to go back into short dresses. And once that happens I'll curtsy like some sweet young thing, and when the officers come over from Rathenow I'll get on Colonel Goetze's lap and ride, gee-up, gee-up, and why not? He's three quarters uncle and only one quarter admirer anyway. It's your fault. Why haven't I got any proper dresses? Why don't you make a lady of me?'

'Would you like that?'

'No.' Saying which, she ran up to her mother, threw her arms round her impetuously and kissed her.

'Not so wild Effi, not so passionate. It always worries me when I see you like this ...' And her mother seemed seriously intent on giving further expression to her cares and anxieties. But she didn't get so far, because just at that moment three young girls came in at the iron gate in the churchyard wall and walked up the gravel path towards the roundel and the sundial. All three waved to Effi with their parasols and hurried up to Frau von Briest to kiss her hand. She asked a few quick questions and then invited the girls to keep them, or at least Effi, company for half an hour, 'I have things to see to, and young people are happiest left to themselves. So, I'll take my leave.' And so saying she climbed the stone steps leading from the garden to the wing.

And with that the young people were on their own.

Two of the young girls – plump little persons whose curly golden red hair admirably matched their freckles and equable temper – were the daughters of Jahnke, the assistant schoolmaster whose sole interests were the Hanseatic

League, Scandinavia and Fritz Reuter, a fellow Mecklenburger and his favourite writer, in emulation of whom, with Mining and Lining in mind, he had given his twins the names Bertha and Hertha. The third young lady was Hulda Niemeyer, Pastor Niemeyer's only child; while more ladylike than the other two, she was also boring and conceited, a lymphatic blonde with somewhat protuberant, stupid eyes that somehow always seemed to be searching for something, which was why Klitzing of the Hussars had said of her, 'Doesn't she look as if she were expecting the Archangel Gabriel at any moment?' Effi felt that the somewhat critical Klitzing was only too accurate, but refrained nonetheless from making any distinction between her three friends. That was the last thing she had in mind at the moment. 'This boring old embroidery. Thank goodness you're here,' and she put her elbows on the table.

'But we've driven your mamma away,' said Hulda.

'Not really. You heard her, she was going anyhow, she's expecting a visitor you see, some old friend from when she was a girl, I'm going to tell you about that later, a love-story complete with hero and heroine, and ending in renunciation. You'll be amazed, you won't believe your ears. I've seen him too, Mamma's old friend, over in Schwantikow. He's a Landrat, and very handsome and manly.'

'That's the main thing,' said Hertha.

'Of course it's the main thing, "women should be womanly, men should be manly" – that's one of Papa's favourite sayings, as you know. Now help me tidy this table, otherwise I'll be in trouble again.'

In a trice all the skeins were packed into the basket, and when they were all seated again, Hulda said, 'Well then Effi, it's time now, let's have this tale of love and renunciation. Or is it not really that bad?'

'A tale of renunciation is never bad. But unless Hertha takes some of these gooseberries I can't start, she can't keep her eyes off them. Help yourself, as many as you like, we can pick more later, only don't throw the skins away, or better still, put them on this newspaper supplement here, then we'll make it into a paper bag and get rid of the whole lot. Mamma can't stand it if she sees skins lying everywhere, she always says you could slip on them and break a leg.'

'Don't believe it,' said Hertha, addressing herself to the gooseberries with a will.

'Nor do I,' Effi agreed. 'Just think, I fall at least two or three times every day, and I've never broken anything. Proper legs don't break so easily, mine certainly don't, nor yours, Hertha. What do you think, Hulda?'

'One shouldn't tempt Providence. Pride comes before a fall.'

'There's the governess again, you're a real old maid.'

'Well, it won't stop me getting married, perhaps sooner than you.'

'Think I care. Do you imagine that's what I'm waiting for? That's all I need. Anyway, I'm going to have someone, maybe quite soon. I'm not worried. Only the other day little Ventivegni from across the way said, "What do you bet we'll be getting together this year for somebody's Wedding Eve!"'

'And what did you say to that?'

'"It's possible of course," I said, "quite possible; Hulda is the oldest and might get married any day." But he wouldn't have any of that and said, "No, it will be quite another young lady – who is as dark as Hulda is blond." And he gave me a very serious look as he said it... But how did I get on to all this, I'm forgetting the story.'

'Yes, you do keep going off at a tangent; maybe you don't want to tell us after all.'

'Oh I want to all right, but it's true of course, I do keep getting off the subject, because it's all rather strange, in fact, it's almost romantic.'

'But didn't you say he was a Landrat?'

'That's right, a Landrat. And his name is Geert von Innstetten, Baron von Innstetten.'

All three burst out laughing.

'What are you laughing at?' said Effi, put out, 'What's that supposed to mean?'

'Oh Effi, we didn't mean any offence, not to you and not to the Baron. Did you say Innstetten? And Geert? Nobody around here is called anything like that. These old aristocratic names can be so funny.'

'Yes indeed, my dear. But that's the aristocracy. They don't have to care, and the further back they go the less they have to care. You mustn't mind if I say you don't understand these things. We'll still be friends. So it's Geert von Innstetten, and a baron. He's exactly the same age as Mamma, to the day.'

'And how old is your Mamma then?'

'Thirty-eight.'

'A nice age to be.'

'Yes, it is, especially if you still have Mamma's looks. She's a beautiful woman, really, don't you think? And the way she has everything just so, and is always so poised and refined, never puts her foot in it like Papa. If I were a young lieutenant, I would fall in love with Mamma.'

'But Effi, how can you say such a thing?' said Hulda, 'That's against the fourth commandment.'

'Nonsense. How can that be against the fourth commandment? I think Mamma would be pleased if she knew I'd said something like that.'

'That may well be,' Hertha interjected, 'but let's get on with the story.'

'All right, be patient, I'm just going to start... So, Baron Innstetten. He wasn't quite twenty and he was stationed in Rathenow and was a regular guest on all the estates here, though his favourite was grandfather Belling's place in Schwantikow. It wasn't of course because of Grandfather that he called so often, and when Mamma talks about it, anybody can see who the real attraction was. And I think it was mutual.'

'So what happened then?'

'What happened was what was bound to happen, what always happens. He was still far too young, and when Papa came on the scene he was already a Ritterschaftsrat and had Hohen-Cremmen, so there wasn't really much to think about and she accepted him and became Frau von Briest... And the rest, what came after that, you know... The rest is me.'

'Yes, the rest is you, Effi,' said Bertha. 'Thank goodness for that, we wouldn't have had you if things had been otherwise. So you must tell us, what did Innstetten do, what became of him? He didn't take his own life, otherwise you wouldn't be expecting him today.'

'No, he didn't take his own life. But it was a bit like it.'

'Did he try?'

'No, he didn't. But he wasn't inclined to stay in the neighbourhood any longer, and it must have put him off army life in general. It was peacetime after all. To cut a long story short he resigned his commission and went off to study law, "really made a meal of it" as Papa puts it; but when the war of 1870 came along he joined up again, with the Perlebergers, mark you, not with his old regiment, and he got the Iron Cross. As you would expect, because he's very dashing. And immediately after the war he went back to his files, and they say Bismarck thinks highly of him, and the Kaiser too, and that's how he came to be a Landrat, for the district of Kessin.'

'Kessin? I don't know any Kessin near here.'

'No, it isn't in our part of the country, it's a fair way from here, in Pomerania, Eastern Pomerania in fact, not that that means anything, because it's a coastal resort (everywhere's a coastal resort up there) and this holiday trip Baron Innstetten is making is a kind of tour of his cousins or something. He wants to see old acquaintances and relatives.'

'He's got relatives here?'

'Yes and no, depends how you look at it. There are no Innstettens here, in fact there are no Instettens left at all, I don't think. But he has some distant cousins on his mother's side here, and mainly I think he wanted to see Schwantikow and the Bellings' house again, which hold so many memories for him. He was over there yesterday, and today he's coming to Hohen-Cremmen.'

'And what does your father say to that?'

9

'Nothing. He's not like that. And he knows Mamma. He just teases her.'

At that moment it struck noon, and before the chimes had stopped, Wilke, the Briests' old butler and general factotum, appeared with a message for Effi: 'Her ladyship would like Miss Effi to make herself presentable in good time. The Baron will arrive at one o'clock sharp.' And as he announced this Wilke began to clear the ladies' work-table, reaching first for the sheet of newspaper the gooseberry skins were lying on.

'No Wilke, don't do that, we're going to see to the skins... Hertha, it's time to make the paper bag; and put in a stone so it all sinks. Then we'll have a long funeral procession and bury the bag at sea.'

Wilke smiled. 'A real caution, our young lady' he must have been thinking; but Effi, placing the bag in the middle of the swiftly tidied tablecloth, said: 'Now each of the four of us takes a corner and we sing something sad.'

'Yes, well, you say that, Effi. But what exactly are we supposed to sing?'

'Anything; it doesn't matter, except that it must have a rhyme with "ee"; "ee" is the vowel for keening. So we'll sing:

> "In the deepest deep,
> Let it peacefully sleep."'

And as Effi solemnly intoned this litany, all four began to move towards the jetty, climbed into the boat that was moored there, and from that slowly lowered the bag and its stone weight into the pond.

'Hertha, your guilt is now consigned to the deep,' said Effi, 'oh and that reminds me, this is how they used to drown poor unfortunate women, from boats like this, for infidelity of course.'

'But not here.'

'No, not here,' Effi laughed, 'that kind of thing doesn't happen here. But in Constantinople it does, now I come to think of it, you must know that just as well as I do, you were there when ordinand Holzapfel told us about it in geography.'

'Yes,' said Hulda, 'Holzapfel was always talking about that kind of thing. But then that's the kind of thing you forget.'

'Not me. I remember that kind of thing.'

2

They continued to talk in this vein for a while, recalling with indignation and satisfaction lessons they had attended together and a whole series of Holzapfel's improprieties. There would have been no end to it had Hulda not suddenly said, 'But it's high time you went in Effi. You look, well, how shall I put it, you look as if you had just come from picking cherries, all crumpled and crushed; linen always gets so many creases, and with that big white floppy collar... yes, I've got it, you look like a cabin-boy.'

'Midshipman, if you please. I must have something for my nobility. Anyway, midshipman or cabin-boy, Papa promised me a mast the other day, right here by the swing, with spars and rigging. Won't that be something, and I'll put my own pennant on the masthead, and no-one is going to stop me. And Hulda, you'll shin up the other side and at the top we'll shout hurrah and kiss one another. Splice the mainbrace, won't that be fun!'

'"Splice the mainbrace"... listen to that... You really do talk like a midshipman. But I wouldn't dream of climbing up after you, I'm not such a daredevil. Jahnke is right when he says there's a lot of the Bellings in you, from your mother's side. I'm just a pastor's daughter.'

'Oh, get away with you. Still waters run deep. Do you remember the time Cousin Briest was here, still a cadet, but grown up for all that, and you slid all the way along the barn roof? And why was that? I'm not going to let on. Come on, let's have a swing, two on each end, I don't think the ropes will snap, or if you don't want to – for I can see you pulling long faces – we'll play tag. I still have a quarter of an hour. I don't want to go in yet, just to say good afternoon to a Landrat, and a Landrat from Eastern Pomerania at that. He's a bit old too, he could almost be my father, and if he really lives in a seaport, which is what they say Kessin is, then he ought to prefer me in my sailor suit, he ought almost to take it as a special token of respect. When princes receive – or so Papa tells me – they always put on the uniform of wherever their guest comes from. So not to worry... I'm going to hide and the bench here is home.'

Hulda had a few reservations, but before she could speak, Effi was off up the nearest gravel path, dodging to left and right until suddenly she was gone. 'Effi, that doesn't count. Where are you? We're not playing hide and seek, we're playing tag.' And with these and similar protestations her friends ran after her, far beyond the roundel and the two plane trees on the side, until the elusive Effi burst from her hiding place and, because she was now

11

behind her pursuers, effortlessly reached the bench and was home with 'one, two, three'.

'Where were you?'

'Behind the rhubarb clumps, they've got such big leaves, even bigger than a fig-leaf.'

'Shame on you!'

'No, shame on you, because you've lost. Hulda with those big eyes of hers didn't spot me, helpless as usual.' And with that Effi flew over the roundel again in the direction of the pond, perhaps with the intention of hiding behind a thick hazel-hedge that was growing there, so that she could make a wide detour round the churchyard and the front of the house and get back to the wing and home. She had it all nicely worked out, but alas, before she was even half-way round the pond she heard her name being called from the house, and looking round, saw her mother waving from the stone steps with her handkerchief. A moment later Effi was standing in front of her.

'There you are still in that tunic of yours and our visitor is here. You never keep to time.'

'*I* keep to time, it's your visitor who hasn't. It's not one yet, not by a long chalk,' and turning to the twins (Hulda was lagging far behind) she shouted, 'Just carry on, I'll be straight back.'

A moment later Effi was in the large garden-room which took up almost the entire wing of the house.

'Mamma, you mustn't scold like that. It really is only half-past. Why has he come so early? A gentleman never comes late, but still less too early.'

Frau von Briest was visibly embarrassed, but Effi clung to her and caressed her and said, 'I'm sorry, I'll hurry now, you know how quick I can be, and in five minutes Cinderella will be transformed into a princess. He can surely wait or talk to Papa that long.'

And with a nod to her mother she made to trip light-footedly up the little iron staircase which led from the garden-room to the upper floor. But Frau von Briest, who could be unconventional herself when necessary, suddenly held Effi back as she was going, looked at the charming, youthful creature, hot from the excitement of the game, standing there in front of her, a picture of life at its freshest – and in a confidential tone said, 'Maybe it's as well if you just stay as you are. Yes, just stay as you are. You look very nice like that. And even if you didn't, you look so unprepared, not made up at all, and that's what matters at a moment like this. I have something to tell you, my sweet Effi...' and she took her child by both hands... 'I have to tell you that –'

12

'But Mamma, what's the matter? You're frightening me.'

'What I have to tell you is that Baron von Innstetten wants to marry you.'

'Wants to marry me? Is he serious?'

'It's not the kind of thing to be joked about. You saw him the day before yesterday, and I think you liked him. Of course he is older than you, which is a good thing all in all, and he is a man of character, position and sound morality, and if you don't say no, which I would hardly expect from my clever Effi, then at twenty you'll have a position others don't reach until they're forty. You'll go far further than your mamma.'

Effi said nothing; she was searching for words. But before she could find them she heard her father's voice from the adjoining room, which was in the rear of the main house, and Ritterschaftsrat von Briest, a well-preserved man of pronounced bonhomie in his fifties, stepped over the threshold of the garden-room – with him Baron Innstetten, slim, dark-haired and of military bearing.

Effi, seeing him, began to tremble nervously; but not for long, because almost at the very moment Innstetten approached her with a friendly bow, the golden red heads of the twins appeared round the Virginia creeper that half-obscured the window, and Hertha, the cheekier of them, called into the room, 'Come back Effi.' Then she ducked down and the two sisters jumped off the arm of the bench they had been standing on back down into the garden, and all that could be heard was their subdued giggling and laughter.

3

On that same day Baron Innstetten had become engaged to Effi Briest. The jovial father of the bride to be, adjusting with difficulty to the solemnity of his role at the engagement dinner which followed, had proposed a toast to the young couple, and this gave Frau von Briest a disturbing sensation about the heart, probably conjuring up times scarcely eighteen years past. But not for long. It couldn't be her, so now, instead of her, it was her daughter – just as good, all in all, perhaps even better. For life with Briest was quite tolerable, even if he was a shade prosaic and lapsed on occasion into frivolity. Towards the end of the meal – ice-cream was already being passed round – the old Ritterschaftsrat stood up again and proposed that the formal mode of address be dropped within the family. Whereupon he embraced Innstetten and gave him a kiss on the left cheek. But this was not the end of it for he went on to recommend intimate names and titles for use within the family, setting up a sort of scale of familiarity which naturally respected the established rights of individual cases. Thus for his wife the continuation of 'Mamma' would be best (for there were some young mammas), whereas he himself would resist the honourable title of 'Papa', strongly preferring to be simply Briest, which was so nice and short. And as for the children – and at this word, meeting the eye of Innstetten who was barely a dozen years his junior, he had to give himself a jolt – well, Effi would be Effi and Geert Geert. Geert, if he was not mistaken, meant a tall, slender stem, and that made Effi the ivy that would cling to it. The couple looked at one another in some embarrassment at these words, coupled in Effi's case with an expression of adolescent amusement, but Frau von Briest said, 'Briest, say what you like and propose what toasts you will, but if you please, spare us your poetic images, that's outside your province.' Cautionary words which found more agreement than dissent in Briest. 'You may be right, Luise.'

As soon as they rose from table Effi took her leave and went to call at the pastor's. On the way she told herself, 'I expect Hulda will be annoyed. I've beaten her to it after all – and she has always been vain and conceited.' But Effi's expectations were not quite accurate; Hulda kept her composure and behaved very well, leaving it to her mother to voice any misgivings or irritation, and the pastor's wife did indeed make some very strange remarks. 'Yes, well, that's the way of it, of course. If it couldn't be the mother it will have to be the daughter. We've seen it all before. Old families stick together, and to those that have shall be given.' Old Niemeyer, deeply embarrassed at this stream of pointed, uneducated, ill-mannered remarks, once more had cause to regret having married a housekeeper.

From the pastor's Effi naturally went on to schoolmaster Jahnke's; the twins had been on the look-out for her and met her in the front garden.

'Well Effi,' said Hertha, as all three walked up and down between the French marigolds blooming to left and right, 'well Effi, how do you feel now?'

'How do I feel? Oh all right. We're already on Christian name terms. He's called Geert by the way, but I've told you that already, I seem to remember.'

'Yes, you have. But I feel so uneasy about it all. Is he really the right one?'

'Of course he's the right one. You don't understand these things Hertha. Anybody is the right one. Provided he is an aristocrat and has a position and good looks, naturally.'

'My goodness Effi, the way you talk. It's quite different from how you used to talk.'

'Yes, used to.'

'So you're quite happy now?'

'If you've been engaged for two hours, you're always quite happy. At least that's what I think.'

'And you don't have the feeling it's at all – how shall I put it – a little embarrassing?'

'Yes, it is a little embarrassing, but not very. And I think I'll get over it.'

After making these calls at the pastor's and the schoolmaster's houses, which didn't take half an hour, Effi went back home where they were about to have coffee on the veranda facing the garden. Father-in-law and son-in-law paced up and down the gravel paths between the two plane trees. Briest spoke of the problems of a Landrat's post; he had been offered several, but he had turned each one down. 'Being able to do just as I want has always been the most important thing for me, or at least more important, if you'll pardon me Innstetten, than always keeping a weather eye on those above me. For what you have to do then is watch and take note of your superiors, not to mention their superiors. That's not for me. Here I take life as it comes and rejoice in every green leaf, in the Virginia creeper growing up the window there.'

He said more of the same, with all sorts of digs at officialdom, excusing himself from time to time with a varyingly reiterated 'Sorry Innstetten'. Innstetten nodded mechanically in agreement, but his mind was scarcely on these matters as he glanced repeatedly in a kind of fascination at the Virginia creeper climbing up the window to which Briest had just alluded, and as he dwelt on this it was as if he saw the golden red heads of the girls again among the tendrils, and heard once more their 'Come back Effi'.

He didn't believe in signs and that kind of thing, on the contrary, he entirely rejected all superstition. But he nonetheless couldn't escape from these three words, and as Briest continued to hold forth, he couldn't get away from the notion that that little incident had been more than mere chance.

Innstetten, who had taken only a short leave of absence, had departed the next day, after promising to write every day. 'Yes, you must do that,' Effi had said, and these were words from the heart, since she had for years known nothing lovelier than getting lots of letters, for example on her birthday. Everybody had to write to her on that day. Little messages in a letter, such as 'Gertrude and Clara also send their best wishes' were not permissible; Gertrude and Clara, if they wanted to stay friends, had to see to it that there was an individual letter with its own stamp, if possible – for her birthday was in the holiday period – a foreign one, from Switzerland or Karlsbad.

Innstetten, as promised, actually did write every day; but what made getting his letters especially agreeable was that all he ever expected in reply was a brief note once a week. And that he received, full of charming trivia which invariably gave him great delight. Such serious matters as had to be discussed

15

ealt with by Frau von Briest and her son-in-law; arrangements for the ...ding, the decorating, and the equipment of the kitchen and the house-...ld in general. Innstetten had already been in post for almost three years, and his house in Kessin, though not elegantly appointed, was furnished as befitted his position, which made it advisable to gain a picture, in correspondence, of all that was already there, so as not to buy anything superfluous. Finally, when Frau von Briest was fully informed about these things, mother and daughter decided on a trip to Berlin to, as Briest put it, 'assemble the trousseau' for Princess Effi. Effi looked forward very much to spending some time in Berlin, especially since Father had consented to their staying at the Hôtel du Nord. 'Whatever it costs can be deducted from equipping the house. Innstetten has everything anyway.' Effi, in contrast to her mother who had put such petty concerns aside once and for all, had, without for a moment considering whether he meant it seriously or as a joke, enthusiastically agreed and her thoughts were far more occupied with the impression the two of them, mother and daughter, would make at the luncheon table, than with Spinn and Mencke, Goschenhofer or the other firms on the provisional shopping list. And her demeanour corresponded to her gleeful imaginings as the big week in Berlin finally arrived. Cousin Briest of the Alexander Regiment, an extremely animated young lieutenant who took the *Fliegende Blätter* and kept a collection of its best jokes, put every off-duty hour at their disposal, so they sat with him at the corner window of Kranzler's or, at respectable times, in the Café Bauer and then drove in the afternoon to the Zoological Garden to look at the giraffes, of whom Cousin Briest, whose first name incidentally was Dagobert, liked to say, 'They look like aristocratic old maids.' Every day went according to plan, and on the third or fourth day the National Gallery was on the agenda, because Dagobert wanted to show his cousin *The Isle of the Blessed*. 'Cousin Effi is on the brink of marriage, but it might nevertheless be just as well to make the acquaintance of "The Isle of the Blessed" beforehand.' His aunt gave him a clip with her fan, but accompanied it with such a benign look that he had no cause to change his tone. These were heavenly days for all three, not least for Cousin Briest who was a wonderful chaperon with a knack for quickly smoothing over any little disagreement. There was never any shortage of such differences of opinion, as these things go, between mother and daughter, but they never arose, happily, during the shopping they had come to do. Whether they were buying six of any item or three dozen, Effi was always in agreement with her mother, and when they discussed the prices of what they had just bought on the way home Effi regularly got the figures mixed up. Frau von Briest, usually so critical, even of her own beloved daughter, not only took this lack of interest lightly, she even saw it as an advantage. 'None of these things means much to Effi,' she told herself, 'Effi isn't demanding; she lives in her own imagination and dreams, and if Princess Friedrich Karl drives past and gives her a friendly greeting from her carriage, it's worth more to her than a whole chest of linen.'

This was quite true, but it was only half the truth. Everyday possessions didn't mean much to Effi, but when she and her mother strolled up and down Unter den Linden looking at the most beautiful window displays and then went into Demuth's to purchase various things for the trip to Italy that was planned for immediately after the wedding, it was then that she revealed her true character. She liked only what was most elegant, and if she couldn't have the best she would do without the second best, because second best meant nothing to her. Yes, she was capable of doing without, her mother was right about that, and doing without had an element of the undemanding; but when, exceptionally, it came to really wanting something, that something always had to be quite out of the ordinary. And in *this* she was demanding.

4

Cousin Dagobert was at the station when the ladies set out on the return journey to Hohen-Cremmen. They had been happy days, particularly since they had not had to suffer disagreeable relatives who were scarcely of the proper class. 'For Aunt Therese,' Effi had said on their arrival, 'we must be incognito this time. We can't have her coming here to the hotel. Either the Hôtel du Nord or Aunt Therese; you can't have both.' Her mamma had finally agreed with her, indeed to seal their agreement, she had even given her darling a kiss on the forehead.

With Cousin Dagobert it had of course been quite another matter: besides having the swagger of a Guardsman, he had above all, with the aid of the special good humour that is almost traditional in officers of the Alexander Regiment, been able to provide stimulation and amusement for mother and daughter alike, and their good mood lasted right to the end. 'Dagobert,' said Effi as they were leaving, 'you must come to my Wedding Eve, and bring some friends. Because after the theatricals – and I don't want you coming with any old rag, tag and bobtail – there's to be a ball. And you have to bear in mind that my first grown-up ball may also be my last. So without at least six of your comrades, first-class dancers to a man, you won't get in. And of course you can get back on the early-morning train.' Her cousin promised all this, and so they parted.

About midday the two ladies arrived at their Havelland station out in the

Luch and in half an hour drove over to Hohen-Cremmen. Briest was happy to have his wife and daughter home again and asked one question after another, mostly not waiting for an answer, but instead launching into an account of what had happened to him in the meantime. 'Earlier you mentioned "The Isle of the Blessed" at the National Gallery – well, we've had something of the sort here while you were away: Pink the steward and the gardener's wife. Naturally I had to sack Pink, reluctantly I may say. It really is awkward that these things always happen at harvest time. And in every other respect Pink was an unusually capable fellow, though this wasn't the place for him, unfortunately. But that's enough of that; Wilke's getting hot under the collar.'

At table Briest was a better listener; the understanding they had struck up with Effi's cousin, about whom they had much to tell, met with his full approval, their attitude to Aunt Therese with less. But they could see clearly that for all his disapproval he was in fact amused; for a little prank like this was much to his taste and Aunt Therese really was a figure of fun. He raised his glass and clinked it with his wife and daughter. When they had risen from the table and a few of the prettiest purchases were unpacked in front of him and presented for his verdict, he continued to show great interest, which even survived, or at least didn't wholly evaporate, as he ran his eye over the bill. 'A trifle expensive, or should we just say very expensive. But not to worry. It all has such chic, I mean it's so stimulating, I have the distinct feeling that if you were to give me a case like that and a travelling rug for Christmas, we two would be in Rome ourselves at Easter, having our honeymoon again after eighteen years. What do you think Luise? Shall we follow their example? Better late than never.'

Frau von Briest made a gesture as if to say 'Incorrigible', and left him to his own sense of shame, which however was not great.

It was the end of August, the wedding day (October 3rd) was coming closer; in both the big house and in the vicarage and the school the preparations for the Wedding Eve went ahead without let-up. Jahnke, true to his passion for Fritz Reuter, had come up, as something 'particularly meaningful' for the occasion, with the idea of having Bertha and Hertha appear as Mining and Lining from *Ut mine Stromtid*, speaking *Plattdeutsch* of course, whereas Hulda was going to do the elder-tree scene from *Das Käthchen von Heilbronn*, with Lieutenant Engelbrecht of the Hussars as Wetter vom Strahl. Niemeyer, who could claim to have fathered the idea, hadn't hesitated for a moment to rewrite the scene to make it apply decorously to Innstetten and Effi. He himself was satisfied with his work and listened after the read-through to friendly comments from all concerned, with the exception however of his old friend and patron Briest, who, after listening to the mixture of Kleist and Niemeyer, protested vigorously, though not on literary grounds. '"Lord and master" here, "lord and master" there. What's it all supposed to mean? It can only give rise to misunderstandings, it distorts the whole thing. Innstetten is unquestionably an excellent specimen of humanity, a man of character and verve, but the Briests – excuse the Berlinism Luise – the Briests didn't come in with the cat either. We're a historic family – thank the Lord, I may add – and the Innstettens are *not*; the Innstettens are just old – ancient aristocracy if you like, but what is ancient aristocracy? I don't want a Briest, or at least a character in a Wedding Eve sketch in whom everybody is bound to see a reflection of our Effi – I don't want a Briest constantly going on, directly or indirectly, about her lord and master. Innstetten would have to be a Hohenzollern in disguise, at the very least, and there are such things. But he's not one of them, so I can only repeat, it's a distortion of the situation.'

And in fact Briest stuck to this view with peculiar tenacity for quite a time. Only after the second rehearsal, when Käthchen, already half in costume, wore a close-fitting velvet bodice, was he moved, never having been averse to a little homage to Hulda, to remark that 'Käthchen was coming along nicely', a turn of phrase that was pretty well as good as a truce, or at least was moving in that direction. That all these things were kept secret from Effi goes without saying. With more curiosity on her side, it would all have been impossible, but Effi had so little desire to find out about the preparations and the planned surprises that she declared emphatically to her mother that 'she was happy to wait and see', and when the latter expressed doubt, Effi terminated the conversation with the repeated assurance that this was indeed so. And why not? It was just a theatrical performance, and it couldn't be as lovely and poetic as the *Cinderella* they had seen on their last evening in Berlin, no, as lovely and poetic it couldn't be. On that occasion she really had wanted to take part herself, if only to make a chalk mark on the ridiculous schoolmaster's back. 'And how lovely the last act was – "Cinderella awakens as a princess" – well, a countess at least, it was just like a fairy tale.' She often talked like this, mostly with increased animation on each occasion she mentioned it, and the secrecy and constant whisperings of her friends annoyed her. 'I wish they took themselves less seriously and had more time for me. When it comes to it, all they'll do is forget their lines and I'll be nervous for them and ashamed that they're my friends.'

As she mocked them in this vein, it was obvious that Effi was not greatly bothered about the Wedding Eve or the wedding. Frau von Briest had pause for thought, but it didn't become a real worry, because Effi, and this was a good sign, was preoccupied with her future and, imaginative as she was, would indulge in quarter-hour descriptions of her life in Kessin, in which, incidentally, much to the amusement of her mother, a rather curious notion of Eastern Pomerania found expression, or perhaps was shrewdly calculated to evoke such an impression. It seemed to amuse her to think of Kessin as half-way to Siberia, where the ice and snow never quite melted.

'Goschenhofer sent the last of the things today,' said Frau von Briest as she sat as usual with Effi in front of the wing at the work-table on which the pile of linen and underwear constantly grew, while the newspapers, which just took up space, became fewer and fewer. 'I hope you have everything now Effi. But if you are still nursing any little wishes, now is the time to let us know, within the hour if possible. Papa has sold the rape for a good price and he's in an unusually good mood.'

'Unusually? He's always in a good mood.'

'In an unusually good mood,' her mamma repeated, 'which must be taken advantage of. So tell me. There were several times in Berlin when I had the impression that there was something or other you particularly wanted.'

'Well, Mamma dear, what can I say. Really, I have everything I need, I mean everything I need *here*. But since it seems I am destined to go so far north… and I must say I have nothing against it, on the contrary I'm looking forward to the northern lights and the brighter gleam of the stars… since it seems I am destined for it, I would really quite like a fur coat.'

'But Effi dear, that's all silly nonsense. You're not going to Petersburg or Archangel.'

'No, but it's on the way…'

'Well, that's true. You will be on the way. But what does that mean? When you go from here to Nauen, you're on the way to Russia. Well, if that's what you want, a fur coat you shall have. But first, just let me advise you against it. Fur coats are for older people, even your old mamma is too young for one, and if you turn up at seventeen in mink or marten in Kessin, they'll think it's fancy dress.'

This conversation took place on September 2nd, and would have continued had it not chanced to be Sedan Day. In the event they were interrupted by fifes and drums, and Effi, who had heard earlier about the planned parade but had forgotten, suddenly dashed from the work-table past the roundel and the pond to a little balcony built on the churchyard wall which had six steps no wider than the rungs of a ladder leading up to it. In a trice she was at the top, and there was the entire school with Jahnke gravely on the right wing while out in front, at the head of the column, marched a little drum-major with an expression on his face as if it had fallen to him to fight the Battle of Sedan all over again. Effi waved her hand▚ greeting did not fail to salute back with the gleamin▚

A week later mother and daughter were again sitting in their old plac▚ busy with their work. It was a wonderful day; the heliotrope in the or▚ mental bed round the sundial was still in bloom, and the light breeze that was blowing wafted its fragrance over to them.

'Oh how good I feel here,' said Effi, 'I feel so good and I'm so happy; I can't imagine heaven being better. And besides, who knows if they have such marvellous heliotropes in heaven.'

'Effi, you mustn't talk like that; you get that from your father, nothing's sacred for him, just the other day he said Niemeyer looks like Lot. Disgraceful. And what is it supposed to mean? In the first place he doesn't know what Lot looked like, and secondly it's hugely offensive to Hulda. It's a good job Niemeyer has only one daughter, so the whole thing collapses. In one particular he is right – in what he says about "Lot's wife", the pastor's good lady, who again managed to ruin Sedan Day entirely with her presumption and foolishness. Which reminds me that our conversation was interrupted when Jahnke marched past with the school – at least I don't imagine the fur coat you spoke of was the only thing you want. So tell me, treasure, what else have you in mind?'

'Nothing, Mamma.'

'Nothing at all?'

'No, nothing at all; seriously… Though if there has to be something…'

'Well…'

'Well, it would be a Japanese screen with black and gold birds on it, all with long crane's bills… And then maybe a globe for our bedroom, the sort that casts a red glow.'

Frau von Briest was silent.

'There you are, Mamma, now you're silent and you look as if I've said something really improper.'

'No Effi, not improper. Least of all in front of your mother. For I do know you. You are a little person full of imagination, and you like to paint pictures of the future, and the more colourful they are, the more beautiful and desirable they seem. That much was clear the day we bought the things for your trip. And now you think it would be wonderful to have a screen in the bedroom with all manner of fabulous creatures, all bathed in the half-light of a red lamp. It all seems like a fairy tale and you want to be a princess.'

Effi took her mamma's hand and kissed it. 'Yes Mamma, that's me.'

'Yes, that's you. I know. But my dear Effi, in life we must be cautious, espe-

to Kessin, a small place where there is
t, they'll laugh at that kind of thing. And
n't take to you, and there are bound to be
bringing, or possibly something even worse.'
then, and no globe. But I must confess I had
and poetic, everything bathed in a red glow.'
ved. She stood up and kissed Effi. 'You're a child.
at's how you imagine it. Reality is different, and it's
t instead of light and a red glow there is darkness.'
t to reply when Wilke came with the letters. One was
fro͟   Innstetten. 'Ah, from Geert,' said Effi, putting the letter
away a͟n͟   ͟ing in a composed tone, 'but you will allow me to place the
piano diagon͟ly in the room. I'm keener on that than the open fireplace
Geert has promised me. And the picture of you, I'm going to have that on
an easel; I can't be entirely without you. Oh yes, and I'll be homesick for you,
perhaps even on the honeymoon trip, but quite certainly in Kessin. They say
there isn't a garrison, not even a medical corps captain, so it's a good thing
it's at least a seaside resort. Cousin Briest's mother and sister always go to
Warnemünde and I'm pinning my hopes on that, for I don't see why he
shouldn't reroute them to Kessin. Reroute, that has the ring of the general
staff, but I think he has ambitions in that direction anyway. And then he'll
naturally come with them, and stay with us. By the way, in Kessin there's a
big steamer, somebody recently told me, that sails to Sweden twice a week.
And on board ship they hold a ball, they have a band naturally, and he's a
very good dancer.'

'Who?'

'Dagobert of course.'

'I thought you meant Innstetten. But anyhow, it's time we found out
what he has to say... You still have the letter in your pocket.'

'So I have. I had almost forgotten.' And she opened the letter and ran her
eye over it.

'Well Effi, nothing to say? I don't see a radiant smile, you're not even
laughing. And he always writes such bright and amusing letters, not all wise
and paternal.'

'I wouldn't permit any of that. He has age and I have youth. I would
shake my finger at him and say, "Geert, just think which is better."'

'And then he would answer, "What *you* have Effi is better." For he is not
only a man of the finest manners, he is also just and sensible and knows very
well what youth means. He always says that and he is attuning himself to
youth, and if he continues to do so when you are married, then it will be an
ideal marriage.'

'I think so too Mamma. But can you imagine, I'm almost ashamed to say it, I'm not really in favour of what is known as an ideal marriage.'

'That's just like you. What are you actually in favour of then?'

'I'm… well, I'm for share and share alike, and naturally for love and affection too. And if it can't be love and affection, for love, as Papa says, is just stuff and nonsense (which I don't actually believe), well then I'm for wealth and a grand house, a *very* grand house, where Prince Friedrich Karl comes for the shooting, either elk or capercaillie, or where the old Kaiser will call and have a gracious word for all the ladies, even the young ones. And when we're in Berlin I'll be for court balls and gala evenings at the opera, always close to the big central box.'

'Is this just high spirits or a mood talking?'

'No Mamma, I'm absolutely serious. Love comes first, but right after it comes brilliance and honour, and then come diversions – yes, diversions, always something new, always something to make me laugh or cry. The thing I can't stand is boredom.'

'How did you manage to put up with us then?'

'Oh Mamma, how can you say such a thing? Of course in the winter when our dear relatives call and stay for six hours or even longer, and Aunt Gundel and Aunt Olga look me up and down and pronounce me impudent – Aunt Gundel once actually said that to me – yes, well at times like that it's not very nice I have to admit. But otherwise I've always been happy here, *so* happy…'

And as she said this she fell to her knees before her mother, sobbing violently, and kissed both her hands.

'Get up Effi. These are just moods young girls get at your age, especially with a wedding in the offing and the uncertainty it entails. And now read me the letter, even if it doesn't contain anything very special, and perhaps not even any secrets.'

'Secrets,' laughed Effi and jumped up, suddenly in an entirely different mood. 'Secrets! Yes, he does keep trying, but most of what he writes I could put on the noticeboard at the town hall where his official announcements are posted. Geert isn't a Landrat for nothing.'

'Go on, read it.'

'"Dear Effi…" That's how he always starts, and sometimes he also calls me his "little Eve."'

'Go on, read it… I want to hear you read it.'

'Well, here goes:

Dear Effi,
The closer we come to our wedding day the fewer your letters. When the

23

post comes I always look first for your handwriting, but as you know (and I didn't intend it to be otherwise), as a rule in vain. The workmen are in the house at the moment doing up the rooms, just a few, for when you come. Most of it will be done when we're away. Madelung the decorator who is doing everything is an eccentric, I'll tell you about him one of these days, but what I really want to tell you is how happy I am about you, my sweet little Effi. I'm impatient to be off, the dear old town is getting more and more quiet and lonely. The last of the bathers left yesterday, he was bathing at 9 degrees in the end and the life-guard was always relieved when he came out safely. They were worried that he might have a stroke which could give the resort a bad name, as if the waves were worse here than elsewhere. I am so happy when I think that in four weeks I'll be sailing with you from the Piazetta to the Lido, or to Murano where they make glass beads and beautiful jewellery. And the most beautiful piece will be yours.

My regards to your parents and a most affectionate kiss to you from

your

Geert

Effi folded the letter again to put it back in the envelope.

'That's a very nice letter,' said Frau von Briest, 'and the way he always strikes the right balance is another thing in his favour.'

'Yes, the right balance, that's him.'

'Let me ask you, my dear Effi, do you wish the letter didn't strike the right balance, do you wish he was more affectionate, maybe effusively affectionate?'

'No, no, Mamma. Really and truly no, that's not what I want. It's better the way it is.'

'It's better the way it is. The way you make that sound. You're so strange. And earlier you were crying. Is there something on your mind? There's still time. Don't you love Geert?'

'Why shouldn't I love him? I love Hulda, I love Bertha, and I love Hertha. And I also love old Niemeyer. And that I love you goes without saying. I love everybody who wishes me well and is kind to me and spoils me. And I expect Geert will spoil me too. In his own way of course. He already wants to give me jewellery in Venice. He hasn't the slightest inkling that I don't care about jewellery. I prefer to climb or swing, especially when I'm afraid something's going to snap or collapse and I might fall. It wouldn't have to cost me my neck.'

'And do you love Cousin Briest too perhaps?'

'Yes, a lot. He always amuses me.'

24

'And would you have liked to marry Cousin Briest?'

'Marry him? My goodness no. Part of him's still a boy. Geert is a man, a handsome man whom I can show off in society and who is going to be something in the world. What can you be thinking of Mamma?'

'Well, that's all right Effi, I'm pleased. But you do have something on your mind.'

'Perhaps.'

'Well, tell me what it is.'

'You see Mamma, it's no bad thing that he's older than me, and may even be a good thing: he isn't old and he's fit and healthy and so dashing and soldierly. And I might almost say that I'm all in favour of him, if only... well if only he were a bit different.'

'How do you mean Effi?'

'Well, how do I mean; now you mustn't laugh at me. Something I heard just recently over at the pastor's house made me think of it. We were talking about Innstetten, and suddenly old Niemeyer furrowed his brow, but it was with respect and admiration, and said, "Yes, the baron. He's a man of character, a man of integrity."'

'And so he is Effi.'

'Exactly. And I think Niemeyer went on to say he's a man of principle. And that, I imagine, is a bit more. Oh, and I... I haven't any. You see Mamma, there's something about all this that worries and frightens me. He's so good and kind to me and he's so considerate, but... I'm afraid of him.'

5

The days of celebration at Hohen-Cremmen were in the past; everyone, including the young couple, had gone away on the evening of the wedding day.

The Wedding Eve party had pleased everybody, especially the performers, among whom Hulda had been the delight of all the young officers, both the Hussars from Rathenow and their somewhat more critical comrades from the Alexander Regiment. Yes, it had all gone off nice and smoothly, almost exceeding expectations. Except that Bertha and Hertha had sobbed so violently that Jahnke's verses in *Plattdeutsch* were pretty well lost to the audience. But even that was no great loss. Certain connoisseurs were even of the opinion that this was the real thing; sobbing and forgetting your lines und unintelligibility – this was always the way (and above all with such fetching redheads) the most resounding triumphs were pulled off. Cousin Briest had a quite special triumph to be proud of in the role he had written for himself.

He had appeared as a shop assistant from Demuth's who had discovered that the young bride intended to travel to Italy directly after the wedding and consequently wished to deliver a travelling case. The case of course turned out to be a giant box of sweets from Hövel's. They had danced until three in the morning, an occasion for old Briest, talking more and more as the effect of the champagne reached its peak, to make all sorts of remarks about the torch-dances that were still kept up at various courts, and about the curious custom of dancing till one's garters dropped, remarks which showed no sign of abating and went from bad to worse until in the end they reached such a pitch that the boom quite definitely had to be lowered. 'Pull yourself together Briest,' his wife whispered in his ear with an unmistakable note of seriousness, 'you're not here to make risqué remarks, but to do the honours of the house. This is a wedding, not a shooting party.' Whereupon Briest replied he couldn't see much difference; and anyway he was feeling happy.

The wedding day itself had gone off well too. Niemeyer has spoken excellently, and one of the old gentlemen from Berlin, who was on the edge of the court circle, had, on the way back from the church to the house for the reception, made observations to the effect that it was quite remarkable how thick on the ground talent was in a state like ours. 'I view this as a triumph for our schooling, and perhaps even more so for our philosophy. When I think that this Niemeyer, an old village pastor who looked like a pauper when he stood up... now tell me, my friend, didn't he speak like a court chaplain? The tact, the art of antithesis, just like Kögel, even superior to him in feeling. Kögel is too cold. Of course a man in his position has to be cold. What is it that brings us down in life? It's always heat.' The dignitary to whom these words were addressed was still unmarried and doubtless for that reason involved in his fourth 'affair', so he naturally agreed. 'Only too true, dear friend,' he said. 'Too much heat!... quite excellent... Reminds me of a story I must tell you later.'

The day after the wedding was a bright October day. The morning sun gleamed and yet it was autumnally cool, and Briest, who had just breakfasted in the company of his wife, rose from his place and stood with both hands behind his back facing the steadily dying embers in the fireplace. Frau von Briest, with a piece of wool-work in her hands, also drew her chair up to the fire and said to Wilke as he came in to clear the breakfast table, 'Now Wilke, once you have cleared up everything in the drawing-room, and that has priority, see that the cakes are sent down to the village, the walnut-cake to the pastor's and the plate of little cakes to Jahnke's. And be careful with the glasses. The fine crystal ones I mean.'

Briest, already on his third cigarette and looking very well, declared, 'There's nothing so good for one as a wedding, provided of course it isn't one's own.'

'I don't know Briest, how you can say such a thing. It's a surprise to me that you think you've been suffering in your marriage. I can't think why.'

'Luise, play the game. But I won't be provoked, not even by that kind of thing. Anyway, it's not us we should be talking about, we didn't even go on a honeymoon. Your father was against it. But now Effi's on her honeymoon. Enviable. Off on the ten o'clock train. They must be passing Regensburg by now, and I think we can take it he'll run through the principal art treasures of the Valhalla collection for her, without getting off the train of course. Splendid chap, Innstetten, but he does have a thing about art, whereas Effi, bless her, is a child of nature. He'll put her through it, I fear, with his enthusiasm for art.'

'Husbands always put you through it. And there are far worse foibles than an enthusiasm for art.'

'Quite, quite. But don't let's argue about that. It's a vast subject. And then people are so different. Now you, it would have suited you down to the ground. You would have been a better match all round for Innstetten than Effi, really. Pity, it's too late now, of course.'

'How charming of you, except that it's quite inappropriate. And be that as it may, what's in the past is in the past. He's my son-in-law now and no good can come of harking back to our younger days.'

'I was just trying to cheer you up.'

'Very kind. But quite unnecessary. I feel cheered up already.'

'You're in a good mood then?'

'I think I can say that. But you mustn't spoil it. So what is it? I can see you have something on your mind.'

'Were you happy about Effi? Were you happy about the whole affair? She was so strange, half child, almost, then full of self-confidence and not at all as deferential as she might be to a man of his standing. The only explanation I can think of is that she doesn't fully appreciate the man she's got. Or is it just that she doesn't really love him? That would be bad. For with all his good points, he's not the man to win her love with easy charm.'

Frau von Briest silently counted the stitches in her canvas. Finally she said, 'Briest, that's the most sensible thing I've heard from you in the last three days, and that includes your after-dinner speech. Yes, she had me wondering too. But I think we can stop worrying.'

'Did she pour out her heart to you?'

'I wouldn't quite put it like that. She felt the need to talk, but not the need to express her innermost feelings, and she sorts out many things for herself; she's communicative and reserved at the same time, secretive almost; altogether a very odd mixture.'

'I agree entirely. But if she didn't say anything, how do you know?'

'I just said she didn't pour out her heart. A general confession, baring the soul, that kind of thing isn't in her. It all came out in fits and starts, quite suddenly, and then it was over. But precisely because it was so involuntary and seemed to come out by sheer chance is why it was so important to me.'

'So when was this, what was the occasion?'

'It must have been just three weeks ago now. We were sitting in the garden, busy with all sorts of items for the household, large and small, when Wilke brought out a letter from Innstetten. She put it in her pocket, and I had to remind her a quarter of an hour later that she had a letter at all. Then she read it, scarcely showing a flicker of interest. I can tell you, my heart sank, so much so that I needed reassurance, as much as is possible in these matters.'

'Very true, very true.'

'What is that supposed to mean?'

'Well, I only meant... But it doesn't matter. Just carry on, I'm all ears.'

'So I asked her straight out how matters stood, and, knowing what she's like, I knew I had to avoid sounding solemn and keep everything as light as possible, almost make a joke of it, so I asked casually whether she would perhaps rather be marrying Cousin Briest who had courted her so very assiduously in Berlin.'

'And?'

'You should have seen her at that. Her immediate response was a saucy laugh. She said her cousin was really just an overgrown cadet in a lieutenant's uniform. And a cadet she could never love, let alone marry. And then she talked of Innstetten who was suddenly the epitome of all masculine virtue.'

'And how do you explain that?'

'Quite simply. Although she's so bright and vivacious, almost passionate, maybe even because of this, she's not someone for whom love is the important thing, or at least not what we would term love. She talks about it of course, dwells on it even, in a tone of conviction up to a point, but only because she has read somewhere that love is the highest thing, the most beautiful, most splendid thing. It could be that she just has it from Hulda, sentimental soul that she is, and is parroting it. But she doesn't feel anything much for all her talk. It may well be that it's still to come, God forbid, but it's not there yet.'

'So what is there? What does she feel?'

'In my opinion and as she herself says, two things: a love of pleasure, and ambition.'

'Well, that can be accommodated. That's a relief.'

'Not to me. Instetten is ambitious for promotion – I wouldn't call him a careerist, he's not that, he's too dignified for that, but he's ambitious for promotion, and that will satisfy Effi's ambition.'

'Well, there you are. That's good, isn't it?'

'Yes, that's good! But it's only half of it. Her ambition will be satisfied, but what about her desire for fun and adventure? I have my doubts. For her hourly little amusements and stimulation, for all that takes away boredom, the arch-enemy of a young person of wit and imagination, for all that Innstetten has very little to offer. He won't leave her stranded in an intellectual desert, he's too clever and too experienced for that, but he won't be much fun either. And the worst of it is, he won't even seriously address the problem of what is to be done. Things will be all right for a while and no great harm will be done, but then she'll notice and she'll feel insulted. And then I don't know what will happen. For soft and accommodating as she is, there's something reckless in her that will risk anything.'

At that moment Wilke came in from the drawing-room and announced that he had counted everything and all was present and correct, except for one of the fine crystal goblets which had been broken the previous day at the toast when Miss Hulda had clinked glasses too hard with Lieutenant Nienkerken.

'Only to be expected, she's always in a dream, and that romantic scene under the elder tree didn't improve matters. A silly girl, I just don't understand Nienkerken.'

'I understand him perfectly.'

'He can't possibly marry her.'

'No.'

'Well, what's the point?'

'It's a vast subject, Luise.'

This was on the day after the wedding. Three days later a little scribbled card arrived from Munich with just initials for names.

Dear Mamma,

Visited the Pinakothek this morning. Geert wanted to go on to the other gallery which I won't mention because I'm not sure how to spell it and I don't like to ask. He's an angel to me and explains it all. Everything is very beautiful but it's tiring. It will probably get easier in Italy and be better. We're staying at the 'Four Seasons' and Geert said, 'It's autumn outside, but with you I have spring.' I thought that was very clever. He is very attentive altogether. Of course I have to be too, especially when he's talking or explaining something. He knows everything so well too, without even looking it up. He talks of you with delight, especially Mamma. Hulda he finds a little coy; but he is very taken with old Niemeyer. A thousand greetings from your quite exhilarated but also rather weary

Effi

Cards like this arrived daily, from Innsbruck, Verona, Vicenza, Padua, and every one started, 'Today we visited the famous local art gallery', or if it wasn't a gallery, it was an arena or a church, Santa Maria something or other. From Padua a proper letter arrived along with the card.

Yesterday we were in Vicenza. One has to visit Vicenza because of Palladio; Geert tells me that all things modern have their roots in him. Only with regard to architecture of course. Here in Padua (where we arrived this morning) he muttered to himself several times in the hotel coach, 'In Padua he lies buried,' and he was surprised I had never heard the words. In the end he said it was all right really and an advantage that I knew nothing about it. He's very fair. And above all, he is an angel to me, not at all condescending and not at all old. I still have pains in my feet and all the standing and looking things up in front of paintings is rather a strain. But it has to be. I'm very much looking forward to Venice. We're staying five days there, maybe even a whole week. Geert has already been enthusing about the pigeons on St Mark's Square, and how you can buy bags of peas to feed the beautiful creatures. He says there are pictures of this, with beautiful blond girls, 'Hulda's type' he says. Which makes me think of the Jahnke girls. Oh what I wouldn't give to be back in our yard, sitting on a coach shaft feeding *our* pigeons. You mustn't have the fantail with the big crop killed, I want to see her again. Oh it's so beautiful here. It's supposed to be the most beautiful place of all.

Your happy but somewhat weary

Effi

Frau von Briest, when she had read the letter, said, 'Poor child, she's homesick.'

'Yes,' said Briest, 'she is. All that damned travelling around...'

'What's the point of saying that now? You could have prevented it. But that's you all over, always wise after the event. Locking the stable door after the horse has bolted.'

'Oh Luise, don't say things like that. Effi is our daughter, but since the 3rd of October she has been Baroness Innstetten. And if her husband and our son-in-law wants to go on a honeymoon and spends the trip recataloguing the pictures in every gallery he visits, there's nothing I can do about it. That's what marriage is all about.'

'Aha – now you admit it. With me you've always denied, I repeat, always denied that women are in a situation of constraint.'

'Yes, I have Luise. But why bring that up now? It's really too vast a subject.'

6

In the middle of November – they had reached Capri and Sorrento – Innstetten's leave ran out, and it was consistent with his character and practice to keep exactly to time. So on the 14th he and Effi arrived on the early morning express in Berlin, and Cousin Briest was there to greet them and suggest they spend the two hours they still had before the departure of the Stettin train on a visit to the St Privat panorama, which might be followed by a light meal. Both suggestions were gratefully accepted. At midday they were back at the station where, after the customary but fortunately never serious invitation to 'come over sometime' had been made both by Effi and Innstetten, they took leave of one another with warm handshakes. Effi was still waving goodbye from the carriage as the train pulled out. Then she made herself comfortable and closed her eyes; only occasionally did she sit up and give Innstetten her hand.

It was a pleasant journey and the train reached Klein-Tantow on time; from there a highway led over to Kessin ten miles away. In summer, especially during the bathing months, people preferred to go by water, taking an old paddle-steamer down the Kessine, the little river from which Kessin took its name; on October 1st the *Phoenix* – of which the local people had long wished in vain that it might one passengerless day be true to its name and go up in flames – regularly ceased service, for which reason Innstetten had already sent a telegram from Stettin to his coachman Kruse: 'Five pm Klein-Tantow station. If weather fine open carriage.'

And now it was fine and when they arrived Kruse was waiting in an open carriage to greet them with the deference required of a gentleman's coachman.

'Now then, Kruse, everything in order?'

'Yes sir, at your service sir.'

'Well Effi, if you'd like to get in.' And as Effi did as instructed and one of the railwaymen stowed a little hand-case at the front beside the coachman, Innstetten gave instructions to send the rest of the luggage on the omnibus.

Immediately afterwards he too took his seat, and – wishing to show the common touch – asked a bystander for a light and shouted, 'Off we go, Kruse.' Their route went across the track, which had several lines at the crossing, diagonally along the railway line and presently past an inn by the highway which bore the name 'The Prince Bismarck'. At this point the road forked, branching right to Kessin, left to Varzin. In front of the inn stood a broad-shouldered man of medium build in a fur coat and a fur hat; the latter, as the Landrat drove past, he raised with great dignity. 'Who was that?' said Effi, who was highly interested in everything she saw, and consequently in the best of moods. 'He looked like a *starost*, not that I've ever seen a *starost* I must confess.'

'No matter Effi. You're very close, just the same. He really does look like a *starost*, and in fact he is something of the sort. He's half Polish you see, his name is Golchowski, and when we have the elections here, or a hunt, he's in his element. Actually he's a very dubious customer whom I wouldn't trust out of my sight and who probably has a lot to answer for. But he likes to act the loyal subject, and when the gentry from Varzin go by, he all but prostrates himself in front of their carriages. I know Prince Bismarck loathes him. But what can one do? We can't offend him because we need him. He has the whole constituency in his pocket and knows how to run an election like nobody else, and he's supposed to be well off. And to cap it all he's a money-lender, which the Poles usually aren't; quite the contrary as a rule.'

'But he looked handsome.'

'Yes, he's handsome all right. Most people here are handsome. They're of good-looking stock. But that's the best you can say for them. Your people in the Mark are an unprepossessing and morose lot, and their manner is less respectful, in fact it's not in the slightest respectful, but when they say yes they mean yes and when they say no they mean no, and you can rely on them. Here nothing is clear-cut.'

'Why are you telling me this? Now that I'm going to have to live with them here?'

'No you won't, you won't hear or see much of them. Because town and country are very different here, and you will only get to know our towns-people, the good people of Kessin.'

'The good people of Kessin. Is that sarcasm, or are they really so good?'

'I wouldn't go so far as to say they are really good, but they're different from the others; they have no similarity whatsoever with the country folk.'

'And how does that come about?'

'Because they are quite different people, of different stock with different ways. If you go inland, what you find are so-called Kashubians, whom you may have heard of, a Slav people who have been here for a thousand years and maybe much longer. But all the people who live in the little shipping and trading towns along the coast are immigrants from far away, who care little about the Kashubian hinterland because there's nothing there for them, their concerns are elsewhere. What concerns them is where their trade is, and since they trade with the whole world and are in communication with the whole world, you find people among them from all corners of the globe. Which goes for Kessin too, backwater though it is.'

'But this is delightful, Geert. You keep calling it a backwater, but now, if you haven't been exaggerating, I find that it's a completely new world. All sorts of exotic things. Isn't that right? That's what you meant, isn't it?'

He nodded.

'A whole world, I say, with perhaps a Negro or a Turk, or perhaps even a Chinaman.'

'A Chinaman too. What a good guess. We may still have one, we certainly did have; he's dead now, buried in a little plot with a railing round it next to the churchyard. If you're not afraid I'll show you his grave sometime. It's in the dunes with just some marram grass round it and a little immortelle here and there, and the sound of the sea all the time. It's very beautiful and very eerie.'

'Yes, eerie – I would like to know more about it. Or maybe rather not, I invariably start imagining things and then I have dreams, and I don't want to see a Chinaman approaching my bed tonight when I hope I'll be sleeping soundly.'

'Well, he won't.'

'Well, he won't. Listen to that. How odd it sounds, as if it were somehow possible. You're trying to make Kessin interesting for me, but you're rather overdoing it. Are there many foreigners like that in Kessin?'

'A great many. The whole town consists of foreigners like that, people whose parents or grandparents lived somewhere else altogether.'

'How very peculiar. Tell me more, please. But nothing sinister. A Chinaman, I think, is always a bit sinister.'

'Yes, that's true,' laughed Geert. 'But the rest of them, thank goodness, are quite different, nice and well-behaved, a little too wrapped up in business, too obsessed with their own advantage and always ready with none too reliable bills of exchange. Yes, you've got to watch them. But they're easy to get on with. And to show you that I haven't been making this up, I'll give you a small sample list of inhabitants.'

'Yes Geert, do that.'

'Well, not fifty paces from us, our gardens are actually next to one another, we have Macpherson, the engineer who has charge of the dredger, a Scotsman, a genuine Highlander.'

'And does he look like one?'

'No, thank goodness, he's a wizened little man, of whom neither his clan nor Walter Scott would be especially proud. And then, living in the same house as Macpherson, there's an old surgeon, Beza by name, actually he's just a barber; he's from Lisbon where the celebrated General de Meza comes from – Meza, Beza, you can hear they're compatriots. And then up the river at the Bulwark – that's the quay where the ships tie up – there's a goldsmith called Stedingk who's descended from an old Swedish family; indeed, I believe there are even imperial counts who bear that name, and then, and after this I'm going to stop, there's good old Dr Hannemann who is of course a Dane and was in Iceland for a long time and has written a short book about the last eruption of Hekla or Krabla.'

'But that's marvellous, Geert. It's like six novels, it's more than one can cope with. It sounds very dull and bourgeois at first but in fact it's quite out of the ordinary. And then you must have people, because after all it's a sea-port, who aren't just surgeons or barbers or things like that. There must be captains, a flying Dutchman or…'

'You're quite right. We even have a captain who was a pirate with the Black Flags.'

'Never heard of them. What are the Black Flags?'

'They're people out in Tongking and in the South Seas… But now that he's back among real people again his manners are of the best and he's rather entertaining.'

'I would be afraid of him though.'

'You needn't be, never, not even when I'm away or at tea with Prince Bismarck, for, apart from everything else we have, we also, thank goodness, have Rollo…'

'Rollo?'

'Yes, Rollo – which makes you think of the Norman Duke, assuming you've heard about that sort of thing from Niemeyer or Jahnke. Well, ours is something like that. He may just be a Newfoundland, but he's a wonderful dog, who loves me and will love you. For Rollo has good taste. And as long as you have him by your side you're safe and nothing can harm you, no living creature, and no dead one. But look at the moon over there, isn't it beautiful?'

Effi, who was silently sunk in herself, drinking in each word, half avidly, half fearfully, now sat up and looked over to where the moon had risen behind white but rapidly disappearing clouds. The big, copper-red disc stood behind a copse of alders, casting its light on a broad sheet of water formed here by the Kessine. Or perhaps it was a lagoon fed by the sea beyond.

Effi was spellbound. 'Yes, you're right Geert, it's beautiful. But it's sort of uncanny too. In Italy I never had this impression, not even when we were crossing from Mestre to Venice. There was water and swamp and moonlight there too, and I thought the bridge was going to collapse but it wasn't so spooky. Why is that? Is it just because it's the north?'

Innstetten laughed. 'We're seventy miles further north than Hohen-Cremmen here and you'll have to wait a while for the first polar bear. I think you're feeling the strain of the long journey, what with the St Privat panorama and the story of the Chinaman and everything.'

'You didn't tell me any story.'

'No, I just referred to him. But the mere mention of a Chinaman is a story in itself…'

'Yes,' she laughed.

'And anyhow you're almost there. Do you see the little house ahead with the light? It's a blacksmith's. There's a bend in the road there. And once we're round the bend you can see the Kessin spire, or rather both of them…'

'There are two?'

'Yes. Kessin is going up in the world. It has a Catholic church now too.'

Half an hour later the carriage stopped at the Landrat's residence at the opposite end of the town, a plain, rather old-fashioned half-timbered house whose front looked out on the main street leading to the bathing beaches, while the gable end looked down on a copse known as the 'Plantation', which lay between the town and the dunes. This old-fashioned half-timbered house was Innstetten's private residence and not the Landrat's office; that lay diagonally opposite, on the other side of the street.

Kruse had no need to announce their arrival by three knocks with the stub of his whip; watch had been kept for some time from door and windows for the arrival of the master and his wife, and before the carriage drew up the entire household was assembled on the threshold, a stone slab which took up the whole width of the pavement, at their head Rollo, who began circling the carriage the moment it stopped. Innstetten first helped his young wife to descend, and then, giving her his arm, walked past the servants with a friendly greeting, and the latter then followed the couple into the hall with its splendid old wall-cupboards. The maid, a pretty woman no longer entirely youthful and whose plumpness became her just as well as the dainty cap on her blond hair, assisted her mistress in laying aside her muff and taking off her coat, and was just bending down to help her off with her fur-lined rubber boots when Innstetten said, 'The best thing will be for me to introduce all the staff, with the exception of Frau Kruse – I suspect she must be with her black hen again as ever – who doesn't like meeting people.' Everybody smiled. 'But never mind Frau Kruse, this is Friedrich who has been with me since I was at university... Isn't that right Friedrich, wonderful times weren't they... and this is Johanna, a compatriot of yours from the Mark, assuming you allow anyone from the Pasewalk district to qualify, and this is Christel to whom we entrust our creature comforts morning and evening, and she knows about cooking, I can assure you. And here we have Rollo. Eh Rollo, how are you?'

It seemed as if Rollo had just been waiting to be addressed like this, for the moment he heard his name he gave a yelp of pleasure, stood upright and put his paws on his master's shoulders.

'That's enough, Rollo, that's enough. But look here, this is your mistress; I have already told her all about you, and I've said you are a beautiful animal and will look after her.' And at this Rollo went down and sat in front of Innstetten, looking up curiously at the young woman. And when she stretched out a hand to him he nuzzled it.

During these introductions Effi had found time to look round. She seemed entranced by all she saw, and dazzled by the superabundance of light. In the front half of the hall there were four or five wall-lamps, the lamps themselves very primitive, of unadorned tin which made their glow all the brighter. Two astral lamps draped with red veils, a wedding present from Niemeyer, stood on a folding table that had been placed between two oak cupboards; in front of them were the tea things with the little burner already lit under the kettle. But there was much, much more besides, some of it very strange. Across the hall ran three beams which divided the ceiling into as many separate fields; from the one nearest the front hung a ship in full sail with a high poop and cannon ports, and further on a giant fish seemed to swim in the air. Effi took her umbrella and gently poked the monster, setting it in slowly swinging motion.

'What's that, Geert?' she asked.

'It's a shark.'

'And the thing right at the back, that looks like a big cigar outside a tobacconist's?'

'It's a young crocodile. But you'll have plenty of time to examine all that tomorrow; now come and let's have a cup of tea. You must be frozen, even with all your travelling-rugs and blankets. It was distinctly cold at the end.'

He gave Effi his arm, and as the two maids withdrew, leaving just Friedrich and Rollo, they turned left into the master's living room and study. Effi was just as surprised here as she had been out in the hall; but before she could utter a word, Innstetten drew back a curtain, and behind it was a second, somewhat larger room with a view of the courtyard and garden. 'This is yours now Effi, Friedrich and Johanna have done what they could to arrange it to my specifications. I find it quite tolerable and I should be happy if you liked it too.'

Effi extracted her arm from his and stood on tiptoe to give him a heart-felt kiss.

'Poor little me, how you spoil me. This grand piano, and this carpet, I do believe it's Turkish, and the aquarium with the little fishes, and the flower-table. Something to spoil me wherever I look.'

'Yes, my dear Effi, you will just have to get used to it, that's what being young and pretty and charming is for, and the good people of Kessin will have discovered that, goodness knows how. For as far as the flower-table is concerned at least, I'm not guilty. Friedrich, where did the flower-table come from?'

'Gieshübler the chemist... There's a card with it.'

'Ah, Gieshübler, Alonzo Gieshübler,' said Innstetten with a laugh and almost animated as he handed the card with its somewhat strange-sounding name to Effi. 'Gieshübler, I forgot to tell you about him – by the by, he has a doctorate, but he doesn't like people to use his title; he claims it just annoys the real doctors, and he's probably right. Anyway, you'll meet him I imagine, in fact quite soon. He's a character, the best we have here, an aesthete and something of an original, but above all he's all heart, and that's always the main thing. But never mind all that, let's sit down and have tea. Where shall it be? Here in my room or over in yours? For that's the extent of the choice. Small and narrow is my hut, as the poet says.'

Effi sat down without reflection on a little corner sofa. 'We'll stay here today, and today you'll be my guest. Or let's do it this way: tea regularly in my room, breakfast in yours. Then we'll each get our due, and I wonder where I'll like it best.'

'That's really a question of morning or evening.'

'Absolutely. But it's how the question is posed, or perhaps what pose we adopt towards it, that's the point.'

And she laughed and nestled up close to him and made to kiss his hand.

'No Effi, for goodness sake don't do that. I'm not interested in being an object of respect, that's for the townspeople in Kessin. For you I'm...'

'What?'

'Let's drop the subject. I must watch what I say in future.'

7

It was broad daylight when Effi wakened next morning. She had to make an effort to focus on her surroundings. Where was she? Of course, in Kessin in Landrat von Innstetten's house, and she was his wife, Baroness Innstetten.

Sitting up she looked about herself with curiosity; the previous evening she had been too tired properly to take in all the half strange, half old-fashioned things that surrounded her. Two pillars supported the ceiling-beam, and green curtains closed off the alcove-like sleeping area where the beds stood from the rest of the bedroom; only in the middle was there no curtain, or it was drawn back, enabling her to view things comfortably from her bed. And there between two windows, reaching up to the ceiling, was the narrow pier-glass, while towering to its right over towards the wall on the hallway side was the black, tiled stove, which – that much she had noticed the previous evening – was still stoked from the outside in the time-honoured way. She could now feel the heat it was radiating. How lovely it was, to be in one's own home; she hadn't felt such a sense of well-being during the entire trip, not even in Sorrento.

But where was Innstetten? All was silent around her, nobody there. All she could hear was the tick-tock of the little pendulum clock and an occasional rumble in the stove which led her to conclude that a few fresh logs were being fed in from the hallway. Gradually she remembered that Geert had said something the previous evening about an electric bell, which it didn't then take her long to find; right beside her pillow was the little white ivory button which she pressed gently.

Johanna appeared immediately. 'You rang, my lady?'

'Oh Johanna, I think I must have overslept. What time is it? It must be late.'

'Just gone nine.'

'And the Master...' she couldn't bring herself to speak straight off of her 'husband'... 'the Master must have been very quiet, I didn't hear a thing.'

'That he was. And your ladyship will have been sleeping very soundly. After the long journey...'

'Yes I was. And the Master, is he always up so early?'

'Always my lady. He's very strict about that; he can't bear sleeping late, and when he goes to his room over there the stove has to be warm, and there must be no waiting for the coffee.'

'So he has already breakfasted?'

'Oh no my lady... the Master...'

Effi realized her question would have been better left unasked and her conjecture that Innstetten might not have waited for her unuttered. She felt as if she should make amends for this error as best she could, and after she had got up and sat down in front of the pier-glass she resumed the conversation, saying, 'The Master is quite right of course. Early to rise was the rule in my parents' house too. There can never be order in the day when people lie in in the morning. But the Master won't be too severe with

38

me; I couldn't sleep last night for a long time, and I was even a bit afraid.'

'What's that my lady? What was the matter?'

'There was a very strange noise coming from above me, not loud but very penetrating. At first it sounded as if long dresses were sweeping over the floorboards, I was so worked up I thought several times I could see white satin shoes. It was as if there was dancing up there, but all very quiet.' As this conversation proceeded, Johanna looked over the young woman's shoulder into the tall, narrow mirror so as to be able to observe Effi's expression better. Then she said, 'Yes, it's in the upstairs room. We used to hear it in the kitchen too. But we don't hear it any longer; we've got accustomed to it.'

'Is there something special about it?'

'Oh heaven forbid, not in the slightest. For a while we didn't rightly know where it was coming from, and the vicar looked embarrassed, though Dr Gieshübler always just laughed about it. But now we know that it's the curtains. The room is rather close and musty so the windows are always left open except when it's stormy. That means there's almost always a strong draught up there blowing the old white curtains – which are far too long – back and forth across the floor. It sounds like silk dresses, or satin shoes, as your ladyship just remarked.'

'Of course that's what it must have been. But I still don't understand why the curtains aren't taken down. Or they could be shortened. It's such a strange sound and it gets on your nerves. And now Johanna, please give me the little towel and dab my forehead. Or get the spray from my travelling case… Ah, that's nice and refreshing. I shall go over now. He's still there isn't he, or has he gone out?'

'The Master was out, my lady, over at his office I believe. But he's been back for a quarter of an hour. I shall tell Friedrich to serve breakfast.'

And with that Johanna left the room, while Effi took another look in the mirror and then crossing the hall, which in the daylight had lost much of the magic of the previous evening, entered Geert's room.

He was sitting at his desk, a somewhat cumbersome roll-top bureau which, as it was an heirloom from his parents' house, he was loth to part with. Effi went up behind him and hugged and kissed him before he had time to get up from his chair.

'Up already?'

'Up already, you say. You're making fun of me of course.'

Innstetten shook his head. 'Why would I do that?' But it pleased Effi to accuse herself and she refused to listen to her husband's assurances that his 'Up already' had been sincerely meant. 'You surely remember from our trip that you never had to wait for me in the morning. During the day of course is another matter. It's true I'm not very punctual, but I'm no lie-abed. In that, I think, my parents brought me up well.'

'In that? In everything my sweet Effi.'

'You're just saying that because it's still our honeymoon... but no, we're beyond that. My goodness Geert, I hadn't thought of that, we've been married more than six weeks already, six weeks and a day. Yes, well, that makes it different, I won't take it as flattery, I'll take it as the truth.'

At that moment Friedrich entered, bringing the coffee. The breakfast table was placed diagonally in front of a little right-angled sofa that just fitted into one corner of the living-room. Here they both sat down.

'The coffee is excellent,' said Effi, at the same time surveying the room and its furnishings. 'This is like hotel coffee, or like Bottegone's... you remember, in Florence, with the view of the cathedral. I must write to Mamma about this, we don't have coffee like this at Hohen-Cremmen. In fact, Geert, I'm just realizing what a distinguished marriage I've made. At home everything only just passed muster.'

'Nonsense Effi, I never saw a better run house than yours.'

'And then the way you live. When Papa bought his new gun-cabinet and hung a buffalo's head over his desk with old Wrangel below it (he was adjutant to the old man once, you know) he thought it was the last word, but when I look around me here, then what we thought was Hohen-Cremmen grandeur seems very plain and ordinary. I don't know what to compare it all with; even last night when I only got a fleeting look at it, it made me think all kinds of things.'

'What kinds of things, may I ask?'

'Ah, what kinds of things. But you mustn't laugh. I once had a picture book with a Persian or Indian prince (he was wearing a turban) sitting cross-legged on a red silk cushion with a big red silk bolster behind him which bulged out to right and left, and the wall behind the Indian prince was bristling with swords and daggers and leopardskins and shields and long Turkish muskets. And look, that's just what it looks like here, and all that's needed to make the resemblance perfect is for you to sit cross-legged.'

'Effi, you're a dear, sweet creature. You don't know how much I find you so, and how dearly I want to show you that every minute of the day.'

'Well, there's plenty of time for that, I'm only seventeen and I don't intend to die just yet.'

'Not before me, at least. Of course, if I were to die, I would prefer to take you with me. I don't want to leave you to anyone else; what do you think of that?'

'I must give that some thought. Or rather, let's drop the subject. I don't

40

like talking about death, I'm for life. And now tell me, what's life like here? On the way you told me all sorts of strange things about town and country, but about the life we're going to lead here – not a word. I can see of course that everything is different here from Hohen-Cremmen and Schwantikow, but in the "good town of Kessin", as you always call it, there must also be society of some kind, people for us to consort with. Are there people of good family in the town?'

'No, my dear Effi; that side of things is going to be a great disappointment to you. We have a few aristocratic families living in the neighbourhood, and you'll meet them, but here in town there's nobody.'

'Nobody at all? I can't believe it. There must be three thousand of you here, and among three thousand people, apart from Beza the barber (that's his name, isn't it?), there must be some kind of élite, dignitaries or something of the sort.'

Innstetten laughed. 'Oh, dignitaries, we have those. But in the light of day they don't amount to much. Of course we have a clergyman and a district judge and a headmaster and a chief pilot, probably adding up to a round dozen people with posts of that sort, good souls for the most part, but they're not exactly refined. And that just leaves the consuls.'

'Just the consuls? Really Geert, how can you say "just the consuls". That's something very high and mighty, I might even say fearsome. The consuls are the ones with that axe aren't they, sticking out of a bundle of rods?'

'Not quite Effi. They're called lictors.'

'That's right, they are called lictors. But consuls were rather distinguished and quite high in the legal system. Brutus was a consul, wasn't he?'

'Yes, Brutus was a consul, but ours aren't very like him; they confine their activities to trading in sugar or coffee, or opening a case of oranges and selling them at ten pfennigs each.'

'Not possible.'

'It certainly is. They're shrewd small tradesmen who are quickly to hand with advice when a foreign ship comes in and is totally foxed by some business procedure, and once they've been of service to some Portuguese or Dutch ship, they soon end up official representatives of these foreign states, so we have as many consuls in Kessin as there are ambassadors and envoys in Berlin, and on holidays, and there are a lot of holidays here, they run up all the flags, and on bright, sunny mornings, you'll see all Europe showing the flag on our roofs, and the stars and stripes and the Chinese dragon to boot.'

'You're in the mood for mockery, Geert, and you may be right. But for my small part, I must confess I find all this quite delightful, it certainly puts our Havelland towns in the shade. When it's the Kaiser's birthday the flags are only ever black and white with a little red at best, but nothing that can compare with the world of flags you're talking about. Anyway, as I've already said to you, I find over and over again that things here are all very foreign, and I haven't heard or seen anything yet that didn't fill me with amazement, starting last night with that quaint ship out in the hall and the shark behind and the crocodile, and this room of yours. All so oriental, I have to say it again, like an Indian prince's apartments…'

'If you like. I congratulate you, princess…'

'And then the gallery upstairs with those long curtains that brush over the floor.'

'But what do you know about that, Effi?'

'Nothing except what I've just told you. It must have been for about an hour when I woke up in the night, I seemed to hear shoes sliding across the floor, and dancing and perhaps even music. But all very quiet. And I told Johanna that this morning, just by way of excuse for sleeping so late. And she told me it came from the long curtains in the gallery upstairs. I think we should just trim a bit off the curtains and have done with it, or at least close the windows; the storms will be starting soon. Mid-November is the time for them after all.'

Innstetten stared straight ahead in some slight embarrassment and seemed undecided whether he should respond to all this. In the end he chose to be silent. 'You're quite right Effi, we'll shorten the long curtains upstairs. But there's no hurry, especially since it's not certain that it will help. It may be something else, something in the chimney, or woodworm or a polecat. For we have polecats here. In any event, before we start changing things you'll have to take a look at the household here, I'll show you round of course; we can do it in a quarter of an hour. And then you can dress for our friend Gieshübler, just a little, for you're really at your most charming just as you are; it's past ten and I would have to be very wrong about him if he didn't call at eleven or at midday at the latest to lay his most devoted respects at your feet. That's the kind of language he indulges in. As I've already told you, he's a capital fellow who will be a friend to you, if I'm any judge of you and him.'

8

Eleven was long past; but Gieshübler had not yet put in an appearance. 'I can't wait any longer,' Geert, whom duty called, had said. 'If Gieshübler does still come, be as cordial as possible and everything will go swimmingly; he mustn't be made to feel embarrassed; if he's bashful he either gets tongue-tied or says the oddest things; but if you can win his trust and put him in a good humour he will talk like a book. I know you'll do it. Don't expect me before three; there are all kinds of things to be done over there. And we must think about the room upstairs again; but it will probably turn out best to leave it as it is.'

With that Innstetten went off and left his young wife alone. She sat, leaning back slightly, in a cosy corner by the window, leaning her arm, as she looked out of the window, on a little flap pulled out of the roll-top bureau. The street was the main road to the beach which meant that in summertime it was full of life, but now in the middle of November everything was empty and silent and only a few poor children whose parents lived in some of the thatched cottages on the outermost edge of the 'Plantation' clattered past the Innstettens' house in their clogs. Effi however did not feel lonely at all, for her imagination was still working on the wonderful things she had seen shortly before on her inspection tour of the house. This tour had begun with the kitchen whose stove proved to be of modern manufacture, while an electric cable ran across the ceiling to the maid's room – both had been recently installed. Effi had been very pleased when Innstetten told her about them, but then they had gone from the kitchen back into the hall and from there out into the courtyard, half of which was not much more than a narrow alley between the two side wings. Everything else relating to the household and its management had been accommodated in these wings, on the right the maid's room, the servants' room, the laundry room, and on the left between the stable and the coach-house the coachman's rooms that were occupied by Kruse's family. Above this, in a loft, the hens were housed, and a flap on the roof above the stable enabled the pigeons to go in and out. All this Effi had looked at with much interest, but this interest was far exceeded when after returning from the yard to the front of the house she had, under Innstetten's guidance, climbed the steps that led upstairs. The staircase was crooked, rickety and dark; the landing by contrast into which it opened almost seemed cheerful because it had a great deal of light and a fine view of the landscape: to one side, out over the roofs of the edge of the town and the 'Plantation' to a Dutch windmill standing high on a dune, to the other on to the Kessine which at this point, just before its estuary, was quite broad and made a stately impression. It was impossible not to be impressed, and Effi had not stinted in giving lively expression to her delight. 'Yes, very beautiful, very picturesque,' Innstetten had answered without further comment and had then opened the two halves of a slightly out-of-true double door which led to the right into the so-called gallery. This ran the whole length of the house; front and rear windows stood open and the long curtains already mentioned swept

43

back and forth in the strong draught. At the centre of one of the side walls a fireplace protruded with a large stone base, while on the opposite wall a few tin lamps hung, each with two openings for the light, just like the ones in the hallway; but everything was gloomy and neglected. Effi was somewhat disappointed and said so, declaring that rather than this abandoned, shabby gallery, she would like to see the rooms on the other side of the landing. 'There's absolutely nothing to see there,' Innstetten had answered, opening the doors nonetheless. Here there were four rooms, each with a single window, all distempered yellow, just like the gallery and just as empty. Except for one in which there were three rush-bottomed chairs with the seats gone; on the back of one of them a little picture an inch or so high had been stuck, showing a Chinaman in a blue jacket with baggy yellow breeches and a flat hat on his head. Effi saw it and asked, 'What's the Chinaman doing there?' Innstetten himself seemed surprised by the picture and assured her he didn't know. 'That's something Christel must have stuck on, or Johanna. Some kind of game. You can see it's been cut out of a child's reading book.' Effi agreed and was only surprised that Innstetten was taking it all so seriously, as if it really mattered. Then, taking another look at the gallery, she had expressed the view that it was a pity to have it all standing empty. 'Downstairs we only have three rooms, and if anybody comes to visit we'll be stuck. Don't you think the gallery could be made into two nice guest rooms? It would be just the thing for Mamma; she could sleep at the back and would have the view of the river and the two moles, and at the front she would have the town and the Dutch windmill. All we have in Hohen-Cremmen is an old German mill. What do you think? Next May Mamma will very likely be coming.'

Innstetten had been in agreement with all this but all he had said at the end was, 'That's all very well, but it's probably better in the long run to put Mamma across the road, where the Landrat's office is; the whole first floor is empty, just as it is here, and she would be more independent there.'

So that was the result of their first tour of the house; then Effi had gone across to dress, not quite as quickly as Innstetten had expected, and now she was sitting in her husband's room, her mind preoccupied alternately with the little Chinaman upstairs and with Gieshübler, who still hadn't appeared. A quarter of an hour earlier to be sure, a little man with crooked shoulders, almost to the point of deformity, but wearing a short, elegant fur coat and a tall top hat, very smoothly brushed, had passed by on the other side of the street and looked over at their window. But that couldn't have been Gieshübler! No, the man with the crooked shoulders and yet such an air of distinction must have been the president of the high court, and she did in fact remember once having seen such a person at a reception at Aunt Therese's, and then it occurred to her that Kessin only had a district judge.

While she was still engrossed in these thoughts, the object of them, who had apparently first taken a morning stroll round the Plantation – or was he trying to pluck up courage? – reappeared, and a minute later Friedrich came to announce the chemist Gieshübler.

'Show him in.'

The poor young woman's heart was beating, because she was appearing for the first time as a wife, and indeed as the first wife of the town.

Friedrich helped Gieshübler out of his fur coat and then opened the door again.

Effi held out her hand as the embarrassed Gieshübler made his entrance, and he kissed it a shade impetuously. The young woman seemed immediately to have made a powerful impression on him.

'My husband has already told me… But this is my husband's room I'm receiving you in… he's over in the office and may be back any minute… May I invite you to join me in my room.'

Now Gieshübler followed Effi's lead into the next room where she pointed to one of the armchairs, herself sitting down on the sofa. 'I can't tell you what pleasure your beautiful flowers and your card gave me yesterday. I stopped feeling a stranger here at once, and when I mentioned it to Innstetten, he said he thought we would be thoroughly good friends.'

'Did he indeed? The good Herr Landrat. Yes, the Herr Landrat and you, my dearest lady, are a case, if I may make so bold, of two dear hearts finding one another. For I know your esteemed spouse for the man he is, and your disposition, my dearest lady, is plain to see.'

'Let us hope you are not seeing with too friendly an eye. I am very young. And youth…'

'Oh, dearest lady, say nothing against youth. Youth, even in error, is charming and beautiful, and age, even in its virtues, is of no great worth. Personally, I can't speak authoritatively in this matter – of age perhaps, but not of youth, for I was never really young. People of my sort are never young. I may say that that is the saddest part of the matter. One has no courage, one has no faith in oneself, one scarcely dares ask a lady to dance, because one wants to spare her the embarrassment, and so the years run by, and one grows old, and one's life was poor and empty.'

Effi gave him her hand. 'Oh, you mustn't talk like that. We women are not as bad as that.'

'Oh no, certainly not…'

'And when I recall,' Effi went on, 'all that I've experienced… which isn't a lot, for I've never gone out much and I've lived most of my life in the country… but when I recall it, I find that in the end we always love what deserves to be loved. And of course I see instantly that you are different from others, we women have a sharp eye for that. In your case it may be that your name contributes to the effect. That was always one of our dear Pastor Niemeyer's favourite claims; he used to say that one's name, particularly one's Christian name, has a mysterious determining influence, and Alonzo Gieshübler, I mean it opens up a whole new world, yes, I might even say, if you'll allow me, Alonzo is a romantic name – it's in Weber's *Preziosa*.'

Gieshübler smiled with quite uncommon contentment and found the courage to set aside his top hat, which was much too tall for his proportions and which, up to that point, he had been rotating in his hands. 'Yes, my dearest lady, there you hit it.'

'Oh, I understand. I've heard about the consuls Kessin is supposed to be so full of, and in the house of the Spanish consul your father presumably met the daughter of a seafaring *capitano*, some Andalusian beauty I imagine. Andalusian women are all beautiful.'

'It was just as you suppose, my lady. And my mother really was beautiful, though it's hardly for me to undertake to prove this. But when your esteemed spouse came here three years ago, she was still alive, and the fire was still in her eyes. He'll corroborate this for me. I take more after the Gieshüblers, people outwardly unprepossessing, but otherwise tolerably sound. We're in our fourth generation in these parts, a full century, and if there were a chemists' aristocracy…'

'You would be in a position to lay claim to it. I for my part take your case as proven, indeed for proven without any reservation. People like us, who come from old families, find it easiest to do this, because we, at least that's how my father and mother brought me up, take pleasure in accepting any noble-mindedness, no matter where it comes from. I was born a Briest, and I am descended from the Briest who carried out the attack on Rathenow – you may perhaps have heard of it – on the day before the battle of Fehrbellin…'

'Oh certainly, my dearest lady, that's a special interest of mine.'

'So I'm a Briest. And my father, if he's said it to me once, he's said it a hundred times: Effi (that's my name you see), Effi, he says, this is the heart of it, just this – when Froben switched horses he was of the nobility, and when Luther said "Here I stand" he was certainly of the nobility. And I think, Herr Gieshübler, Innstetten was quite right when he assured me that we would be true friends.'

At this all Gieshübler wanted to do was make a declaration of love and ask to be allowed to fight and die for her like El Cid or some similar *campeador*. But since none of that was possible and his heart could take no more, he stood up and reached for his hat, which he fortunately found instantly, and, after repeatedly kissing her hand, beat a rapid retreat without uttering another word.

9

That had been Effi's first day in Kessin. Innstetten gave her half a week to settle in and write a variety of letters to Hohen-Cremmen, to Mamma, to Hulda, to the twins; then however their visits in the town had begun, which in part (it was raining so heavily just then as to make this unusual behaviour permissible) they accomplished in a closed coach. When this round was complete it was the turn of the landed aristocracy. This lasted longer, because with the mainly long distances involved only one visit could be made in a day. They called first on the Borckes at Rothenmoor, then they went to Morgnitz, Dabergotz and Kroschentin, where they made their duty calls on the Ahlemanns, the Jatzkows and the Grasenabbs. A few others followed, among whom old Baron von Güldenklee at Papenhagen was included. The impression Effi gained was the same everywhere: mediocre people of mainly dubious affability, who, while they pretended to discuss Bismarck or the Crown Princess, were actually examining Effi's dress, which was found by some to be too pretentious for so young a lady, by others to be not quite discreet enough for a lady of her station. The Berlin style, they noted, was indeed all too evident: a concern for externals and a remarkable embarrassment and insecurity when it came to bigger issues. At the Borckes' in Rothenmoor and then by the families in Morgnitz and Dabergotz she was pronounced to be 'infected with rationalism', while by the Grasenabbs in Kroschentin she was declared outright to be an 'atheist'. Old Frau von Grasenabb, it must be conceded, a South German, née Stiefel von Stiefelstein, had made a half-hearted attempt to redeem Effi for 'deism'; Sidonie von Grasenabb however, an old maid of forty-three, had intervened brusquely, 'I'm telling you mother, she's an an out-and-out atheist, not a jot less, and that's that', whereupon the old lady, who was afraid of her own daughter, had prudently fallen silent.

The whole round of visits had lasted something like two weeks and it was December 2nd when, at an advanced hour, they returned to Kessin from the last of them. This had been to the Güldenklees at Papenhagen, on which occasion it had been Innstetten's unavoidable lot to discuss politics with old Güldenklee. 'Ah, my dear Landrat, when I think how times have changed. On this day a generation ago, more or less, there was another second of

December and the good Louis Napoleon, Napoleon's nephew – *if* that was what he was and he wasn't descended from some other quarter entirely – was blazing away at the Paris mob. Well, one could forgive him *that*, he was the right man for that, and I swear by the motto "Everybody gets no more nor less than his just deserts." But then when he lost his sense of proportion in 1870 and without so much as a by your leave decided to have a go at *us*, that, Baron, if I may say so, was, how shall I put it, a piece of downright insolence. But he got his comeuppance. Our old fellow up there doesn't take insolence, *he's* on our side.'

'Yes indeed,' said Innstetten, who was wise enough to pretend to take such Philistine ramblings seriously, 'the hero and conqueror of Saarbrücken didn't know what he was doing. But you mustn't be too hard on him personally. Who, in the final estimate, is master in his own house? Nobody. I am already adjusting to the thought of handing over the reins of government to someone else, and Louis Napoleon, well, he was just putty in the hands of his Catholic wife, or let's say rather his Jesuit wife.'

'Putty in his wife's hands, and then she thumbed her nose at him. Of course he was, Innstetten. But you're not going to exonerate that puppet just because of that? He has been judged and the judgment stands. In a general way nobody has yet proved,' and with these words his gaze somewhat anxiously sought the eye of his better half, 'whether the rule of women may not actually be an advantage; the wife of course has to be up to it. And who was this wife? She wasn't a wife at all, the best that can be said is that she was a lady, which says it all; the word "lady" almost always has an unpleasant after-taste. This Eugénie – and I shall ignore her connection with the Jewish banker, for I loathe people preening themselves on their virtue – had a touch of the *café chantant*, and if the city she lived in was Babel, then she was the whore of Babylon. I don't wish to be more explicit, for I know,' and he bowed to Effi, 'what I owe German womanhood. Pardon me, dear lady, for even touching on these things in your hearing.'

Such had been the course of the conversation after they had dealt with the election, the rapeseed crop and Nobiling, and now Effi and Innstetten were sitting at home again chatting for another half-hour. The two maids were already in bed for it was nearly midnight.

Innstetten was walking up and down in a short dressing-gown and Morocco slippers; Effi was still in her formal dress; her fan and gloves lay beside her.

'Yes,' said Innstetten, and he stopped pacing up and down, 'we really ought to celebrate today, but I can't quite think how. Should I play you a triumphal march, or set the shark out there swinging and carry you in triumph across the hall? Something has to happen, for you know, that was the last visit.'

'Thank goodness for that,' said Effi. 'But the feeling that we have peace and quiet now is celebration enough, I think. Only you could give me a kiss. But you never think of that. All the long way never a touch, frosty as a snowman. And always that cigar of yours, nothing else.'

'Don't go on, I'll try to be better, all I want to know at the moment is what you feel about the whole business of who to see and cultivate. Are you drawn to one or the other of them? Did the Borckes outdo the Grasenabbs, or the other way round, or are you for old Güldenklee? What he had to say about Eugénie made a very pure and noble impression, did it not?'

'What's this, Herr von Innstetten, do I detect mockery? I'm getting to know quite another side of you.'

'And if our gentry don't come up to the mark,' Innstetten went on without batting an eyelid, 'how do our local dignitaries stand? What did you think of the Club? That's what it comes down to in the end. I saw you the other day talking to our district judge – he's a lieutenant in the reserves, simpers a bit but he might perhaps be tolerable if he could only get away from the idea that his appearance on the right flank was responsible for the retaking of Le Bourget. And his wife! She's held to be the Club's best Boston player and she has the prettiest counters too. So Effi, again, how is it to be in Kessin? Are you going to get used to it? Will you be well-liked and secure my majority if I decide to stand for the Reichstag? Or are you for the hermit's life, for keeping yourself from the Kessiners, both the townspeople and the landed gentry?'

'I think it will be the hermit's life for me, unless the Chemist under the Sign of the Moor can cajole me out of it. That will lower me even further in Sidonie's estimation, but I must accept that; this is a battle that must be fought. I stand or fall with Gieshübler. It sounds funny, but he really is the only person you can talk to, he's the only real person here.'

'That he is,' said Innstetten. 'How well you can discriminate.'

'Would I have *you* otherwise?' said Effi and slipped her arm through his.

That was on the 2nd of December. A week later Bismarck was at Varzin and by then Innstetten knew that until Christmas and even beyond there could be no thought of quiet days for him. The prince had had a soft spot for him since their Versailles days and often invited him over to dine when he had visitors, but also on his own, for the youthful Landrat with his outstanding good manners and astuteness found equal favour with the princess.

The first invitation was for the 14th. There was snow on the ground and for this reason Innstetten decided to make the two-hour journey to the station, from which there was a further hour to go by rail, in the sleigh. 'Don't wait up for me Effi. I can't possibly be back before midnight; probably it will be two or later. But I won't disturb you. Take care until I see you tomorrow morning.' And with that he climbed on to the sleigh and the two pale tan Graditzers raced off through the town and then inland towards the station.

This was the first long separation, almost twelve hours. Poor Effi. How was she to spend the evening? Early to bed was dangerous, then she might wake up and not be able to get to sleep again, and she would listen to every sound. No, best get really tired first and then sleep soundly. She wrote a letter to Mamma and then went to see Frau Kruse whose disturbed condition – she would often have the black hen on her lap until far into the night – filled Effi with sympathy. Her gesture of friendliness, however, was not for one moment returned by the woman as she sat silent and still, brooding to herself in her overheated room, so Effi, once she realized that her visit was more of an intrusion than a pleasure, went away, only pausing to ask the sick woman if she needed anything. But she refused all offers.

It was now evening and the lamps were already lit. Effi went to the window of her room and looked out at the copse with glittering snow lying on its branches. She was totally absorbed by this picture and quite oblivious to what was happening in the room behind her. When she turned round she noticed that Friedrich had laid a place without making a sound and had placed a cabaret service on the sofa-table. 'Oh, yes, supper, well, I suppose I'll have to sit down to it.' But she had no appetite so she stood up again and once more read through the letter she had written to Mamma. If she had felt lonely before, she now felt doubly so. What would she not have given to see the Jahnke redheads come through the door, or even Hulda? Hulda was of course always so sentimental and normally only concerned with her own triumphs, but dubious and contestable though these triumphs might be, she would at that moment dearly have liked to hear about them. In the end she opened up the grand piano to play, but it was no use. 'No, it will just make me utterly melancholy, better to read.' And so she looked for a book. The first one she could lay her hands on was a fat red travel guide, years out of date, possibly from Innstetten's time as a lieutenant. 'Yes, I'll read some of this, there's nothing more calming than books like this. The only thing I don't like about them is the maps, but I'll take care to avoid all that excruciating small print.' And so she opened the book at random at page 153. Next door she could hear the tick-tock of the clock and outside Rollo who, since it had turned dark, had abandoned his post in the shed and today as every evening lay stretched out on the large woven mat outside the door of her bedroom. Her awareness of his proximity diminished her sense of abandonment, she almost recovered her good humour, and started to read straight away. The page that lay open before her was an account of the Hermitage, the well-known margrave's summer residence near Bayreuth; that tempted her – Bayreuth, Richard Wagner – so she read on. 'Among the pictures in the Hermitage, one more claims our attention, not for its beauty but for its age and for the person it represents. It is a considerably darkened portrait of a woman, with a small head and severe, somewhat uncanny features, in a ruff which seems to carry the head all by itself. Some hold it to be of an old margravine from the end of the fifteenth century, others are of the opinion that it is the Countess of Orlamünde; there is agreement on the fact that it is a picture of a figure who has attained a certain notoriety in the history of the Hohenzollerns under the name of the "White Lady".'

'Just my luck,' said Effi, pushing the book aside, 'I want to settle my nerves and the first thing I read is the story of the White Lady, whom I've been afraid of for as long as I can remember. But since I've opened up a horror story, I may as well read it to the end.'

And she opened the book again and read on. '…This particular portrait (whose subject has such a part to play in Hohenzollern family history) plays its part as a picture in the history of Hermitage castle itself, and this is probably connected with the fact that it hangs on a secret door, concealed from outsiders' eyes, behind which is a staircase leading up from the cellars. It is said that when Napoleon spent the night here, the "White Lady" stepped out of the frame and approached his bed. The Emperor is said to have sat up in terror and called for his adjutant, and to the end of his days he referred in great indignation to this *maudit château*.'

'I must stop trying to calm myself by reading,' said Effi. 'If I read any more I'm sure to come to a vaulted cellar where the devil has ridden off on a wine-cask. I believe there's a lot of that kind of thing in Germany, and of course a guide-book is bound to have assembled it all. So I'll just shut my eyes and try as best I can to recreate my Wedding Eve: when the twins couldn't go on for tears, when Cousin Briest, while everyone was looking uneasily at each other, managed to insist with astonishing dignity that such tears were the key to paradise. He really was charming and always so full of high spirits… And now what about me! Here of all places. Oh, I'm not cut out to be a grand lady. Mamma, she'd have fitted in here, she'd have set the tone as a Landrat's wife should, and Sidonie Grasenabb would have been all adulation and wouldn't have given a fig whether she was a believer or not. But me… I'm a child and I'll always remain one. I once heard that was a good thing. But I don't know if it's true. One should always fit in wherever one finds oneself.' At this moment Friedrich came in to clear the table.

'What time is it Friedrich?'

'It's getting on for nine, my lady.'

'Oh well, that's good. Send Johanna to me.'

'Your ladyship requires me?'

'Yes Johanna. I want to go to bed. It's still early really. But I'm so lonely. Please put this letter in the post and when you get back it will be time. And even if it isn't.'

Effi took the lamp and went across to her bedroom. Of course, there on the rush-mat was Rollo. When he saw Effi coming he rose to make way and brushed his ears against her hand. Then he lay down again.

Johanna had meanwhile gone over to the Landrat's office to post the letter. She hadn't been in any hurry on the way, indeed she had gone as far as to have a chat with Frau Paaschen, the clerk's wife. About the young lady of the house, naturally.

'What's she like, then?' Frau Paaschen asked.

'Very young, that's what she's like.'

'Well, that's no bad thing, in fact just the opposite. The young ones, and this is what's good about them, are always standing in front of the mirror preening themselves and trying things on, so they don't notice anything or hear anything and they haven't yet got to be so that they go about counting the candle-ends and seeing you don't get a kiss because no one kisses them any more.'

'Yes,' said Johanna, 'that's how my last mistress was and quite without cause. But there's nothing like that about our young lady.'

'Is he very affectionate to her?'

'Oh very. As you can imagine.'

'But he leaves her all on her own…'

'Yes, my dear Paaschen, but you mustn't forget… there's Prince Bismarck. And he's a Landrat after all. And perhaps he intends to go further.'

'I'm sure he does. And so he will. There's something about him. That's what Paaschen always says, and he's a good judge of folk.'

By the time this errand across the street to the office was over, a quarter of an hour had probably passed, and when Johanna returned, Effi was already sitting in front of the pier-glass waiting.

'You took a long time, Johanna.'

'Yes my lady… I am sorry my lady… I ran into Frau Paaschen over there, and I stayed and passed the time a little. It's so quiet here. You're always glad when you see anyone you can exchange a few words with. Christel is a good soul but she never talks, and Friedrich is so dim and so cautious too that he'll never come out with anything. Of course you have to know when to keep quiet, and Frau Paaschen is so nosy and so very common, actually not at all my type; but one is happy to see or hear anything.'

Effi sighed, 'Yes, Johanna, that's truly the best thing…'

'Your ladyship has such beautiful hair, so long and silky.'

'Yes it's very soft. But that's not good, Johanna. Hair and character go together.'

'They do indeed, my lady. And a soft character is better than a hard one. I have soft hair too.'

'Yes Johanna, And yours is blond too. That's what men like best.'

'Oh that depends a lot, my lady. Many have a weakness for black too.'

'That's true,' laughed Effi, 'I've found that too. It has probably all got to do with something entirely different. But blondes always have a fair complexion, as you do, Johanna, and I'll bet you have plenty of suitors. I'm very young but even I know that. And then I have a friend who was blond, flaxen-haired really, blonder than you, she was a clergyman's daughter...'

'Oh yes...'

'Johanna, what do you mean "Oh yes". It sounded rather suggestive and strange, you surely don't have anything against clergyman's daughters... She was a very pretty girl, that was what our officers all thought – we had officers, you see, red Hussars from Rathenow in fact – and she knew how to dress, black velvet bodice and a flower, a rose or a heliotrope, and if she hadn't had such big, protuberant eyes... oh, you should have seen them, Johanna, at least as big as this' (and Effi laughed as she pulled her right eyelid) '– but for that she would have been a real beauty. She was called Hulda, Hulda Niemeyer, and we weren't as close as all that, but if I had her here now and she was sitting there on the little corner sofa, I would chat with her till midnight or later. I so long for...' and at this she drew Johanna's head closer to her... 'I'm so afraid.'

'Oh, it'll pass, my lady, we've all felt it.'

'You've all felt it? What does that mean Johanna?'

'...And if your ladyship is really so afraid, I can sleep here. I'll take the straw mat and turn a chair over for a headrest, and I'll sleep here until morning, or until the Master gets back.'

'He isn't going to disturb me. He especially promised that.'

'Or I'll just sit on the corner sofa.'

'Yes, that might be all right. No, it won't do. The Master mustn't know I'm afraid, he doesn't like it. He always wants me to be brave and decisive, just like him. But I can't; I was always susceptible... Of course I can see I'll have to make an effort and do his bidding in this instance and indeed in everything... And I do have Rollo. He's lying outside the door.'

Johanna nodded at each word and then lit the candle that was standing on Effi's bedside table. Then she took the lamp. 'Does your ladyship require anything further?'

'No Johanna. The shutters are properly closed, aren't they?'

'Just drawn to, my lady. Otherwise it's so dark and stuffy.'

'Very well.'

And at that Johanna withdrew; Effi got into bed and pulled the bed-clothes tightly round her.

She left the candle burning, because she did not propose to go to sleep just yet, but intended, just as she had done earlier with her Wedding Eve, to review her honeymoon trip and go over everything again in her mind's eye. But things did not turn out as she had imagined, and she had only just got to Verona and was looking for the house of Juliet Capulet when she dropped off. The stump of candle in the little silver candlestick gradually burned down, then flared one last time and went out.

Effi slept very soundly for a while. But suddenly she sat up with a loud cry, in fact she heard the cry herself, just as she heard Rollo barking outside; from down the hallway his 'woof, woof' sounded, muffled and almost fearful. She felt as if her heart were standing still; she could not call out and just at this moment something flitted past her and the door leading to the hall-way flew open. But the moment of her greatest terror was also the moment of liberation, because instead of something dreadful, it was Rollo that came up to her, seeking her hand with his muzzle and, once he had found it, lying down on the rug spread out at her bedside. Effi herself had pressed the bell-push three times with her other hand and in less than half a minute Johanna was there, barefoot, her skirt over her arm and a large check shawl thrown over head and shoulders.

'Thank goodness you're here, Johanna.'

'What was it my lady? Your ladyship has had a dream.'

'Yes, a dream. I must have had a dream... but there was something else too.'

'And what was that, my lady?'

'I was sleeping soundly, and suddenly I sat up and called out... perhaps it was a nightmare... nightmares run in the family, Papa has them too and frightens us with them, though Mamma just says he should get a grip on himself, which is easier said than done... so, I sat up, roused from my sleep and cried out, and when I looked round as best I could in the dark something rushed past my bed, just there, just where you're standing Johanna, and then it was gone. And if I really ask myself what it was...'

'Well, what was it then my lady?'

'And if I really ask myself... I don't like to say this Johanna... but I think it was the Chinaman.'

'The one from upstairs?' Johanna tried to laugh, 'our little Chinaman, the one Christel and me stuck on the back of the chair? Oh, your ladyship *was* dreaming, and even if you were awake it all came out of the dream.'

'I would like to think so. But at exactly the same moment Rollo barked outside, so he must have seen it too, and then the door flew open and the dear, faithful animal bounded towards me as if he had come to save me. Oh it was awful, my dear Johanna. And I'm so alone, and so young. Oh if only I had somebody here with a shoulder to cry on. But so far away from home… Oh, away from home.'

'The Master may be here any time.'

'No, he mustn't come; he mustn't see me like this. He might laugh at me and I could never forgive him for that. It was so terrifying, Johanna… you must stay here now… But don't wake Christel or Friedrich. Nobody must know.'

'Or maybe I could fetch Frau Kruse, she never sleeps, she sits there all night.'

'No, no, she's one of them too. All that business with the black hen, it's the same kind of thing; no, she mustn't come. No Johanna, stay here, just you. And it's a good thing the shutters are just drawn to. Throw them open, and make it good and loud, I want to hear a noise, a human noise… I know it sounds funny but I have to call it that… and then open the window a little so that I have some air and light.'

Johanna did as she was bidden, and Effi sank back into her pillows and soon afterwards into a lethargic sleep.

10

Innstetten had not got back from Varzin until six in the morning and, fending off Rollo's demonstrations of affection, had retired as quietly as possible to his room. Here he made himself comfortable and all he would allow was for Friedrich to cover him with a travelling rug. 'Wake me at nine.' And at that hour he had duly been wakened. He got up quickly and said, 'Bring me breakfast.'

'Her ladyship is still asleep.'

'But it's late. Has something happened?'

'I don't know. All I know is that Johanna had to sleep in her ladyship's room last night.'

'In that case send Johanna in.'

So in came Johanna. She had the same rosy complexion she always had, and seemed not to have been especially affected by the night's events.

'What's happened with your mistress? Friedrich tells me something happened and you slept over there.'

55

'Yes sir. Her ladyship rang three times, quite quickly, all at once, so I thought there must be something amiss. And so there was. She must have had a dream, or maybe it was the other thing.'

'What other thing?'

'Oh, you know sir.'

'No, I don't know. At any rate it's time to make an end of all that. And how did you find my wife?'

'She seemed beside herself, clutching Rollo's collar with her arms round him as he stood by her ladyship's bedside. And the dog was frightened too.'

'And what had she been dreaming, or come to that, what had she heard or seen? What did she say?'

'It had sort of flitted by her, quite close.'

'What? Who?'

'Him from upstairs. Him from the gallery, or that little room.'

'Nonsense I say. Always the same stuff and nonsense; I don't want to hear any more of it. And after that you stayed with my wife?'

'Yes sir. I made a bed on the floor right beside her. And I had to hold her hand, and then she got to sleep.'

'And she's still sleeping?'

'Quite soundly.'

'That I find worrying, Johanna. Sleep can help you recover, but it can also make you ill. We must wake her, carefully of course, so she isn't frightened again. And tell Friedrich not to bring breakfast, I shall wait until the Mistress is here. And use some discretion.'

Half an hour later Effi appeared. She looked charming, very pale, and she was leaning on Johanna. But when she saw Innstetten she rushed to him and hugged and kissed him. And as she did so tears streamed down her cheeks. 'Oh Geert, thank goodness you're here. Now everything is all right again. You mustn't go away again, you mustn't leave me alone again.'

'Effi my dear – put it down Friedrich, I'll see to everything – Effi my dear, it's not just a whim or thoughtlesssness when I leave you alone, it's because that's how it has to be; I have no choice, I'm a civil servant, I can't just say to Prince Bismarck or the Princess, Your Highness, I can't come, my wife gets so lonely, or my wife is afraid. If I said that it would show us in a ridiculous light, certainly me, and you too. But have a cup of coffee first.'

Effi drank some and that visibly revived her. Then she grasped her husband's hand again and said, 'You're right; I can see it's not done. In addition to which we're aiming higher. I say we, because really I'm more set on it than you…'

56

'All wives are,' laughed Innstetten.

'Well, that's agreed; you'll accept invitations just as you have been doing, and I'll stay here and wait for my "lord and master", which reminds me of Hulda under her elder tree. I wonder how she is?'

'Ladies like Hulda are always all right. But what else were you going to say?'

'I was going to say that I'll stay here, and even alone if need be. But not in this house. Let's move. There are such nice houses on the Bulwark, there's one between Consul Martens' and Consul Grützmacher's, and there's one on the marketplace, directly opposite Gieshübler; why can't we live there? Why here? When we had friends or relatives visiting, I often heard them say that in Berlin people move because of piano-playing next door, or cockroaches, or because the caretaker's wife was unfriendly; and if people move for a little thing like that...'

'A little thing? A caretaker's wife? Don't say that...'

'If it can be done for things like that, then it can be done here too, where you're the Landrat and everybody does what you want and many people are indebted to you. Gieshübler would certainly help us, even if it were only for my sake, for he would be sorry for me. So say it Geert, tell me we're giving up this haunted house, this house with its...'

'Chinaman, you mean. You see, Effi, the dreadful word can be uttered without making him appear. What you saw, or what flitted past your bed, as you would have it, was the little Chinaman the maids stuck on the chair-back upstairs; I bet he was wearing a blue jacket and a flat hat with a shiny button on top.'

She nodded.

'There you are, a dream, a hallucination. And I suppose Johanna told you yesterday about the wedding up there...'

'No.'

'So much the better.'

'She didn't tell me a thing. But I can see from all this that there *is* something odd about this place. And then there's the crocodile; it's all so uncanny here.'

'That first evening when you saw the crocodile you thought it was like something out of a fairy tale...'

'Yes, I did then...'

'...Besides Effi, I can't leave here, even if it were possible to sell the house or arrange an exchange. It would be just like refusing invitations to Varzin. I can't have people in the town here saying Landrat Innstetten is selling his house because a little Chinaman stuck on a chair appeared as a ghost at his wife's bedside. I'd be finished, Effi. There's no recovering from ridicule like that.'

57

'Yes Geert, but are you so sure there's no such thing?'

'I wouldn't say that. It's one of those things you either believe in or, preferably, don't. But assuming there is such a thing, what harm does it do? The fact that there are germs floating around in the air, as you'll have heard, is much worse and much more dangerous than all this spectral activity. That is if spectres are active and such things really exist. And I'm surprised to find such an aversion and fear in *you* of all people, a Briest. You're behaving as if you came of some petty bourgeois family. Ghosts are a mark of distinction, like a family tree and so forth, and I know families who would just as soon part with their coat of arms as their "White Lady", who may just as easily be black.'

Effi said nothing.

'Well Effi. No answer?'

'What am I supposed to answer? I've given in to you and shown willing, but I still think you, for your part, could show me more sympathy. If you knew just how much I need that. I suffered a lot, really a lot, and when I saw you I thought that would be the end of my fears. But all you can say is, you don't want to appear ridiculous, to the Prince or to the town. It's not much comfort. Very little indeed, I find, even less so since you've ended up contradicting yourself and not only seem to believe in these things yourself, but actually to be demanding that I take an aristocratic pride in your ghost. Well, I don't. And when you say there are families who value their ghost as highly as their coat of arms, that's just a matter of taste; I value my coat of arms more. We Briests don't have a ghost, thank goodness. The Briests were always very good people, which has probably got a lot to do with it.'

The argument might well have gone on and led to the first serious ill-feeling between them, had Friedrich not come in to give her ladyship a letter. 'From Herr Gieshübler. The messenger is awaiting an answer.'

All trace of displeasure vanished from Effi's face instantly; the mere mention of Gieshübler's name did her good, and her sense of well-being increased as she ran her eye over the letter. First of all it wasn't a letter but a *billet*, addressed in the most wonderful copperplate hand to 'Frau Baronin von Innstetten, née von Briest', and instead of a seal there was a little picture of a lyre with a rod sticking in it. The rod might also have been an arrow. She handed the *billet* to her husband who equally admired it.

'Well, read it.'

Effi broke the wafer and read:

Esteemed lady, dear Frau Baronin,

58

Permit me, in offering you my most obedient respects this morning, to add a humble request. A dear friend of mine of many years' standing, a daughter of our dear town of Kessin, Fräulein Marietta Trippelli, will arrive on the mid-day train and tarry in our midst until tomorrow morning. She intends to be in Petersburg on the 17th and to give a series of recitals in that city until the middle of January. Prince Kochukov is once again offering her the hospitality of his residence. Kindly disposed towards me as always, Fräulein Trippelli has agreed to spend the evening at my humble abode and to give a rendering of some *Lieder*, wholly of my choice (for she permits no difficulty to deter her). Might the Frau Baronin possibly condescend to grace this musical evening with her presence? At seven o'clock. Your esteemed spouse, whose presence I feel I can count upon with certainty, will lend his support to my humble request. Others present, only Pastor Lindequist (who will accompany) and of course the old pastor's widow Frau Trippel.

I remain, Madam, your most devoted servant,

A. Gieshübler

'Well?' said Innstetten, 'Yes or no?'

'Yes, of course. This will take me out of myself. And anywhow I can't refuse my dear Gieshübler when it's his very first invitation.'

'Agreed. So Friedrich, tell Mirambo, who presumably brought the *billet* round, that we should be honoured.'

Friedrich went out. When he had gone Effi asked, 'Who is Mirambo?'

'The real Mirambo is a robber-chief in Africa... Lake Tanganyika if your geography stretches to that... but ours is just Gieshübler's general factotum who keeps the stove stoked, and this evening he will probably be on duty in tails and cotton gloves.'

It was evident that this little incident had had a positive effect on Effi and had restored her light-heartedness in large measure, but Innstetten was intent on contributing something more to promote her further convalescence. 'I'm glad you said yes, and said it so quickly and unhesitatingly, and now I want to make another suggestion to bring you completely back to normal. I can see there is still something bothering you from last night, and it doesn't suit my dear Effi, so we must get rid of it, for which purpose there's nothing better than fresh air. The weather is splendid, fresh and mild at the same time, there's hardly a breath of wind; what do you say to going for a ride, but a long one, not just down to the Plantation, and in the sleigh of course, with the white snow-blankets, and we'll put on the bells, and if we're back by four you can have a rest, and at seven we'll be at Gieshübler's listening to Miss Trippelli.'

Effi took his hand. 'How good you are Geert, and how considerate. I must have seemed very childish to you, or at least very childlike; first for my fears, and then for suggesting that you sell the house, and then, what's worse, that you put off the Prince. That you should fob off the Prince – it's laughable. For after all he's the man who determines our fate. Mine too. You can't imagine how ambitious I am. Actually it was sheer ambition that made me marry you. But you don't have to look so serious about it. I love you too... how does it go when you pick a flower and pluck the petals? He loves me *un peu, beaucoup, à la folie.*'

And she laughed gaily. 'So now tell me,' she went on, when Innstetten still said nothing, 'where is it to be?'

'I thought to the railway station, but taking a detour, then back along the highway. And at the station we'll eat, or better still at Golchowski's, in the Prince Bismarck Inn – we passed it, if you remember, the day we arrived. It's always good to call in on these people, and then I can discuss the election with your *starost*, as you've christened him, and if he personally isn't up to much, he does keep an orderly tavern and an even better table. Eating and drinking is something the people here understand.'

It was almost eleven when they had this conversation. At twelve Kruse drew up at the door with the sleigh and Effi climbed in. Johanna wanted to bring a foot-muff and furs, but with all that was still weighing on her, Effi was so much in need of fresh air that she waved everything aside and made do with a double blanket. Innstetten however said to Kruse, 'We want to go to the station, where we two both were this morning. They'll be surprised up there, but there's no harm in that. I think we'll drive along the Plantation here and then turn left towards the Kroschentin church spire. Give the horses their head. We must be at the station by one.'

And they followed this course. Smoke hung over the white roofs of the town, for there was almost no movement in the air. Utpatel's mill too was only turning slowly, and they flew past it, close by the churchyard with its berberis bushes whose tips, hanging over the railings, brushed Effi as they passed, scattering snow all over her travelling rug. On the other side of the lane was a plot with a railing, not much bigger than a flower bed, with nothing to be seen in it but a young pine-tree sprouting at its centre.

'Is somebody buried there too?' asked Effi.

'Yes, the Chinaman.'

Effi shuddered; it was as if she had been stabbed. But she had strength enough to control herself and asked with apparent calm, 'Ours?'

'Yes, ours. He naturally couldn't be buried in the parish churchyard, and so Captain Thomsen, who was his friend, you might say, bought this plot and had him buried here. There's a stone too, with an inscription. All before

60

my time, of course. But they still talk about it.'

'So there is something in it. A story. You said something of the sort this morning. In the long run it would be best for me to hear what it is. As long as I don't know what it is, with the best will in the world I am still a prey to my own imaginings. Tell me the truth. The truth can never be such a torture as my imagination.'

'Bravo Effi. I didn't want to talk about it. But now it has come up of its own accord, which is good. And in any case there's really nothing to it.'

'All the same to me; nothing, or a lot or a little. Just get on with it.'

'Easier said than done. The beginning is always the hardest part, with stories too. Let's see, I think I'll start with Captain Thomsen.'

'Yes, and...'

'Well, Thomsen, whom I've already mentioned to you, was on the so-called China run for many years, carrying cargoes of rice between Shanghai and Singapore, and he must have been sixty when he arrived here. I don't know whether he was born here or had other connections here. To cut a long story short he arrived, sold his ship, an old tub that he didn't get much for, and bought a house, the one we now live in. For out there in the wide world he had become a wealthy man. And that's where the crocodile and the shark came from, and the ship too of course... Well, there was Thomsen, a very dapper fellow (at least so they tell me) and well-liked. Among others by Kirstein the mayor, and especially by the pastor in Kessin at that time, a Berliner who had come shortly before Thomsen and had his share of hostility to contend with.'

'I can believe that. I see it too; they're so strict and self-righteous here. I think it's the Pomeranian way.'

'Yes and no, it depends. There are some districts where they're not strict at all, and there anything goes... But look Effi, the Kroschentin church spire is just in front of us. Shouldn't we forget about the station and just call on Frau von Grasenabb? If my information is correct, Sidonie is not at home. So we could risk it...'

'What can you be thinking of Geert, I ask you? It's heavenly flying along like this, and I can actually feel myself being liberated and shedding all my fears. And now I am to give it all up just to drop in on these old folk and in all probability cause them embarrassment. For heaven's sake, no. Apart from which, what I really want is to hear this story. So, we were with the Captain, whom I imagine to be a Dane, or an Englishman, very spruce, with a white stand-up collar and immaculate white shirts...'

'Quite right. That's how they describe him. And with him he had a young person of about twenty, whom some say was his niece though most say she was his granddaughter, which in fact, if you take their years into account, is hardly possible. And besides the granddaughter or niece there was also a Chinaman, the same one who rests among the dunes and whose grave we passed just now.'

'Yes, and…'

'Well, this Chinaman was the servant in Thomsen's house, and Thomsen thought so highly of him that he was more of a friend than a servant. And things went on like this for years. Then suddenly it was rumoured that Thomsen's granddaughter, who was called Nina, I think, was to marry according to the old man's wishes, and it was to be another captain. And this turned out to be so. There was a big wedding in the house, the pastor from Berlin married them, and Utpatel the miller, who was a nonconformist, and Gieshübler, whom people in town didn't fully trust when it came to religion, were invited, and above all many captains and their wives and daughters. And as you can imagine spirits ran high. In the evening there was dancing and the bride danced with everyone, with the Chinaman as well in the end. Then suddenly the word went round that she had gone, the bride that is. And she had indeed gone away somewhere or other, but nobody knows what happened. And two weeks later the Chinaman died and Thomsen bought the plot that I showed you and he was buried there. The pastor from Berlin is supposed to have said they could have gone ahead and buried him in the Christian churchyard, for he had been a very good man, just as good as the others. Who he actually meant by "the others", Gieshübler told me, nobody really knew.'

'But in this matter, I am wholly against the pastor; one mustn't say that kind of thing, because it's imprudent and out of place. That's something not even Niemeyer would have said.'

'And they did in fact hold it very much against the pastor, whose name incidentally was Trippel, so it was actually fortunate he died soon afterwards, otherwise he would have lost his post. For the town, in spite of having chosen him, was against him just as you are, not to speak of the Consistory.'

'Trippel you say? Then there's a connection with Pastor Trippel's widow whom we're going to meet tonight?'

'Of course there's a connection. He was her husband and the father of Miss Trippelli.'

Effi laughed. 'Trippelli! Now I can see it all clearly at last. Gieshübler wrote that she was born in Kessin; but I thought she was the daughter of an Italian consul. We have so many foreign names here. But it turns out she's plain German, daughter of Trippel. Is she really so distinguished that she could dare to italianize her name like that?'

'Fortune favours the brave. In any case, she's not at all bad. She spent a few years in Paris with the celebrated Viardot, and it was there she met the

Russian prince. Russian princes are very enlightened, above trivial class prejudice, and Kochukov and Gieshübler – whom she calls "uncle" by the by, and one might almost say he's a born uncle – these are really the two who made little Marie Trippel what she is now. It was through Gieshübler she got to Paris, and then Kochukov transformed her into Trippelli.'

'Oh Geert, how exciting it all is, and what a mundane existence I led in Hohen-Cremmen! Never anything out of the ordinary.'

Innstetten took her hand and said, 'You mustn't talk like that Effi. Towards ghosts you can adopt whatever attitude you please. But beware of what's out of the ordinary, or what people choose to call out of the ordinary. What appears to you so tempting – and I include in that a life such as Miss Trippelli leads – that is something that as a rule costs you your happiness. I know very well how much you love and cherish Hohen-Cremmen, but still you often make fun of it and have no idea of the meaning of those quiet days at Hohen-Cremmen.'

'Oh yes, I have,' she said. 'I know very well. I just like to hear about something different now and then, and when I do I'm seized by a desire to take part in it. But you're quite right. And really I have a great longing for peace and quiet.'

Innstetten wagged his finger. 'My one and only Effi, it's your imagination again. Always some new fancy, first this, then that.'

11

The outing went as planned. At one o'clock the sleigh stopped down by the railway embankment outside the Prince Bismarck Inn, and Golchowski, delighted to see the Landrat in his establishment, saw to it personally that an excellent lunch was prepared. At the end of the meal, when the dessert and Tokay had been served, Innstetten called over the landlord, who had appeared from time to time to ensure that everything was in order, and asked him to sit down and tell them what had been happening. For this Golchowski was just the man; not an egg was laid for ten miles around that he didn't know about. And so it proved to be on that day too. Sidonie Grasenabb, Innstetten's surmise had been right, had, just as she had done the previous Christmas, gone to spend four weeks at the 'Court Chaplain's'; he also reported that Frau von Palleske had had to dismiss her chambermaid instantly and ignominiously for an embarrassing involvement, and things were bad with old Fraude – they were saying that he had just had a fall, but actually it had been a stroke, and his son, who was stationed at Lissa with the Hussars, was expected home at any moment. After this chit-chat, turning to more serious matters, they had got on to Varzin. 'Yes,' said Golchowski, 'just imagine the Prince running a paper-mill! It's all very odd; in actual fact he can't stand writing, and printed paper even less, and now he has acquired a paper-mill.'

'True enough my dear Golchowski,' said Innstetten, 'but in life you can never get away from contradictions like that. And being a prince and achieving greatness doesn't help at all.'

'No, no, greatness doesn't help at all.'

Probably this conversation about the Prince would have continued had not the railway signal-bell announced the imminent arrival of a train. Innstetten looked at the time.

'What train is that, Golchowski?'

'It's the Danzig express; it doesn't stop here, but I always go up and count the coaches, and sometimes there's somebody I know standing at a window. Just beyond my yard there are some steps up the embankment to lineman 417's hut...'

'Oh, we'll take advantage of that,' said Effi. 'I love watching trains...'

'Well then my lady, it's high time.'

And so all three of them went out and took up position, when they got to the top, beside the lineman's hut in a strip of garden which at the moment was under snow, though a space had been shovelled clear. The lineman was there already with his flag in his hand. And now the train raced through the station and in the next instant was passing the strip of garden. Effi was so excited that she saw nothing and was left as if spellbound, looking after the last coach which had a brakeman sitting on top.

'At six-fifty it gets into Berlin,' said Innstetten, 'and an hour later, if the wind is in the right direction, the folk at Hohen-Cremmen will hear it rattling past in the distance. Would you like to be on it, Effi?'

She said nothing. But when he looked over at her he saw that there was a tear in her eye.

As the train raced by, a heartfelt longing had come over Effi. Though she had every advantage, she still had the feeling she was in an alien world. And even when she took delight in one thing or another there, she would immediately afterwards become aware of what she missed. Over there was Varzin, and in the other direction the Kroschentin church spire was glinting, and beyond was the Morgenitz spire, and there the Grasenabbs and the Borckes lived and *not* the Bellings and *not* the Briests. 'Yes, *them*!' Innstetten had been quite right about her rapid fluctuations of mood, and now she saw again all that

64

lay behind her, as if transfigured. But although she had gazed after the train filled with longing, she was far too mercurial to dwell on it for long, and even on the way home, as the red ball of the setting sun poured out its glow on the snow, she felt freer again; everything seemed fresh and beautiful, and by the time she had returned to Kessin and was stepping into Gieshübler's hall-way almost on the stroke of seven, she was not merely at one with herself, her mood was almost exuberant, to which the aroma of valerian and flag-root that pervaded the house might have in some measure contributed.

Innstetten and his wife had appeared punctually, but despite their punc-tuality they had arrived after the other guests; Pastor Lindequist, old Frau Trippel and Miss Trippelli herself were already there. Gieshübler – in a blue tail-coat with matt gold buttons, and pince-nez sporting a broad black rib-bon that lay across his brilliant white piqué waistcoat like some knightly order – Gieshübler was having difficulty mastering his excitement. 'May I make the introductions: Baron and Baroness Innstetten, Frau Pastor Trippel, Fräulein Marietta Trippelli.' Pastor Lindequist, whom they all knew, stood aside smiling.

Miss Trippelli, in her early thirties, very masculine in appearance and of a distinctly humorous disposition, had until the introductions occupied the place of honour on the sofa. The introductions over however, going towards a high-backed chair that stood nearby, she said, 'If your ladyship would be so good as to assume the burdens and hazards of your office. For one might well,' and she pointed to the sofa, 'speak of "hazards" in this instance. I've been telling Gieshübler this for donkey's years, with alas no effect; kind as he is, he is also quite, quite stubborn.'

'But Marietta…'

'This sofa, you see, which first saw the light of day fifty years ago, is con-structed according to an obsolete trap-door principle, and if one entrusts oneself to it without previously erecting a tower of cushions beneath one, one disappears down the trap, or at least far enough to leave one's knees tow-ering up like a monument.' All this Miss Trippelli delivered with an equal measure of bonhomie and assurance in a tone designed to convey: 'You may be Baroness Innstetten, but I am Miss Trippelli.'

Gieshübler was extremely fond of his artist friend and thought highly of her talents; but all his enthusiasm could not blind him to the fact that she had been vouchsafed only a modest portion of social refinement. And such refinement was precisely what he himself cultivated. 'Marietta dear,' he intervened, 'you have such a charming and amusing way of talking about these things; but on the subject of my sofa you are quite wrong, and let the experts decide between us. Even a man like Prince Kochukov –'

'Oh please, Gieshübler, leave *him* out of it. Why always Kochukov? If you

65

go on, her ladyship is going to suspect that I belong to the prince – who, by the way, is only one of the lesser princes and has no more than a thousand souls, or rather used to have (in the old days when they still counted souls) – she is going to suspect that I'm soul one thousand and one. No, it's really not like that; you know my motto Gieshübler, "Press on regardless". Kochukov is a good chap and he's my friend, but he doesn't understand the first thing about art and matters of that sort, certainly not about music, though he composes masses and oratorios – when they dabble in art most Russian princes incline to the religious or the orthodox – and questions of furnishing and interior decoration certainly rank among the many things of which he has no understanding. Something only has to be colourful and cost a great deal of money and anyone can sell it to him as a thing of beauty, that's how much class he has.'

Innstetten was enjoying himself, and Pastor Lindequist's satisfaction was plain for all to see. But her daughter's forthright tone caused good old Frau Trippel one embarrassing moment after another, while Gieshübler felt the conversation was taking such an awkward turn that termination was indicated. An end best served by some musical items. It could be assumed Marietta would not choose Lieder of objectionable content, and even if she did, her artistry was such that it would ennoble the content. So he intervened: 'Dear Marietta, I have ordered our little repast for eight. That leaves three quarters of an hour, unless you perhaps prefer to sing us a jolly song as we eat, or perhaps to leave it until we have left the table…'

'Gieshübler, I ask you. You, an aesthete. There is nothing more unaesthetic than singing on a full stomach. In addition to which – and I know you are a man of culinary discrimination, indeed a gourmet – in addition to which it all tastes better when you have the thing behind you. Art first, then walnut ice, that's the proper order.'

'Then I may bring you the music, Marietta?'

'Bring the music? If I know you Gieshübler, you'll have whole bookcases full of music, and I can't sing you the entire collection. Music indeed! Which music, Gieshübler, that's what matters. And make sure it's in the right range, alto…'

'I'll find it.' And he busied himself at a cabinet, pulling out drawer after drawer while Miss Trippelli moved her chair round the table to the left, so that she was sitting close to Effi.

'I'm curious to know what he'll bring,' she said. At this Effi experienced a slight sense of embarrassment.

'I rather imagine,' she answered, taken aback, 'something by Gluck, something quite dramatic… Indeed, my dear Fräulein, if I may make so bold as to comment, I am surprised to hear that you are only a singer. I should have thought that your particular talents were very much for the stage. Your appearance, your presence, your voice… I haven't seen much of that sort of thing, only on short visits to Berlin… when I was still half a child. But I should have thought Orpheus or Kriemhild or the Vestal Virgin…'

Miss Trippelli shook her head, gazing into abysses, but failed to produce a response, because just at that moment Gieshübler reappeared and presented her with half a dozen scores which his friend took and discarded in quick succession. ' "Erl-King"… ah, bah; "Mill-stream, peace to your babbling"… But Gieshübler, I ask you, you're a marmot, you've been asleep for seven years… And Löwe's ballads; not exactly the latest thing either. "The Bells of Speyer"… Oh, all that ding, dong, ding, really it's just cheap sensationalism, it's tasteless and passé. Ah, but here we have "Sir Olaf"… now that's all right.'

And she stood up, and sang 'Olaf' to the pastor's accompaniment with great assurance and bravura, receiving applause all round.

Other similarly romantic pieces were then found, 'Flying Dutchman', 'Zampa', and then the 'The Boy on the Heath', all things that she sailed through serenely with consummate virtuosity; Effi seemed spellbound by words and music alike.

When Miss Trippelli had finished the 'The Boy on the Heath', she said 'That will be enough,' a pronouncement she uttered with such finality that neither Gieshübler nor anybody else had the temerity to make any further request of her. Least of all Effi. She merely said, after Gieshübler's friend had sat down beside her again, 'If only I could finds words to say, my dear Fräulein, how grateful I am to you. All so beautiful, so assured, so accomplished. But there is another thing, if you will pardon me, that I admire almost more than all that, and that is the serenity with which you are able to perform these pieces. I am so susceptible to impressions that I'm all a-quiver at the merest mention of ghosts and can scarcely recover my self-control. And you perform these things so powerfully, so shatteringly and are yourself perfectly cheerful and good-humoured.'

'Yes, my lady, art is like that. Not to speak of the theatre from which, mercifully I may say, I have been preserved. For, proof as I quite certainly feel myself to be against its temptations – it is fatal for one's reputation, and that is the best thing we have. In addition to which it blunts one's sensibilities, as colleagues have assured me a hundred times. They go about poisoning and stabbing one another, and then Romeo whispers a bad joke in the dead Juliet's ear, or a malicious bit of gossip, or presses a little billet doux into her hand.'

'I find it incomprehensible. And to come back to what I am indebted to

you for this evening, for example the ghostly bit in "Olaf", I can assure you
that when I have an anguished dream, or when I think I can hear the faint
sound of dancing or music above my head when there's really no-one there,
or when someone slips past my bed, I am beside myself and can't forget it for
days.'

'Yes, my lady, what you are describing is something quite different, something real, or something that could be real. A ghost which stalks through a
ballad doesn't scare me, but a ghost which stalks through my room is a very
unpleasant matter, to me or anyone else. Our feelings in that regard are
exactly the same.'

'So have you had that experience too?'

'Certainly. At Kochukov's too. And I've made it a condition this time that
I sleep somewhere else, perhaps in the English governess's room. She's a
Quaker, so I'm bound to be safe.'

'You think these things are possible then?'

'My dear lady, when you've reached my age and taken the knocks I have
– been to Russia and even spent six months in Romania – you think anything is possible. There are so many bad people, and so you find the other
thing too, you might say the one goes with the other.'

Effi listened with attention.

'I come,' continued Miss Tripelli, 'of a very enlightened family – except
that Mother never quite went along with it – but nevertheless Father said to
me at the time of that business of the spirit-writing, "Listen Marie, there is
something in this." And he was right, there is something in it. In fact they're
lurking all round us, right and left, behind and in front of us. You'll find
out.'

At that moment Gieshübler came and offered Effi his arm, Innstetten
took Marietta and Pastor Lindequist followed with the widow. In which
order they sat down to eat.

12

It was late when the party broke up. Soon after ten Effi had said to Gieshübler, 'It must be time to go; Fräulein Trippelli mustn't miss her train, so
she must set out from Kessin at six,' but Miss Trippelli, who was standing
beside her at these words, had protested with her own brand of uninhibited
volubility against such tender consideration on her behalf. 'Ah, your ladyship
thinks people like us need regular sleep, but this is not so; what we need regularly is applause and seats sold at high prices. Yes, you may laugh. Besides

– it's something one learns – I can sleep in my compartment, in any situation and on my left side at a pinch, without even having to undo my dress. Of course I am never confined; bosom and lungs must be free at all times, and above all the heart. Yes, my lady, that is the main thing. And moreover, anyway with sleep, it's not the amount that counts, it's the quality; a good five minute nap is better than tossing and turning for five hours, now to the right, now to the left. Incidentally, one sleeps wonderfully well in Russia, in spite of the strong tea. It must be the air that does it, or the late dinners, or the way they spoil one. There are no worries in Russia; in that – the money is the same in both – Russia is better than America.'

After this declaration from Miss Trippelli, Effi had desisted from any further suggestion that they should go, and so midnight had come round. Their farewells – they were in high spirits – were hearty, with a fair measure of familiarity.

The way from the chemist's at the Sign of the Moor to the Landrat's residence was rather long; it was made shorter by Pastor Lindequist's asking if he might accompany Innstetten and his wife part of the way, considering a walk under the stars in the heavens the best way to overcome the effects of Gieshübler's hock. They walked along, indefatigably citing the most diverse Trippelliana; Effi started it with what had stuck in her memory, and next it was the pastor's turn. An ironist, he had, after questioning her on a variety of quite worldly matters, finally enquired as to Miss Tripelli's views on religion, and been informed that she recognized only Orthodoxy. Her father, it was true, had been a rationalist, almost a free-thinker, which is why he would have preferred to have the Chinaman in the parish churchyard; she for her part held the opposite opinion, though she enjoyed the great advantage of believing nothing at all. But decisive as she was in her lack of belief, she was at all times aware that it was a special luxury, in which one might only indulge as a private person. Where the state was concerned such laxity ended, and if she were to have control of the Ministry of Education or a regional church assembly, she would proceed with unremitting severity. 'I feel I have something of a Torquemada in me.'

Innstetten was highly amused and for his part related that he had studiously avoided ticklish matters like dogma, concentrating instead on moral issues. The main topic of their conversation had been the seductiveness of any kind of public appearance, the constant vulnerability, to which Miss Trippelli had blithely replied, taking up the second half of the sentence only, 'Yes, constant vulnerability; especially of the voice.'

In this way the Trippelli evening had passed before them once more by the time they parted, and it was to be three days before her telegram to Effi from Petersburg called Gieshübler's friend to mind again. It read: 'Madame la Baronne d'Innstetten, née de Briest. Bien arrivée. Prince K. à la gare. Plus épris de moi que jamais. Mille fois merci de votre bon accueil. Compliments empressés à Monsieur le Baron. Marietta Trippelli.'

Innstetten was delighted and the expression he gave to his delight was more fulsome than seemed appropriate to Effi.

'I don't understand you Geert.'

'Because you don't understand Miss Trippelli. The authenticity of the woman is priceless; it's all there down to the last dot on the *i*.'

'So you think it's all play-acting.'

'What else? All calculated for wherever she chances to be, for Kochukov and for Gieshübler. Gieshübler will probably set up a fund for her, or perhaps just leave her a legacy.'

The musical soirée at Gieshübler's had taken place in the middle of December, and immediately after that the preparations for Christmas began, and Effi, who otherwise might have found these days hard to face, was thankful to have a household of her own with needs that had to be satisfied. There were questions to be asked, thinking to be done, purchases to be made, all of which kept dark thoughts at bay. The day before Christmas Eve presents arrived from Hohen-Cremmen from her parents, and all sorts of little gifts from the schoolmaster's house had been packed in the same box; beautiful pippins from a tree that Effi and Jahnke had grafted several years earlier, then brown wrist and knee warmers from Bertha and Hertha. Hulda just sent her a few lines with the excuse that she still had to knit a travelling rug for X. 'Which is simply not true,' said Effi, 'I'll bet X doesn't even exist. Why can't she stop surrounding herself with admirers who aren't there?'

And so Christmas Eve arrived.

Innstetten put up the decorations for his young wife himself, the tree was lit and a little angel hovered high up in the air. There was also a crib with pretty little banners and inscriptions, one of which referred discreetly to a happy event expected at the Innstetten residence in the coming year. Effi read it and blushed. Then she went up to Innstetten to thank him, but before she could do so a *Julklapp* thudded into the hallway, an old Pomeranian Christmas custom: a large box concealing a world of delights. In the end they found the main thing, a dainty box of fondants with all sorts of little Japanese pictures pasted all over it, and inside it, as well as its spiced contents, a little piece of paper on which was written:

> At Christmas there came three kings,
> And what the little blackamoor brings
> From under the blackamoor chemist's sign
> Is neither myrrh nor incense fine,

But fondants of the choicest flavours –
Pistachio and almond – as special favours.

Effi read it twice or three times with much pleasure. 'There is something especially agreeable about a good soul's attentions. Don't you think so Geert?'

'I certainly do. In fact it's the only thing that gives one real pleasure, or should give one real pleasure. For apart from that we're all up to our ears in inanities of all sorts. I am too. But I suppose we are what we are.'

The first day of the holiday was church day, on the second they were out at the Borckes' where everybody was present with the exception of the Grasenabbs who didn't want to come 'because Sidonie wasn't at home,' which everyone considered to be rather an odd excuse. Some even muttered, 'On the contrary, that would have been a good reason to come.' On New Year's Eve there was the Club Ball at which Effi could not fail to appear, nor did she wish to, for the ball would give her the chance to see the town's flora and fauna all assembled in one place at last. Johanna was fully taken up in preparing her mistress's ball gown, Gieshübler, who, apart from everything else, had a hothouse, sent camellias, and Innstetten managed to fit in a visit upcountry to the Papenhagen estate where three barns had burnt down.

It was quite silent in the house. Christel, with nothing to do, had sleepily drawn a footstool up to the fire, and Effi retired to her bedroom where she sat down between mirror and sofa at a little writing table that had been specially set up for her, to write to Mamma, whom she had so far sent only a card thanking her for her Christmas present and letter, but no other news for weeks now.

Kessin, December 31st

My dear Mamma,
This is probably going to be a long letter, for it's a long time – the card doesn't count – since you heard from me. The last time I wrote I was still deep in Christmas preparations, now the Christmas season is over. Innstetten and my dear friend Gieshübler did everything they could to make Christmas Eve as pleasant as possible for me, but I still felt a bit lonely and my anxiety turned my thoughts to you. In fact even with all I have to be thankful and bright and happy about, I don't seem to be able to shake off a feeling of loneliness, and if I used to make fun of Hulda's sentimental tears, perhaps rather more than was called for, I'm now being punished for it by having to struggle with those very same tears myself. For Innstetten must not see them. But I am sure this will all get better when there is more life in our household, which there will be my dear Mamma. What I recently hinted at is now a certainty and Innstetten gives me daily

proof of his joy at it. How happy I am at the prospect myself I don't have to tell you, because when it happens there will be life and distraction around me, or as Geert puts it, I'll have 'a darling toy'. He is probably right in his choice of word, but he would be better not to use it, for it always causes me a little stabbing pain and reminds me how young I am, and that I still half belong in the nursery. I cannot rid myself of this idea (Geert thinks it's unhealthy) which somehow manages to turn what should be my greatest happiness into something more like a constant source of embarrassment to me. Yes my dear Mamma, when the dear Flemming ladies recently enquired about all sorts of things, I felt I was sitting an examination I was rather badly prepared for, and I think too that I gave some pretty stupid answers. I was in a bad temper too. For a great deal that looks like sympathy is really only curiosity, and seems the more impertinent because I still have a long time to wait for the happy event, well into the summer. The first few days of July, I think. Then you must come here, or better still, as soon as I am more or less on my feet again, *I* shall come back, I'll take a holiday and be off to Hohen-Cremmen. Oh, how I'm looking forward to it and the Havelland air – it's almost always cold and raw here – and every day I'll go on a drive into the Luch with its reds and yellows, I can already see the baby reaching out its hands, for it is sure to feel then that that is where its real home is. But I'm only writing this *to you*. Innstetten must know nothing of it, and I must ask even you to forgive me for wanting to bring the baby to Hohen-Cremmen and already announcing my intention today, instead of pressing a heartfelt invitation on you, my dear Mamma, to come to Kessin, which every summer has fifteen hundred visitors for the sea bathing, ships flying every conceivable flag and even a hotel in the dunes. But I'm not inhospitable, that's not why I offer so little hospitality, I haven't turned my back on the Briest tradition to that extent, it's simply this Landrat's house of ours, which, pretty and out of the ordinary as it is, isn't actually a proper house at all, just an apartment for two people and scarcely that, for we don't even have a dining-room, which is quite awkward when a couple of people come to visit. We do have more accommodation on the first floor, a large gallery and four small rooms, but they are all rather uninviting and I would call them lumber rooms if there were any lumber in them; but they are absolutely empty apart from a few rush-seated chairs, and they make a very strange impression to say the least. Now you will probably think that that could all be changed quite easily. But it can't be changed; for the house that we live in is… a haunted house; there, now it's out. I beg you, by the way, not to comment on this item of information when you write back, for I always show Innstetten your letters and he would be beside himself if he discovered I had written this to you. I wouldn't have done so, especially since I have had such a peaceful time for several weeks now and have stopped being afraid; but Johanna tells me it always comes back, when somebody new appears in the house that is. And I can't expose you to such a danger, or if that's an exaggeration, to such a peculiar and disagreeable disturbance! I'm not going to bother you with the story itself today, at least not in any detail. It's about an old ship's captain, a so-called China hand, and his grand-daughter who was engaged to a young captain here for a short time and suddenly disappeared on her wedding day. That wouldn't be so bad. But what's more important, her father had brought a young Chinaman back with him from China, first as his servant, then as the old man's friend, and he died shortly after she disappeared and was buried at a lonely spot by the churchyard. I drove past there the other day, but I turned away quickly and looked in the other direction because otherwise I think I would have seen him sitting there on the grave. For, oh my dear Mamma, I really did see him once, or at least I think I did, when I was fast asleep and Innstetten had gone to visit Prince Bismarck. It was dreadful; I wouldn't like to go through that again. I can't very well invite you to come to a house like this, pretty as it otherwise is (it's nice and comfortable, but uncanny at the same time, very odd). And Innstetten, although I came round to his point of view about most of this, has not, this much I think I may say, behaved quite properly in the matter. He wanted me to see all this as an old wives' tale and laugh at it, but then suddenly he seemed to believe in it all him-self and came up with the strange proposal that I should consider a resi-dent ghost like this as a mark of distinction, of ancient aristocratic pedi-gree. But this I can't and won't do. Kind and considerate as he usually is, on this point he is neither kind nor considerate. For there is something behind it all, this much I know from Johanna and also from Frau Kruse. She's our coachman's wife and she sits in an overheated room all the time with a black hen. Which in itself is frightening enough. So now you know why *I* want to come to *you* as soon as the time comes. Oh, how I wish the time would come soon. There are so many reasons why I wish that. This evening it's the New Year's Eve Ball, and Gieshübler – the only nice per-son here, in spite of having one shoulder higher than the other, or really a bit more than that – Gieshübler has sent me some camellias. Maybe I shall dance after all. Our doctor says it would do me no harm, on the contrary. And Innstetten has agreed too, which rather surprises me. And now love and kisses to Papa and all my other dear ones. A happy New Year.

Yours ever,

Effi

73

13

The New Year's Eve Ball had lasted into the early morning and Effi had been widely admired – although not as unrestrainedly as her bouquet of camellias which everybody knew to have come from Gieshübler's hothouse. After the New Year's Eve Ball everything stayed as it had been before, with scarcely any attempt at social contact, and the winter was felt to be long indeed. Visits from neighbouring gentry occurred only seldom, and the return visits duty required were always preceded by the remark, in a semi-mournful tone, 'Well Geert, if it really has to be, but I shall die of boredom.' Words with which Innstetten could only ever agree. What was said on these afternoon visits about family, children and even farming was not so bad, but when it came to church matters, and the pastors who were in attendance were treated like little popes, or so esteemed themselves, then Effi's patience snapped and she thought sorrowfully of Niemeyer who was always restrained and modest, in spite of the fact that on all the bigger ceremonial occasions people said he had what it took to be appointed to the 'cathedral'. With the Borckes, the Flemmings, the Grasenabbs, friendly as the general attitudes of these families – apart from Sidonie Grasenabb – were, no real rapport with anyone was established, and as far as pleasure, amusement or even a feeling of passable well-being was concerned, things would have been pretty bad had it not been for Gieshübler. He looked after Effi like her own small Providence, and she was grateful to him for it. He was naturally, as well as everything else, a keen and attentive newspaper-reader, not to mention the leading light in the magazine circle, so hardly a day went by without Mirambo bringing a large white envelope with a variety of papers and journals in which the appropriate parts had been underlined, mostly with a fine light pencil line, or occasionally a thick blue line with an exclamation or question mark beside it. And he did not stop there; he sent figs and dates too, bars of chocolate in shiny paper tied with red ribbons, and when something particularly beautiful came into bloom in his hothouse he would bring it round himself and spend a happy hour chatting with the young woman he found so congenial and for whom he had all the finer feelings of love rolled into one, a father's love, an uncle's, a teacher's and an admirer's. Effi was moved by all this and mentioned it in her letters to Hohen-Cremmen so often that her mother began to tease her about being 'in love with an alchemist'; but this well-meant teasing was wide of the mark, indeed its effect was almost painful, because it brought home to her, if only dimly, what was actually lacking in her marriage: marks of devotion or encouragement, little attentions. Innstetten was kind and good, but he was no lover. He felt he loved Effi, and knowing in good conscience that this was so absolved him from making any special effort. It had almost become the rule that when Friedrich brought in the lamp he would withdraw from his wife's room to his own. 'I still have some tricky business I must deal with.' And then he would go. The door-curtain was of course drawn back so that Effi could hear the rustling of his files or the scraping of his pen, but that was all. Rollo would then come and lie in front of her on the hearthrug, as if to say, 'I'll have to look after you again, nobody else will.' Then she would bend down and quietly say, 'Yes, Rollo, we're alone.' At nine Innstetten would appear again for a cup of tea, usually with the newspaper in his hand, and talk of the Prince, who again had many irritations, especially with that Eugen Richter whose attitude and language were quite intolerable, and go through the list of honours and appointments, taking exception to most of them. Then he would talk about the elections and how lucky he was to have a constituency where there was still some respect. When he was done with that, he would ask Effi to play something, a bit of *Lohengrin* or *The Valkyrie*, for he was a Wagner enthusiast. Why he had been drawn to this composer was uncertain; some said it was his nerves, for down to earth as he might seem, he was actually of a nervous disposition, others put it down to Wagner's stand on the Jewish question. Probably both were right. By ten fatigue would be setting in and Innstetten would essay one or two tired if well-intended caresses, which Effi permitted, without in any real sense reciprocating.

In this way winter passed, April came and the garden beyond the yard began to turn green, which pleased Effi; she just couldn't wait for the summer, with the walks on the beach and the visitors who came for the sea bathing. When she looked back, the Trippelli evening at Gieshübler's and then the New Year's Eve Ball, yes, all that had been passable, quite pleasant; but the months after that, well, they had left a lot to be desired, above all they had been so monotonous that she had once even written to Mamma:

Can you imagine Mamma, I'm almost reconciled to our ghost? Of course I wouldn't like to go through that dreadful night again, when Geert was over at Prince Bismarck's, certainly not that; but being constantly alone, and absolutely nothing happening, well, it's not easy, and occasionally when I wake up in the night I listen for a moment, just to see if I can hear the shoes gliding over the boards up there, and if it's all quiet I'm almost disappointed and I tell myself, I wish it would come back, but not too awful and not too close.

It was in February that Effi had written this, and now it was almost May. Over in the Plantation things were coming to life again and the finches could be heard singing. In the same week too the storks came, and one glided slowly over the house and settled on a barn next to Utpatel's mill. That was its perch of old. This event too Effi reported, writing now as she did much more often to Hohen-Cremmen, and in the same letter she said at the end:

Something, my dear Mamma, which I almost forgot: the new district commandant of the Landwehr – whom we've had for about four weeks now – or do we really have him? That is the question, and an important question too, though you may laugh, indeed you are bound to laugh, since you don't know the desperate state our social life here is still in. Or at least mine, since I have not been able to get on any terms with the families here. Perhaps my fault, not that it makes any difference. The fact remains, it's a desperate state of affairs, and that's why all these winter months I've been looking forward to the new district commandant as a saviour and bringer of solace. His predecessor was a monster, with bad manners and worse morals, and as if that wasn't enough, he was always hard up too. We all suffered the whole time under him, Innstetten even more than me, and when at the beginning of April we heard that Major Crampas, that's the new man's name, was here, we fell into one another's arms as if nothing bad could ever happen again in dear old Kessin. But as I've already said, even though he's here, it seems nothing is going to come of it. Crampas is married and has two children of ten and eight, his wife is a year older than him, say forty-five. That in itself wouldn't matter, there's no reason why having a maternal friend shouldn't be wonderfully entertaining for me. Miss Trippelli was almost thirty and we got on very well. But this can't happen with Crampas's wife, a commoner incidentally. She is always out of sorts, almost melancholy (just like Frau Kruse, of whom she greatly reminds me), and all because of jealousy. Crampas is apparently a man who has had many affairs, a ladies' man, which I always find ridiculous, and I would find it ridiculous on this occasion too, if he hadn't had a duel with one of his comrades for just that sort of reason. His left arm was shattered just below the shoulder and you can't miss it, though the operation, Innstetten tells me (I think they call it a resection and it was done by Wilms), was hailed as a masterpiece of the art. Both of them, Herr and Frau Crampas, paid their call on us a fortnight ago; it was a very awkward situation, for Frau Crampas watched her husband so closely that he was considerably embarrassed and I totally. On his own he can be very different, animated and high-spirited – which I had the chance to see for myself when he was with Innstetten three days ago, and I followed their conversation from my room. Afterwards I spoke to him too. The complete cavalier, very suave. Innstetten was in the same brigade with him during the war, and they often saw one another north of Paris at Count Gröben's. Yes, my dear Mamma, that could have been a chance to start a new life in Kessin; and the Major doesn't have the Pomeranian prejudices either, though I've heard he comes from Swedish Pomerania. But that wife of his! It's impossible to see the Major without her, but with her it's equally impossible.

Effi had been quite right, and in fact no closer contact with the Crampases developed. They met out at the Borckes' family place, then briefly at the station and a few days later on the boat on an outing to a large beech and oak forest near the Breitling known as 'the Schnatermann'; but there was no more than a brief exchange of greetings, and Effi was delighted at the signs of the season starting at the beginning of June. There was of course still a shortage of holidaymakers – bathers usually only appeared in ones and twos before Midsummer's Day – but the preparations themselves helped pass the time. In the Plantation the roundabout and the shooting stalls were erected, the boatmen caulked and painted their boats, each little apartment got new curtains, and the rooms that were situated in damp spots and had dry rot under the floorboards were treated with sulphur and aired.

In Effi's house too, on account of an awaited new arrival quite other than the summer visitors, there was a certain agitation all round; even Frau Kruse wanted to be involved as far as she could. But Effi took lively exception to this, saying: 'Geert, don't let Frau Kruse touch anything; no good can come of it and I'm worried enough already.' Innstetten granted her all she asked, saying that Christel and Johanna had plenty of time to see to everything, and to divert his young wife's thoughts in a different direction he dropped the whole subject of preparations and asked instead whether she had noticed that a holidaymaker had moved in opposite, not the first but nevertheless one of the first.

'A gentleman?'

'No, a lady who has been here before, in the same apartment each time. She always comes early because she can't stand it when everywhere is so full.'

'I won't say I can't see her point. So who is it then?'

'It's Registrar Rode's widow.'

'That's strange. I always thought registrars' widows were poor.'

'Yes,' laughed Innstetten, 'they are as a rule. But here you have an exception. At any rate she has more than her widow's pension. She always arrives with a great deal of luggage, infinitely more than she needs, and she seems to be a quite peculiar woman, eccentric and ailing, and very shaky on her feet. She is unsure of herself because of this, and always has an elderly servant with her, strong enough to look after her, or carry her if anything happens. She has a new one this year. Another very stocky person once again, a bit like Miss Trippelli, but stouter.'

'Oh, I've seen her. Nice brown eyes, trusty and faithful when they look at you. But just a bit dim.'

'That's right, that's her.'

It was the middle of June when Innstetten and Effi had this conversation. From then on every day brought a further influx of holidaymakers, and as always about this time of year, walking out to the Bulwark to wait for the steamer's arrival became a sort of daily routine for the Kessin folk. Effi of course, Innstetten being unable to accompany her, had to forego this, but at least she had the pleasure of seeing some animation in the street leading to the beach and the Strand Hotel, hitherto so empty of people, and in order to keep it under constant review she was much more than usual in her bedroom, from whose windows she could best see everything. Johanna stood at her side and had an answer to more or less everything she wanted to know; since most of the visitors came back every year, the maid could not only supply their names but sometimes a little story about them too.

This was all amusing and entertaining for Effi. However, on Midsummer's Day itself, just before eleven in the morning, when usually the traffic from the steamer was flooding by at its most colourful, instead of married couples, children and hackney carriages piled with suitcases, it happened that a carriage draped in black and followed by two mourners' coaches came from the centre of the town down the street leading to the Plantation, and stopped at the house opposite the Landrat's residence. For Registrar Rode's widow had died three days earlier, and her relatives from Berlin, who had been informed with the greatest promptitude, had decided on arrival that they would not have the deceased transported to Berlin, but would bury her in Kessin in the churchyard in the dunes. Effi stood at her window and looked with curiosity upon the oddly solemn scene that unfolded opposite. The arrivals from Berlin were two nephews and their wives, all about forty, give or take a year, and of enviably healthy complexion. The nephews in well-fitting frock-coats could pass muster, and the sober, businesslike attitude revealed in their whole bearing was becoming rather than off-putting. But the two wives! They were visibly intent on showing Kessin what real mourning was, and were wearing long crêpe veils that reached to the ground and at the same time hid their faces. And now the coffin, on which lay a few wreaths and even a palm frond, was placed on the carriage and the two married couples took their seats in the coaches. Into the first – along with one of the mourning couples – Lindequist climbed too; behind the second coach walked the landlady and beside her the stout woman whom the deceased had brought to Kessin to minister to her. The latter was extremely and it seemed genuinely upset, even if the emotion in question was not exactly grief; but in the case of the landlady, a widow who was sobbing with the utmost violence, it was almost excessively clear that the possibility of an extra gratuity was what she had in mind all the time, in spite of being in the happy position, much envied by other landladies, of being able to relet the apartment, for which she had already drawn rent for the whole summer.

Effi, as the funeral cortège set off, went into the garden behind the yard to rid herself, among the beds edged with box, of the impression of lifelessness and lovelessness the whole scene across the street had made on her. When this failed, a desire to take a longer walk than the monotonous stroll round the garden seized her, the more so since the doctor had said taking plenty of exercise in the open air was the best thing she could do in view of what she had to come. Johanna, who was in the garden with her, brought her a shawl, hat and parasol, and with a friendly 'good morning' Effi stepped out of the house and walked towards the copse, beside whose broad, paved central lane a narrower path ran down to the dunes and the hotel on the beach. Along the wayside there were benches and she availed herself of each of them, for walking was a strain for her, especially as the hot midday hour had now come. But sitting comfortably and watching the ladies driving by in their finery, she revived again. For seeing people enjoying themselves was vital as air to her. When the copse ended the very worst part of the way was of course yet to come, sand, and more sand, and nowhere a trace of shade; but fortunately boards and planks had been put down here, so she arrived at the Strand Hotel, though hot and tired, nonetheless in a good mood. Inside lunch was being taken in the dining-room, but here outside all was silent and empty, which was as she at that moment preferred it. She ordered a glass of sherry and a bottle of Biliner water and gazed out at the sea, which was shimmering in the bright sunshine, while at its edge it rolled on to the beach in little waves. 'Bornholm is across there, and beyond it Visby, which Jahnke always used to tell me such marvellous things about in the old days. Visby he rated almost more highly than Lübeck or Wullenweber. And beyond Visby is Stockholm, where the Stockholm Bloodbath took place, and then

79

come the great rivers and then the North Cape, and then the midnight sun.' And at that moment she was seized by a desire to see it all. But then her thoughts returned to what she had so soon to come and she was almost aghast. 'It's sinful, being so frivolous and thinking such thoughts and indulging in these daydreams when I should be thinking about what's about to happen. Maybe I shall be punished for it, and we'll both die, me and the child. And the carriage and the two coaches won't stop across the road then, they'll stop at our house... No, no, I don't want to die here, I don't want to be buried here, I want to go to Hohen-Cremmen. Lindequist, good as he is – I would rather have Niemeyer; he baptized me, and confirmed me and married me, and he ought to bury me too.' At this a tear fell on her hand. Then she laughed again. 'I'm still alive and I'm only seventeen, and Niemeyer is fifty-seven.'

From the dining-room she could hear the clatter of crockery. But suddenly she thought she heard chairs being pushed back; perhaps people were leaving the table, and she wanted to avoid meeting anyone. So she too rose quickly from her seat to return to the town by a roundabout route. This route passed close by the churchyard in the dunes, and as the gate chanced to be open, she went in. Everything was in bloom here, there were butterflies flying over the graves and high in the air a few gulls soared. It was so beautiful and still that she was immediately inclined to linger by the first graves, but since the blazing sun was getting hotter by the minute, she went further up towards a shady path formed by trailing willows and a profusion of weeping ashes by the graves. When she came to the end of this path she saw on her right a fresh mound of sand with four or five wreaths on it, and close beside it, beyond the line of trees, was a bench on which sat the good, stout person who had followed the Registrar's widow's coffin beside the landlady as the last mourner. Effi recognized her immediately and was moved in her heart to see the good, faithful person, as she thought she must surely be, if she was to be found here in the blazing heat of the sun. It must have been nearly two hours since the funeral.

'This is a hot spot you've found for yourself,' said Effi, 'much too hot. And it would just take a little bad luck and you'd have sunstroke.'

'That would be the best thing that could 'appen.'

'How so?'

'That would see me out of this world.'

'I don't think you should say that, even if you are unhappy or if somebody dear to you has died. You were probably very fond of her?'

'Me? Of 'er? God forbid.'

'But you are very sad. There must be a reason.'

'That there is, my lady.'

'You know me?'

'Yes, you're the Landrat's wife from across the road. Me and the old lady used to talk about you all the time. Towards the end she couldn't no more, because she couldn't get 'er breath properly, it was 'er chest, most likely water on it; but while she could talk she didn't 'alf go on. Right old Berlin gossip she was...'

'A good woman?'

'No; I'd tell a lie if I said that. But there she lies and you're not supposed to speak ill of the dead, especially when they're barely at rest in the grave. Still, she'll be at rest all right! But she was a bad lot, and she was quarrelsome and penny-pinchin', and she didn't provide for me neither. And them relatives who came down from Berlin yesterday... quarrellin' 'alf the night, they were... they're another bad lot, they're a thoroughly bad lot. Rotten, the lot of them, greedy and graspin' and 'ard-'earted; and stuck-up and unfriendly, and full of personal remarks when they paid me wages, and they only did that because they 'ad to because there are only six days to go till the start of the next quarter. Otherwise I wouldn't 've got nothin', or just 'alf or even a quarter. Nothin' out of the kindness of their 'earts. And a torn five mark note is all they gave me for my fare back to Berlin; I suppose it'd just about be enough if I went fourth class and sat on my case. Well, I'm not goin' to. I'm just goin' to sit 'ere and wait till I die... Dear God, I thought I was goin' to 'ave peace now, and I'd 've stuck it out with the old girl. And it's all come to nothin' again and it's back to the grindstone. And me a Catholic into the bargain. I'm sick of it, I wish I was lyin' where the old girl's lyin' and she could go on livin' in my place... Now she would 'ave liked to go on livin'; slave-drivers like 'er, gaspin' for air, they're the ones who like livin'.'

Rollo, who had come with Effi, had in the meantime sat down in front of this person, his tongue hanging out, and was looking at her. Now that she had stopped talking he got up, took a step forward and laid his head on her knee.

The person was instantly as if transformed. 'Dear God, what that means to me. If it isn't a creature who 'as time for me, who 'as a friendly look for me and lays 'is 'ead on my knee. Dear God, it's a long time since anythin' like this 'appened to me. So what's your name then, old boy? What a fine chap you are.'

'Rollo,' said Effi.

'Rollo; that's odd. But what's in a name? I've an odd name too, Christian name that is. That's all the likes of us 'ave.'

'What is your name then?

'My name's Roswitha.'

'Yes, that is unusual, isn't it...'

'Yes, quite right my lady, it's a papish name. And I'm papish too, that's another thing. From Eichsfeld. And bein' papish makes things even more difficult and 'ard to take. A lot of people don't want papish maids, because they're always runnin' off to church. "Always at confession, but never a word about the main thing." Oh Lord, how often 'ave I 'eard that, first when I was in service in Giebichenstein, and then in Berlin. But I'm a bad Catholic, I've lapsed completely, maybe that's why I'm in such a bad state; yes, you can't neglect your faith, you 'ave to go along with it right and proper.'

'Roswitha,' Effi repeated the name and sat down on the bench beside her. 'What are you going to do now?'

'Oh, my lady, what can I do? There's nothin' for me to do. Really and truly I just want to sit 'ere and wait till I drop dead. That'd be the best thing. And then people would think I loved the old soul like a faithful dog and couldn't part from 'er grave and just stayed there and pined away. But that'd be wrong. You don't pine away for old women like that; I just want to die because I can't live.'

'I want to ask you something Roswitha. Are you what they call "fond of children"? Have you ever had to do with small children?'

'Certainly I 'ave. They're what I like best of all. With these old Berlin women – God forgive me my sin, for she's dead now and stands before the throne of God, an' could 'ave me called to account – ah, old women like that are dreadful, the things you 'ave to do for 'em, it's enough to turn your stomach, but such a dear little thing, a wee thing like a doll peeping at you with its little eyes, that's somethin' different, that warms the cockles of your 'eart. When I was in 'alle I was wet-nurse to the salt works director's wife, and in Giebichenstein I bottle-fed twins; yes, my lady, I know all about that, it's second nature to me.'

'Well, Roswitha, let me tell you something, you're a good, faithful person, I can see that, a little on the blunt side, but there's no harm in that, some of the best are like that, and I instantly felt I could trust you. Would you like to come with me? I feel as if you've been sent by God. I'm expecting a little one quite soon now, may God help me, and once the child is here it will have to be cared for and looked after and maybe even nursed. You never know, though I hope it won't come to that. What do you think? Will you come with me? I can't imagine I'm wrong about you.'

Roswitha had jumped up and taken the young woman's hand and was kissing it impetuously. 'So there is a God in 'eaven, and when the need is greatest, help is nearest. You'll see, my lady, it'll be all right; I'm a decent woman and I've got good references. You'll see that when I bring you my book. The very first day I saw your ladyship, I thought to myself, "now if you could find that kind of service", and now I've found it. Oh my dear Lord, oh Blessed Mary, Mother of God, who would have dreamt it when we laid that old woman in the earth and the relatives went off and left me sittin' 'ere.'

'You can often count on the unexpected, Roswitha, and it's not always bad. And now we must go. Rollo is getting impatient, he keeps running to the gate.'

Roswitha was ready on the instant, but went over to the grave again, muttered something and crossed herself. And then they went down the shady path and back to the churchyard gate.

Opposite was the enclosure with the railings round it, the white stone gleaming and glinting in the afternoon sun. Effi could now look at it more calmly. The path led on between the dunes a little way, until, just short of Utpatel's mill, she reached the edge of the copse. She turned left there, and taking a diagonal avenue known as the 'Reeperbahn', walked with Roswitha towards the Landrat's residence.

14

In less than a quarter of an hour they had reached the residence. When they both stepped into the cool hallway, Roswitha seemed overwhelmed at the sight of all the strange objects hanging up there; Effi however forestalled further comment. 'Roswitha, you go in there. That's the room we sleep in. First of all I want to go over to my husband in the Landrat's office – that's the big house next to the little one you've been staying in – and tell him that I'd like to entrust the care of the child to you. He's sure to be agreeable to all this, but I must have his consent first. And when I have, we'll move him out, and you can sleep along with me in the alcove. I think we'll get on with one another.'

Innstetten, when he heard what was proposed, quickly and good-humouredly said, 'You did right Effi, and if there is nothing wrong with her record, we'll take her on the strength of her honest face. It's not often that's deceptive, thank goodness.'

Effi was very happy to meet with so little difficulty. 'It's going to be all right now,' she said, 'I'm not afraid any longer.'

'Afraid of what Effi?'

'Oh, you know… But things you imagine are the worst, worse than anything sometimes.'

Roswitha moved in that very hour, bringing what few belongings she had over to the Landrat's residence where she installed them in the alcove. At the end of the day she went to bed early and, tired as she was, fell asleep straight away.

The next morning Effi – who had been living with her fears again for some time (for it was just full moon) – enquired how Roswitha had slept and whether she had heard anything.

'What?' the latter asked.

'Oh, nothing. I just meant something like the noise of a broom sweeping, or of someone slithering across the floorboards.'

Roswitha laughed, which made a particularly good impression on her young mistress. Effi was of staunchly Protestant upbringing and would have been very shocked if anyone had found anything Catholic in or about her; but she nevertheless believed that Catholicism protects us better against some things 'like those things upstairs'; indeed, this consideration had been quite a significant factor in her plan to take Roswitha into the house.

They adjusted quickly to one another, for an agreeable side of Effi, as of most young country ladies from the Mark, was that she liked to be told all sorts of little stories, and the registrar's widow with her penny-pinching and her nephews and their wives provided an inexhaustible fund of them. Johanna too liked to listen.

She however, while Effi often laughed aloud at the more outrageous bits, would just smile, registering silent amazement that her ladyship should take such delight in all this silly chatter; her amazement, however, which went hand in hand with a pronounced sense of superiority, was a blessing and meant that no arguments about seniority could arise. Roswitha was simply a figure of fun, and to have been jealous of her would have been like being jealous of Rollo for his position of friendship.

In this manner a week passed, full of gossip and almost comfortable in that Effi looked forward to what awaited her personally with less anxiety than before. Nor did she think that it was so close. The beginning of the next week saw an end of the gossip and comfortable times; then it was all fetching and carrying, even Innstetten came out of his habitual reserve, and on the morning of the 3rd of July a cradle stood by Effi's bed. Dr Hannemann patted the young woman's hand and said, 'Today is Königgrätz Day; a pity it's a girl. But there's enough time for the other, and the Prussians have plenty of victory anniversaries.' Roswitha may have been thinking along similar lines, but in the meantime her joy at what was there was quite unalloyed, and without further ado she called the child Wee Annie, which the young mother took to be a sign. 'It must have been inspiration that Roswitha hit on just that name.' Even Innstetten could think of no objection, and so they talked of Little Annie long before the christening day ever came. Effi, who intended to be with her parents at Hohen-Cremmen from the middle of August on, would have liked to delay the christening until then. But it could not be done; Innstetten could not get leave, so, in spite of the fact that it was Napoleon's birthday – some families found this inappropriate – the 15th of August was named for the ceremony, in the church, naturally. The banquet which followed was held in the big Club House on the Bulwark, the Landrat's residence not having a reception room for such a gathering, and all the local gentry were invited and indeed attended. Pastor Lindequist proposed a charming toast to mother and child which was generally admired, Sidonie von Grasenabb taking the opportunity to remark to her neighbour, an aristocratic old Assessor of the strict persuasion, 'Yes, his speeches on these occasions are all right, but he couldn't answer to man or God for his sermons, he's all half-measures, one of those who are damned because they're lukewarm. I'm not quoting the exact words from the Bible.' Immediately afterwards old Herr von Borcke too stood up to toast Innstetten. 'Ladies and gentlemen, these are difficult times we live in. Rebellion, defiance, indiscipline wherever you look. But as long as we still have men, and, I may add, wives and mothers too' – and at this point he bowed with an elegant wave of his hand to Effi – 'as long as we still have men like Baron Innstetten, whom I am proud to call my friend, then things will go on, and this old Prussia of ours will survive. Yes, my friends, Pomerania and Brandenburg, together we'll see it through and stamp on the venomous head of the dragon revolution. Staunch and true, we shall prevail. Our brother Catholics whom we must respect, even as we struggle against them, have their Rock of St Peter, but we have our *Rocher de Bronze*. Baron Innstetten, long may he live!' Innstetten thanked him quite briefly. Effi said to Major Crampas, who was sitting next to her, that the remark about the Rock of St Peter was probably a compliment to Roswitha and she would ask old Justizrat Gadebusch afterwards if he shared her opinion. Crampas inexplicably took this remark seriously and advised against an appeal to the Justizrat, which Effi found uncommonly amusing. 'I really thought you were a rather better mind-reader than that.'

'Oh, my dear lady, faced with beautiful young women who are not yet eighteen, one's reading quite lets one down.'

'Now you've really put your foot in it, Major. You can call me a grandmother, but references to my not yet being eighteen I can never forgive.'

When they had left the table, the late afternoon steamer came down the Kessine and berthed at the landing-stage opposite the hotel. Effi sat with Crampas and Gieshübler over coffee with all the windows open, watching the show. 'Tomorrow morning at nine that same ship will take me upstream, and by midday I'll be in Berlin, and by evening at Hohen-Cremmen, with

Roswitha walking beside me and holding the child in her arms. I hope she won't be crying. Oh, what spirits I'm in already! Dear Gieshübler, were you ever as happy to see your parents' house again?'

'Yes, I know the feeling, dear lady. Except that I wasn't bringing a little Annie, because I didn't have anyone to bring.'

'That'll come,' said Crampas, 'let's clink glasses, Gieshübler; you're the only sensible person here.'

'But Major, all we have left is the cognac.'

'So much the better.'

15

Effi had left for Hohen-Cremmen in the middle of August; at the end of September she was in Kessin again. Occasionally in the intervening six weeks she had felt a desire to be back; but once she was, and stepped into the dark hallway into which only wan light from the staircase fell, she was suddenly beset with fear again, and she said quietly, 'You don't get this wan, yellow light at Hohen-Cremmen at all.'

A few times during her days back at home she had felt a longing for the 'haunted house', but all in all life had been filled with happiness and contentment. With Hulda of course, who couldn't get over still having to wait for a husband or fiancé, she had not got on so well, but with the twins on the other hand so much the better, and more than once, playing ball or croquet with them, it had quite gone out of her head that she was married at all. These had been brief intervals of happiness. But best of all she had enjoyed standing on the swing as it flew through the air, just as in the old days, and the feeling 'now I'm going to fall' had given her a strange tingling sensation, a shudder of sweet danger. When at last she jumped off the swing, she would walk with the two girls as far as the bench in front of the schoolhouse, where she would tell old Jahnke, who soon joined them, about her life in Kessin, which was half Hanseatic and half Scandinavian, and whatever else quite different from Schwantikow or Hohen-Cremmen.

These were the little daily diversions, in addition to which there were occasional trips out to the Luch in its summer profusion, mostly in the shooting-carriage; above all there were the chats Effi had almost every morning with her mother. For these they would sit in the big airy drawing room, Roswitha rocking the child and singing all sorts of lullabies in Thuringian dialect which nobody could properly understand, perhaps not even she herself; Effi and Frau von Briest would draw their chairs over to the open window and look, as they talked, down on to the park, the sundial or the dragonflies hovering almost motionless over the pond, or on to the flagstone path where Herr von Briest sat beside the projecting flight of steps reading the papers. Every time he turned a page he would first take off his pince-nez and wave a greeting up to his wife and daughter. When he reached the last paper, usually the *Havelland Advertiser*, Effi would go down and either sit beside him or stroll with him through the park and gardens. On one such occasion they went over from the gravel path to a little monument standing to one side, which Briest's grandfather had had erected in commemoration of the Battle of Waterloo, a rusty pyramid with a cast of Blücher on the front and one of Wellington on the back.

'Do you take strolls like this in Kessin,' asked Briest, 'and does Innstetten accompany you and tell you all sorts of things?'

'No Papa, I don't take strolls like this. It's impossible because we only have a small garden behind the house which is really hardly a garden at all, just a few flower-beds with box borders, and vegetable patches with three or four fruit trees in them. Innstetten isn't that way inclined, and anyway he doesn't intend to be in Kessin much longer.'

'But child, you must get some exercise and fresh air, that's what you're used to.'

'I do. Our house stands by a copse that they call the Plantation. I go walking there a lot, and Rollo goes with me.'

'Always Rollo,' laughed Briest. 'If one didn't know better, one might almost think Rollo was closer to your heart than your husband and child.'

'Oh Papa, that would be awful, even though – I have to admit – there was a time when I couldn't have managed without Rollo. That was when… well, you know… Then he as good as saved my life, or at least that's what I imagined, and since then he's been my good friend whom I rely on quite particularly. But of course he's only a dog. And people do come first, naturally.'

'Yes, that's what they always say, but I have my doubts. The whole question of animals is a very tricky area, and the last word hasn't been spoken yet. Believe me Effi, it's a vast subject. And when you think of somebody having an accident on the water, or worse still, when the ice is breaking up, and he has a dog with him, one like Rollo, it doesn't give up until it has the unfortunate fellow back on dry land. And if the fellow is already dead, then it lies beside the body and yelps and whines till somebody comes, and if nobody comes it lies beside the body until it dies itself. And that's what these animals always do. Now if we take human beings! God forgive me the sin, but I'm afraid it does sometimes seem to me that God's other creatures are better than man.'

'But Papa, if I were to repeat that to Innstetten…'

'I wouldn't do that if I were you Effi…'

'Rollo would save me of course, but Innstetten would save me too. He's a man of honour, after all.'

'That he is.'

'And he loves me.'

'Of course, of course. And where there's love, that love is reciprocated. That is how it is. It surprises me though that he hasn't even taken leave and popped over on a visit. With such a young wife…'

Effi blushed, because she thought exactly the same. But she didn't like to admit it. 'Innstetten is so conscientious, I think he wants to be well thought of, and he has his plans for the future; Kessin is just a step on the way. And then after all, I won't run away from him. He has me already. And if you are too affectionate – what with the difference in years – people do tend to smile.'

'Yes Effi, they do. And you just have to accept that. Incidentally, don't mention any of this to anyone, not even to Mamma. It's all so difficult, what to do, what not to do. That's a vast subject too.'

They had had conversations like this more than once during Effi's stay at her parents' house, but their effect was fortunately short-lived, and the somewhat melancholy impression re-entering the Kessin house for the first time had made on Effi evaporated equally quickly. Innstetten proved to be full of little attentions, and when tea had been taken and all the town gossip and love-stories had been discussed in a most light-hearted vein, Effi hung on his arm affectionately as they went through to continue chatting, with more anecdotes about Miss Trippelli who had recently been in lively correspondence with Gieshübler again, which always indicated some new strain on her constantly overdrawn bank balance. Effi was very animated during the conversation, feeling herself to be quite the young wife, and was pleased to be free of Roswitha for an indefinite period, as she had been moved out to the servants' quarters.

Next morning she said, 'The weather is fine and mild, and I hope the veranda on the side facing the Plantation is still in good order and we can sit out and have breakfast in the open. We shall have to come indoors soon enough, and the winter in Kessin really is four weeks too long.'

Innstetten was in full agreement. The veranda of which Effi had spoken, and which might more correctly have been called a marquee, had been erected in the summer, three or four weeks before Effi's departure for Hohen-Cremmen, and consisted of a large wooden platform, open at the front, with a vast canopy overhead and canvas curtains to left and right which could be drawn back and forth on rings along an iron rod. It was a charming spot, admired all summer long by the holiday-makers who had to pass this way.

Effi had settled in a rocking chair and said, as she pushed the coffee-tray sideways towards her husband, 'Geert, be so good as to do the honours today; I find it so lovely in this rocking chair that I don't want to get up. So make a little effort, and if you're really pleased to have me back, I'll think of a way to make it up to you.' And as she spoke she smoothed the damask cloth and laid her hand on it, and Innstetten took it and kissed it.

'How did you actually manage without me?'

'None too well Effi.'

'You're just saying that and putting on a long face, but in fact it's not true at all.'

'Effi now...'

'Which I shall prove to you. For, if you had had just a little bit of longing for your child – not to mention myself, for after all, what is one to a lord and master who was a bachelor for so long, and was in no hurry...'

'Well?'

'Yes Geert, if you had had the slightest twinge of longing, you wouldn't have left me sitting all alone for six weeks in Hohen-Cremmen like a widow, with nobody there but Niemeyer and Jahnke and the occasional visitor from Schwantikow. And as for the Rathenowers, not one of them came – you would think they were afraid of me or I was too old for them.'

'Oh Effi, what a way to talk. Do you know, you're a little coquette?'

'Thank the Lord that you say so. That's the best thing to be for you men. And you're no different from the others, even if you do put a solemn and respectable face on it. I know very well, Geert... in actual fact you're...'

'Well, what?'

'Well, I prefer not to say. But I can see right through you; in actual fact you are, just as my Schwantikow uncle once said, an affectionate soul born under the lovers' star, and Uncle Belling was quite right when he said it. You just don't want to show it, you think it's not proper and spoils one's career. Am I close to the mark?'

Innstetten laughed. 'Not so far off. You know Effi, you seem quite different. Until little Annie came you were a child, but suddenly...'

'Well?'

'Suddenly it's as if you'd been exchanged for someone else. But it suits you, I'm quite bowled over. Effi, do you know something?'

'What?'

'There is something seductive about you.'

'Oh Geert, my one and only Geert, what a splendid thing to say; now there's really a warm glow in my heart… Pour me another half cup… Are you aware that's what I've always wanted to be. We have to be seductive, otherwise we are nothing…'

'Did you think of that?'

'I could have. But I got it from Niemeyer…'

'From Niemeyer! Heavens above, what a pastor! No, they don't make them like that here. But how did *he* come to say that? It's the kind of thing some Don Juan, some heartbreaker would have said.'

'Yes, who knows,' laughed Effi… 'But isn't that Crampas coming? And from the beach. He surely hasn't been bathing? On the 27th of September…'

'He often does that kind of thing. Sheer bravado, that's all it is.'

Meanwhile Crampas was almost up to them and greeted them.

'Good morning,' Innstetten called to him. 'Come on, come closer.'

Crampas came up to them. He was in civilian dress and kissed Effi's hand as she continued to rock her chair. 'Excuse me, Major, for neglecting the honours of the house; but the veranda isn't the house, and ten in the morning is really not a respectable time. In that situation one is less formal, or if you prefer, more intimate. And now take a seat and account for your activities. From your hair now, of which one might wish you had more, it's clear to one and all that you have been bathing.'

He nodded.

'Irresponsible,' said Innstetten, half in earnest, half joking. 'Only four weeks ago you were involved in that business with Heinersdorf, the banker who also thought the sea and those spectacular waves would respect him for his millions. But the gods are jealous of one another, and Neptune didn't hesitate to side against Pluto, or at least against Heinersdorf.'

Crampas laughed. 'Yes, one million marks! My dear Innstetten, if I had *that* kind of money, I wouldn't actually have risked it; for beautiful as the weather is, the water is only nine degrees. But people like me, with an overdraft of a million, if you'll pardon the modest boast, we can take that kind of liberty without fear of the gods' jealousy. And we can take comfort from the old saying "A man born for the rope is safe in the water."'

'But Major, you shouldn't, if you'll permit me, stick your neck out in such utterly prosaic fashion. Of course there are those who think that… I mean what you've just said… that everybody more or less deserves it. Nonetheless Major, for a major…'

'It's not a traditional way to die. Admittedly, dearest lady. Not traditional and in my case not even very probable – so, all just quotation, or more precisely a *façon de parler*. And yet there was some sincerity in it, when I said just now the sea won't claim me. I'm quite certain that I shall die a proper, and I hope an honourable soldier's death. Only a gipsy prophecy for the moment, but it chimes somehow with my own conscience.'

Instetten laughed. 'That's going to present problems Crampas, unless you intend to serve with the Grand Turk, or under the Chinese dragon. They're still at it out there. Here history is over for the next thirty years, believe me – and anybody who wants to die a soldier's death –'

'– will have to order a war from Bismarck. I know all that Innstetten. But that would be a trifle for you. It's the end of September now, in ten weeks at the most the Prince will be in Varzin again, and since he has a *faible* for you – I resist the vernacular term for fear of looking down the barrel of your pistol – you will be able to fix up an old comrade from Vionville with a little war. The Prince is only human after all, and a little persuasion can go a long way.'

Effi had been rolling breadcrumbs into little balls during this conversation, throwing them like dice, and making patterns with them to indicate that a change of subject would be desirable. Nonetheless Innstetten seemed inclined to respond to Crampas's jocular remarks, which made Effi decide to intervene directly. 'I can't see, Major, why we should concern ourselves with the manner of your death; life is closer to us, and for the time being is a much more serious matter.'

Crampas nodded.

'It's a good thing you admit I'm right. How are we to live here? *That* is for the moment the question, *that* is more important than anything else. Gieshübler has written to me about this, and if it were not indiscreet and vain, for there are all sorts of other things in the letter too, I would show you it… Innstetten doesn't need to read it, for he has no feeling for these things… incidentally his handwriting is quite flawless and his mode of expression makes you think of an education at an old French court, not the Old Market Place in Kessin. And the fact that he has a deformity and must be the only man here still wearing white jabots – I wonder where he gets somebody to iron them – all fits perfectly. Well, Gieshübler wrote to me about plans for club-evenings and an organizer called Crampas. And that, Major, that I like better than the soldier's death, to say nothing of the other.'

'I couldn't agree more. And the winter cannot be other than splendid, if we can be assured of your ladyship's support. Miss Trippelli is coming…'

'Miss Trippelli? Then I'm superfluous.'

'Not at all, dearest lady. Miss Trippelli can't sing week in, week out, it would be too much both for her and for us; variety is the spice of life, a truth which, of course, every happy marriage seems to contradict.'

'If there are any happy marriages, apart from mine…' and she gave Innstetten her hand.

'Variety then,' Crampas went on. 'And to ensure that we and the Club, whose vice-chairman I have the honour to be at the moment, achieve that, we must have proven contributors. If we join forces we'll stand this whole backwater on its head. The plays have already been selected: *War in Peace*, *Monsieur Hercules*, Wilbrandt's *Young Love*, perhaps Gensichen's *Euphrosyne*. You as Euphrosyne, me as Goethe in old age. You'll be astonished at my tragic rendering of the poet prince... if "tragic rendering" is the right expression.'

'I don't doubt it. I've learnt from my alchemist and secret correspondent's letter that, among many other things, you also occasionally write poetry. I was surprised at first...'

'Because you didn't think I looked the poet.'

'No. But since I've discovered that you go bathing at nine degrees, I've changed my mind... nine degrees in the Baltic beats the Castalian Spring...'

'The temperature of which is unknown.'

'Not to me; at least nobody is going to contradict me. But now I must get up. Here comes Roswitha with Wee Annie.'

And she stood up quickly and went to meet Roswitha, took the child from her arms and held her proudly and happily aloft.

16

The days were fine and stayed fine well into October. One consequence of this was that the marquee-cum-veranda outside came into its own, so much so that the morning hours at least were regularly spent there. About eleven the major would drop by, first to enquire about her ladyship's health and for a spot of scandalmongering, he was wonderful at that, and then to arrange a ride with Innstetten, frequently inland up the Kessine to the Breitling, but more often down to the moles. When the gentlemen were away Effi would play with the child or leaf through the newspapers and magazines Gieshübler continued to send her, or perhaps write a letter to Mamma, or say, 'Roswitha, let's take Annie for a walk', and Roswitha would harness herself to the basket perambulator and pull it a few hundred paces into the copse with Effi walking behind, to a place strewn with chestnuts which they gathered for the child to play with. Effi was rarely in town; there wasn't really anyone there for her to chat to, once another attempt to break the ice with Frau von Crampas had failed. The major's wife remained shy and withdrawn.

So things went for some weeks until Effi suddenly announced her wish to be permitted to go riding too; it was something she loved, and asking her to do without something that meant so much to her, simply because there would be talk in Kessin, was too much. The major thought it was a capital idea, and Innstetten, though clearly less taken with it and objecting repeatedly that they wouldn't be able to find a lady's horse, had to give in when Crampas confidently insisted that they should leave that to him. And true enough, one was found, and it was bliss for Effi to be able to gallop along the beach where the signs segregating 'gentlemen's bathing' from 'ladies' bathing' now stood impotently. Rollo was mostly in the party too, and on occasion they took a rest on the beach or felt the urge to proceed some of the way on foot, so it was agreed they would take along the necessary servants, and the major's batman, an old Treptow Uhlan called Knut, and Innstetten's coachman Kruse were turned into grooms, somewhat imperfectly, since, to Effi's dismay, they dressed them up in an apology for livery which left their real occupations all too apparent.

It was already the middle of October by the time they first sallied forth in fully equipped cavalcade, with Innstetten and Crampas in front and Effi between them, then Kruse and Knut and finally Rollo, though he was soon ahead of everybody as he disliked trotting behind. When they had passed the now deserted Strand Hotel and soon afterwards, keeping to the right, reached the mole on the nearer side by a path along the beach over which moderate breakers were foaming, they felt a desire to dismount and walk out to the head of the mole. Effi was first out of the saddle. Between the two stone causeways the broad Kessine flowed sedately to the sea that lay before them, its sunlit surface ruffled by only an occasional gentle wave.

Effi had never been out here, for when she had arrived in Kessin the previous November it was already the stormy season, and when summer came she had been in no condition for long walks. Now she was delighted, finding everything grand and magnificent and indulging in disparaging comparisons of the Luch with the sea, picking up pieces of driftwood whenever she could, to hurl them either to the left into the sea or to the right into the Kessine. Rollo was always happy to dash after them for his mistress; suddenly however his attention was attracted to quite another quarter, and creeping forward cautiously, almost timidly, he suddenly pounced on an object that came into view in front of him, in vain of course, for at the same moment, from a sunlit rock overgrown with green seaweed about five paces away, a seal slipped noiselessly down into the sea. For a short while they could still see the head, then that too disappeared.

They were all excited, and Crampas began to imagine a seal-hunt, announcing they should bring shotguns next time, since these creatures had a tough skin.

'Can't be done,' said Innstetten, 'harbour police.'

'What a thing to say,' laughed the major. 'Harbour police! The authorities we have here will surely turn a blind eye, all three of them. Does everything have to be so fiendishly legal? Rules and regulations are always a bore.'

Effi clapped her hands.

'Yes Crampas, that's your style, and Effi, you can see, applauds you. Naturally; women are always the first to call the police, but they won't hear anything of the law.'

'That's a time-honoured woman's privilege, Innstetten, and we won't change it.'

'No,' Innstetten laughed, 'nor do I want to. No point trying to wash off the leopard's spots. But someone like you, Crampas, who've grown up under the banner of discipline and know very well that obedience and order are of the essence, a man like you really shouldn't talk like that, not even in jest. Of course you're sublimely indifferent, and you think there's no immediate danger of the heavens caving in. And they won't, not right away. But one day they will.'

Crampas was momentarily embarrassed, for he thought this had been said with something particular in mind, which was not the case. Innstetten was simply delivering one of his little moral lectures as he was wont to do. 'In these matters I admire Gieshübler, always the cavalier,' he said in a more conciliatory tone, 'but without ever forgetting his principles.'

The major was in control of himself again and said in his usual tone, 'Yes, Gieshübler, the best chap in the world, and with even better principles, if that's possible. But what's the reason when all's said and done? Why? Because he has his "handicap". Normal people are for frivolity. Indeed, without a bit of frivolity life isn't worth a charge of buckshot.'

'Well, mark my words Crampas. It sometimes comes to that.' And he looked at the major's shortened left arm.

Effi had heard little of this conversation. She had gone to the spot where the seal had lain and Rollo was standing beside her. Then both looked from the rock out to sea and waited for the 'mermaid' to appear again.

At the end of October the election campaign began, which prevented Innstetten from taking part in further excursions, and Crampas and Effi would also have had to desist in deference to the good people of Kessin, had not Knut and Kruse been there by way of a guard of honour. And so the riding continued into November.

There had of course been a change in the weather and a constant nor'wester drove cloud masses overhead and the sea foamed mightily, but there was still no rain or cold, so these outings under grey skies with the roar of the waves were almost more beautiful than before with the sun shining and the sea calm. Rollo bounded ahead, spattered now and then with spray, and the veil of Effi's riding hat fluttered in the wind. In this weather talking was virtually impossible; but when they turned away from the sea into the shelter of the dunes, or better still into the pine woods which lay even further inland, it was quiet, Effi's veil no longer fluttered and the narrow path forced the two riders close together. This gave the opportunity, as they were slowed to a walk by roots and stumps, to resume the conversation interrupted by the roar of the waves. Crampas, an accomplished conversationalist, reminisced about the war and his regiment and told stories about Innstetten and his idiosyncrasies – because of his seriousness and his buttoned-up approach he had never, according to Crampas, really fitted into the merry band of comrades, so that he had always been more respected than loved.

'Yes, I can imagine,' said Effi, 'it's fortunate that respect is the main thing.'

'Yes, in its place. But it really isn't appropriate in every situation. And then of course there were always his mystical leanings, which sometimes gave offence, first because soldiers don't have much time for that sort of thing, and then because we had the impression, perhaps wrongly, that he wasn't quite so committed to it as he would have us believe.'

'Mystical leanings?' said Effi. 'What exactly do you mean by that, Major? He surely didn't hold prayer meetings and play the prophet. Not even like the one in that opera – I forget his name.'

'No, he didn't go that far. But maybe it's better to drop the subject. I wouldn't like to say something behind his back that could be misconstrued. Especially since these are things that can quite well be discussed in his presence, things which might be blown up willy-nilly into something peculiar when he isn't here to interrupt at any moment and contradict or for that matter laugh at us.'

'Now you're being cruel, Major. How can you put my curiosity on the rack like that. First you say he's something, then he isn't. And mystical leanings! Does he have visions?'

'Have visions! I wouldn't exactly say that. But he was very fond of telling us ghost stories. And when he had got us all worked up, and actually put the wind up some of us, suddenly it was as if he had only been taking a rise out of the gullible ones. To cut a long story short, it reached a point where I said straight out to him one day, "Come on, Innstetten, it's all an act. You don't fool me. You're having us on. You don't believe it any more than we do really, but you want to make yourself interesting, and you've got the idea that not being run-of-the-mill goes down better with the top brass. They can't have nondescript types in the higher echelons. And with your eye for the main chance you looked round for a way to be out of the ordinary, and came up with ghosts.""'

Effi said not a word, and the major was finally put out by this. 'My dear lady is silent.'

'Yes.'

'Am I permitted to ask why? Have I given offence? Or do you find me unchivalrous, indulging in a little gossip about an absent friend, that much I would admit, despite my protests. But there you do me an injustice, in spite of everything. We can pursue this subject freely in his hearing as far as I'm concerned, and I'm prepared to repeat every word I've just said.'

'I can believe it.' And now Effi broke her silence and told everything she had been through in the house, including how odd Innstetten's response had been. 'He didn't say yes, he didn't say no, and I couldn't get any sense out of him.'

'The same old Innstetten,' laughed Crampas. 'That's what he was like in the old days when we were stationed together in Liancourt and later in Beauvais. He was living in an old episcopal palace – and by the by, this might interest you, it was a Bishop of Beauvais, rejoicing in the name of "Cochon", who condemned the Maid of Orleans to be burnt at the stake – and never a night passed without Innstetten going through some kind of incredible experience. Or half going through it. It might have been nothing. And I can see he's still acting on the same principle now.'

'All right. And now for a serious question Crampas, to which I want a serious answer: how do you explain all this?'

'Now there, my dear lady…'

'No evasions, Major. This is all very important to me. He's your friend and I'm your friend. I want to know what it's all about. What goes through his mind?'

'Well, my lady, God can see into people's hearts, but a major on the regional staff of the volunteer reserve can't see into anything much. How can I solve such psychological riddles? I'm a simple man.'

'Oh, Crampas, don't be so silly. I may be too young to know much about people; but I would have to be back at my confirmation, almost even my christening, to mistake you for a simple man. You're the very opposite, you're a dangerous character…'

'That's the most flattering thing you could say to a man well past forty, who's teetering on the brink of the retired list. So let's see, what goes through Innstetten's mind…'

Effi nodded.

'Well, if I have to commit myself, what goes through his mind is that a man like Landrat Baron Innstetten who might any day be given some senior ministerial post or the like, for believe me he's aiming high, that a man like

Baron Innstetten can't live in an ordinary house, can't live in a cottage, for that, if you'll pardon me, is what the Landrat's residence actually is. So he gives it a little enhancement. A haunted house can never be ordinary... That's the first thing.'

'The first thing? For goodness sake, is there more to come?'

'Yes.'

'I see, well, I'm all ears. But let it be something good, if possible.'

'I'm not quite sure about that. It's delicate, risqué almost, especially for your ears, my dear lady.'

'That makes me even more curious.'

'Well then. The thing is, my dear lady, besides his burning desire to make a career for himself, whatever the cost, even if he has to recruit his own private ghost, Innstetten has one other passion: he always has to improve everybody, he's a born pedagogue, and the proper place for him, with Basedow to the left of him and Pestalozzi to the right (though he's more religious than either), would have been the College at Schnepfenthal or Bunzlau.'

'And he wants to improve me too? Improve me by exposing me to a ghost?'

'Improve is perhaps not the right word. But yes, in a roundabout way, improve you.'

'I don't follow you.'

'A young wife is a young wife, and a Landrat is a Landrat. He's often on the road in his district, and then the house is alone, uninhabited. But a ghost is like a cherub with a sword...'

'Ah, now we're out of the wood at last,' said Effi. 'And there's Utpatel's mill. There's only the churchyard to pass now.'

Soon afterwards they went down the sunken path between the churchyard and the plot with the railing round it, and Effi looked across to the stone and the pine-tree where the Chinaman lay.

17

It struck two as they got back. Crampas took his leave and rode into the town, stopping in front of his house on the market square, while Effi changed from her outdoor clothes and tried to sleep; but she couldn't, as her irritation was greater than her fatigue. For Innstetten to muster a ghost so as not to live in an absolutely ordinary house might pass at a pinch, that fitted in with his desire to distinguish himself from the crowd; but the idea of using the ghost to improve her, that was really too much, it was almost insulting. And 'improvement', that much was clear to her, was only half the story, the lesser half; what Crampas had meant was more, much more, it was a kind of device calculated to frighten her. Here was a total lack of goodness of heart, verging on cruelty. The blood rushed to her head and she clenched her little fingers, suddenly determined to make plans; but presently she had to laugh again. 'What a child I am! What guarantee have I that Crampas is right! Crampas is amusing because he has a malicious tongue, but he's unreliable, just a poseur, he's not a patch on Innstetten when all's said and done.'

At that moment Innstetten drove up, home earlier than usual. Effi sprang to her feet to greet him in the hallway with particular affection, for she had the feeling that she had to make up for something. Yet she couldn't fully get over what Crampas had told her, and for all her affection, as she listened to him with seeming interest, she kept thinking to herself 'So the ghost is calculated, it's a ghost to keep me in order.'

But it went out of her mind in the end and she relaxed and listened to what he had to tell her.

By now it was the middle of November, and the nor'wester increased to gale force, blowing so hard against the moles for a day and a half that it forced the Kessine back against the Bulwark and flooded the streets. But after it had blown itself out the bad weather subsided and a few more sunny late autumn days followed. 'Who knows how long they will last,' Effi said to Crampas, and so they decided to go for another ride the next morning; Innstetten meant to join the party too, as he had a free day. Their intention was to go first to the mole where they would dismount and take a short walk on the beach, rounding it off with breakfast in the lee of the dunes where there was no wind.

At the appointed hour Crampas rode up to the Landrat's residence; Kruse was already holding his mistress's horse and she swiftly climbed into the saddle, making Innstetten's excuses as she did so; he couldn't come after all: there had been another big fire the night before in Morgenitz – the third in three weeks, deliberate it would seem – and he had had to go out there, to his great chagrin, for he had been really looking forward to this ride, which would probably be the last of the autumn.

Crampas expressed his regret, perhaps just for something to say, perhaps genuinely, for reckless though he was in his amorous adventures, he was still a good fellow to his friends. Superficially, of course. To help a friend one minute and deceive him five minutes later were things his concept of honour had no trouble in accommodating. He did both the one and the other with astounding bonhomie.

The outing took its usual route through the Plantation. Rollo ran ahead, then came Crampas and Effi, followed by Kruse. Knut was missing.

'What have you done with Knut?' Effi asked.

'He has mumps.'

'That's remarkable,' laughed Effi. 'Actually he's always looked as if he had mumps.'

'Very true. But you should see him now. Or rather you shouldn't. For mumps are infectious, even the sight of them is enough.'

'Don't believe it.'

'There are a lot of things young women don't believe.'

'And then again they believe a lot of things they'd be better off not believing.'

'Is that directed at me?'

'No.'

'Pity.'

'That "pity" is you all over. You know, Major, I really believe you would think it was quite in order if I made you a declaration of love.'

'I wouldn't go as far as that. But I would like to see the man who didn't wish for something along those lines. Thoughts are free, and wishes too.'

'I doubt that. And anyway, there's quite a difference between thoughts and wishes. Thoughts as a rule are something kept in the background, whereas wishes are on the tip of your tongue.'

'Not *that* old comparison.'

'Oh Crampas, you're... you're...'

'A fool.'

'No. There you go exaggerating again. But you're something else. In Hohen-Cremmen we always used to say, myself included, there was nothing vainer than an ensign in the Hussars at eighteen –'

'And now?'

99

'Now I would say there's no-one vainer than a major in the local reserve at forty-two.'

'In saying which the two years you graciously concede make up for all the rest. I kiss your hand.'

'Yes, "I kiss your hand", that's absolutely the right turn of phrase for you. That's what they say in Vienna. And I got to know the Viennese in Karlsbad four years ago where they courted me outrageously although I was only a young thing of fourteen. If you knew what I heard then.'

'Nothing undeserved, I'm sure.'

'If that were true, then what I'm supposed to feel flattered by would be rather rude... But look at the buoys bobbing and dancing in the water out there. The little red flags have been taken in. Last summer, on the few occasions I ventured as far as the beach, when I saw the red flags, I said to myself, that's Vineta, that's where Vineta *must* be, those are the tops of the towers...'

'That's because you know Heine's poem.'

'Which one?'

'The one about Vineta.'

'No, I don't know it; I really don't know very much at all. Unfortunately.'

'And you have Gieshübler and the magazine circle! Anyhow, Heine gave the poem another name, "Sea Spectre" or something like that. But it was Vineta he meant. You'll forgive me if I tell you the story – as he passes the spot, he, the poet that is, is lying on the deck of a ship looking down into the water, and there he sees narrow medieval streets with women in hoods tripping along, and they all have hymnbooks in their hands and are on their way to church, and all the bells are ringing. And when he hears that, he is seized with longing to go into the church with them, even if it's only because of their hoods, and in his desire he cries out and is on the point of plunging in. But at that moment the captain grabs his leg and shouts, "Doctor, are you possessed by the Devil?"'

'But that's wonderful. I'd like to read it. Is it long?'

'No, it's actually quite short, a bit longer than "You have diamonds and pearls" or "Fingers soft and lily-white"...' and he gently touched her hand. 'But long or short, what descriptive power, what vividness! He's my favourite poet and I know him by heart, not that I go in for poetry much, though I've dabbled in it myself, for my sins. But Heine's different: it's real life somehow, and above all he knows about love, which is the main thing in the end. Not that he's one-sided in that respect...'

'What do you mean by that?'

'I mean he's not only interested in love...'

'Well, even if he were one-sided in that, it wouldn't be the worst thing in the world. What else is he interested in?'

'He's very much for the romantic, which comes close behind love and in some people's view can't be separated from it. Not that I believe that. For his later poems, which have been called "romantic", in fact he himself called them that, these romantic poems are full of executions; often, it's true, as a consequence of love. But mainly for other grosser motives, among which I would count politics, which is almost always gross, as the main one. Charles I for example carries his head underneath his arm in one of these poems, and the story of Vitzliputzli is even grislier...'

'Who?'

'Vitzliputzli. You see Vitzliputzli is a Mexican god, and when the Mexicans had taken twenty or thirty Spaniards prisoner, those twenty or thirty had to be sacrificed to Vitzliputzli. That's the way things were out there, local custom, ritual, it was all over in a flash, belly open, heart out...'

'No Crampas, you must stop talking like that. It's improper and disgusting. And just when we're about to have breakfast.'

'Speaking for myself, I'm not affected at all, and my appetite depends entirely on the menu.'

With these words, exactly according to plan, they reached a bench that had been set up half in the lee of the dunes with a very primitive table in front of it, two posts with a board across them. Kruse, who had ridden on ahead, had already set out the meal; rolls and slices of cold roast meat with a bottle of red wine, beside which stood two pretty, delicate glasses, small and gold-rimmed, the kind you bring back from the seaside or buy as souvenirs at a glass factory.

They dismounted. Kruse, who had tied the reins of his own horse round a stunted pine, walked up and down with the other two horses, while Crampas and Effi sat down at the set table, with an open view of the beach and the mole through a narrow gap in the dunes.

The half-wintry November sun poured out its wan light on a sea still agitated in the aftermath of the storm, and the breakers reared. Every now and then a gust of wind carried the spray right up to them. Marram grass grew around, and the bright yellow of the immortelles stood out, despite their similar hue, from the yellow sand where they grew. Effi played hostess. 'Sorry Major, to have to present these rolls to you in a basket lid...'

'The giver, not the gift is what matters.'

'Well, it was Kruse's idea. And you're here too Rollo. Our supplies don't seem to have taken account of you. What are we going to do about Rollo?'

'I think we'll give it all to him, out of sheer gratitude, on my part at least. For you see my dearest Effi...'

Effi looked at him.

'For you see my dear lady, Rollo has reminded me of what I wanted to

101

tell you as a continuation of, or rather a companion piece to Vitzliputzli –
except that it is much more piquant because it's a love story. Did you ever
hear of a certain Pedro the Cruel?'

'Vaguely.'

'A kind of Bluebeard.'

'Oh lovely, just the type we all like to hear about; I can still remember what
we used to say about my friend Hulda Niemeyer, whose name you know;
which was that she didn't know any history except for the six wives of Henry
VIII, the English Bluebeard, if that name does him justice. And she really did
have all six off by heart. And you should have heard her pronounce their
names, especially Elizabeth's mother's – so terribly embarrassed you'd have
thought it was her turn next… But now, tell me the story of Don Pedro…'

'Yes, well, at Don Pedro's court there was a dark, handsome Spanish
knight who wore the Cross of Calatrava on his chest – which meant more or
less the same as the Order of the Black Eagle and the *Pour le Mérite* rolled
into one. This cross was part of the whole thing, they had to wear it all the
time, and this particular Knight of Calatrava, with whom the Queen was
naturally secretly in love…'

'Why naturally?'

'Because we're in Spain.'

'I see.'

'And this particular Knight of Calatrava, as I was saying, had a most beautiful dog, a Newfoundland, although there wasn't any such thing at the time,
for it all happened a hundred years before the discovery of America. A most
beautiful dog then, let's say like Rollo…'

Rollo barked when he heard his name and wagged his tail.

'This went on for many a day. But the secret love affair, which didn't
remain all that secret, it seems, was eventually too much for the King, and
because he couldn't bear the Knight of Calatrava – for he wasn't just cruel,
he was a jealous old stick, or if that's not the word for a king, and still less for
my kind listener, Frau Effi, he was consumed with envy – he decided to have
the Knight of Calatrava secretly executed for his secret love.'

'I don't blame him.'

'I don't know about that, my dear lady. Listen to what happened next.
Some things are acceptable, but to my mind the King went too far, well
beyond the limit. He pretended he was going to hold a celebration to honour the knight, in recognition of his heroic deeds and valour in war. There
was a long, long table, and all the grandees of the realm sat at that table with
the King in the middle, and opposite him was the place for the man in
whose honour it had been arranged – the Knight of Calatrava, the man they
had gathered to celebrate that day. And since, although they had waited

some good while for him, he still didn't appear, the festivities had to begin without him and one place remained empty – the empty place directly opposite the King.'

'And then?'

'And then, just imagine my dear lady, as the King, this two-faced Pedro, is about to rise and express his regret that his "dear guest" is still missing, the servants' screams of horror are heard outside on the stairs, and before anyone knows what has happened, something bounds along the long table, jumps on to the chair, and deposits a severed head at the unoccupied place, and over this head Rollo stares at the man sitting opposite, the King. Rollo had accompanied his master on his last walk, and at the moment when the axe fell, the faithful hound had seized the head as it dropped, and now here he was, our friend Rollo at the long banqueting table, accusing the royal murderer.'

Effi had gone quite silent. Finally she said, 'Crampas, that's all very beautiful in its way, and because it's beautiful, I'll forgive you. But you would do better and please me more if you told me different stories. Even by Heine. Heine surely didn't write poems only about Vitzliputzli and Don Pedro and this Rollo of *yours* – for mine wouldn't have done such a thing. Come on Rollo. Poor thing, I can't look at you without thinking about the Knight of Calatrava whom the Queen secretly loved… Call Kruse please and have him put the things back in the saddle-bags, and on the ride back, you must tell me something different, something quite different.'

Kruse came up. But as he went to take the glasses Crampas said, 'One of the glasses, *that* one there, you can leave. I'll take that myself.'

'Yes, sir.'

Effi, who had heard this, shook her head. Then she laughed. 'Crampas, what do you think you're doing? Kruse is stupid enough not to give it a second thought, and even if he does, he'll see nothing in it, fortunately. But that doesn't give you the right to the glass… that thirty-pfennig glass from the Josephine factory.'

'You may mock the price, that just increases its value to me.'

'Always the same. For such a humorist you have an odd sense of humour. If I understand you correctly, you're intending – it's so ridiculous I'm almost ashamed to say it – you see yourself as the King of Ultima Thule, long before your time.'

He nodded with a roguish smile.

'Well, if you must. We all have our little ways; you know very well what I mean. But I have to say that the role you see fit to cast *me* in is too unflattering. I don't want to run around as the rhyming appendage of the King of Thule. Keep the glass by all means, just don't draw any conclusions that might be compromising for me. I shall tell Innstetten about this.'

103

'You won't do that, my dear lady.'

'Why not?'

'Innstetten is not the man to take this kind of thing as it ought to be taken.'

She looked at him sharply for an instant. But then she lowered her eyes in confusion, almost in embarrassment.

18

Effi was displeased with herself and glad it was settled that these outings together would cease from now on for the rest of the winter. When she considered what had been said, touched upon or hinted at over all these weeks and months, she could find nothing to reproach herself with in any direct way. Crampas was a clever man, sophisticated, humorous, free, free in a good sense too, and it would have been petty and mean-spirited to be strait-laced and insist on the rules of strict propriety at every moment. No, she could not accuse herself of having responded to his manner, yet she had just a slight sense of having escaped danger and congratulated herself that it all seemed to be behind her now. For that they should meet frequently *en famille* was scarcely likely, Crampas's domestic situation more or less precluded that, and meetings in the homes of neighbouring gentry in prospect for the winter could only be occasional and fleeting. Effi worked all this out to her growing satisfaction and came to the conclusion that she would not grieve unduly at having to do without what the major's company offered. In addition to which Innstetten informed her that his visits to Varzin would not take place this year: Prince Bismarck was going to Friedrichsruh, which he seemed to be favouring more and more; on the one hand he regretted this, on the other he welcomed it – now, he said, he could devote himself wholly to his home life, and if she didn't object, they would retrace their Italian journey again using the notes he had made. Such recapitulation was really essential, for it was only then that one made everything lastingly one's own, and retrospective study could even give conscious existence to things only fleetingly glimpsed, which one scarcely knew one still harboured in one's soul. He elaborated further on this and added that Gieshübler, who knew the whole 'boot of Italy' down to Palermo, had asked to be allowed to join them. Effi, who would have far, far preferred an ordinary evening just chatting together, without the 'boot of Italy' (they were even going to hand round photographs), was a little strained in her answer; Innstetten however, quite wrapped up in his plan, noticed nothing and went on, 'It won't of course just be Gieshübler, we must

104

have Roswitha and Annie with us too, and if I think of us sailing up the Canale Grande and hearing the gondoliers singing far off in the distance, while a few feet away Roswitha is bending over Annie, treating her to a rendition of "Buhküken von Halberstadt" or some such thing, then we may have some fine winter evenings to look forward to with you sitting at my side, knitting me a nice woollen cap. What do you say to that, Effi?'

Such evenings were not merely planned, they went ahead, and would in all probability have gone on for many weeks had not the harmless Gieshübler in his innocence, despite his horror of ambiguous dealings, been the servant of two masters. The one was Innstetten and the other was Crampas, and if he accepted Innstetten's invitation to the Italian evenings, not least because of Effi, with genuine delight, then the delight with which he obeyed Crampas was even greater. For according to Crampas's plan, *One False Step* was to be performed before Christmas, and when they were about to have their third Italian evening, Gieshübler used the occasion to talk to Effi, who was to play the part of Ella.

Effi was galvanized; what were Padua and Vicenza to that! Effi was not for reheated leftovers; fresh dishes were what she longed for, variety. But as if a voice within had called, 'Take care!' she asked in the midst of her joy and excitement, 'Was it the major who thought up this plan?'

'Yes. As you know, my lady, he was elected unanimously to the entertainments committee. So at long last we can look forward to an agreeable winter at the Club. He's ideal for the job.'

'And is he going to be in the play too?'

'No, he turned that down. A pity, I have to say. For he is good at everything and would be an absolutely wonderful Arthur von Schmettwitz. He's only going to produce.'

'So much the worse.'

'So much the worse?' Gieshübler repeated.

'Oh you mustn't take me so seriously, it's just a manner of speaking and I really mean the opposite. On the other hand of course there is something overpowering about the major, he likes to do things over your head. And then you have to act the way *he* wants, and not the way you want yourself.'

She carried on in this vein, tying herself up in one contradiction after another.

One False Step was duly performed, and because they had only two weeks (the last week before Christmas was excluded), everybody made an effort and it went off wonderfully; the cast, above all Effi, were rewarded with generous applause. Crampas had indeed contented himself with producing, and, strict as he had been with all the others during rehearsals, he had

105

scarcely interfered with Effi's acting at all. Either he had been informed by Gieshübler of his conversation with Effi, or he had himself noticed that Effi was studiously avoiding him. He was clever and knew enough about women not to disturb things that were taking their natural course, a course with which experience had made him all too familiar.

After the evening's performance at the Club they broke up late, and it was past midnight when Innstetten and Effi arrived home. Johanna was still up to help them, and Innstetten, who preened himself in no small way about his young wife, told Johanna how charming the Mistress had looked and how well she had acted. It was a pity he hadn't thought of it before – she and Christel and even Frau Kruse, the old bat, could easily have watched from up in the music gallery; there had been a large number of people there. Then Johanna went out and Effi, who was tired, lay down. Innstetten however, who felt like chatting, drew up a chair and sat down at his wife's bedside, looking at her amiably and holding her hand in his.

'Yes Effi, that was a lovely evening. A lovely play, I found it so amusing. And to think it was written by a Kammergerichtsrat, you would hardly credit it. And from Königsberg, no less. But what pleased me most was my enchanting little wife who turned every head.'

'Oh Geert, don't talk like that. I'm quite vain enough already.'

'Vain enough, that may be true. But not as vain as the others by a long chalk. And that's in addition to your seven beauties, as Hans Sachs put it…'

'We all have seven beauties…'

'Just a slip of the tongue; you can multiply that figure by itself.'

'How gallant you are Geert. If I didn't know you, I might be afraid. Or is there something behind it all?'

'Have you a guilty conscience then? Been listening behind the door?'

'Oh Geert, I really do get scared,' And she sat bolt upright in bed and stared at him. 'Shall I ring for Johanna to bring us tea? You're so fond of it before you go to bed.'

He kissed her hand. 'No Effi. After midnight not even the Kaiser may call for tea, and you know I don't like to make more demands on people than is necessary. No, I just want to look at you and be glad that I've got you. There are times when one is more keenly aware of the treasure one has. You might after all have been like poor Frau Crampas; what an awful woman she is, friendly to no one, and she would have liked to wipe you off the face of the earth.'

'Oh Geert, please, you're just imagining that. The poor woman! I didn't notice anything.'

'That's because you don't have an eye for that kind of thing. But it was just as I say and very awkward for poor Crampas, who avoided you all the time and scarcely gave you a glance. Which is very unnatural, first because he's a ladies' man through and through, and then, when it comes to ladies like you, why, they're his particular passion. And I'll wager nobody knows that better than my little wife herself. When I think of the lively chit-chat – if you'll forgive the expression – when he used to come to the veranda in the morning or when we went riding along the beach or walking on the mole. It's just as I say, he didn't dare today, he was afraid of his wife. And I don't blame him. The major's wife is a bit like our Frau Kruse, and if I had to choose between the two of them, I don't know which it would be.'

'I know who I would choose; there's a difference between the two of them. The major's poor wife is unhappy, Frau Kruse is uncanny.'

'And you're more for unhappiness?'

'Quite definitely.'

'Well, let me tell you, it's a matter of taste. It's easy to see you have never been unhappy. Anyway, Crampas has a knack of conjuring the poor woman away. He always finds a way of leaving her at home.'

'But she was there today.'

'Today yes. There was no way round it. But I arranged an outing to Ring, the head forester's, with him, Gieshübler and the pastor on Boxing Day, and you should have seen the skill with which he proved to his wife that she would have to stay at home.'

'Is it going to be gentlemen only then?'

'Heaven forbid. No, I would draw the line at that. You are to come and two or three other ladies, not counting the ones from the estates.'

'In that case it's truly unkind of him, Crampas I mean, and that kind of thing always comes home to roost.'

'Sometimes it does. But I think our friend is one of those who don't lose any sleep over things to come.'

'Do you think he's a bad person?'

'No, not bad. Almost the opposite, at any rate he has his good points. But he's half-Polish, as good as, and not entirely reliable, not in anything actually, least of all with women. He's a gambler. Not at the gaming table, but he gambles his way through life, you have to watch him like a hawk.'

'I'm glad you've told me this. I shall be on my guard with him.'

'Yes. But don't overdo it; that won't help. Be natural, that's always best, and of course better still is character and firmness, and if I may be permitted so starchy an expression, a pure soul.'

She looked at him wide-eyed. Then she said, 'Yes, of course. But let's not say any more, not about all these things I can take no pleasure in. You know, I seemed to hear that dancing up above just then. Strange how it keeps coming back. I thought that you were only joking about all that.'

'I wouldn't say that Effi. But be that as it may, one just has to keep one's life in order and have no reason to be afraid.'

Effi nodded and suddenly recalled what Crampas had said to her about her husband being a 'pedagogue'.

Christmas Eve came and went just as in the previous year; presents and letters arrived from Hohen-Cremmen; Gieshübler again paid homage with a poem, and Cousin Briest sent a card, a snowscape with telegraph poles and a little bird sitting huddled on the wires. There were treats for Annie too, a tree with lights, and the child reached out her little hands to it. Innstetten was relaxed and jolly and seemed to revel in the joys of domesticity, lavishing much attention on the child. Roswitha was surprised to see the Master at once so affectionate and so good-humoured. Effi too spoke and laughed a lot, but none of it came from her innermost soul. She felt depressed and didn't know who to hold responsible for it, herself or Innstetten. There had been no Christmas greeting from Crampas; actually she was pleased, but then again not pleased, his attentions filled her with a certain apprehension and she was put out by his indifference; she could see that all was not as it should be.

'You're so restless,' said Innstetten after a while.

'Yes. Everybody has treated me so well, you most of all; it depresses me, because I feel I don't deserve it.'

'That's not something to agonize about, Effi. It comes down to one thing in the end: what you get is what you deserve.'

Effi listened intently, and her bad conscience prompted her to ask herself whether he had deliberately put it in such an ambiguous way.

Later, towards evening, Pastor Lindequist called to offer congratulations and enquire about the outing to the head forester's at Uvagla, which of course had to be a sleighride. Crampas had offered him a place in his sleigh, but since neither the major nor his groom, who was to take charge of the horses as well as everything else, knew the way, it was suggested that they might all make the trip together, with the Landrat's sleigh in the lead and Crampas's following on. And Gieshübler's too, probably. For Mirambo, to whom friend Alonzo, normally so cautious, seemed inexplicably intent on entrusting himself, probably had less knowledge of the paths than even the freckled Treptow Uhlan. Innstetten, who was tickled by these embarrassing little details, was fully in agreement with Lindequist's proposal and arranged that he would drive across the market square at two o'clock precisely and lead off the convoy without further ado.

This arrangement was duly observed and promptly at two, as Innstetten crossed the market square, Crampas first greeted Effi from his own sleigh and then fell in behind Innstetten's. The pastor sat beside him. Gieshübler's sleigh with Gieshübler himself and Dr Hannemann followed, the first in an elegant buffalo coat trimmed with marten, the latter in a bearskin coat that had clearly seen thirty years' sevice. Hannemann had been a ship's doctor in his younger days on the Greenland run. Mirambo sat at the front, rather on edge because he was unused to handling a sleigh, just as Lindequist had predicted.

In two minutes they were past Utpatel's mill.

Between Kessin and Uvagla (where according to legend a Wendish temple had once stood) lay a strip of woodland that was scarcely more than half a mile wide but seven miles long, with the sea along its right side, and a wide sweep of extremely fertile and well-cultivated land stretching as far as the horizon on its left. Here, on the landward side, the three sleighs now flew along, at some distance from a few old coaches in front, in which in all probability other invited guests sat, also bound for the head forester's. One of these coaches was easily recognizable with its high, old-fashioned wheels – it was from Papenhagen. Of course. Güldenklee was rated the best speaker in the district (better than Borcke, even better than Grasenabb), a man who could not well be absent from any festive occasion.

The trip went by quickly – the gentry's coachmen made an effort, not wishing to be overtaken – so that at three they were already drawing up at the head forester's. Ring, an imposing gentleman in his mid-fifties with a military manner, who had been through the first campaign in Schleswig under Wrangel and Bonin and had distinguished himself at the storming of the Danewerk, stood in the doorway and welcomed his guests, who, after they had taken off their coats and greeted the lady of the house, sat down first at a long coffee-table on which there were elaborately piled pyramids of cakes. The head forester's wife, by nature a very apprehensive or at best very timid woman, was just the same in the role of hostess, to the quite obvious annoyance of the inordinately vain head forester who favoured self-assurance and panache. Fortunately he contained his displeasure, for what his wife lacked his daughters more than made up for, two very pretty young things of thirteen and fourteen who took after their father. The elder especially, Cora, immediately started flirting with Innstetten and Crampas, both of whom fell in with the game. Effi was annoyed at this, and then ashamed at having been annoyed. She was sitting next to Sidonie von Grasenabb and said, 'Strange, I was like that too when I was fourteen.'

Effi was expecting Sidonie to contradict this or at least express reservations. Instead she said, 'I can imagine.'

'And the way her father spoils her,' Effi went on, just for something to say to cover a certain embarrassment.

Sidonie nodded. 'That's at the root of it. No discipline. It's a sign of the times.'

At this point Effi made no further comment.

Coffee was quickly taken and they got up to go for a half hour's walk in the surrounding forest, first visiting a game enclosure. Cora opened the gate and had hardly gone in before the deer came up to her. It was all quite charming, just like a fairy tale. But the young girl's vanity as she posed for effect prevented any spontaneous response, above all from Effi. 'No,' she said to herself, 'I wasn't like that. Maybe I did lack discipline as that awful Sidonie just hinted, maybe other things too. They were too kind to me at home. They loved me too much. But one thing I can say, I never put on airs. Hulda did. That's what I didn't like about her when I saw her again this summer.'

On the way back from the forest to the head forester's it began to snow. Crampas joined Effi and expressed his regret that he had not yet had a chance to greet her. At the same time he pointed to the big heavy snowflakes that were falling and said, 'If it goes on like this we'll be snowed up here.'

'That wouldn't be the worst thing that could happen. Ever since I was a child the idea of being snowed up has had pleasant associations for me, associations of help and protection.'

'That's new to me my dear lady.'

'Yes.' Effi went on, trying to laugh, 'ideas are a funny thing, they don't just come from one's personal experience, but also from things one has heard somewhere or just happens to know. You're well-read Major, but in the case of one poem – not quite Heine's "Sea Spectre" or "Vitzliputzli" I admit – I do seem to be one up on you. The poem is called "God's Wall", and I learnt it by heart from our pastor at Hohen-Cremmen many, many years ago, when I was still quite small.'

'"God's Wall"', Crampas repeated. 'A nice title, and what's it about?'

'A little story, quite short. There was a war somewhere, a winter campaign, and an old widow who lived in great fear of the enemy prayed for God to "build a wall round her" to protect her from her country's enemies. And God had the house buried in snow, and the enemy passed it by.'

Crampas was visibly disconcerted and changed the subject.

By the time it was getting dark they were all back in the head forester's house.

19

They sat down at table just after seven, and everyone was delighted when the Christmas tree, a pine covered with countless silver balls, was lit again. Crampas, who was not familiar with the Rings' house, was filled with admiration. The damask, the wine-coolers, the fine silverware, it all gave an impression of grandness, far beyond the normal circumstances of a head forester, and the reason was that Ring's wife, timid and shy though she was, came of a family of wealthy Danzig grain merchants. That was where most of the pictures round the room came from too: the grain merchant and his wife, the banqueting hall of the Teutonic Knights in Marienburg and a good copy of the famous Memling altarpiece in St Mary's in Danzig. Oliva Abbey was there in duplicate, once in oil and once carved in cork. Besides all this, above the sideboard there hung a much darkened portrait of old Nettelbeck, part of the modest furnishings of Ring's predecessor in office who had died only a year and a half earlier. At the time when, as was usual, an auction was held, nobody had wanted the picture of the old fellow until Innstetten, annoyed at this disrespect, had bid for him. Whereupon Ring's patriotism too had returned, and so the old defender of Kolberg had stayed in the head forester's house.

The portrait left much to be desired; otherwise, as already suggested, a sheen verging on opulence was everywhere manifest, and this was matched by the meal that was served. Everyone seemed to enjoy it, with the exception of Sidonie. She was sitting between Innstetten and Lindequist and when she caught sight of Cora, she said, 'There's that insufferable brat Cora again. Just look at her, Innstetten, the way she presents the little wine glasses, the affectation of it, she could be a waitress any day. Quite intolerable. And the way your friend Crampas is looking at her! That's where it all starts. I ask you, where will it end?'

Innstetten basically agreed with her but found the tone she used for all her comments so offensively tart that he remarked sarcastically, 'Yes, my dear lady, where will it end? *I* can't imagine either' – whereupon Sidonie turned away from him to her neighbour on the left, 'Tell me Pastor, is that fourteen-year-old flirt in your class already?'

'Yes my dear lady.'

'Well, I'm afraid you must permit me to tell you that yours cannot be the right approach. I know it's very difficult these days, but I also know that those upon whom the nurture of young souls is incumbent frequently fail to bring the appropriate seriousness to the task. So there we are, the blame rests squarely with the parents and teachers.'

Lindequist, adopting the same tone as Innstetten, said she was absolutely right, but the spirit of the times was just *too* strong a force.

'Spirit of the times!' said Sidonie. 'Don't use that expression to me. I can't bear to hear it, it's an admission of utter weakness, a declaration of bankruptcy. I've seen it all; never grasp the nettle, avoid anything unpleasant. For duty is not easy. So people all too readily forget that we shall be called to account for what has been entrusted to us. Active intervention my dear Pastor, discipline. The flesh is weak of course, but...'

At that moment English roast beef appeared and Sidonie took a generous helping, not noticing Lindequist's smile. And since she failed to notice it, it is not surprising that she carried on regardless, 'All that you see here was bound to turn out like this; it was all muddled and wrong from the start. Ring, Ring – unless I'm mistaken there was once a legendary king of that name over in Sweden or somewhere like that. Just look at him, isn't he behaving as if he was a direct descendant, and his mother, whom I knew in her time, used to take in ironing in Köslin.'

'I don't see anything wrong in that.'

'See anything wrong? I don't either. Anyway, there are worse things. But I think the least I expect from you, as a man of the cloth, is that you acknowledge that there is a social order to be observed. A head forester is not much more than a forester, and no forester has wine-coolers and silver the like of this; it's all quite inappropriate, and leads to children growing up like our Fräulein Cora here.'

Sidonie, prepared as ever to prophesy doom when the spirit moved her to unleash her pent-up wrath, would have launched there and then into her Cassandra act on the future, had not the steaming punchbowl – with which these Christmas reunions at the Rings' were always concluded – at that moment appeared on the table, and with it the Christmas pastries, ingeniously stacked so that they far outdid the pyramid of cakes served with the coffee a few hours earlier. And now Ring himself, who had until then kept somewhat in the background, went into action with radiant solemnity and began filling the glasses in front of him, tall cut crystal goblets, pouring in a virtuoso arc, a feat that Frau von Padden who, though sadly absent on this occasion, was always good for an instant *aperçu*, had once called the '*remplissage en cascade à la Ring*'. The liquid would curve golden red, and not a drop would be lost. And so it was today. Finally, when they all duly had their glasses in their hands – including Cora who had in the meantime installed herself with her golden red tresses on 'Uncle Crampas's lap – the old gentleman from Papenhagen rose, as is the custom at festivities of this sort, to propose a toast to his dear head forester. There were all sorts of rings, he began, tree rings, curtain rings, wedding rings and as far as engagement rings were concerned – for now the time had probably come to mention them – there was fortunately every guarantee that one would be visible in this house in a very short time, adorning the ring-finger (in this case a ring-finger in two senses) of a pretty little fistikins...

'Outrageous,' muttered Sidonie to the pastor.

'Yes my friends,' Güldenklee went on, raising his voice, 'there are many sorts of rings, and there is even a story we all know, which is called the story of the "three rings", a Jewish story, which, like all that liberal fiddle-faddle, has caused and continues to cause nothing but confusion and disaster. May God help us in this. And now let me conclude, for I don't wish to strain your patience and indulgence unduly. I'm not in favour of these three rings, my friends, I'm for *one* ring, for *one* ring who is all that a ring should be, a ring who sees all that is good in this old Pomeranian circle of ours, all who stand with God for King and Fatherland – and there are still some of them (loud acclamation) – who sees all that assembled round this his hospitable table. *That's* the Ring I'm for. Here's to him!'

Everybody joined in the toast and surrounded Ring who, while it lasted, had to hand over the *remplissage en cascade* to Crampas who was sitting opposite; the tutor however dashed from his place at the lower end of the table to the piano and struck up the first bars of the Prussian anthem, where-upon they all rose and solemnly joined in: 'I am a Prussian... a Prussian will I be.'

'It's a beautiful song,' said old Borcke to Innstetten immediately after the first verse, 'they don't have anything like that in other countries.'

'No,' said Innstetten, who didn't much hold with this kind of patriotism, 'in other countries they have other things.'

They sang all the verses, then it was announced that the carriages were at the door, and immediately afterwards everybody rose so as not to keep the horses waiting. For 'consideration for the horses' took precedence over all else in the district of Kessin too. In the hallway stood two pretty maids, Ring set store by that kind of thing, to help the guests on with their fur coats. Everybody was in high spirits, some more than a little merry, and the dispersal of the guests into their various vehicles seemed about to be accomplished swiftly and smoothly, when suddenly it was announced that Gieshübler's sleigh was not there. Gieshübler himself was far too polite to appear con-cerned, far less make a fuss; in the end, since somebody had to say it, Cram-pas asked what the trouble was.

'Mirambo can't drive,' said the groom. 'When he was harnessing the horses the one on the left kicked him in the shins. He's lying yelling in the stable.'

Naturally Dr Hannemann was called; he duly went out and after five minutes assured them with the true surgeon's aplomb, 'Yes, Mirambo must stay behind; the only thing for it at this stage is rest and cold compresses. Absolutely no cause for concern otherwise.' That was some consolation, but didn't solve the awkward problem of how Gieshübler's sleigh was to be driven back, until Innstetten announced that he would stand in for Mirambo and personally convey the two luminaries, the doctor and the chemist, safely to their destination. Amid much laughter and some rather inebriated jokes at the expense of the most obliging Landrat in the land who was even willing to be parted from his young wife to be of assistance to a friend, this suggestion was accepted, and Innstetten with Gieshübler and the doctor in the back took the lead again. Crampas and Lindequist followed, and when Kruse drove up next with the Landrat's sleigh, Sidonie approached Effi smiling and asked, since there was now an empty seat, if she might ride with her. 'It's always so stuffy in our coach; that's how my father likes it. And besides, I should so like to have a chat with you. But just as far as Quappendorf. Where the road to Morgnitz branches off, I'll get out and I'll have to get back into our uncomfortable old crate. And besides, Papa smokes.'

Effi was not much pleased with this company and would rather have made the journey alone; but she had no choice, and so Fräulein Sidonie climbed in and hardly had the two ladies taken their seats when Kruse gave the horses a crack of his whip, and they set off down the head forester's drive, from which they had a magnificent view of the sea, down some rather steep dunes towards the beach road which ran in an almost straight line for five miles to the Kessin Strand Hotel and then took a right turn through the Plantation and on into the town. No snow had fallen for a few hours, the air was fresh and the dim light of the crescent moon fell on the wide expanse of the darkening sea. Kruse drove along the very edge of the water, sometimes cutting through the foam on the breakers, and Effi, who was shivering a little, wrapped herself up tighter in her cloak, maintaining a prolonged and deliberate silence. She knew very well that the talk about the 'stuffy coach' had simply been a pretext, and that Sidonie had only joined her in order to tell her something unpleasant, which she was in no hurry to hear. Besides, she really was tired, perhaps from the walk in the forest, perhaps from the head forester's punch too. Persuaded by Frau von Flemming who had been sitting beside her, she had addressed herself to it with a will. So she pretended to be asleep, closed her eyes and leaned her head further and further to the left.

'You shouldn't lean so far to the left, my dear lady. If the sleigh goes over a stone you'll be thrown out. Your sleigh doesn't even have a safety strap, I see, not even the hook for one.'

'I can't bear safety straps, there's something rather prosaic about them. And then, the idea of being thrown out appeals to me, especially straight into the breakers. Rather a chilly bath of course, but what of it... Can you hear anything by the way?'

'No.'

'You don't hear something like music?'

'An organ?'

'No, not an organ. That would make me think it was just the sea. No, it's something else, an infinitely delicate sound, almost like a human voice...'

'It's a hallucination,' said Sidonie who judged that the moment had come for her to strike. 'You're ill, it's your nerves. You're hearing voices. Pray God that you may hear the right voice too.'

'I hear... well, of course it's too silly, I know, otherwise I'd imagine I'd heard the mermaids singing... But tell me, what's that? There's something flashing high up into the sky. It must be the northern lights.'

'Yes,' said Sidonie. 'Your ladyship behaves as if it were one of the wonders of the world. It's no such thing. And if it were, we have to be on our guard against the cult of nature. It's lucky by the way that we're out of range and don't have to listen to the head forester, that vainest of men, talking about the northern lights. He'd imagine the heavens were doing it for his benefit, I'll be bound, to add a still more festive touch to his festivities. He's a fool. Güldenklee could have found something better to do than toast him. And now he's currying favour with the church, he recently made a presentation of an altar-cloth. Perhaps Cora had a hand in the embroidery. These hypocrites are to blame for everything, because their material interests are always uppermost and are added to the burden of those of us who are earnestly trying to save their souls.'

'It's so difficult to see into people's hearts.'

'Yes. It is. Except that in some cases it's quite easy.' Saying which she directed a penetrating look at the young woman, indeed one that bordered on effrontery.

Effi was silent and turned aside impatiently.

'I say, in some cases it's quite easy,' repeated Sidonie, who had achieved her object, and so continued with an unruffled smile, 'and our head forester is one of those transparent puzzles. I pity anybody who brings up children as he does, but there is *one* good thing about it, namely that it's all plain to see in his case. And it's just as true of his daughters. Cora will go to America and become a millionairess, or a Methodist preacher; whichever it is, she's a lost woman. I've never seen a fourteen-year-old...'

At that moment the sleigh stopped and when the two ladies looked round to discover what the matter was, they noticed that to their right, about thirty paces from them, the other two sleighs had also stopped – farthest away on the right the one Innstetten was driving, closer to them Crampas's.

'What is it?' asked Effi.

Kruse turned half-round and said, 'The Schloon, m'lady.'

'The Schloon? What's that? I don't see anything.'

Kruse shook his head from one side to the other as if to say the question was more easily asked than answered. In which he was right. For nobody could say in so many words what the Schloon was. But at this awkward moment Fräulein Sidonie quickly came to his assistance, knowing as she did all about everything in these parts including, naturally, the Schloon.

'Yes, my dear lady,' said Sidonie, 'things look bad. Not so much for me, I shall get through easily enough; because the coaches will be along soon, and they have big wheels and anyway our horses are used to this. But with these sleighs it's a different matter; they get bogged down in the Schloon, so for better or worse you will have to make a detour.'

'Bogged down! I'm afraid, my dear Fräulein Sidonie, I still don't see at all. Is the Schloon a crevasse or something that will swallow up man and beast? I can't imagine anything like that in this part of the world.'

'Well, it *is* something very like that, but on a smaller scale; the Schloon is actually nothing but a miserable little stream that comes down here on the right from Lake Gothen and trickles through the dunes. In the summer it sometimes dries up completely and you drive over it without even noticing.'

'And in the winter?'

'Ah well, in the winter it's a different story; not always, but often. Then it turns into a Soog.'

'Goodness me, all these names, these words!'

'Then it turns into a Soog, which is at its worst when the wind is blowing off the sea. Then the wind drives the sea water up into the little channel, but not so that you can see it. That's the worst part of the whole thing. That's what's really dangerous. It all happens underground and the sand on the beach is saturated and full of water to a fair depth. And if you try to cross a stretch of sand like that, which actually isn't sand any more, you sink in as if it were a marsh or a bog.'

'I know about that,' said Effi brightly. 'It's just like our Luch', and in the midst of her fears she had a sudden sense of melancholy pleasure.

As this conversation was going on Crampas had got down from his sleigh and walked over to Gieshübler's which had stopped on the far right, to arrange with Innstetten what was to be done now. Knut, he announced, was willing to chance going through, but Knut was stupid and didn't know what he was talking about; it was something local people must decide. Innstetten, to Crampas's astonishment, was also for 'chancing it', they had to give it another try – he had seen it before, it was always the same story: these folk had some superstition based on their fears, which were quite unjustified. And it wasn't to be Knut, who didn't know what he was doing, but Kruse who would take another run at it, and Crampas was to climb in with the ladies (there was a small seat free at the back), to be on hand if the sleigh overturned. That was after all the worst that could happen.

Crampas now appeared alongside the two ladies with the message from Innstetten and laughed as he carried out his orders, installing himself as instructed on the small seat, which was actually only a cloth-covered rail, and shouting, 'Off we go then Kruse!'

Kruse had already brought the horses back a hundred paces and was hoping to bring the sleigh through safely by taking a good run at it. But the moment the horses touched the Schloon they sank over their ankles into the sand, and had difficulty in backing out again.

'It can't be done,' said Crampas, and Kruse nodded.

While all this was happening the coaches had come up at last, the Grasenabbs' in the lead, and once Sidonie had taken her leave with a brief word of thanks to Effi and had taken her back seat facing her father who was smoking his Turkish pipe, the coach advanced on the Schloon without further ado; the horses sank in deep, but the wheels cleared all danger easily, and in less than half a minute the Grasenabbs were trotting away on the other side. The other coaches followed. Effi looked after them, not without envy. But not for long, because in the meantime a solution had been worked out for the sleighs too, a simple one: Innstetten had decided not to force the issue further, but to take the more peaceful alternative, a detour. Exactly, then, what Sidonie had envisaged in the first place. The Landrat's orders rang out incisively from the right: to stay for the time being on the present side and follow him through the dunes to a wooden bridge further up. When both drivers, Knut and Kruse, had received the message, the major, who had descended with Sidonie to be of assistance, came back to Effi and said, 'I can't leave you alone, my lady.'

Effi was momentarily undecided, then moved quickly from one side to the other and Crampas took the seat to her left.

All this might perhaps have been open to misinterpretation, but Crampas knew women well enough not to flatter his own vanity. He could see quite clearly that Effi was only doing the one thing that was proper in the circumstances. It was impossible for her to refuse his company. And so they raced after the other two sleighs, always staying close to the water, with thick dark woods towering on the other side. Effi looked at them and assumed they would eventually travel along the far, landward side of the forest, exactly the same way as they had come in the early afternoon. Innstetten now had other plans however, and as soon as his sleigh was over the wooden bridge, instead of taking the outer path, he turned into a narrower one through the thick woods. Effi shuddered. Up to that point she had had air and light about her, but not any longer, now the dark treetops arched over her. She began to shake and clenched her fingers together to get a hold on herself. Thoughts and images flashed through her mind, and one of them was the little mother in the poem 'God's Wall', and just as the mother prayed, so too did she pray now that God might build a wall round her. Twice or three times the prayer passed her lips, but then all of a sudden she realized that these words were lifeless. She was afraid, but at the same time she felt as if she were under a spell from which she had no wish to escape.

'Effi,' she heard softly in her ear, his voice quivering. Then he took her hand and opened her fingers which she still held clasped together, and covered them with passionate kisses. She felt as if she were about to faint.

When she opened her eyes again they were out of the wood, and a short distance away she heard the bells of the sleighs hurrying on ahead. They became more and more audible, and as they turned from the dunes into the town just before Utpatel's mill, the little houses with their snow-covered roofs lay on their right.

Effi looked around, and the next moment the sleigh stopped in front of the Landrat's house.

20

Innstetten, who had watched Effi closely as he lifted her from the sleigh, though he had avoided any utterance about the strange ride à deux, was up early next morning and tried to master the displeasure, which still lingered, as best he could.

'Did you sleep well?' he said, when Effi came to breakfast.

'Yes.'

'Good for you. I can't say the same myself. I dreamt you had an accident with the sleigh in the Schloon, and Crampas tried to rescue you; at least that's how I have to describe it, but he went down with you.'

'The way you said all that was quite peculiar, Geert. There's some hidden reproach behind it and I can guess why.'

'How very remarkable.'

'You don't think it was right for Crampas to come and offer us his help.'

'Us?'

'Yes, us. Sidonie and me. You must have completely forgotten that it was

118

you who sent Crampas. And once he was sitting opposite me, uncomfortably enough by the way on that painfully narrow rail, was I supposed to turn him out when the Grasenabbs arrived and then all of a sudden the journey went on? I would have made myself look ridiculous, and that's something you're so sensitive about. You'll recall that with your concurrence I've gone riding with him on many occasions, and on this occasion I was supposed not to ride with him? It's wrong, we used to say at home, to show distrust towards a gentleman.'

'Towards a gentleman,' said Innstetten pointedly.

'Isn't he one? You yourself called him a cavalier, in fact a perfect cavalier.'

'Yes,' Innstetten went on, his voice becoming more friendly, though there was still a slight edge of derision in his tone. 'A cavalier he is, and a perfect cavalier he most definitely is. But a gentleman! My dear Effi, a gentleman is something rather different. Have you ever seen a trace of the gentleman in the man? I haven't.'

Effi avoided his gaze and said nothing.

'We seem to be of one mind. And in any case, as you said, it was my own fault; I wouldn't call it a *faux pas*, not exactly a happy expression in the circumstances. So, my fault and it won't happen again, not if I can help it. But you too, if I may offer a word of advice, should be on your guard. He's a man who doesn't think twice about what he does and says, and he has his own ideas about young women. I know him of old.'

'I shall bear in mind what you've said. Only, I think you misjudge him.'

'I do *not* misjudge him.'

'Or me,' she said with an effort, and tried to meet his gaze.

'Nor you either, my dear Effi. You're a charming young woman, but firmness isn't exactly your speciality.'

He got up to go. As he reached the door Friedrich came in to deliver a note from Gieshübler, which was of course addressed to the baroness. Effi took it. 'A secret correspondence with Gieshübler,' she said. 'Further grounds for jealousy for my lord and master. Or isn't it?'

'No, not quite, my dear Effi. I'm foolish enough to make a distinction between Crampas and Gieshübler. They are not of the same carat. Carats can be a measure of purity in people too. I personally, if I may say so, far prefer Gieshübler's white jabot, although nobody wears jabots any more, to Crampas's golden red sapper's beard. But I don't imagine that's the woman's view.'

'You think us weaker than we are.'

'A comfort that is for practical purposes extraordinarily inconsequential. But let's drop this. Read the letter instead.'

And Effi read:

May I enquire how my dear lady finds herself? All I know is that you safely escaped the Schloon: but there were hazards enough in travelling through the woods. Dr Hannemann is just back from Uvagla and has set my mind at rest regarding Mirambo; yesterday he thought the injury was more serious than he wanted to tell us, but not today. It was a delightful trip.

In three days we shall celebrate New Year. We shall have to make do without festivities the like of last year's; but there will of course be a ball, and to have you favour the dancers with an appearance would bring joy to the entire assembly, not least to

Your humble servant,

Alonzo G.

Effi laughed. 'Well, what do you say?'

'What I said before, that I prefer to see you with Gieshübler than with Crampas.'

'Because you take Crampas too seriously and Gieshübler not seriously enough.'

Innstetten wagged a finger at her in jest.

Three days later it was New Year's Eve. Effi appeared in a charming ball-gown, one of her Christmas presents; she did not dance, but took a seat with the older ladies for whom armchairs were provided close by the musicians' gallery. From the aristocratic families with whom the Innstettens consorted for preference no one had come, because shortly before a little contretemps had occurred with the town's Club committee, which had yet again been accused by old Güldenklee of 'radical tendencies'; three or four other aristocratic families had come however, who were not members but always came as guests, and whose estates lay on the other side of the Kessine; some of them had travelled a long distance over the frozen river, and they were delighted to join in the celebrations. Effi sat between the widow of old Ritterschaftsrat von Padden and the somewhat younger Frau von Titzewitz. The Ritterschaftsrat's widow, a wonderful old lady and a real eccentric, attempted to counterbalance what nature had bestowed on her from the heathen, Wendish side, especially in the form of prominent high cheekbones, with strict observance of the Germanic Christian faith. She carried this strictness to such lengths that even Sidonie von Grasenabb seemed like a freethinker by comparison, but against this – perhaps because the Radegast and Swantowit branches of the family were united in her – she had the old von Padden sense of humour which had reposed in the family like a blessing for many a year, and delighted all who came into contact with her, even if they were opponents in church and politics.

'Now tell me my child,' said the Ritterschaftsrat's widow, 'how is life treating you, really?'

'Well, my lady, I have a most excellent husband.'

'I know. But that doesn't always help. I also had an excellent husband. What about here? No hostility?'

Effi was startled and touched at the same time. There was something uncommonly pleasant in the free and natural tone in which the old lady spoke, and the fact that she was such a devout woman made it even more pleasant.

'Oh, my lady…'

'There you are, you see. I've seen it before. It's always the same. Times don't change, not in that. And perhaps that's how it should be. For the main thing, my dear young woman, is to fight. One always has to wrestle with one's natural instincts. And when one has them down and almost wants to cry out, because it's so painful, that's when the sweet angels rejoice.'

'Oh, my lady, it's sometimes so hard.'

'Of course it's hard. But the harder it is the better. You should be pleased. The call of the flesh remains, and I have grandsons and granddaughters so I see it every day. But my dear woman, to conquer oneself in the faith, that's what matters, that is the real thing. Our old Martin Luther, that man of God, showed us that. Do you know his *Table Talk*?'

'No, my lady.'

'I'll send you it.'

At this moment Major Crampas came up to Effi and begged to pay his compliments. Effi blushed to the roots of her hair, but before she could answer, Crampas said, 'May I ask you, my lady, to introduce me to the ladies?'

Effi told them Crampas's name and he, already completely *au fait*, made light conversation, recalling all the Paddens and Titzewitzes he had ever heard of. At the same time he apologized for not yet having visited those residing on the other side of the river and introducing his wife; but it was strange, he said, what a power water had to separate. It was the same with *la Manche*, the Straits of Dover…

'What?' said old Frau von Titzewitz.

Crampas felt it inappropriate to go into explanations which would not have achieved anything, and went on, 'For twenty Germans who go to France, there still isn't one who goes to England. It's the water; I repeat, water has the power to divide.'

121

Frau von Padden, scenting a suggestive allusion with fine instinct, wanted to intercede on behalf of water, but Crampas, with growing eloquence, continued to talk and drew the ladies' attention to the beautiful Fräulein von Stojentin, 'who was without doubt the queen of the ball', his glance actually resting momentarily on Effi in admiration as he spoke. Then he quickly took his leave, bowing to all three in turn.

'A handsome man,' said Frau von Padden. 'Does he visit you?'

'Occasionally.'

'A really handsome man,' Frau von Padden repeated. 'A trifle too sure of himself. And pride goes before a fall… But just look, he's going to dance with Grete Stojentin. He's too old really, at least in his mid-forties.'

'He's nearly forty-four.'

'Oho, you seem to know him rather well.'

It suited Effi very well that the new year, right at the beginning, brought all sorts of excitements. Since New Year's Eve a keen north-easterly had been blowing, which in the following days increased almost to gale force, and on the third of January in the afternoon it was reported that a ship had missed the entrance to the harbour and foundered a hundred yards from the mole; it was said to be English, out of Sunderland, and apparently had seven men on board; the pilots, try as they might, could not round the mole, and launching a boat from the beach was completely out of the question, the breakers were far too rough. That sounded bad enough. But Johanna, who had brought the news, also had comfort to hand: Consul Eschrich with the rescue gear and the rocket battery was on his way already and success was assured; the distance was not quite as great as back in '75, and it had worked then, when they even managed to save the poodle, and it had been really touching to see how overjoyed the dog was, how over and over again it licked the captain's wife with its red tongue, and licked the dear little child that wasn't much older than Wee Annie.

'Geert, I must go out there too, I must see this,' Effi had declared instantly, and both had set out so as not to be too late. Their arrival was well-timed; for just as they reached the beach from the Plantation, the first shot was fired, and they could quite clearly see the rocket that carried the land-line flying under the stormclouds and over the ship and falling on the far side. All hands busied themselves on deck, and with the light line they hauled out the thicker cable with the basket, and it wasn't long before the basket was coming back, completing a kind of circuit, and one of the sailors, a slim, pretty fellow with an oilskin sou'wester, was safe on dry land being questioned avidly, while the basket went on its way again to fetch the sec-

122

ond man, and then the third, and so on. They were all rescued and Effi, walking home with her husband half an hour later, could have thrown herself down on the dunes and had a good cry. There was room in her heart for a noble sentiment once again, and she was infinitely cheered that it was so.

That had been on the third. On the fifth there was a new source of excitement for her, albeit of quite another sort. Coming out of the town hall, Innstetten had met Gieshübler, who as well as everything else was of course a town councillor and a magistrate, and in the course of conversation he had discovered that the War Ministry had enquired what stance the municipal authorities might take if the matter of a garrison were to be raised. If the response were positive enough, that is if they would undertake to provide barracks and stabling, they might be allocated two troops of Hussars. 'Now Effi, what do you say to that?' Effi was as if spellbound. All the innocent happiness of her childhood suddenly rose up before her again, and at that moment she felt as if red Hussars – for they were red too, just like the ones at home at Hohen-Cremmen – were no less than the ultimate guardians of paradise and innocence. And all the while she said nothing.

'Aren't you going to say anything, Effi?'

'Yes, it's strange Geert. But it makes me so happy, I can't speak for joy. Will it really happen? Will they really come?'

'There's a long way to go, of course, before it's settled, indeed Gieshübler was of the opinion that his colleagues the city fathers didn't deserve it at all. Instead of being unanimously pleased at the honour, or if not the honour at least the advantages, they came up with all sorts of "ifs" and "buts" and were stingy about the new buildings; indeed Michelsen the gingerbread-baker went so far as to say it would ruin the town's morals, and anybody with a daughter would have to take precautions and put bars on his windows.'

'It's unbelievable. I never saw people with better manners than our Hussars; really Geert. Well, you know that yourself. And this Michelsen wants to put up bars everywhere. Does he have any daughters?'

'Yes indeed, three. But all of them are *hors concours*.'

Effi laughed more heartily than she had for a long time. But it didn't last, and when Innstetten went out and left her alone she sat down at her child's cradle and her tears fell on the pillows. It was all descending on her again, and she felt like a prisoner, as if she would never escape.

She suffered greatly and wanted to free herself from it all. But although she was capable of strong feelings, strength was not in her nature; she lacked tenacity, and all her good impulses quickly subsided. And so she drifted on, one day because there was nothing she could do about it, the next because she didn't want to. The forbidden, the mysterious had her in its thrall.

And so it came about that she, by nature so frank and open, slipped fur-

123

ther and further into duplicity and play-acting. There were moments when she was appalled at how easy it was becoming. Only in one respect did she remain unchanged: she could see it all clearly and never glossed things over. Once, late in the evening she stepped in front of the mirror in her bedroom; light and shadows were flickering back and forth and Rollo barked outside, and for a moment it was as if someone were looking over her shoulder. But she quickly remembered herself. 'I know what it is; it wasn't *him*', and she pointed a finger at the haunted room upstairs. 'It was something else... my conscience... Effi, you're a lost woman.'

But there was no stopping it, the ball was rolling, and what happened one day determined what happened the next.

About the middle of the month, invitations to the country arrived. The order that was to be observed in this had been agreed among the four families with whom the Innstettens consorted for preference; the Borckes were to lead, the Flemmings and the Grasenabbs to follow, and the Güldenklees to conclude. A week in between each visit. All four invitations came the same day, and were evidently intended to give an impression of order and mature consideration, possibly also of a special bond of friendship uniting them all.

'I shan't be there Geert, because of the cure I've been taking for weeks now, you must make my excuses in advance.'

Innstetten laughed. 'The cure. I'm to blame it on the cure. That may be the pretext, the real reason is, you don't want to go.'

'No, there's more honesty in it than you allow. It was you who wanted me to consult the doctor. I did so, and now I have to follow his advice. The good old doctor thinks I'm anaemic, strangely enough, and you know I drink water with iron every day. If you think of lunch at the Borckes', possibly with potted head and jellied eels, you're bound to see it would be the death of me. And surely you wouldn't want to treat your Effi like that. Of course there are times when...'

'Effi, please...'

'Anyhow, and this is the only good thing about it, I'm looking forward to being able to accompany you part of the way each time you go, at least to the mill, or to the churchyard, or even to the corner of the woods, where the side road from Morgnitz comes in. And then I'll get down and stroll back again. It's always nicest in the dunes.'

Innstetten agreed, and when the carriage drew up three days later she got in too and kept her husband company as far as the corner of the woods. 'Ask him to stop here Geert. You go on up to the left now, and I'm going right, down to the beach and back through the Plantation. It's a fair distance, but not too far. Dr Hannemann tells me every day exercise is the main thing, exercise and fresh air. And I rather think he's right. Give my regards to everybody; except Sidonie, in her case don't bother.'

The drives on which Effi accompanied her husband to the corner of the woods were repeated every week; but in the intervening time too Effi insisted on strictly observing what the doctor ordered. Not a day passed when she did not take her prescribed walk, mostly in the afternoon when Innstetten became engrossed in the newspapers. The weather was agreeable, the air fresh and mild, the sky clouded over. She went alone as a rule and said to Roswitha, 'Roswitha, I'm just going down the road, then to the right to the square with the merry-go-round; I'll wait for you there, come and meet me. And then we'll come back along the birch avenue or the Reeperbahn. But don't come unless Annie is asleep. And if she isn't asleep, send Johanna. Or never mind, it's not necessary, I'll manage on my own.'

The first day of this arrangement they did meet. Effi was sitting on a wooden bench that ran the length of a long wooden shed, looking across at a low, half-timbered house, yellow with black-painted beams, a hostelry with a modest clientèle, townspeople who would drink their glass of beer or play solo there. It was barely getting dark, but the windows were already lit, and the light from them fell on the piles of snow and a number of trees on one side. 'Look, Roswitha, how beautiful it looks.'

On a few days they met again in the same place. Mostly however, when Roswitha arrived at the merry-go-round and the wooden shed, there was no-one there, and when she got back Effi would come out to her in the hallway and say, 'Wherever have you been Roswitha? I've been home for ages.'

Thus some weeks passed by. The matter of the Hussars had been more or less dropped, because of the difficulties made by the town council; but since the negotiations had not been quite terminated and had recently been handed over to another authority, the General Staff, Crampas had been summoned to Stettin to give his views on the subject. From there he wrote to Innstetten on the second day: 'Forgive me Innstetten, if I took French leave. It all happened so quickly. I shall incidentally try to spin the whole thing out, for it's a relief to get away once in a while. Give my regards to your good lady, my gracious patron.'

He read the note aloud to Effi. She didn't react. At length she said, 'It's just as well.'

'What do you mean?'

'That he's gone away. He always says the same old thing. When he gets back he'll at least have something new to say for a bit.'

Innstetten cast a sharp glance at her. But he noticed nothing and his suspicions were allayed once more. 'I'm going away too,' he said after a while, 'to Berlin in fact; maybe, like Crampas, I'll be able to bring back something new. My dear Effi always wants to hear something new; she's bored in our good old Kessin. I'll be gone for a week, perhaps a day longer. And don't be afraid... it really won't come back... You know what I mean, up there... And if it does, you have Rollo and Roswitha.'

Effi smiled to herself, and there was a touch of melancholy in her smile. She involuntarily thought of the day when Crampas had first told her he was just putting on an act, manipulating her fears about the ghost. The great pedagogue! But wasn't he right? Wasn't the act justified? And all kinds of conflicting thoughts, good and bad, went through her mind.

On the third day Innstetten departed.

As to what he might intend in Berlin, he had said nothing.

21

Innstetten had been away for only four days when Crampas returned with the news that the higher authorities had finally abandoned their intention of transferring two troops of cavalry to Kessin; so many little towns applied for cavalry garrisons, and these were Blücher's Hussars no less, that they had come to expect any such offer to be met with open arms, not with hesitation. When Crampas reported this, the council looked somewhat embarrassed, and only Gieshübler enjoyed a moment of triumph, for he relished the setback for his colleagues' philistinism. Among the ordinary folk a mood of dissatisfaction spread when the news came out, indeed even some consuls with daughters were momentarily displeased, but on the whole the matter was soon forgotten, perhaps because the other current question: 'What's Innstetten up to in Berlin?' was of more interest to the population of Kessin, or at least to its dignitaries. They were reluctant to lose the Landrat who was generally well-liked, yet quite fantastic rumours were circulating, cultivated and spread by Gieshübler, even if he was not their originator. Among other things Innstetten was said to be going to Morocco as head of a legation whose gifts would include not just the usual vase with Sanssouci and the Neues Palais on it, but more importantly, a large ice-making machine. This seemed so plausible in view of the temperatures prevailing in Morocco that the whole story was believed.

Effi heard about it too. In days not so long before it would have amused her; but the state of her soul since the turn of the year had made her incapable of laughing freely and spontaneously at that kind of thing. Her features had taken on quite a different expression and the half-appealing, half-mischievous childlike look she had had even as a married woman was gone. The walks to the beach and the Plantation, which she had given up while Crampas was in

Stettin, she took up again after his return, not allowing even bad weather to deter her. As before it was arranged that Roswitha would come as far as the end of the Reeperbahn or the vicinity of the churchyard to meet her, but they missed one another even more frequently than before. 'I could scold you for never finding me, Roswitha. But it doesn't matter; I'm not afraid any more, not even at the churchyard, and I've never yet met a soul in the woods.'

This was said on the day before Innstetten came back from Berlin. Roswitha paid little heed, preferring to busy herself hanging garlands over the doors; even the shark was given a spruce branch and looked even more remarkable than usual. Effi said, 'That's right, Roswitha, he'll be pleased with all this greenery when he gets back tomorrow. Should I go walking again today? Dr Hannemann insists and is always saying I don't take it seriously enough, otherwise I would look better; I don't really feel like it today, it's drizzling and the sky is so grey.'

'I'll bring your raincoat, your ladyship.'

'Yes, do that! But don't come after me today, we never manage to meet,' she said laughing. 'You really are hopeless at it, Roswitha. And I don't want you catching cold, and all for nothing.'

So Roswitha stayed at home, and since Annie was asleep, she went over to Kruse's to have a chat with his wife. 'Dear Frau Kruse,' she said, 'you were goin' to tell me more of that story about the Chinaman. You couldn't yesterday, what with Johanna bein' 'ere an' 'er always so 'igh and mighty, this isn't for 'er. There was somethin' between them, I think, the Chinaman and Thomsen's niece I mean, that's if she wasn't 'is granddaughter.'

Frau Kruse nodded.

'Either,' Roswitha went on, ''is love wasn't returned' – Frau Kruse nodded again – 'or maybe it was, and when the time came the Chinaman just couldn't stand the thought of it suddenly bein' over. For they're 'uman too, even if they are Chinese, so I suppose it's just the same for them as it is for us.'

'Just the same,' Frau Kruse affirmed, and she was about to tell her story to confirm this, when her husband came in and said, 'Mother, pass me the bottle with the leather polish, would you; I've got to have the harness gleaming for when the Master gets back tomorrow; he don't miss a thing, and even if he don't say nothing, you can tell he's noticed.'

'I'll get you it, Kruse,' said Roswitha. 'There's somethin' your wife's just goin' to tell me; but it'll not take long, and then I'll come and bring you it.'

Roswitha did then come out into the yard a couple of minutes later with the bottle of polish in her hand, and stopped beside the harness that Kruse had just hung over the garden fence. 'Mercy me,' he said as he took the bottle from her hand, 'it's not doin' a lot o' good, what with this constant drizzle. The shine just goes. But what has to be done has to be done.'

'It 'as indeed. What's more, Kruse, that's proper polish, you can see that with 'alf an eye, proper polish don't stay tacky, it dries right off. And then if it's foggy tomorrow, or wet, it don't matter. But that business with the Chinaman, it's a queer tale, I must say.'

Kruse laughed. 'Stuff and nonsense is what it is Roswitha. And my wife's always tellin' stories like that instead of seein' to what she should, and then when I go to put on a clean shirt, a button's missin'. It's been like that as long as we've been here. Nothin' in her head but these stories, and on top of that there's the black hen. And the black hen don't lay no eggs. Come to think of it, what's it goin' to lay eggs with? Never gets out and cock-a-doodle-do on its own's not enough to do the trick. That's more'n you can ask of any hen.'

'Just you listen to me Kruse, I'm goin' to tell your wife all this. I always took you for a respectable man, and now you go sayin' a thing like that about cock-a-doodle-do. Men are always worse than you think. By rights I should take that there brush and paint a black moustache on you.'

'Well now Roswitha, I wouldn't have nothin' against that, not from you,' and Kruse, who most of the time stood on his dignity, seemed about to slip into a far more playful tone when he suddenly caught sight of the baroness, today coming from the other side of the Plantation, and just at that moment passing the garden fence.

'Hello Roswitha, what a lively mood you're in. What's Annie doing then?'

'She's sleepin' my lady.'

But as she said it, Roswitha went red and quickly broke off the conversation and made for the house to help her mistress change. For it was by no means certain that Johanna would be there. She spent more time over at the 'office' these days, because there was less to do at home, and Friedrich and Christel were too boring for her and never had anything to say.

Annie was still asleep. Effi bent over her cradle, let Roswitha take off her hat and coat and sat down on the little sofa in her bedroom. She slowly smoothed back her damp hair, put her feet on a low chair which Roswitha had slipped into place, and said, visibly enjoying this relaxation after rather a long walk, 'I must remind you Roswitha that Kruse is a married man.'

'I know my lady.'

'Yes, the number of things one knows, and still one behaves as if one didn't. Nothing can come of it.'

'Nothin' was ever supposed to come of it my lady...'

'If you're banking on her illness, you're in for a rude awakening. That sort live longest. And then she has her black hen. Beware of that, it knows everything, and it tells all it knows. I don't know, it gives me the shudders. And I'll bet it's got something to do with all that up there.'

'Oh I don't think so. But it's dreadful just the same. Kruse's always against

128

'is wife, but nothin' 'e says is goin' to make me change my mind about that.'

'What did he say?'

'He said it's just mice.'

'Well, mice are bad enough. I can't stand mice. But I distinctly saw you and Kruse together, chatting familiarly, and I do believe you were about to paint a moustache on him. That's getting rather familiar. And where will it leave you in the end? You're still a presentable person, and you have a little something. But be careful, that's all I'm saying. What really happened to you that first time? Is it something you can tell me?'

'Oh yes, that I can. But it was dreadful. And it's because it was so dreadful that your ladyship needn't worry about Kruse. When you've been through what I 'ave you've 'ad enough of that kind of thing and you watch out. I still dream about it sometimes, and it leaves me like a wet rag the next day. Such terrible fear…'

Effi had sat up and was resting her head on her arm. 'Well, tell me. What happened exactly? With you people it's always the same story, I know that from home…'

'Yes, it probably always starts the same, and I'm not sayin' what 'appened to me was anythin' special, or anythin' like that. But when they came and accused me to my face and suddenly I 'ad to say, "Yes, I am," that was dreadful. Mother I could bear, but Father, who 'ad the village smithy, strict 'e was, and when 'e 'eard 'e was furious. 'E came at me with an iron 'e'd just taken out of the fire and was goin' to kill me. I screamed and ran up to the loft and 'id, and I lay there tremblin' and only came down when they called up and told me to. And I 'ad a younger sister who kept pointin' at me and sayin' what a disgrace I was. And then when the child was due I crept into the barn next door, because I didn't dare stay at 'ome. Some strangers found me lyin' there 'alf-dead and carried me indoors and up to my bed. And on the third day they took away my baby, and when I asked where it was, they told me it was bein' well looked after. Oh my lady, may Mary Mother of God preserve you from misery like that.'

Effi started and looked wide-eyed at Roswitha. But she was more alarmed than indignant. 'What a thing to say! I'm a married woman, you know. You mustn't say such things, it's not done, it's improper.'

'Oh my lady…'

'Just tell me what happened to you. They had taken your child. You had got that far…'

'And then, after a few days, somebody came out from Erfurt and drove up to the mayor's and asked if there was a wet-nurse to be 'ad. And the mayor, may the Lord reward him, said yes, and the strange gentleman took me away there and then, and from that time on I saw better days; even with the Registrar's widow it was bearable, and I ended up 'ere with you my lady. And that was best, best of all.' And as she said this she came over to the sofa and kissed Effi's hand.

'Roswitha, you mustn't keep kissing my hand, I don't like it. And just watch out for Kruse. You're normally such a good, sensible person... With a married man... no good ever comes of it.'

'Oh my lady, God and 'is saints guide us in mysterious ways, and the misfortune that comes our way 'as its good side too. And those it don't improve are beyond 'elp... I really don't mind men so much...'

'There you are Roswitha, you see.'

'But if I 'ad to go through all that again with Kruse, there would be nothin' for it, I would just go and drown myself. It was too dreadful. The 'ole thing. And what became of the poor mite? I don't believe she's still alive; they let 'er die, and it's my fault.' And she threw herself down by Annie's cradle and rocked the child back and forth and sang her *Buhküken von Halberstadt* over and over again.

'Don't,' said Effi, 'don't sing any more, I have a headache. But bring me the papers. Or has Gieshübler sent over any magazines?'

'Indeed 'e 'as. The fashion magazine was on top of the pile. We 'ad a look at it, me and Johanna, before she went over. Johanna's always so cross because she can't 'ave anythin' like that. Shall I bring the fashion magazine?'

'Yes, bring it and bring the lamp too.'

Roswitha went out, and Effi, left alone, said to herself, 'To think what we turn to, to get by. A pretty lady with a muff, and another with a half-veil; fashionable dolls. But there's nothing better for taking my mind off other things.'

The next morning a telegram came from Innstetten saying that he was coming on the second train and so would not be in Kessin before evening. The day went by in constant agitation; fortunately Gieshübler came in the afternoon and helped to pass an hour. Finally at seven o'clock the carriage drove up, Effi stepped outside and greetings were exchanged. Innstetten was in a state of excitement that was unusual for him, and this meant that he failed to see the embarrassment mingled with Effi's warm reception. Inside in the hallway the lamps and candles were burning, and the tea things that Friedrich had already set down on one of the tables between the cupboards gleamed with the reflected glow.

'It looks just as it did when we arrived here. Do you still remember that, Effi?'

She nodded.

'Except that the shark with his spruce branch is behaving more calmly today, and Rollo's conducting himself with restraint too and not putting his paws on my shoulders any more. What's wrong with you Rollo, old boy?'

Rollo rubbed against his master's legs on his way past and wagged his tail.

'He's not pleased about something, either it's me or other people. Well, I suppose it must be me. Anyway, let's go in.' And he stepped into his room, and sitting down on the sofa, asked Effi to sit beside him. 'It was so nice in Berlin, unexpectedly so; but all the time I was enjoying myself I was still longing to be back. And how well you're looking! A little pale and a little changed, but it suits you.'

Effi blushed.

'And now you're blushing too. But it's just as I say. Before you could sometimes look like a spoilt child, and now all of a sudden you look like a woman.'

'I'm pleased to hear that Geert, but I think you're just saying it.'

'No, not at all, you must accept the credit, if it's something creditable...'

'I should think so.'

'And now guess who sends you greetings.'

'That's not hard Geert. And in any case we wives, I count myself among them now that you're back again' – and she gave him her hand and laughed – 'we wives are good at guessing. We're not as slow as you.'

'Well, who then?'

'Cousin Briest of course. He's the only person I know in Berlin, not counting my aunts whom you won't have called on, and who are much too envious to send their greetings. Haven't you found that old aunts are always envious?'

'Yes Effi, that's true. And when you say that, I hear my old Effi again. For you know, the old Effi, the one who still looked like a child, was also much to my taste. Just as much as my lady wife is today.'

'Was she indeed? And if you had to choose between the two...'

'That's a question for scholarly research, I don't intend to get involved in that. But here's Friedrich with the tea. How I've been longing for this moment! And I said as much too, to your cousin Briest no less, when we were sitting in Dressel's toasting you in champagne... Your ears must have been burning... and do you know what your cousin replied?'

'Something foolish, no doubt. That's his forte.'

'That's the blackest ingratitude I've heard in my whole life. "Here's to Effi," he said, "my beautiful cousin... You know, Innstetten, what I'd most like would be to challenge you to a duel and shoot you dead. For Effi is an angel, and you've deprived me of that angel." And as he said it he looked so serious and mournful that one could almost have believed him.'

'Oh, I know that mood that takes him. How many glasses had you had?'

'I don't remember, and possibly I wouldn't have known even at the time. But I do believe he was being absolutely serious. And it might even have been the right thing. Don't you think you would have got on well with him?'

'Got on well with him? That's not saying much Geert. But I'm almost sure I wouldn't even have got on well with him.'

'Why not? He really is a very delightful and pleasant chap and he's even quite clever.'

'Yes, he's all that…'

'But…'

'But he's a bit silly. And that's not a quality we women appreciate, not even when we're half children, which is how you've always seen me, and maybe still do, in spite of my progress. Silliness is not for us. Men should be men.'

'I'm glad to hear it. By Jove, that puts one on one's mettle. And by happy chance I can claim to have just come from something that was very like being put on my mettle, or at least will require it in the future. Tell me, what would you say to a ministry?'

'A ministry? That can be one of two things. It can be people, clever, distinguished gentlemen who govern the country, and it can also just be a building, a palazzo, a Palazzo Strozzi or Pitti, or if you don't care for them, some other palace. You can see, I didn't go on my Italian journey for nothing.'

'And could you bring yourself to live in such a palazzo? I mean in such a ministry?'

'Goodness gracious Geert, they haven't made you a minister? Gieshübler said something of the sort. And of course Prince Bismarck can do anything. My goodness, has he actually managed that, and me only eighteen?'

Innstetten laughed. 'No Effi, not a minister, we're not as far as that yet. But it may be that I'll prove to have all kinds of talents, and then it won't be impossible.'

'So not for the moment, not a minister yet?'

'No. And I have to say we won't even live in the Ministry, but I shall be at the Ministry every day, just as now I'm at the Landrat's office, and I shall report to the Minister and travel with him when he goes to inspect the provincial authorities. And you'll be the wife of a Ministerialrat and live in Berlin, and in six months' time you'll almost have forgotten being here in Kessin with nothing but Gieshübler and the dunes and the Plantation.'

Effi said nothing, her eyes only grew wider; there was a nervous twitch at the corner of her mouth and her whole delicate frame quivered. Suddenly she slid down from her seat in front of Innstetten, hugged his knees and in a tone as if she were praying said, 'Thank God.'

Innstetten paled. What was this? Something that had been with him on and off for weeks was back and could be read so clearly in his eyes that Effi was alarmed by it. She had been swept away by a noble sentiment that was little short of a confession of guilt and had said more than she should have. She had to counteract that again, had to find something, some way out, whatever the cost.

'Get up Effi. What's wrong?'

Effi stood up quickly. She didn't resume her place on the sofa, but instead pulled up a high-backed chair, evidently because she didn't feel she had the strength to hold herself erect without support.

'What's wrong?' Innstetten repeated. 'I thought your days here had been happy. And now you exclaim "Thank God" as if the whole thing here had been an ordeal. Was *I* an ordeal for you? Or was it something else? Tell me.'

'I don't know how you can still ask Geert,' she said, trying her utmost to control the tremor in her voice. 'Happy days! Of course there were happy days, but there was another kind too. I've never been completely free from fear here, never. It's not two weeks since I saw it over my shoulder again, the same face, the same sallow complexion. And these last nights, with you away, it came back again, not the face, but the shuffling, and Rollo barked again, and Roswitha heard it too and came to my bedside and sat by me, and we only nodded off again when it was getting light. This house is haunted, and I was meant to believe that business about the ghost – for you're a pedagogue. Yes Geert, that's what you are. But never mind that, all I know is I've been afraid in this house for a whole year and more, and when I get away from here, I'll expect to be rid of all that and be free again.'

Innstetten's eyes had not left her and he had followed every word. What did she mean, 'you're a pedagogue'? – and the other thing she had said just before, 'and I was meant to believe that business about the ghost'. What was all that? Where did it come from? And he felt that slight suspicion of his stir again and settle in more firmly. But he had lived long enough to know that all signs are deceptive and that in our jealousy, despite its hundred eyes, we more often go wrong than in the blindness of our trust. It could well be just as she said. And if it was, why shouldn't she exclaim, 'Thank God!'

And so, quickly reviewing all the possibilities, he overcame his suspicions and reached out to her across the table. 'Forgive me Effi, but all that took me so much by surprise. All my fault, of course. I've always been too wrapped up in my own affairs. We men are all self-centred. But that is going to change. There's one good thing about Berlin: it has no haunted houses. Where would they come from? And now let's go over and see Annie; otherwise Roswitha will accuse me of being an unfeeling father.'

Listening to these words, Effi had gradually grown calmer, and the feeling that she had successfully extricated herself from a danger of her own making restored her resilience and composure.

22

Next morning they had breakfast together rather later than usual. Innstetten had got over his irritation and worse, whilst Effi existed so entirely within her feeling of liberation that she had not only recovered her facility for simulating a degree of good humour, but almost her former spontaneity as well. She was still in Kessin, and yet she felt as though it lay far behind her.

'I've been thinking about it Effi,' said Innstetten, 'you're not entirely wrong in all you said against our house here. It may have been good enough for Captain Thomsen, but not for a spoilt young woman; everything old-fashioned, no room for anything. You'll be better off in Berlin, with a proper reception room, not like the gallery here, and a hallway and staircase with tall stained-glass windows, Kaiser Wilhelm with crown and sceptre, or something religious perhaps, Saint Elizabeth, or the Virgin Mary. Let's say the Virgin Mary, we owe it to Roswitha.'

Effi laughed. 'So be it. But who's going find us a place? I can't very well send Cousin Briest to look. Or my aunts for that matter! Anything's good enough as far as they're concerned.'

'Yes, house-hunting. A thankless task to impose on anyone. I'm afraid you'll just have to go yourself.'

'And when, do you think?'

'Mid-March.'

'Oh, that's far too late Geert. Everything will have gone by then. The good places are hardly going to wait for us.'

'That's true. But I only got back yesterday, so I can't very well say "Go tomorrow." It just wouldn't do, and it wouldn't suit me either; I'm pleased to have you again.'

'No,' she said, gathering the coffee service together noisily to conceal her rising embarrassment, 'no, that wouldn't do, not today or tomorrow, but one day soon. And as soon as I find something, I'll be straight back. But there's one more thing, Roswitha and Annie must come with me. It would be best of all if you could come too. But it can't be done, I can see that. And it won't be a long separation. I already know where I'm going to take an apartment...'

'Yes? Tell me.'

'That's my secret. I want to have a secret too. Then I can surprise you with it.'

At that moment Friedrich came in with the post. It was mostly official communications and newspapers. 'Ah, there's a letter for you too,' said Innstetten. 'And if I'm not mistaken, it's your mother's writing.'

Effi took the letter. 'Yes, it's from Mamma. But it's not postmarked Friesack; look, it clearly says Berlin.'

'So it does,' laughed Innstetten, 'You're acting as if it's a miracle. Your mother must be in Berlin, and she's written her darling a letter from her hotel.'

'Yes,' said Effi, 'you're probably right. But I'm almost afraid, and I don't take any comfort in what Hulda Niemeyer always used to say on the subject: that it's better to fear than to hope. What do you think Geert?'

'Not quite up to the mark for a pastor's daughter. But do read the letter. Here's a paper-knife.'

Effi slit open the envelope and read:

My dear Effi,

I've been here in Berlin for 24 hours; consultations with Schweigger. As soon as he saw me he congratulated me, and when I asked in astonishment what for, I was told that Wüllersdorf, the permanent secretary, had just been to him and told him Innstetten had been posted to the Ministry. I'm a little annoyed at hearing this from a third party. But I'm so proud and so happy for you that you're forgiven. I always knew (even when I. was still with the Rathenowers) that he was destined for great things. And now *you* are going to reap the benefit. You must naturally have a place of your own, newly furnished. And if, my dear Effi, you feel my advice can be of assistance, come up as soon as you can make time. I'm staying a week to take a cure here, maybe a little longer if it doesn't have the desired effect; Schweigger is being somewhat vague about it. I've taken a private apartment in Schadowstrasse; there are still vacant rooms beside mine. I'll tell you about the problem with my eye when I see you; all I'm concerned about at the moment is the future of the pair of you. Briest will be absolutely delighted, he puts on a show of indifference to these things, but really it means more to him than to me. Kind regards to Innstetten, kiss Annie from me – perhaps you will bring her with you.
As always,
Your affectionate and loving mother,
Luise von B.

Effi laid the letter aside and said nothing. She was clear about what she was going to do; but she didn't want to be the one to say it, she wanted Innstetten to do that, then she would give her hesitant assent.

Innstetten fell right into the trap. 'Well Effi, why so silent?'

'Oh Geert, there are two sides to everything. On the one hand I'd be so happy to see Mamma again, perhaps in a few days' time. But there's so much against the idea too.'

'What?'

'Mamma, as you know, has such fixed ideas and she only knows her own wishes. With Papa she has always been able to get her own way. But I want a place that's to *my* taste, and newly furnished to suit *me*.'

Innstetten laughed. 'Is that all?'

'Well, that would be enough. But it isn't all.' And at this point she collected herself and looked him in the eye and said, 'And then Geert, I don't want to leave you again straight away.'

'Minx, you're just saying that because you know my weak spot. But we all have our vanity, so I'll believe it. I'll believe it, but at the same time I'll play the heroic role of renunciation. Go as soon as you think fit, as soon as your heart will allow.'

'You mustn't talk like that Geert. "Your heart will allow" – what's that supposed to mean? You're as good as forcing me to play the sweet young thing who, out of pure coquetry, must reply, "Oh Geert, then I can never go." Or something of the sort.'

Innstetten wagged a finger at her. 'Effi, you're too subtle for me. I always thought you were a child, and now I see that in fact, like most women, you've got the measure of your husband. But let's drop the subject, or as your Papa always used to say, "that's too vast a subject." Just tell me when you're going.'

'Today's Tuesday. Let's say Friday on the midday boat. Then I'll be in Berlin by evening.'

'Settled. And when will you be coming back?'

'Well, let's say Monday evening. That's three days.'

'Can't be done. That's too soon. You can't do everything in three days. And your mother won't let you go so soon anyway.'

'Well, when I choose then.'

'All right.'

And with that Innstetten rose to go across to the Landrat's office.

The days until her departure flew by. Roswitha was very happy. 'Oh my lady, Kessin, well… it's not Berlin, is it? And them 'orse-trams. And when the bell rings and you don't know whether to go right or left, sometimes I thought it was all goin' to run right over me. No, there's nothin' like it 'ere. I do believe some days we don't see 'alf a dozen people. And never anythin' but the dunes and out there the sea. It roars and roars, but that's all there is to it.'

'Yes Roswitha, you're right. It roars and roars all the time, but it's no life really. And you get all sorts of foolish ideas. You can't deny it, that business with Kruse was not proper.'

'Oh my lady…'

'Now I'm not going to enquire into that any further. You won't admit it, which is only natural. And don't take too few things with you. In fact you can take all of your things and Annie's too.'

'I thought we were coming back.'

'Yes, I am. The Master wishes it. But you can perhaps stay, at my mother's. Just make sure she doesn't spoil Annie too much. She was sometimes very strict with me, but a grandchild…'

'And Wee Annie's so sweet. Nobody can resist 'er.'

That was on Thursday, the day before their departure. Innstetten was away and was not expected back until the evening. In the afternoon Effi went into town as far as the market square, and there she went into the chemist's and asked for a bottle of *sal volatile*. 'One never knows who one will be travelling with,' she said to the old assistant to whom she usually chatted and who adored her as Gieshübler himself did.

'Is Dr Gieshübler at home?' she went on to ask, after she had put the bottle in her bag.

'Indeed, my lady; he's in the next room, reading the newspapers.'

'I wouldn't be disturbing him?'

'Oh never.'

And Effi went through to a small high room with shelves round it on which there were all sorts of flasks and retorts; on one of the walls there were alphabetically ordered boxes with iron rings on the front in which prescriptions were kept.

Gieshübler was delighted and embarrassed. 'What an honour. Here among my retorts. May I invite your ladyship to be seated for a moment?'

'Of course, Gieshübler, but really just for a moment. I want to say goodbye.'

'But my dearest lady, surely you'll be back. Just for three or four days, I heard…'

'Yes dear friend, that's the intention, and it's arranged that I'll be in Kessin again in a week at the latest. But it's also possible I may *not* come back. I don't have to tell you that there are a thousand possibilities… I can see you're about to tell me I'm too young… young people die too. And then there are so many other things. So I want to take my leave of you as if it were for ever.'

137

'But my dearest lady…'

'As if it were for ever. And I want to thank you, dear Gieshübler. For me you've been the best thing about this place, because of course you're the best person there is here. And if I live to be a hundred, I'll never forget you. I've felt lonely here at times, and sometimes I've had a heavy heart, heavier than you can imagine; I haven't always done the right thing; but from the very first day, whenever I have seen you, I've felt better in body and spirit.'

'But my dear lady.'

'And I wanted to thank you for that. I've just bought a bottle of *sal volatile*; sometimes there are very peculiar people in your compartment who won't even let you open the window – and then perhaps if my eyes fill with tears – for they sometimes go to your head, the salts I mean – I'll think of you. Good-bye dear friend, and give my regards to your lady friend, Miss Trippelli. I've thought of her often these last weeks, and of Prince Kochukov. It's an odd relationship though. But I can see how it must… And do keep in touch. Or I'll write.'

With that Effi left. Gieshübler accompanied her out into the square. He seemed dazed, so much so that he entirely failed to notice several puzzling things she had said.

Effi went back home. 'Bring me the lamp Johanna,' she said, 'but take it into my bedroom. And then a cup of tea. I'm so cold, and I can't wait until the Master comes back.'

Both were brought in. Effi was already sitting at her little writing-table, pen in hand with a sheet of paper before her. 'Put the tea on the table over there please Johanna.'

When Johanna had left the room again, Effi locked herself in, looked in the mirror for a moment, then sat down again. And now she wrote:

I am leaving tomorrow by boat and this note is to say good-bye. Innstetten expects me back in a few days, but I'm *not* coming back, ever… And you are aware of the reason… It would have been best if I had never set eyes on this corner of the earth. I entreat you not to construe this as a reproach; the guilt is all mine. When I look at your domestic situation… *your* behaviour may be excusable, not mine. My guilt weighs very heavy on me. But I may yet escape from it. That we have been transferred from here I take as a sign that I may yet be accorded mercy. Forget what has happened, forget me.

Yours,

Effi

She ran her eye over the lines once more. They seemed strangely formal, but that was how it had to be; it was to indicate that there was no longer any bridge between them. Then she put the note in an envelope and went to a house between the churchyard and the corner of the woods. A thin column of smoke rose from the delapidated stump of the chimney. She handed in the note.

When she got back Innstetten was already there and she sat down with him and told him about Gieshübler and the *sal volatile*.

Innstetten laughed. 'Where did you get your Latin from Effi?'

The ship, a small sailing ship – the steamers only operated in the summer – left at twelve. Innstetten and Effi were on board a quarter of an hour early, as were Roswitha and Annie.

They had more luggage than a trip planned for so few days seemed to call for. Innstetten talked to the captain; Effi, in a raincoat and a light grey travelling hat, stood on the afterdeck near the wheel, and from there surveyed the Bulwark and the pretty row of houses that ran along the Bulwark's line. Directly opposite the landing-stage was Hoppensack's Hotel, a three-storey building whose yellow flag with cross and crown on it hung limply from the gabled roof in the still, rather misty air. Effi looked up at the flag for a while, then her eye glided down and finally came to rest on a group of people gathered curiously on the Bulwark. At that moment the bell was rung. It was an odd feeling for Effi as the boat slowly started to move, and when she surveyed the landing-stage once more she saw that Crampas was standing in the front row. She was startled to see him, but pleased as well. He, for his part, his whole bearing changed, was visibly moved and waved earnestly to her, a greeting she returned equally earnestly, though at the same time most amicably; as she did so there was an appeal in her eyes. Then she went quickly to her cabin where Roswitha had already installed herself with Annie. Here, in the somewhat stuffy interior, she remained until they had left the river and sailed into the wide bay of the Breitling; then Innstetten came and called her up on deck to see how magnificent the view was just there. So she went up. Grey clouds hung over the surface of the water and only occasionally was there a half-veiled glint of sunlight through the cloud cover. Effi's thoughts went back to the day, fifteen months before, when she had driven along the shore of this self-same Breitling in an open carriage. A short span of time, and often such a quiet and lonely life. And yet the things that had happened since then!

And so they sailed up the waterway and by two they were at or at least very near the station. When soon afterwards they passed the Prince Bismarck Inn, Golchowski was once more standing in the doorway, and he did not fail to accompany the Landrat and his lady to the steps up the embankment. At the top the train had not yet been announced and Effi and Innstetten walked up and down the platform. Their conversation centred on the question of where to live; they were agreed on the district and that it had to be between the Tiergarten and the Zoological Garden. 'I want to hear the song of the finches, and the parrots too,' said Innstetten, and Effi concurred.

Then they heard the signal and the train drew in; the stationmaster was most obliging and Effi was given a compartment to herself.

Another handshake, a wave of a handkerchief, and the train drew out again.

23

Friedrichstrasse station was crowded; but nonetheless, Effi had recognized her mother from the compartment, and Cousin Briest beside her. Their joy at the reunion was great, waiting in the luggage hall was not too severe a test of their patience, and in little more than five minutes their cab was trundling alongside the horse tram rails into Dorotheenstrasse in the direction of Schadowstrasse where the *pension* stood on the first corner. Roswitha was overjoyed, and delighted at Annie who stretched her little hands out towards the lights.

Then they were there. Effi was given her two rooms, not as expected beside Frau von Briest, but off the same lobby, and when everything had been put away properly, and Annie was safely tucked up in her cot, Effi reappeared in her mother's room, a little drawing-room with a fireplace and a modest fire in the grate, the weather being mild, almost warm. Three places were set at a round table with a green-shaded lamp, and on a little side-table stood the tea things.

'Your apartment is charming, Mamma,' said Effi as she sat down opposite the sofa, only to get up again immediately afterwards and busy herself at the tea table. 'May I play the waitress again?'

'Of course you may, my dear Effi. But just for you and Dagobert. For my part, I must abstain, which is not at all easy.'

'I understand, because of your eyes. Tell me Mamma, what is it that's wrong with them? In the cab, and it did rattle so, we talked the whole time about Innstetten and our grand career, far too much and it won't do, believe me; your eyes are more important to me, and in one respect, thank goodness,

I find them quite unaltered. When you look at me they're just as kind as ever.' And she rushed over to her mamma and kissed her hand.

'Effi, you're so impetuous. Just the same old Effi.'

'Oh no Mamma. Not the same at all. I wish I were. Marriage changes one.'

Cousin Briest laughed. 'I don't see much change, cousin; you're prettier than ever, that's all. And I don't imagine it's put an end to your impetuousness yet either.'

'The same old cousin,' Frau von Briest affirmed; Effi herself wouldn't hear of it and said, 'Dagobert, for all your talents, you don't know much about people. It's strange. You officers don't seem to understand people, the young ones certainly don't. All you look at is yourselves and your recruits, and of course the horses in the case of the cavalry. That bunch know absolutely nothing.'

'But cousin, where does this wisdom come from? You don't know any officers. Kessin, I read somewhere, decided to do without the Hussars it was to be allocated, incidentally a unique phenomenon in the history of the world. Or are you talking about the old days? You were still half a child then, when the Rathenow officers came over to visit.'

'I could say that children are the most observant. But I won't, that's all beside the point. What I want to know is how Mamma's eyes are.'

Frau von Briest proceeded to tell them that the eye specialist had diagnosed congestion in the brain. That was what was causing the blurring. It was to be brought under control by diet; beer, coffee, tea – all to be cut out, and she was to have local blood-letting from time to time, then it would soon improve. 'He said a fortnight or so. But I know doctors' forecasts. A fortnight means six weeks, and I'll still be here when Innstetten arrives and you move into your new apartment. And I can't deny that that's the best thing about all this, indeed the only thing that reconciles me in advance to what I suspect will be a long course of treatment. So just look for something really nice. I thought of Landgrafenstrasse or Keithstrasse, elegant but not too expensive. For you will have to be careful with money. Innstetten's post is very prestigious, but it doesn't bring in all that much. And Briest is complaining too. Prices are falling, and he tells me every day that if they don't bring in protective tariffs he'll have to give up Hohen-Cremmen and get out the begging-bowl. You know how he likes to exaggerate. But help yourself Dagobert, and then if you can, tell us a nice story. People's ailments are always tedious, and even one's nearest and dearest only listen because they've no alternative. I'm sure Effi would like to hear a story too, something from the *Fliegende Blätter* or *Kladderadatsch*, though they say it's not what it used to be.'

'Oh, it's still as good ever. It still has Strudelwit and Prudelwit, and that's enough on its own.'

'My favourite is Charlie Miessnick and Wee Wippy from Bernau.'

'Yes, they're the best. But Wee Wippy, if you'll pardon me, my beautiful cousin, isn't in *Kladderadatsch*, and anyway he's out of a job at the moment, there isn't a war on. Pity. Chaps like me would also like to have a go and get rid of' – and he ran his finger over his uniform from his button-hole to his armpit – 'this awful empty space.'

'Oh, that's all just vanity. Tell us a joke instead. What's the latest?'

'Well, dear cousin, we have a curious state of affairs. It's not everybody's cup of tea. What we have at the moment are Bible jokes.'

'Bible jokes? How do you mean?... The Bible and jokes don't go together.'

'As I said, it's not everyone's cup of tea. But permissible or not, they're all the rage. A passing fad, like plovers' eggs.'

'Well, if it's not too drastic, tell us one, just to see. Can you?'

'Of course I can. And I may even add, you've struck lucky. The one going the rounds at the moment is particularly good, because it's a combination of Scripture and pun. The question in this case – all these jokes take the form of questions by the way – is of the utmost simplicity: "What was our Lord's favourite plaything called?" Now guess.'

'Little lambkin, perhaps.'

'A brave try. You're an ace, Effi. I'd never have thought of that. But you're wide of the mark.'

'Well, what was it then?'

'Our Lord's favourite plaything was called "Gladly", because in the hymn it says "Gladly the cross I'd bear" or "cross-eyed bear", "eyed", e-y-e-d.'

Effi, shaking her head, repeated the phrase and the additional information, but in spite of all her efforts was unable to see the point; she was quite decidedly one of the happy few who are impervious to this kind of wordplay, and so Cousin Briest found himself in the unenviable position of having to point out again and again how the words sounded the same but actually had different meanings.

'Oh I see. You must excuse me for taking so long. But it really is too silly.'

'Yes, it is silly,' said Dagobert sheepishly.

'Silly and in poor taste, enough to put you off Berlin. You leave Kessin to be among proper people again, and the first thing you hear is a Bible joke. Mamma is silent too, which is comment enough. However, I'm going to allow you to make an orderly retreat –'

'Please do, Cousin Effi.'

'– an orderly retreat, and I take it in all seriousness as a good sign that the first thing my cousin Dagobert said to me here was, "Gladly the cross I'd bear." Strange as it may seem, Cousin, though it's a bad joke, I'm grateful to you for telling it.'

Dagobert, having just got off the hook, proceeded to make fun of Effi's earnestness, but desisted when he saw that he was annoying her.

Soon after ten he left, promising to come back next day to ask for his orders.

And as soon as he had gone, Effi too withdrew to her rooms.

The next day was a very fine one, and mother and daughter went out early, first to the eye clinic where Effi sat in the waiting room and occupied herself leafing through an album. Then they went to the Tiergarten and on to the vicinity of the Zoo to look for an apartment in that area. And as it happened they did locate something eminently suitable in Keithstrasse, which was where they had been thinking of from the outset, except that it was a new building, damp and not quite finished. 'It won't do, Effi dear,' said Frau von Briest, 'it must be ruled out simply for health reasons. You don't put in a Geheimrat to dry out plaster.'

Effi, much as she liked the apartment, was in agreement, the more so because a swift solution did not suit her at all, quite the contrary, 'gain time, gain all,' and so a postponement of the whole matter was in fact the best thing that could happen from her point of view. 'We'll bear this apartment in mind though Mamma, it's so nicely situated and it's really exactly what I wanted.' Then the two ladies drove back into town, ate at a restaurant that had been recommended to them and went to the opera in the evening, which the doctor had permitted on condition that Frau von Briest went to listen rather than to watch.

The next few days followed a similar pattern; mother and daughter were genuinely delighted at having each other again and being able to chat to their heart's content after such a long time. Effi had a talent not just for talking and listening, but when really at ease was a most adept scandalmonger, and she more than once recaptured her old high spirits, and her mother wrote home how happy she was to find the 'child' so cheerful and ready to laugh once more; it was like the lovely time they had all had almost two years before all over again, when they were buying her trousseau. Cousin Briest too was quite his old self, she reported. And this was indeed the case, except that they saw less of him than last time, and when asked why, he would maintain, apparently quite seriously, 'Because you're too dangerous for me, cousin.' Every time this happened mother and daughter would subside into laughter, and Effi would say, 'Dagobert, you're still very young of course, but not young enough to court me in that style any more.'

In this way almost two weeks had passed. Innstetten wrote more and more urgently and became quite sharp, even towards his mother-in-law, so Effi realized that further postponement was scarcely possible and they really had to find a place to rent. But what then? There were still three weeks until they moved to Berlin and Innstetten was insisting on her prompt return. There was only one thing for it: some more play-acting, she would have to be ill.

She didn't care for this for a variety of reasons, but it had to be, and once that was clear to her, it was also clear how she was going to play this role, down to the last detail.

'Mamma, Innstetten, as you see, is getting touchy about my absence. I think we have to capitulate and rent somewhere today. And tomorrow I'll travel back. Oh it's so hard for me to leave you.'

Frau von Briest was in agreement. 'And which apartment is it to be?'

'The first one of course, the one in Keithstrasse which I liked so much from the start, and so did you. It probably won't quite have dried out yet, but it's summer now, which is some consolation. And if the dampness gets too bad and I get a touch of rheumatism, there's always Hohen-Cremmen after all.'

'Child, don't tempt Providence; rheumatism can come out of the blue, and you never know what brought it on.'

These words came at just the right moment for Effi. She took the tenancy that very morning and wrote a card to Innstetten saying she would be leaving next day. And sure enough the cases were packed straight away and all preparations made. But when the next morning came, Effi sent from her bed for her mother and said, 'Mamma, I can't travel. I have such aches and pains and it's hurting all down my back, I'm almost inclined to think it's rheumatism. I didn't know it could be so painful.'

'There you are, what did I tell you? Speak of the devil. Yesterday you were thoughtless enough to say it, now you've got it. When I see Schweigger, I'll ask him what you ought to do.'

'No, not Schweigger. He's an eye specialist. That won't do, you never know, he might take it amiss, being consulted about something else. I think it would be best just to wait and see. It might go away. I shall take nothing but tea and soda-water for a whole day, and if that makes me perspire, perhaps I'll get over it.'

Frau von Briest expressed her agreement but insisted that she should have proper nourishment. Not eating anything, which used to be the fashion, was quite wrong and just weakened one; in this particular she was wholly on the side of the new school: good solid meals.

Effi derived no small consolation from these views and sent a telegram to Innstetten in which she spoke of a tiresome turn of events which annoyingly for the moment prevented her return, and then she said to Roswitha, 'Roswitha, you must get some books for me; it won't be difficult, I want old ones, really old ones.'

'Of course my lady. The lendin' library is just next door. What am I to bring?'

'I'll write it down, all sorts of things to choose from, sometimes they don't have the one thing you happen to want.' Roswitha fetched a pencil and paper and Effi wrote down: Walter Scott, *Ivanhoe* or *Quentin Durward*; Cooper, *The Spy*; Dickens, *David Copperfield*; Willibald Alexis, *Baron Bredow's Breeches*.

Roswitha read through the list and in the next room cut off the last line; she was too ashamed for herself and for her mistress to hand over the note in its original form.

The day passed without further incident. Next morning there was no improvement, nor on the third day.

'Effi, we can't go on like this. When something like this gets a hold, you never get rid of it; what doctors quite rightly warn against most is letting things drag on like this.'

Effi sighed. 'Yes Mamma, but who are we to have? Not a young doctor; that would embarrass me, I don't know why.'

'A young doctor is always a little *gênant*, and if he isn't, so much the worse. But you can put your mind at rest; I would suggest a very old one who treated me when I was still at Hecker's Boarding School, which was a good twenty years ago. And he was almost fifty then and had nice grey hair, all curly. He was a ladies' man, but within the bounds of propriety. Doctors who lose sight of those go under, they're bound to; our women, at least society women, still know what's right and proper.'

'Do you think so? I'm always glad to hear good things like that. At times you do hear otherwise. And it must often be hard. And what is the old Geheimrat called? For I take it he is a Geheimrat.'

'Geheimrat Rummschüttel.'

Effi laughed outright. 'Rummschüttel! A shaky doctor for a patient who can't move.'

'Effi, you do say some strange things. You can't be in any great pain.'

'No, not just at the moment; it keeps coming and going.'

Next morning Geheimrat Rummschüttel called. Frau von Briest received him, and when he saw Effi, his first words were: 'The image of her mother.'

The mother was inclined to demur, saying that twenty years and more

145

was a long time; Rummschüttel however stood by his assertion, at the same time assuring them that he didn't have every face engraved on his memory, but once he had registered an impression, that impression was there for good. 'And now my dear Frau von Innstetten, what's the trouble, how can we help?'

'Oh Herr Geheimrat, I can't really tell you what it is. It keeps coming and going. Just at this moment it's as if it had flown away. At first I thought it was rheumatism, but now I'm almost inclined to think it's neuralgia, pains all down my back, and then I can't sit up. My Papa suffers from neuralgia, so I've seen what it's like. Perhaps I've inherited it from him.'

'Very probably,' said Rummschüttel, who had taken his patient's pulse and had been observing her closely but unobtrusively. 'Very probably, my dear lady.' But what he said to himself was, 'Putting it on, a virtuoso performance, a daughter of Eve *comme il faut*.' However, he gave not the slightest indication of this, but said with all the seriousness anyone could have desired, 'Rest and keep warm, that's the best thing I can prescribe. Some medicine, but nothing unpleasant, will do the rest.'

And he stood up to write out the prescription. *Aqua amygdalarum amararum* half an ounce, *Syrupus florum aurantii* two ounces. 'I would ask your ladyship to take half a teaspoonful of this every two hours. It will calm your nerves. And there is one other thing I would insist upon: no mental strain, no visits, no reading.' So saying, he pointed to the book lying beside her.

'It's Scott.'

'Oh well, there's no objection to that. Travel books are best though. I'll call again tomorrow.'

Effi had been perfectly composed and had played her part well. Still, when she was alone again – her mother was seeing the Geheimrat out – the blood rushed to her head; it had been quite obvious to her that he had seen through her play-acting and responded in kind. He was evidently a man well-versed in the ways of the world, who saw everything quite clearly but chose not to notice it all, perhaps because he knew that some things might deserve to be respected. For was there not play-acting that merited respect, and was not her own now just such a case?

Soon afterwards Frau von Briest returned, and mother and daughter jointly indulged in singing the praises of the fine old gentleman who, in spite of his seventy years, they agreed still had something youthful about him. 'Send Roswitha to the chemist's right away... You're only to take it every three hours though, he made a point of telling me that outside. That's how he always used to be, he seldom prescribed anything, and only small amounts; but always something effective, and it helped straight away.'

Rummschüttel came the next day, then every three days because he saw

146

the embarrassment his visits caused the young woman. This won his sympathy, and after the third visit he was certain of his verdict. 'There's something going on here that is forcing this young woman to behave like this.' The days were long gone when he would have taken offence at such behaviour.

When Rummschüttel made his fourth visit, he found Effi up, sitting in a rocking chair with a book in her hand and Annie at her side.

'Ah my dear lady! Delighted. I don't attribute it to the medicine; the fine weather, these fresh bright March days, illness just goes. I congratulate you. And your Mamma?'

'She has gone out Herr Geheimrat, to Keithstrasse, we've taken an apartment there. I'm expecting my husband in the next few days, and I'm greatly looking forward to the opportunity, once we've settled in, of introducing him to you. For I would like to hope that you will agree to look after me in the future too.'

He bowed.

'Although I'm a little worried about the new apartment,' she went on, 'it's a new building. Do you think, Herr Geheimrat, that the damp walls…'

'Not in the slightest, my dear lady. Have the heating kept up for three or four days with all the doors and windows open, then you can risk it, on my responsibility. That neuralgia of yours wasn't too serious. But I'm happy that you were so cautious, for it has given me an occasion to renew an old acquaintance and make a new one.'

He repeated his bow, looked into Annie's eyes with a kind smile and took his leave, asking for his respects to be conveyed to Frau von Briest.

He was hardly gone when Effi sat down at her writing-table and wrote:

Dear Innstetten,
Rummschüttel has just been and told me I'm cured. I am now fit to travel, say tomorrow; but today is already the 24th and you intend to arrive here on the 28th. I am still a bit under the weather. I think you will agree I ought to abandon the journey altogether. Our things are on the way already anyhow, and if I came we would have to stay at Hoppensack's Hotel like visitors. There is the matter of cost to be considered too; expenses are going to mount up in any case; apart from anything else Rummschüttel's bills have to be paid, though we shall keep him as our doctor. A very charming old gentleman by the way. As a doctor he is not considered to be in the front rank; his opponents and rivals call him a 'ladies' doctor'. Which is praise as well as blame; it's not everybody who knows how to treat us. The fact that I can't say good-bye personally to the Kessin people doesn't matter a great deal. I did visit Gieshübler. The

major's wife has always been stand-offish towards me, stand-offish to the point of rudeness; that just leaves the pastor and Dr Hannemann and Crampas. Convey my respects to him. I'm sending cards to the country families; the Güldenklees, you tell me, are in Italy (I can't imagine what they think they will find there), and that just leaves the other three. Make my excuses as best you can. Formalities are your forte and you always manage to strike the right note. As for Frau von Padden with whom I was so taken on New Year's Eve, perhaps I'll write to her myself and express my regrets. Let me know by telegram whether all this meets with your approval.

As ever,

Yours,

Effi

Effi posted the letter herself, as if that in itself might hasten the reply, and next morning the telegram she had requested came from Innstetten, 'Fully agree.' Her heart leapt, she rushed downstairs to the nearest cab-rank. 'Number 1C Keithstrasse.' And the cab flew down Unter den Linden and then Tiergartenstrasse before stopping outside the door of her new apartment.

Upstairs the things that had arrived the day before lay in a jumble, but this did not disturb her, and when she stepped out on to the broad, walled balcony, the Tiergarten lay before her on the far side of the canal bridge, its trees all showing a shimmer of green already. And above, a clear blue sky and a laughing sun.

She trembled with excitement and breathed deeply. Then she stepped back inside from the balcony, lifted her gaze and clasped her hands.

'Now, God willing, a new life! Things are going to be different.'

24

Three days later, quite late in the day, about nine, Innstetten arrived in Berlin. Everybody was at the station, Effi, her mother, Cousin Briest; it was a warm reception and Effi's was the warmest of all, and a world of things had been talked about by the time the carriage they had taken stopped outside the new apartment in Keithstrasse. 'Oh, you've made a good choice here Effi,' said Innstetten as he stepped into the vestibule, 'no shark, no crododile, and I hope, no ghost.'

'No Geert, that's all over now. It's a new time, a new beginning, and I'm not afraid any more and I'm going to be better than I have been and behave more to your liking.' All this she whispered to him as they climbed the carpeted stairs to the second floor. Cousin Briest escorted her mother.

Upstairs some things were still missing, but a homely impression had been achieved nonetheless and Innstetten expressed his pleasure at this. 'Effi, you're a little genius you know,' but Effi would have none of this praise and pointed to her mother, saying she was really responsible. 'That goes here,' she would announce, brooking no denial, and she had invariably been right, which of course had saved a lot of time and kept tempers sweet to the end. Finally Roswitha came in too to greet the Master, taking the occasion to say, 'Fräulein Annie begs to be excused for today' – her little joke, of which she was proud, and indeed it had the desired effect.

And now they all sat down at the table which was already laid, and when Innstetten had poured himself a glass of wine and drunk to 'happy days', clinking glasses with everybody, he took Effi's hand and said, 'But Effi, tell me now, what was all this about your illness?'

'Oh, don't let's bother about that, it's not worth talking about; a little painful, and a proper nuisance, spoiling our plans as it did. But that was all it was, and it's over now. Rummschüttel proved his worth, a fine, delightful old gentleman, as I think I said in my letter. Not a leading light in his field, but Mamma says that's an advantage. And I suppose she's right as she always is. Our good Dr Hannemann wasn't a leading light either, but he always knew what to do. And now tell me, how are Gieshübler and all the others?'

'Who might all the others be? Crampas sends his regards to her ladyship...'

'Ah, how courteous.'

'And the pastor sends his regards; the country gentlemen and their ladies were rather reserved and seemed to hold me responsible for your leaving without saying good-bye. Our friend Sidonie even made pointed remarks, and only the good Frau von Padden, whom I made a special journey to visit the day before yesterday, seemed to be genuinely pleased at your greetings and your declaration of affection. She said you were a charming young woman, but I should watch over you carefully. When I replied that you thought I was more of a "pedagogue" than a husband, she said almost absently to herself, "A little lamb, white as snow." And that was that.'

Cousin Briest laughed, '"A little lamb, white as snow..." There you have it cousin.' And he would have gone on teasing her, but stopped when he saw she was blushing.

The conversation, mostly touching on matters from the past, went on a while longer, and in the end, from one thing and another that Innstetten said, Effi learnt that of the entire Kessin household only Johanna had been prepared to make the move to Berlin. She had of course stayed behind for the moment, but would arrive in the next two or three days with the rest of their things; Innstetten was pleased at her decision, because she had always been the most useful, possessed of a markedly metropolitan chic. Perhaps a little too much of it. Christel and Friedrich had both pronounced themselves too old, and he had from the outset excluded the possibility of even discussing the matter with Kruse. 'What good would a coachman be to us here?' Innstetten concluded. 'A horse and carriage, *tempi passati*, that kind of luxury is a thing of the past in Berlin. We couldn't even have found room for the black hen. Or do I underestimate the apartment?'

Effi shook her head, giving rise to a short pause at which her mother rose; it would soon be eleven and she had a long way to go; no-one was to accompany her though, the cab rank was nearby – a suggestion Cousin Briest of course rejected. Soon afterwards they parted, having arranged to meet the next morning.

Effi was up quite early and – the air was almost warm enough for summer – had had the coffee-table moved over close to the open balcony door, and when Innstetten appeared too she went out on to the balcony with him and said, 'Well, what do you think? You wanted to hear the finches in the Tiergarten and the parrots in the Zoological Garden. I don't know whether they will both do you the favour, but they might. Can you hear that? It came from over there, from that little park over there. It isn't actually the Tiergarten, but very nearly.'

Innstetten was delighted, and as grateful as if Effi had conjured it all up just for him. Then they sat down, and this time Annie joined them. Roswitha required Innstetten to find a great change in the child, which he duly did. And then they chatted on, alternating between people in Kessin and the visits they would have to make here in Berlin, and finally discussing a summer trip, though they had to break off the conversation in time for their rendezvous.

They met as arranged at Helm's opposite the Red Castle, visited various shops, ate at Hiller's and were back home in good time. It had been a pleasant outing together and Innstetten was heartily glad to be part of city life again and feel its effects. The next day, the 1st of April, he went to the Chancellor's Palace to sign the book (he decided against a personal greeting on grounds of tact) and then went on to report at the Ministry where, though it was both socially and officially a very busy day, he was in fact received, indeed his immediate superior favoured him with the most obliging civility. He knew, he said, what a good man he had in him and was sure nothing would ever interfere with their mutual respect and understanding.

In the house too, everything was turning out well. It was a moment of heartfelt regret for Effi to see her mother returning to Hohen-Cremmen after taking her cure for six weeks as had been envisaged from the outset, regret only tempered to some extent by Johanna's arrival in Berlin the same day. That was at least something, and even if the pretty blonde was not as close to Effi's heart as Roswitha with her utter selflessness and infinite good humour, she was held in equally high regard, both by Innstetten and her young mistress, because she served deftly and because of her pronounced and self-assured reserve towards men. Rumour had it in Kessin that her beginnings in life could be traced back to a prominent officer, long since retired, of the Pasewalk garrison, and this was deemed to explain her superior attitudes, her beautiful blond hair and even the general impression of striking shapeliness she made. Johanna shared the joy felt on every side at her arrival, and was quite in agreement with taking over both as housemaid and Effi's lady's-maid just as before, while Roswitha, who in just under a year had more or less mastered all Christel's culinary arts, was to manage the kitchen department. Tending and looking after Annie was to be Effi's own job, at which Roswitha had to laugh. She knew what young women were like.

Innstetten lived entirely for his work and his home. He was happier than in Kessin, because it had not escaped his notice that Effi was behaving in a more cheerful and relaxed manner. And she was able to do this because she felt freer. What was past, it is true, did still enter into her life, but she was not afraid of it any more, or only on much rarer, fleeting occasions, and what remained to tremble on within her gave her bearing a peculiar charm. In everything she did there was a strain of melancholy, a sort of apology, and she would have been happier if she had been able to show it all more openly. But that was not of course permissible.

The social season in the city was not yet over when they started to pay their calls in April, but it was winding down, so they did not quite manage to enter into it fully. In the second half of May it died out completely, and they were even happier than before to meet in the Tiergarten when Innstetten came from work in the lunch hour, or to take a stroll in the Charlottenburg Palace gardens in the afternoon. Effi, as they walked up and down the long frontage between the Palace and the Orangerie trees, always looked at the Roman emperors standing there by the dozen, noting a curious similarity between Nero and Titus, collected pine-cones that had fallen from the weeping spruces, and then went with her husband, arm in arm, as far as the distant Belvedere over by the Spree.

'They say it was haunted once,' she said.

'No, it was just apparitions.'

'That's the same thing.'

'Sometimes it is,' said Innstetten, 'but in actual fact there's a difference. Apparitions are always staged – at least here in the Belvedere that's supposed to have been the case, so your Cousin Briest told me just yesterday – hauntings are never staged, hauntings are natural.'

'So you do believe in them?'

'Of course I believe in them. These things exist. It's just that I'm not sure I believe entirely in what went on in Kessin. Has Johanna shown you her Chinaman yet?'

'What Chinaman?'

'Well, ours. She took it off the back of the chair before we left the old house and put it in her purse. I saw it the other day when she was giving me change for a mark. And she was embarrassed at having to admit that that's what it was.'

'Oh Geert, you shouldn't have told me that. So now we have something like that in our house again.'

'Tell her to burn it.'

'No, I don't like to do that, it wouldn't help anyway. But I will ask Roswitha…'

'What? Oh, I see. I can guess what you mean to do. She's to buy an image of a saint and put it in her purse. Is it something like that?'

Effi nodded.

'Well, do what you like, but don't tell anyone about it.'

In the end Effi said she wasn't going to bother, and continuing to chat about all kinds of things amongst which travel plans for the summer gradually emerged as the main topic, they drove back as far as the Grosser Stern, and then walked down Korso-Allee and the wide Friedrich-Wilhelmstrasse back to their apartment.

It had been their intention to take their holiday early, by the end of July, and to go to the Bavarian Alps where the Oberammergau passion play was to be performed again that year. But it wasn't to be; Geheimrat von Wüllersdorf, whom Innstetten knew from former days and who was now his special colleague, was suddenly taken ill, and Innstetten had to stand in for him. It was the middle of August before everything was sorted out and they could travel; by then it was too late to go to Oberammergau so they opted for a stay on Rügen. 'First of course, Stralsund, where there's Schill, whom you know, and Scheele, whom you don't and who discovered oxygen, not that you need to know that. And then from Stralsund to the Rugard at Bergen, from where, so Wüllersdorf tells me, you have a view of the entire island, and then between the Great and the Little Jasmunder Bodden to Sassnitz. For going to Rügen really means going to Sassnitz. Binz would do perhaps as well, but there – to quote Wüllersdorf again – the beach is nothing but gritty stones and shells, and we want to do some bathing.'

Effi was in agreement with everything Innstetten planned, especially the fact that the entire household was to disperse for four weeks and Roswitha was to go to Hohen-Cremmen with Annie, while Johanna was to stay with her somewhat younger half-brother who had a sawmill near Pasewalk. This meant everyone was suitably accommodated. At the beginning of the next week they at last set out, and were in Sassnitz the same evening. The inn was called 'Fahrenheit Hotel'. 'The prices, one hopes, will be Celsius,' was Innstetten's comment on reading the name, and there was still time for the two of them, in high good humour, to take an evening stroll along the cliffs and look out from a rocky promontory over the silent bay quivering in the moonlight. Effi was enchanted. 'Oh Geert, it's like Capri, it's like Sorrento. Yes, let's stay here. But not in the hotel. The waiters are too grand for me, you feel embarrassed to ask for a bottle of soda-water…'

'Yes, attachés to a man. It will surely be possible to find something private to rent.'

'I think so too. We'll look for something tomorrow.'

The morning was as beautiful as the evening had been and they took breakfast outdoors. Innstetten received several letters which had to be dealt with quickly, so Effi decided to use the time she now had free to look for a place to stay. She first passed a fenced meadow, then some groups of houses and oat fields and finally took a path that dropped down a gulley towards the sea. Where this gulley path met the beach stood an inn overshadowed by tall beeches, not as grand as the Hotel Fahrenheit, really just a restaurant, where because of the early hour everything was deserted. Effi took a seat with a view and had barely taken a sip of the sherry she had ordered when the landlord, half out of curiosity and half out of politeness, came over to engage her in conversation.

'We like it very much here,' she said, 'my husband and I; what a magnificent view out over the bay – the only worry is finding a place to rent.'

'Yes, my lady, that will be difficult…'

'But it's already late in the year…'

'All the same. Here in Sassnitz you certainly won't find anything, I can guarantee that; but further down the coast, where the next village starts, you can see the roofs glinting from here, you might find something.'

'And what's the village called?'

'Crampas.'

Effi thought her ears had deceived her. 'Crampas,' she repeated with an

153

effort, 'I've never heard of that as a placename before... And there isn't anything else in the vicinity?'

'No my lady. Not round here. But further up, to the north, there are more villages and in the inn outside Stubbenkammer they'll certainly be able to give you information. People with places to let always leave their addresses there.'

Effi was glad she had been alone for this conversation, and when she had reported back to her husband soon afterwards, only omitting the name of the village next to Sassnitz, he said, 'Well, if there's nothing around here, we'd best take a carriage (which, incidentally, always makes a good impression at hotels) and move straight on up towards Stubbenkammer. Some idyllic place with an arbour of honeysuckle is probably there just waiting to be found, and if not, there's always the hotel. One's as good as the other when all's said and done.'

Effi was in agreement, and at about midday they reached the inn close to Stubbenkammer which Innstetten had just spoken of and ordered a bite to eat. 'To be served in half an hour. We intend to take a walk first and look at Lake Hertha. There's presumably a guide?'

The answer was in the affirmative and soon a middle-aged man approached our travellers. He looked important and solemn enough to have at the very least officiated in a junior capacity in the service of the goddess Hertha herself.

The lake, ringed with high trees, was quite close by; it was edged with reeds and a profusion of yellow waterlilies floated on the still black surface of the water.

'It really does look as if it had to do with the cult of Hertha, or some such thing,' said Effi.

'Yes my lady... And the stones still there are witness to that.'

'Which stones?'

'The sacrificial stones.'

And as the conversation took its course all three walked from the lake over to a wall that had been cut vertically into the gravel and clay against which several smoothly polished stones leant, each with a shallow depression and several grooves running down it.

'And what are *those* for?'

'They were to let it run away better, my lady.'

'I think we should go,' said Effi, and taking her husband's arm, she walked with him back towards the inn, where, at a place with an open view of the sea, the snack they had ordered was served. The bay lay in sunshine before them, here and there a sailing-boat glided over it, and seagulls swooped one after another round the nearby cliffs. It was very beautiful, as

154

Effi could see, but when she looked beyond the glittering surface she saw once more, to the south, gleaming brightly, the roofs of the long straggling village whose name had so startled her that morning.

Innstetten, without knowing or even suspecting what was going on inside her, could see quite clearly that she was bereft of all joy and pleasure. 'I'm sorry Effi, that you're not really enjoying it here. You can't forget Lake Hertha, especially those stones.'

She nodded. 'Yes, you're right. And I must confess, I've never in my life seen anything that made me feel so sad. We must give up the idea of looking for somewhere. I can't stay here.'

'And yesterday it was the Gulf of Naples and absolutely everything that was beautiful.'

'Yes, yesterday.'

'And today? No trace of Sorrento left today?'

'A trace yes, but only a trace; it's Sorrento as if it were about to die.'

'All right Effi,' said Innstetten and reached out his hand, 'I won't plague you with Rügen, so let's leave it at that. That's settled. There's no need for us to tie ourselves to Stubbenkammer, or Sassnitz or places further down. But where now?'

'I think we should stay another day and wait for the steamer, which, if I'm not mistaken, comes from Stettin tomorrow and sails across to Copenhagen. They say it's fun there, and I can't tell you how much I long for a little fun. Here I feel as if I'll never be able to laugh again, as if I'd never laughed in my whole life, and you do know how I like to laugh.'

Innstetten showed great sympathy with her state of mind, the more so since he mostly fully agreed with her. Beautiful as it was, it really was all very melancholy.

And so they waited for the Stettin steamer and on the third day in the early morning they arrived in Copenhagen and took rooms on Kongens Nytorv. Two hours later they were in the Thorwaldsen Museum, and Effi said, 'Yes Geert, this is beautiful and I'm pleased we made the effort to come here.' Soon afterwards they went to lunch and at the table d'hôte made the acquaintance of a family from Jutland who were sitting opposite them and whose strikingly beautiful daughter, Thora von Penz, immediately attracted not only Innstetten's but also Effi's almost admiring attention. Effi could not stop looking at her big blue eyes and flaxen hair, and when they rose from table an hour and a half later the hope was expressed on the Penzes' side – they unfortunately had to leave Copenhagen that same day – that they might be privileged to welcome the young Prussian couple at Aggerhuus Castle (two miles from the Limfjord), an invitation the Innstettens accepted with scarcely any hesitation. With all this the hours at the hotel passed pleasantly. But that was not the end of the good things that happened on that memorable day of which Effi was to say that it should be marked in red on the calendar. To fill her cup of happiness, the evening brought a performance at the Tivoli Theatre, an Italian pantomime, Harlequin and Columbine. Effi found their antics quite intoxicating, and late in the evening as they were going back to the hotel, she said, 'You know, Geert, now I really feel I'm beginning to come to myself again. Leaving our beautiful Thora aside, when I think of this morning at the Thorwaldsen and Columbine this evening...'

'Which if it comes down to it you liked better than the Thorwaldsen...'

'To be quite candid, yes. I just happen to respond to things like that. Dear old Kessin was a disaster for me. Everything got on my nerves there. In Rügen it was much the same. I think we should stay a few more days here in Copenhagen, with an excursion to Frederiksborg and Elsinore of course, and then across to Jutland; I'm really looking forward to seeing our beautiful Thora again, and if I were a man, I would fall in love with her.'

Innstetten laughed. 'You don't know what I'll do.'

'I wouldn't mind at all. Then there would be competition, and you'd see, I can still rise to that.'

'You don't have to tell me.'

They made the trip. Over in Jutland they drove up the Limfjord as far as Aggerhuus Castle where they stayed three days with the Penzes, and then, in many stages, with stops, some long, some short, in Viborg, Flensburg and Kiel, they returned home via Hamburg, which they loved – not straight to Keithstrasse in Berlin, but first to Hohen-Cremmen where they now wanted to enjoy a well-earned rest. For Innstetten this meant a few days only, for his leave had run out, but Effi stayed a week longer and announced that she didn't intend to return home until the third of October, her wedding anniversary.

Annie had thrived splendidly in the country air, and Roswitha had planned for her to walk to her Mamma in her little boots, which she managed to perfection. Briest was quite the doting grandfather, and warned against being too loving and even more against being too strict and was the same old Briest in every way. However, all his affection was really directed at Effi, who was still very much on his mind – and most of the time when he was alone with his wife too.

'How do you find Effi?'

'As sweet and good as ever. We can't be thankful enough to God for having such a delightful daughter. And how grateful she is for everything, and always so happy to be under our roof again.'

'Yes,' said Briest, 'that's a virtue she has more of than I care for. Actually it's as if this were still her real home. But she has a husband and child and her husband is a gem and the child is an angel, and yet she acts as if Hohen-Cremmen were still the main thing for her, and her husband and a child couldn't compete with us. She's a splendid daughter, but rather too splendid for me. It worries me a bit. And it's not fair on Innstetten. What's actually going on there?'

'What do you mean, Briest?'

'I mean what I mean, and you know what I mean. Is she happy? Or is there something in the way? Right from the beginning I sensed she felt more respect than love for him. And to my mind that's a bad thing. Love may not always last, but respect certainly doesn't. Women actually get annoyed when they have to respect someone; they start by being annoyed, then they get bored and they end up laughing at you.'

'Is this something you've experienced for yourself?'

'I wouldn't say so. I never attracted enough respect for that. But enough of this needling, Luise. Just tell me how things stand.'

'Yes, well Briest, you keep coming back to these things. We've talked about them a dozen times and more, and exchanged views on them, but you keep coming up with this wish to know everything and then the questions you ask are so terribly naive, as if I could see into the deepest depths. What sort of idea do you have about young women, and about your daughter in particular? Do you really think they spread everything out for all to see? Or that I'm that oracle (the name escapes me) or that I instantly hold the truth in my hands, all cut and dried, when Effi has poured out her heart to me? At least that's what they call it, but what do people mean by "pouring out your heart"? The really important thing stays in. She'll take care not to let me into her secrets. And besides, I don't know where she gets it from, but she's... well, she's a very cunning little person, and this cunning of hers is the more dangerous because she's so very delightful.'

'So you admit that... delightful. And good as well?'

'Good as well. Which is to say, full of good-heartedness. How things stand otherwise, I'm not quite sure; I imagine she's inclined to think our dear Lord is a good fellow and comforts herself with the thought that he won't be too hard on her.'

'Do you think so?'

'Yes I do. I also think there's been a big change for the better in her. Her character is what it is, but the circumstances since the move suit her much better and they're becoming much more part of each other's lives. She told me something along those lines, and what's more important for me, I've been able to see it confirmed with my own eyes.'

157

'So what did she say?'

'She said, "Mamma, things are better now. Innstetten has always been a very fine man, there aren't many like him, but I couldn't really get close to him, there was something remote about him. He was remote even when he was being tender. Yes, at those moments most of all; there were times when it made me feel afraid."'

'I know the feeling.'

'What is that supposed to mean Briest? Am I suppposed to have been afraid or are you claiming you were afraid? I find both ideas equally ludicrous…'

'You were going to tell me about Effi.'

'Yes, well, she told me that sense of remoteness had left her, which she was very happy about; that Kessin hadn't been the right place for her, the haunted house and the people up there, one lot too religious, the other lot too dull, but since the move to Berlin she has felt she's in the right place. She said he's the best of men, a bit too old for her and too good for her, but she's got over the hump. That was the expression she used, I was quite struck by it.'

'Why? It's not quite up to scratch, the expression I mean. But…'

'There's something behind it. And she wanted to hint as much to me.'

'Do you think so?'

'Yes Briest; you always think butter wouldn't melt in her mouth. But you're wrong. She likes to be carried along, and if she's riding a good wave, then she's good too. Struggling and resistance are not for her.'

Roswitha came up with Annie and with that the conversation broke off.

This conversation between Briest and his wife took place on the same day as Innstetten had departed from Hohen-Cremmen for Berlin, leaving Effi behind for at least another week. He knew there was nothing quite as beautiful for her as dreaming her time away in carefree and tranquil mood, hearing only kind words and assurance of how delightful she was. Yes, more than anything else, that was what gave her a sense of well-being, and now she savoured it to the full once again, quite gratified despite the total lack of entertainment; visitors were rare, because since her marriage, at least for the young folk, a proper centre of attraction was missing, and even the pastor's house and the school were no longer what they had been in the old days. At the school-house especially everything was half-empty. In the spring the twins had married two teachers who lived near Genthin, a big double wedding with a report on the celebrations in the *Havelland Advertiser*, and Hulda was in Friesack looking after a rich old aunt, who, as is usual in such cases, proved to be much more long-lived than the Niemeyers had imagined. In spite of this Hulda never complained in her letters, not because she had nothing to complain about, but because she did not wish the suspicion to arise that life could treat a person as excellent as herself other than very well. Niemeyer, a weak father, displayed the letters with pride and joy, while Jahnke, who equally lived only for his daughters, had calculated that both young women would produce babies on the very same day, on Christmas Eve no less. Effi laughed heartily and to the prospective grandfather she expressed the wish that she might be invited to be godmother to both grand-children, then she dropped family topics and told him about 'København' and Elsinore, Limfjord and Aggerhuus Castle, and above all about Thora von Penz, who, she could only say, had been 'typically Scandinavian', blue-eyed, flaxen-haired and always in a red velvet bodice, at which Jahnke's expression was transfigured and he repeated over and over, 'Yes, that's what they're like; Germanic through and through, far more German than the Germans.'

On the third of October, her wedding anniversary, Effi meant to be back in Berlin. Now it was the evening before, and on the pretext of packing and preparing everything for the return journey, she had retired to her room relatively early. In actual fact all she wanted was to be alone; much as she liked to chat, there were times too when she longed for peace.

The rooms she occupied on the upper floor looked out on to the garden; in the smaller one Annie and Roswitha were sleeping with the door ajar, in the larger one which she herself occupied, she was pacing up and down; the lower casements of the windows were open, and the little white curtains billowed in the draught and then fell slowly over the back of the chair until the next draught of air freed them again. It was so light that the titles under the pictures in narrow gold frames that hung over the sofa were clearly legible: *The Storming of Rampart 5 at Düppel*, and beside it *King Wilhelm and Count Bismarck on the Heights of Lipa*. Effi shook her head and smiled. 'The next time I'm here, I'll ask for different pictures; I can't stand these battle scenes.' And now she closed one of the windows and and sat down at the other whose casements she left open. What a good feeling all this gave her. The moon stood by the church tower and cast its light on the lawn with the sundial and the beds of heliotrope. All was shimmering silver, and beside the bands of shadow were white bands of light, as white as linen laid out to bleach. The tall clumps of rhubarb were still standing, their leaves an autumn yellow, and she had to think of the day just over two years before when she had been playing here with Hulda and the Jahnke girls. And then, when the visitor came, she had climbed the short flight of stone steps beside the bench, and an hour later she was engaged.

She stood up and went to the door and listened; Roswitha was asleep already, and Annie too.

And all at once, with the child before her, all sorts of images from the days in Kessin flooded into her memory: the Landrat's house with its gable, and the veranda with its view of the Plantation, and she was sitting rocking in the rocking chair; and now Crampas came up to greet her, and then Roswitha came with the child, and Effi took her and held her aloft and kissed her.

'That was the first day, that's when it started.' And with these thoughts going through her head, she left the room where they were both sleeping, sat down at the open window again and and looked out into the silent night.

'I can't get away from it,' she said. 'And the worst thing about it, the thing that makes me despair of myself…'

At that moment the clock in the tower opposite struck and Effi counted the chimes.

'Ten… And tomorrow at this time I'll be in Berlin. And we'll be talking about our anniversary, and he'll be saying sweet, kind, perhaps affectionate things to me. And I'll sit and listen and I shall have this guilt on my soul.'

And she rested her head on her hand and gazed straight ahead and was silent.

'And I shall have this guilt on my soul,' she repeated. 'Yes, I do have it. But is it really weighing on my soul? No. And that's why I'm appalled at myself. What weighs on me is something quite different: fear, mortal fear, the constant fear that I'll be found out some day after all. And besides the fear… shame. I'm ashamed. But just as I don't have a proper sense of remorse, I don't have a proper sense of shame either. I'm only ashamed because of the never-ending lying and deceit; I was always proud that I couldn't lie, and also that I didn't need to lie, lying is so mean-minded, and now I've had to lie all the time, to him and to the whole world, in matters great and small, and Rummschüttel noticed it and shrugged his shoulders, and who knows what he thinks of me, not the best, whatever it is. Yes, I'm plagued by fear, and shame too at my own duplicity. But not shame at my guilt, I *don't* feel that, or not properly, or not enough, and that's what's crushing me, the fact that I don't feel it. If all women are like this, then it's terrible, and if they're not, and I hope they aren't, then things don't look good for me, then there's something wrong in my soul, I don't have the right feelings. And that's what old Niemeyer told me once back in his active days, when I was still half a child: the right feelings, he said, that's what's important, and if you have them then the worst can't happen to you, but if you don't, you're in eternal peril, and what goes by the name of the Devil has us surely in his power. Merciful God, is that how it is with me?'

And she laid her head on her arms and wept bitterly.

When she sat up again, she had grown calmer and she looked out into the garden again. Everything was so still, and a quiet, gentle sound from the plane-trees, as if it was raining, struck her ear.

Some time passed. From the village street a grating voice rang out; the old night-watchman Kulicke was calling out the hours, and when at last he was silent, from the distance she heard the rattling of a train coming nearer and nearer until, two miles away, it passed Hohen-Cremmen. Then the sound faded and finally died away, and there was only the moonlight falling on the lawn, and all that was to be heard was the plane trees rustling as before, as if light rain were falling.

But it was only the movement of the night air.

25

The next evening Effi was back in Berlin and Innstetten met her at the station with Rollo who trotted alongside them as they drove chatting through the Tiergarten.

'I was beginning to think you weren't going to keep your word.'

'But Geert, of course I'd keep my word, that comes before anything else.'

'Don't say that. It's asking a great deal, always to keep your word. And sometimes it's not possible. Just think back. I was expecting you that time in Kessin when you were renting the apartment, and who didn't come but Effi.'

'Ah yes, but that was different.'

She didn't want to say 'I was ill', and Innstetten didn't notice. He had too many other things on his mind, all to do with his post and his social position. 'Actually Effi, our life in Berlin is just beginning now. When we moved here in April the season was petering out and we barely had time to pay our calls. Wüllersdorf was the only close acquaintance we had, and he's a bachelor unfortunately. From June onwards everything goes to sleep and to all the world the shuttered windows say: "Gone to the country"; whether it's true or not makes no difference… So what were we left with? A chat with Cousin Briest, a meal at Hiller's, that's not Berlin life, not really. But that's all going to change now. I've made a note of everybody of the rank of Rat who still has enough go in him to entertain. And that's what we're going to do too. We're going to entertain, and by winter they will all be saying at the Ministry, "Yes, there's no doubt Frau von Innstetten is the most delightful wife in town."'

'Oh Geert, I don't know you like this, you're quite the ardent admirer.'

'It's our wedding anniversary, you must make allowances.'

161

Innstetten seriously intended to replace the quiet life he had led as a Landrat with a more socially active one, for his own sake, and still more for Effi's; but things were slow to start and occasions rare, the right time had not yet come, and at first the best they had from the new life was, just as in the previous six months, their home life. Wüllersdorf often came, as did Cousin Briest, and when they were there they sent up to the Gizickis, a young married couple who lived above them. Gizicki himself was a Landgerichtsrat and his clever, quick-witted wife was a von Schmettau. Now and then they played music, briefly they even tried whist; but they gave it up because they found just chatting more agreeable. The Gizickis had lived in a small town in Upper Silesia until recently, and Wüllersdorf, some years before of course, had been posted to the most far-flung corners of the province of Posen, which was why he was given to quoting the well-known rhyme with such gusto and emphasis:

> Schrimm
> Is grim,
> Rogasen
> You go mad in,
> But being sent to Samter
> Is even damnder.

Nobody was more amused at this than Effi, and it was generally the cue for a whole series of anecdotes about small towns. Kessin came up too, with Gieshübler and Miss Tripelli, head forester Ring and Sidonie Grasenabb, at which Innstetten, if he was in a good mood, could become quite unbuttoned. 'Ah yes,' he would say, 'good old Kessin! It had its characters, that I have to admit, first and foremost Crampas, Major Crampas, quite the beau and a bit of a Don Juan with his red beard, whom my wife, I don't know whether I should say understandably or incomprehensibly, had taken quite a fancy to -' 'Let's say understandably,' Wüllersdorf interjected, 'for I take it he was chairman of the Club and an amateur actor: romantic leads or *bonvivants*. And maybe more, perhaps he was a tenor into the bargain.' Innstetten confirmed this on all counts, and Effi tried to join in the laughter, but it took an effort, and when the guests left and Innstetten retired to his room to work his way through another pile of documents, she would always feel tormented anew by the old thoughts, and have the feeling that she was being pursued by a shadow.

Such anxieties remained with her. But they were less frequent and less acute than before, which was little wonder with the way her life was developing. The affection she encountered not only from Innstetten, but also from people who were not at all close to her, and not least the almost affectionate friendship shown to her by the Minister's wife, herself still a young woman, these were all things that at least mitigated the cares and anxieties of times past, and when a second year had been seen out and the Empress at the opening of one of her new charitable foundations had chosen the 'Frau Geheimrätin' to be one of the ladies-in-waiting, and at the court ball even old Kaiser Wilhelm had addressed a few kind and gracious words to the beautiful young woman 'of whom he had already heard', these cares gradually left her altogether. It had happened once upon a time, but far, far away, as if on another planet, and it all dissolved like a mirage and turned into a dream.

Effi's parents occasionally came on a visit from Hohen-Cremmen and were pleased at the couple's happiness, Annie was growing up – 'as beautiful as her grandmother' said Briest senior – and if there was a cloud in the clear sky, it was that it almost looked as though there were to be no more children after little Annie; so presumably the house of Innstetten (for there was no-one left with the family name) was about to die out. Briest, who treated the survival of other families with scant concern as he really only believed in the Briests, sometimes joked about this and said, 'Yes Innstetten, if things go on like this, Annie will end up marrying a banker (a Christian one I hope, if there are still any left), and His Majesty, in deference to the old baronial line, will have Annie's *haute finance* children recorded for all time as "von der Innstetten" in the *Almanach de Gotha*, or, which is less important, ensure they have a place in Prussian history' – ruminations to which Innstetten responded with a moment's slight embarrassment, Frau von Briest with a shrug of her shoulders and Effi by contrast with hilarity. For proud as she was of her lineage, this applied to her own person only, and an elegant, cosmopolitan and above all very, very rich banker as son-in-law would not have been at all contrary to her wishes.

Yes, Effi took the matter of inheritance lightly, as charming young women do; but when a very long time had gone by – they were in the seventh year of their new position – Frau von Briest finally called in old Rummschüttel, who had something of a reputation in the field of gynaecology. He prescribed Schwalbach. But because Effi had been suffering from a catarrhal infection since the previous winter and had even had her lungs sounded a few times, he concluded by saying, 'Well then, Schwalbach to start with, my dear lady, for say three weeks, then the same length of time in Ems. When you're taking the cure at Ems the Geheimrat can be with you. So the whole thing amounts to three weeks of separation. That's the best I can do for you, my dear Innstetten.'

163

This met with their agreement, and in the event it was decided that Effi would make the trip with Geheimrat Zwicker's wife, 'for the latter's protection' as Briest said, and he was not entirely wide of the mark in this, since Frau Zwicker, though well into her forties, was much more in need of a chaperone than Effi. Innstetten, again tied up deputizing for colleagues on leave, complained he would probably even have to write off the days together in Ems, to say nothing of Schwalbach. Then the departure was set for June 24th, Midsummer's Day, and Roswitha helped her mistress to pack and make a list of her linen. Effi's old love for her was still there, indeed Roswitha was the only person she could talk to freely and without restraint about all that lay behind them, Kessin and Crampas, the Chinaman and Captain Thomsen's niece.

'Tell me Roswitha, you're a Catholic. Don't you ever go to confession?'

'No.'

'Why not?'

'I used to. Never told them nothin' serious though.'

'That's very wrong. It can't do any good then.'

'Oh, my lady, that's what they all did back in our village. Some of 'em just giggled.'

'Have you never felt that it's a good thing, if something is weighing on your soul, that you can be rid of it?'

'No, my lady. That time my father came at me with the red-hot iron, I was really afraid then; but terrible fear is all it was, nothin' else.'

'Not fear of God?'

'Not really, my lady. Once you've been terrified by your father like I was terrified, then you're never as terrified of God. I've always just thought God is good and will help a poor mite like me.'

Effi smiled and dropped the subject, and she found it quite natural that poor Roswitha should talk as she did. What she did say was, 'You know Roswitha, when I come back we must have a serious talk about it. It really was a great sin.'

'About the child and it starvin' to death? Yes my lady, it was. But it wasn't me, it was the others – and anyway, it's all so long ago.'

26

Effi had been away more than four weeks, writing happy, almost high-spirited letters, especially since her arrival in Ems where one was, as she wrote, among real people again, that was to say among men, of whom only the odd specimen was to be seen in Schwalbach. The medical appropriateness of their added presence had naturally, she reported, been raised by her travelling companion, Geheimrätin Zwicker, who had come down heavily against it, all of course with a look in her eye that said more or less the opposite; Frau Zwicker, wrote Effi, was charming, somewhat free, probably with a past even, but highly amusing and one could learn a great deal from her; never, in spite of her twenty-five years, had she felt so much of a child as since her acquaintance with this lady. And she was so well read, even in foreign literature; when for example Effi had recently mentioned *Nana* and asked if it really was so dreadful, Frau Zwicker had replied, 'My dear Baroness, what do you mean, dreadful? There are much worse things than that.' 'She also seemed inclined,' Effi concluded her letter, 'to tell me all about these "worse things". But I wouldn't let her, because I know you think the immorality of our times derives from such things as these and you're probably right. But it wasn't easy. The other thing is that Ems lies in a hollow. We suffer terribly from the heat here.'

Innstetten had read this letter with mixed feelings, slightly amused but also a little put out. This Zwicker woman was not the right person for Effi, who had a strain in her that could be led astray; but he let it pass and did not write to her along these lines, partly for fear of displeasing her, but rather because he told himself it would do no good. Meanwhile he longed for his wife's return and groaned at having not only to perform his own duties 'on the appointed hour's stroke' but others' too, since all the other senior staff were either away or about to go away.

Yes, Innstetten longed for a break from work and loneliness, and there were similar feelings in the kitchen, where Annie preferred to spend her time after school, which was quite natural in that Johanna and Roswitha not only loved the little Fräulein in equal measure, but were also, as always, on the best of terms with each other. This friendship between the two servants was a favourite topic of conversation with various friends of the house, so that Landgerichtsrat Gizicki observed to Wüllersdorf, 'I see this as fresh confirmation of the wise old saying "Let me have men about me that are fat". Caesar was a shrewd judge of character and knew that it takes *embonpoint* to be affable and get on with people.' And this the two maids both had, one could safely say, except that the foreign word which was practically unavoidable in this context was flattering in Roswitha's case, whereas in Johanna's it was simply the *mot juste*. The latter could not in fact really be termed corpulent, just buxom and statuesque, with her blue eyes and her proud, all-conquering air, an expression which quite definitely became her, looking straight ahead over her firmly corseted bosom. Imbued with propriety and decorum, her whole life was lived in the elevating awareness that she was the servant of a good house, and this gave her such a sense of superiority over Roswitha, who was still one part peasant, that when, as occasionally happened, the latter seemed to be accorded preferential treatment, she merely smiled. This preferential treatment – well, if that was the way it had to be sometimes – was an endearing little foible of her mistress's which there was no reason not to grant dear old Roswitha with her eternal tale of her 'father with the red-hot iron bar'. 'If one behaves properly that kind of thing can't happen.' All this went through her head without her ever actually saying it. Theirs was in fact a friendly coexistence. But what really maintained peace and harmony was that the care and almost the education of little Annie had, by tacit agreement, been split between them. Roswitha's was the poetic department, telling her stories and fairytales, while Johanna was responsible for manners, a division that was so firmly established on both sides that disputes scarcely arose, something to which Annie's character itself contributed, since she had a quite distinct tendency to put on the young lady of quality, and in this she could have had no better teacher than Johanna.

To resume then: both maids were equal in Annie's eyes. During this time however, when they were preparing for Effi's return, Roswitha had once again the *soupçon* of an advantage over her rival because the whole matter of the welcome had fallen to her, indeed it was deemed *her* prerogative. This welcome fell into two parts: a floral wreath with a garland on the door, and then the recitation of a poem. The wreath – after they had been undecided for a time between 'W' or 'E.v.I.' – in the end caused no special difficulties (a 'W' woven from forget-me-nots had been favoured), but the question of the poem promised to be much more awkward, and it might have remained unresolved had Roswitha not plucked up her courage and bearded the Landgerichtsrat on the second-floor landing, as he returned from court, with a bold request for a 'verse'. Gizicki, a very kind gentleman, had instantly promised all they requested, and late that same afternoon his cook had handed in the desired verse, the contents of which were as follows:

> Mamma, our longing is long-standing,
> We've waited weeks and days and hours,
> Now we greet you from balcony and landing,

We've woven wreaths of brightest flowers.
Now Papa laughs with happiness,
For the time of wife- and motherlessness
At last, at last to its end has come,
And Roswitha laughs, Johanna too
And Annie jumps right out of her shoe
And calls out, 'welcome, welcome home.'

Of course this stanza had been learned by heart that same evening, but not without subjecting its poetic quality, or lack of it, to critical scrutiny. It had been Johanna's opinion that though the stress on wife and mother had seemed at first to be in order, there was nevertheless something about it that might give offence, and she personally, if she were a wife and mother, would be hurt by it. Annie was somewhat dismayed by this remark and promised to show her school-mistress the poem the next day. She came back with the comment that 'Miss was quite happy with "wife and mother", but absolutely against "Roswitha and Johanna"' – at which Roswitha had declared, 'Miss is a silly ass; that's what comes of too much learning.'

The maids and Annie had the above conversation on a Wednesday, the argument about the disputed line being settled on the same day. The following morning – a letter was expected from Effi to establish the day of arrival which would presumably not be until the end of the following week – Innstetten went to the Ministry. Now it was midday and school was over, and when Annie with her satchel on her back came along Keithstrasse from the canal she met Roswitha in front of the house.

'Let's see,' said Annie, 'which of us can get to the top of the stairs first.' Roswitha would hear nothing of this race, but Annie rushed on ahead, and reaching the top she stumbled and fell so awkwardly that she struck her forehead on the boot-scraper which was right beside the stairs, and began to bleed profusely. Roswitha, panting laboriously after her, tugged the bell violently, and when Johanna had carried the somewhat frightened child inside, they discussed what to do next. 'We should send for the doctor… We should send for the Master… the concierge's daughter Lene must be back from school now too.' These proposals were all rejected as taking too long, they had to do something straight away, so they put the child on the sofa and began to apply cold water to cool her. This seemed to help and they began to calm down. 'Better get 'er bandaged now,' Roswitha said at length. 'The Mistress cut a long bandage when she twisted 'er ankle on the ice last winter, that must still be about –' 'Of course it must,' said Johanna, 'but where do we look for it?... Ah, now, it comes back to me, it's in the sewing-table. It's probably locked, but the lock is child's play; just fetch a chisel Roswitha, we'll force the lid open.' With that they proceeded to wrench off the lid and rifle through the compartments from top to bottom, but there was no sign of the rolled-up bandage. 'I know I've seen it,' said Roswitha, and as she searched on in growing irritation, everything that came to hand landed on the broad window-sill: sewing things, pin-cushions, bobbins of thread and silk, little dried bunches of violets, cards, *billets*, and finally a little bundle of letters lying under the third tray down, right at the bottom, tied with a red silk thread. But they still hadn't found the bandage.

At that moment Innstetten came in.

'Oh dear me,' said Roswitha, standing beside the child in her fright. 'It's nothing sir; Annie fell on the boot-scraper... oh dear me, what's 'er ladyship goin' to say? A good thing she wasn't 'ere when it 'appened.'

Innstetten had meanwhile taken off the temporary compress and saw that it was a deep cut but nothing serious. 'It isn't bad,' he said. 'All the same Roswitha, we must see that Rummschüttel comes. Lene can fetch him, she'll have time now. But what in heaven's name has happened to the sewing-table?'

And now Roswitha told him about the search for the rolled bandage; but she'd give that up now and cut a fresh piece of linen.

Innstetten was in agreement and sat down beside the child after the two maids had left the room. 'You're so wild Annie, you get that from your Mamma. A regular whirlwind. Nothing comes of it, or at least only this kind of thing.' And he pointed to the cut and gave her a kiss. 'You didn't cry though, and that was good, so for that I'll forgive you your wildness... I think the doctor will be here in an hour; just do everything he says, and once he's bandaged you, don't pull it or move it or fiddle with it, and it'll get better quickly, and by the time Mamma gets back everything will be in order again, or nearly. It's a good thing after all that that's not till next week, the end of next week according to what she wrote to me; I've just had a letter from her; she sends you love and kisses and is looking forward to seeing you again.'

'Could you read me the letter Papa?'

'Of course I could.'

But before he had time to, Johanna came in to say that lunch was served. Annie got to her feet with him in spite of her cut, and father and daughter sat down at table.

27

Innstetten and Annie sat facing one another silently for a while; in the end, when he found the silence awkward he asked her a few questions about the headmistress and who her favourite teacher was. Annie answered without much enthusiasm because she sensed that Innstetten's mind was elsewhere. Things only improved after the second course when Johanna whispered to her little Annie that there was something still to come. And good, kind Roswitha, who felt she owed her little treasure something on that unfortunate day, had indeed made something extra, an omelette with apple slices, no less.

The sight of this made Annie a little more talkative and Innstetten's frame of mind too appeared improved when immediately afterwards the doorbell rang and Geheimrat Rummschüttel came in. Quite by chance. He had just dropped in without any inkling of their having sent to ask him to call. The compresses they had applied met with his approval. 'Just send for some lead-water and keep Annie at home tomorrow. The main thing is rest.' Then he asked after Frau von Instetten and what news there was from Ems; he said he would call again next day to see how things were.

When they had risen from table and gone into the next room – where they had been at such pains, in vain as it turned out, to find the bandage – Annie was laid on the sofa again. Johanna came and sat with the child while Innstetten began to clear the countless things that lay in a jumble on the window-sill back into the sewing-table. From time to time he did not know where things belonged and had to ask for help.

'Where were the letters Johanna?'

'Right at the bottom,' she said, 'here in this bit.'

And as his question was answered Innstetten looked more closely than before at the little bundle tied with red thread, which seemed to be composed more of numerous folded-up notes than of letters. He flicked through the edges of the package with thumb and forefinger as if it were a pack of cards, and some lines, actually only odd words, flashed before his eyes. It wouldn't be true to say he recognized it, but he did seem to have seen that handwriting somewhere before. Should he take a look?

'Johanna, could you bring the coffee? Annie will take half a cup too. The doctor didn't say she wasn't to, and what isn't forbidden is allowed.'

As he said this he unwound the red thread and while Johanna left the room, he let the entire contents of the bundle run quickly through his fingers. Only two or three letters were addressed, 'To Frau Landrat von Innstetten.' Now he recognized the writing; it was the Major's. Innstetten knew nothing of any correspondence between Crampas and Effi and everything began to spin in his head. He stuck the bundle in his pocket and went into his room. Several minutes later Johanna tapped lightly on the door to indicate that the coffee was served and Innstetten answered, but that was all; other than that, total silence. Only after a quarter of an hour was he heard again pacing up and down on the carpet. 'What can be wrong with Papa?' said Johanna to Annie. 'The doctor told him it was nothing, didn't he?'

The pacing up and down in the next room seemed never-ending. Finally Innstetten appeared in the other room and said, 'Johanna, look after Annie and see that she stays resting on the sofa. I shall be gone for an hour, or perhaps two.'

Then he looked attentively at the child and left.

'Did you see the look on Papa's face, Johanna?'

'Yes Annie. Something must have annoyed him greatly. He was quite pale. I've never seen him like that.'

Hours went by. The sun was already down and there was only a red glow above the roofs opposite when Innstetten came back. He took Annie's hand, asked her how she felt and instructed Johanna to bring the lamp into his room. The lamp was brought. In the green shade were translucent ovals with numerous different photographs of his wife, pictures which had been taken for the cast at the performance of Wichert's *One False Step* in Kessin. Innstetten turned the shade slowly from left to right and examined each picture in turn. Then he stopped; finding it sultry he opened the balcony door, and finally picked up the bundle of letters again. It seemed that on his preliminary examination he had already picked out a few and placed them on top. These he now read once more under his breath.

Be in the dunes again this afternoon, behind the mill. We can talk at old Frau Adermann's, the house is isolated enough. You mustn't be so afraid of everything. We *too* have rights. And if you say that to yourself firmly enough, I think all your fears will melt away. Life wouldn't be worth living if conventions were always observed just because they happened to be conventions. The best things are all beyond that. Learn to enjoy them.

170

...away, you write, escape. Impossible. I can't leave my wife in the lurch, in poverty on top of everything else. It can't be done, and we must take these things lightly, otherwise we are poor lost souls. Frivolity is the best thing we have. It's all fate. It was meant to be like this. And would you wish it otherwise, wish that we had never met?

Then came the third letter.

...Be at the old place again today. What are my days going to be like here without you? In this desolate backwater. I'm beside myself, but you're right in one thing: it's our salvation, and when all's said and done we should bless the hand that has forced this parting on us.

Innstetten had barely pushed the letters aside again when the bell rang outside. Soon afterwards Johanna announced, 'Geheimrat Wüllersdorf.'

Wüllersdorf entered and saw at a glance that something must have happened.

'Sorry Wüllersdorf,' Innstetten greeted him, 'sorry to have asked you to come over right away today. I don't like disturbing the quiet of anybody's evening, least of all an overworked Ministerialrat. But there was no alternative. Please, make yourself comfortable. Here, have a cigar.'

Wüllersdorf sat down. Innstetten paced up and down again and, in the agitation that consumed him, would have preferred to keep moving, but he could see that that was not possible. So he too took a cigar, sat down opposite Wüllersdorf and tried to be calm.

'There are,' he began, 'two reasons why I've called you: first to deliver a challenge, and secondly, afterwards, to act as my second in the affair; the first is not a pleasant task and the second even less so. What do you say?'

'You know Innstetten, I'm at your disposal. But before we go into the affair, forgive me if I ask the naive question: is this necessary? Haven't we passed the age for you to be holding a pistol in your hand, and me to be aiding and abetting you? But don't misunderstand me, I'm not saying "no". How could I refuse you anything? And now, let's hear what it's all about.'

'It's about a lover of my wife's, a man who was my friend, more or less.'

Wüllersdorf looked at Innstetten. 'Innstetten, that isn't possible.'

'It's more than possible, it's certain. Read these.'

Wüllersdorf ran his eye over the letters. 'These are addressed to your wife?'

'Yes, I found them in her sewing-table today.'

'And who wrote them?'

'Major Crampas.'

'So we're talking about things that happened when you were still in Kessin?'

Innstetten nodded.

'So six years ago, or six and a half years.'

'Yes.'

Wüllersdorf was silent. After a while Innstetten said, 'Those six or seven years seem to have made an impression on you. There is the theory of the time limit of course, but I don't know if this is a case in point.'

'I don't know either,' said Wüllersdorf. 'And I must confess, that seems to me to be the nub of the matter.'

Innstetten looked at him wide-eyed. 'Can you say that in all seriousness?'

'In all seriousness. This isn't a case for indulging in *jeux d'esprit* or dialectical niceties.'

'I'm curious to know what you mean exactly. Tell me frankly where you stand.'

'Innstetten, your situation is terrible, and your life's happiness is gone. But shoot the lover, and your life's happiness is doubly gone, so to speak, and to the pain you already have from the injury you've suffered you will add the pain from the injury you have inflicted. At the heart of the matter is the question, do you absolutely have to do it? Do you feel so offended, wounded, outraged that one of you has to go, him or you? Is that how matters stand?'

'I don't know.'

'You must know.'

Innstetten had jumped to his feet, he walked over to the window and, filled with nervous agitation, tapped on the panes. Then he turned back quickly, went over to Wüllersdorf and said, 'No, that's not how matters stand.'

'Well, how do they stand?'

'The fact of the matter is that I'm infinitely miserable; I've been insulted, scandalously deceived, but in spite of that, I feel no hate at all, much less any thirst for revenge. And when I ask myself why not, the only explanation I find is the years that have passed. People always talk about inexpiable guilt; it's certainly not true, not in the eyes of God, and not in the eyes of men either. I would never have believed that *time*, pure time, could have such an effect. And then there's something else: I love my wife, strange to say, I still love her, and terrible as I find everything that has happened, I'm still so much under the spell of her delightful nature, of that vivacious charm which is all her own that in spite of myself I feel inclined, in my heart of hearts, to forgive her.'

Wüllersdorf nodded. 'Quite with you, Innstetten, would perhaps feel just the same myself. But if you take that attitude to the matter and tell me, "I love this woman so much that I can forgive her anything," and if we also take into consideration that it all happened so long, long ago, like something on another planet, well, Innstetten, if that's the position, why bother with this whole business?'

'Because there's no way round it. I've turned it all over in my mind. We're not just individuals, we're part of a larger whole and we must constantly have regard for that larger whole, we're dependent on it, beyond a doubt. If it were a matter of living in isolation I could let it go; then it would be for me to bear the burden that had been put on me, it would be the end of real happiness, but plenty of people have to live without "real happiness" and I would have to too – and would manage it. You don't have to be happy, that's the last thing you have a right to, and you don't necessarily have to do away with the one who robbed you of your happiness. You can, if you're going to turn your back on society, let him get away with it. But wherever men live together, something has been established that's just there, and it's a code we've become accustomed to judging everything by, ourselves as well as others. And going against it is unacceptable; society despises you for it, and in the end you despise yourself, you can't bear it any longer and put a gun to your head. Forgive me for lecturing you like this, when all I'm saying is what we've all told ourselves a hundred times. But – well, who can actually say anything new! So there it is, it's not a question of hate or anything like that, I don't want blood on my hands for the sake of the happiness that's been taken from me; but that, let's call it that social something which tyrannizes us, takes no account of charm, or love, or time limits. I've no choice. I must.'

'Well, I don't know, Innstetten…'

Innstetten smiled. 'Make up your own mind, Wüllersdorf. It's ten now. Six hours ago, I grant you, the game was still in my hands to play one way or the other, there was still a way out. Now there isn't, now I'm up a blind alley. You could say I've only myself to blame; I should have kept a closer eye on myself, controlled myself, contained it all inside me, battled it out in my own heart. But it came too suddenly, it was too strong, so I can hardly reproach myself for not having been cooler and kept my nerve. I went to your house and left you a note, and at that point the game was out of my hands. From that moment on somebody else had some knowledge of my misfortune and, what's more serious, of the stain on my honour, and after our first words just now somebody else knew it all. And now that somebody else knows, there's no way back for me.'

'Well, I don't know,' Wüllersdorf repeated. 'I don't really like to use such an old cliché, but there's no better way of putting it: Innstetten, I shall be as silent as the grave.'

'Yes Wüllersdorf, that's what people always say. But there's no such thing as confidentiality. And even if you do make the cliché come true and are confidentiality itself towards others, *you* will still know, so what you've just said about agreeing with me and understanding everything I say doesn't save me from you. I am from this moment on, and there's no going back on it, the object of your sympathy – not in itself a pleasant thought – and you will weigh every word you hear me exchange with my wife, whether you intend to or not, and if my wife were to talk about fidelity, or sit in judgment, as wives do, on what other women get up to, I wouldn't know where to look. And supposing I were to take a conciliatory line in some quite ordinary matter of honour because it's "without malice aforethought" or something along those lines, the shadow of a smile will cross your face, or it will at least register a twitch, and you'll be thinking deep down, "Good old Innstetten, it's getting to be a real obsession, this chemical analysis of every offence to determine its insult content, and he *never* finds one with enough irritants in it to be harmful. He's never choked on anything yet," – am I right or wrong Wüllersdorf?'

Wüllersdorf had stood up. 'I find it terrible that you're right, but you *are* right. I won't plague you any further by asking if it has to be. The world is as it is, and things don't take the course *we* want, they take the course *other people* want. All that pompous stuff you hear from some people about "divine justice" is nonsense of course, there's no such thing, quite the reverse: this cult of honour of ours is a form of idolatry, but as long as we have idols we have to worship them.'

Innstetten nodded.

They were together for another quarter of an hour and it was decided that Wüllersdorf should leave the same evening. There was a night train at twelve.

Then they parted with a brief 'Auf Wiedersehen in Kessin.'

28

The following evening, as arranged, Innstetten travelled up. He took the same train as Wüllersdorf the previous day, and soon after five in the morning he was at the station where the road branched off to the left to Kessin. Today, as always while the season lasted, the oft-mentioned steamer, whose first bell Innstetten heard as he reached the bottom of the steps leading down from the railway track, was due to sail just after the train arrived. The walk to the landing stage took less than three minutes; he strode to it, greeted the captain, who looked somewhat embarrassed and must already have heard about the whole thing in the course of the previous day, and took his place near the wheel. Moments later the ship cast off from the quay; the weather was magnificent, bright morning sun, not many passengers on board. He recalled the day when, returning from their honeymoon, he and Effi had driven along the banks of the Kessine here in an open carriage – a grey November day it was then, but he himself was light of heart; now it was the reverse, the light outside, and the grey November day within him. Many, many were the times he had come this way since then, and the peace that lay upon the fields, the breeding stock that looked up in the enclosures as he passed, the people at work, the fertility of the fields, all these things had induced a sense of well-being, and now, in stark contrast, he was glad when some clouds came over and began to dull the laughing blue of the sky. And so they sailed downstream, and soon, after they had passed the splendid expanse of the Breitling estuary, the Kessin church tower hove into sight, and moments later the Bulwark too and the long row of houses with the boats and ships in front of it. And now they had docked. Innstetten took his leave of the captain and strode towards the gangway which had been rolled up to facilitate disembarkation. Wüllersdorf was already there. Each greeted the other without speaking at first, and then they walked across the street to Hoppensack's Inn where they sat down under an awning.

'I booked in here yesterday morning,' said Wüllersdorf, who was disinclined to get straight down to the matter in hand. 'When one thinks what a backwater Kessin is, it's astonishing to find such a good hotel here. I don't doubt that my friend the head waiter here speaks three languages; to judge by his parting and the cut of his waistcoat we may safely assume four – Jean, would you bring us coffee and cognac please.'

Innstetten quite understood why Wüllersdorf was adopting this tone, and he was in agreement with it too, though he could not wholly master his restlessness and involuntarily pulled out his watch.

'We have time,' said Wüllersdorf. 'An hour and a half yet, or almost. I've ordered the carriage for eight-fifteen; it won't take us more than ten minutes.'

'And where?'

'Crampas first suggested a corner of the woods just beyond the churchyard. But then he broke off and said, "No, not there." Then we agreed on a place in the dunes. Right on the beach, there's a dip in the first dune and you can see the sea.'

Innstetten smiled. 'Crampas seems to have picked a beauty spot. He was always that way inclined. How did he take it?'

'Wonderfully well.'

'Arrogant? Frivolous?'

'Neither one nor the other. It shook me Innstetten, I can tell you. When he heard your name he went deathly pale and had to struggle to master his feelings, and I noticed a quiver at the corner of his mouth. But all that was over in an instant, and he got a grip of himself again, and from that moment he was all melancholy resignation. I'm absolutely certain he has the feeling he's not going to come out of this alive, and doesn't want to. If I judge him aright, he loves life and yet he's indifferent to it. He grabs what he can in the passing, but he doesn't set much store by any of it.'

'Who's going to be his second? Or should I say who is he going to bring along?'

'That, once he had recovered his composure, was his main worry. He named two or three local aristocrats, but then rejected them, saying they were too old and too religious, and he would send a telegram to Treptow, to his friend Buddenbrook. And then he came, splendid chap, dashing and yet like a child at the same time. He couldn't calm down and paced up and down in great agitation. But when I had told him everything he said the same as we did, "You're right, it has to be!"'

The coffee came. They had a cigar and Wüllersdorf was again intent on steering the conversation round to more indifferent matters.

'It surprises me that none of the local people have turned up to greet you. I know you were very well-liked. Not even your friend Gieshübler...'

Innstetten smiled, 'You don't know them up here on the coast; half of them are philistines, the other half are slippery customers, not much to my taste; but they do have one virtue, they have manners. And as for dear old Gieshübler. Of course they all know what's going on, and for that very reason they're taking care not to appear curious.'

At that moment a chaise with its hood down came into sight from the left, moving slowly because it was not yet the appointed hour.

'Is that ours?' asked Innstetten.

'Presumably.'

And moments later the carriage stopped outside the hotel and Innstetten and Wüllersdorf stood up.

Wüllersdorf went over to the coachman and said, 'To the mole.'

The mole was in the opposite direction, right instead of left, and this false instruction was only given to avoid any kind of intervention, which was always a possibility. But whether they wanted to turn left or right further on, they still had to go through the Plantation, so their route inevitably led past Innstetten's old home. The house lay more silent that ever; the rooms on the ground floor looked pretty neglected; whatever could it be like upstairs! And the feeling of uncanniness that he had so often fought against in Effi, or else had cause to smile at, now afflicted Innstetten himself, and he was glad when they were past it.

'That's where I lived,' he said to Wüllersdorf.

'It looks strange – desolate and deserted.'

'Indeed. In the town they thought it was haunted, and looking at it today, I don't blame them.'

'What was it all about?'

'Oh, some nonsense: an old ship's captain with a granddaughter or a niece who disappeared one fine day, and then a Chinaman, who may have been her lover, and in the hallway there was a little shark and a crocodile, both suspended on strings and always in motion. Makes a marvellous story, but not now. There are all kinds of other things flitting through my mind.'

'You're forgetting, this could all go off smoothly.'

'It can't. And that isn't what you yourself said a short while ago Wüllersdorf, when you were talking about Crampas.'

Soon afterwards they had passed the Plantation and the coachman was about to turn right towards the mole. 'Go left instead. We'll go to the mole later.'

And the coachman turned left into a wide cart track that ran behind the men's bathing in a straight line to the woods. When they were within three hundred paces of them Wüllersdorf stopped the carriage and they both went ahead on foot, sinking into the grinding sand, walking down a wide cart track which cut at right angles through the three lines of dunes at this point. There were dense clumps of marram grass all around on either side, but round it grew immortelles and a few blood-red pinks. Innstetten stooped and picked one of the wild pinks to put in his buttonhole. 'The immortelles come later.'

They walked on for five minutes. When they had reached the fairly deep hollow between the first two lines of dunes they saw, to their left, the opposing party already there: Crampas and Buddenbrook, and with them the good Dr Hannemann who had his hat in his hand, so that his white hair blew in the wind.

Innstetten and Wüllersdorf walked up the gulley in the sand, Buddenbrook came towards them. They exchanged greetings and the two seconds stepped aside for a brief discussion of the remaining practicalities. The agreement was that they were to advance simultaneously and fire at ten paces. Then Buddenbrook went back to his place; it was all quickly performed; and the shots rang out. Crampas fell.

Innstetten, stepping back a few paces, turned away from the scene. Wüllersdorf had gone over to Buddenbrook and both awaited word from the doctor, who shrugged his shoulders. At that moment Crampas indicated with a gesture that he wanted to say something. Wüllersdorf bent down to him, nodded at the few words that came scarcely audibly from the dying man's lips and then went up to Innstetten.

'Crampas would like to say something to you Innstetten. You must grant him this wish. He has barely three minutes to live.'

Innstetten walked over to Crampas.

'Would you…' These were his last words.

One more agonized but almost friendly flicker in his features and it was all over.

29

On the evening of the same day Innstetten arrived back in Berlin. He had gone straight to the railway station in the carriage he had left on the road across the dunes, without going near Kessin again, leaving it to the two seconds to make the report to the authorities. On the way (he was alone in the compartment) he went over what had happened, reflecting on it all once more; his thoughts were the same as two days earlier, but in reverse order, starting with the conviction that he was in the right and had done his duty, and ending up doubting it all. 'Guilt, if there is such a thing, isn't bound to time or place and can't just lapse from one day to the next. Guilt requires expiation; that makes sense. But a time limit is a half-measure, it's weak, or at least prosaic.' And he clung to this idea for support, repeating to himself that what had happened had to happen. But at the very moment when he was certain of this, he rejected it again. 'There must be some time limit, a time limit is the only sensible approach; and whether it's prosaic into the bargain or not is neither here nor there, what's sensible is usually prosaic. I'm forty-five now. If I had found the letters twenty-five years later, I would have been seventy. Then Wüllersdorf would have said, "Innstetten, don't be a fool." And if Wüllersdorf hadn't said it, Buddenbrook would have, and if *he* hadn't said it I would have said it myself. That much is clear. If you take something to extremes, then you go too far and end up looking ridiculous. No doubt about it. But where does it start? Where is the dividing line? After ten years a duel is still necessary, and they call it honour, and after eleven years, or perhaps after only ten and a half, they call it folly. The dividing line, the dividing line. Where is it? Has it come? Has it already been crossed? When I think of that last look, the resignation, with a smile in spite of his agony, what that look was saying was, "Innstetten, always the stickler for principles… You could have spared me this, and yourself too." And maybe

178

he was right. My soul seems to be saying something like that. Yes, if I'd been filled with mortal hate, if I'd had a burning lust for revenge... Revenge isn't admirable, but it's human, and has a natural human right. As it was, it was all for the sake of an idea, a concept, it was an artificial affair, half play-acting. And now I have to carry on with the act, and send Effi away, and be the ruin of her, and myself too... I should have burnt the letters and the world should never have found out about them. And then when she came back, without any inkling, I should have said, 'Your place is there,' and should have inwardly divorced myself from her. Not in the eyes of the world. There are so many lives that aren't real lives, so many marriages that aren't real marriages... happiness would have gone, but I wouldn't have had to live with that eye with its questioning look and its silent, gentle reproof.'

Shortly before ten Innstetten drew up outside his house. He climbed the stairs and pulled the bell; Johanna came and opened the door.

'How is Annie?'

'Well sir. She's not asleep yet... If you would care to...'

'No, no, don't excite her. I'd rather see her tomorrow morning. Bring me a glass of tea Johanna. Has anybody called?'

'Only the doctor.'

And now Innstetten was alone again. He paced up and down, as was his wont. 'They know everything already. Roswitha is stupid, but Johanna is a smart one. And if they don't know for certain, they've put two and two together and have a shrewd idea. It's curious how many things can become pointers and tell-tales, as if everybody had been there.'

Johanna brought the tea. Innstetten drank it. After all the strain he was dead tired and fell asleep.

Innstetten was up early. He saw Annie, exchanged a few words with her, praised her for being a good patient and then went to the Ministry to report what had happened to his chief. The Minister was most gracious. 'Yes Innstetten, happy the man who comes through what life brings us unscathed; you haven't had your troubles to seek.' He found all that had happened in order and left the consequences to Innstetten.

It was late afternoon before Innstetten got back to the apartment, where he found a few lines from Wüllersdorf.

Arrived back this morning. Experienced a world of things; painful, touching, Gieshübler above all. The most delightful hunchback I've ever met.

179

He didn't say much about you, but your wife, your wife! He couldn't get over it and ended up in tears, the little man. The things that happen. One can only wish there were more Gieshüblers. But there are more of the others. And then the scene at the Major's house – terrible. But not a word about that. One more lesson in the importance of being careful. I shall see you tomorrow.

Yours,
W.

Innstetten was badly shaken after he had read this. He sat down and wrote a few letters himself. When he was finished he rang: 'Johanna, letters for the post-box.' Johanna took the letters and made to go.

'...And then, Johanna, there's another thing: my wife will not be coming back. Others will tell you why not. Annie must know nothing, at least not yet. Poor child. You must break it to her gently that she no longer has a mother. I can't. But do it sensibly. And don't let Roswitha ruin things.'

Johanna stood there, as if quite dazed for a moment. Then she went up to Innstetten and kissed his hand.

When she got back to the kitchen she was quite filled with pride and superiority, almost happiness. The Master had not only told her everything, but at the end he had said, 'Don't let Roswitha ruin things.' That was the main thing, it wasn't that she lacked goodness of heart and even sympathy for the Mistress, but what preoccupied her above all else was the triumph of having a position of a certain intimacy with the Master.

Under normal circumstances flaunting and exploiting this triumph would have been an easy matter, but today it turned out that things were not at all in her favour, so that her rival, without having been taken into the Master's confidence, proved to be the better informed. The concierge below, at just about the same time as this was happening, had called Roswitha into his little room and as soon as she entered had thrust a newspaper before her eyes. 'There Roswitha, there's something for you; you can bring me it back down later. It's only the *Fremdenblatt*: but Lene has gone out to get the *Kleine Journal*. There will be more in that; they always know everything. Imagine Roswitha, who would have thought it?'

Roswitha, not usually at all curious, had made her way as quickly as possible up the back stairs after this exchange and had just finished reading when Johanna joined her.

The latter put the letters Innstetten had just given her down on the table, ran her eye over the addresses, or at least pretended to (for she had long since established to whom they were written), and said with studied nonchalance, 'One is to Hohen-Cremmen.'

'I can imagine,' said Roswitha.

This remark caused Johanna no little astonishment. 'The Master never writes to Hohen-Cremmen ordinarily.'

'Yes, ordinarily. But now – imagine, I just got this from the concierge downstairs.'

Johanna took the paper and read half-aloud a passage marked heavily in ink: 'Just before going to press we heard from a well-informed source that yesterday morning in the seaside resort of Kessin in Eastern Pomerania, a duel took place between Ministerialrat v.I. (Keithstrasse) and Major von Crampas. Major von Crampas was killed. There is alleged to have been a liaison between him and and the Ministerialrat's wife, a beautiful and still very young woman.'

'The things these papers print,' said Johanna, who was displeased that her news had been overtaken by events. 'Yes,' said Roswitha. 'And now people are goin' to read that and call my poor, dear mistress all sorts of things. An' that poor Major. Now 'e's dead.'

'Roswitha, what can you be thinking of? Should he *not* be dead? Or should our dear Master be dead instead?'

'No Johanna, the Master ought to be alive too, everybody ought to be alive. I'm not for shootin' people, I can't even stand 'earin' the bangs. But just think Johanna, it was ages ago, and them letters, as soon as I saw them, I thought there was something funny about them with that red string wound round three or four times and then knotted without a bow – they looked all yellow with age, it was that long ago. We've been 'ere more'n six years now, 'ow can people let such old stories –'

'Oh Roswitha, what do you know about it? And when you get down to it, you're to blame. It all came from the letters. Why did you fetch that chisel and force the sewing-table open? You should never do that; you must never break open a lock that somebody else has locked.'

'You've gone too far now Johanna, accusin' me of somethin' like that straight out, and anyway if it comes to that *you're* to blame, you're the one who came dashin' into the kitchen like a mad thing and told me to break open the sewin'-table because the bandage was in it, that's when I brought the chisel, and now I'm to get the blame. Well I must say…'

'All right, I take it back Roswitha. But don't try your "Poor Major" on me. Poor Major indeed! The sum total of your poor major was worth nothing; people like that with golden red moustaches they're always twirling are never worth a thing and all they do is damage. And when one has always been in service in fine houses – which you haven't Roswitha, that's something you lack – then one knows what is proper and fitting and what honour means, and one knows that when that kind of thing happens, there's no other way, and so there's what they call a challenge issued, and somebody ends up shot dead.'

'Oh, I know all that; I'm not so stupid as you would like to 'ave me. But when it was so long ago –'

'Roswitha, that "so long ago" of yours, that's what shows you don't understand a thing about it. You're always telling the same old story about your father and the red-hot iron bar, and how he came at you, and each time I put a red-hot slug in the iron I think of your father, and I see him wanting to kill you because of the child, which is dead now. Yes Roswitha, you're always talking about it, and next thing you'll be telling Annie the story too, and when Annie is confirmed, she'll certainly hear it, perhaps the very same day. And it annoys me that you've been through all that, when your father was just a village blacksmith who shoed horses or put rims on cart-wheels, and now you come and expect the Master to turn a blind eye to it all, just because it was so long ago. And what does long ago mean? Six years isn't long ago. And our mistress – who isn't coming back, the Master has just told me that – our mistress isn't twenty-six yet, her birthday's in August, and you talk to me about "long ago". And even if she was thirty-six, I can tell you thirty-six is an age when you really have to be careful, and if the Master had done nothing, the best people would have cut him. But you don't know anything about that Roswitha, you don't even know the word.'

'No, I don't know anythin' about that and don't want to neither; but one thing I do know Johanna, you're in love with the Master.'

Johanna gave a forced laugh.

'Yes, go on, laugh. I saw it a long time ago. There's somethin' in your manner. It's a good thing the Master don't notice that kind of thing… The poor lady, the poor lady.'

Johanna was now intent on peace. 'Let it be Roswitha. You're in one of your funny moods; but I know you all have them, you country folk.'

'Maybe we do.'

'I'm going to post the letters now and see downstairs if the concierge has the other paper yet. I did understand you to say he sent Lene for it? There's bound to be more in that. There's next to nothing in this one.'

30

Effi and Geheimrätin Zwicker had been in Ems for almost three weeks, living on the ground floor of a charming little villa. In the shared drawing-room which lay between their two living-rooms and had a view of the garden was a jacarandawood grand piano on which Effi would occasionally play a sonata, and the Geheimrätin occasionally a waltz; she was quite unmusical, restricting herself in the main to rhapsodizing about Niemann's Tannhäuser.

It was a magnificent morning; in the little garden the birds were twittering, and from the house next door in which there was a 'bar', the click of billiard-balls could already be heard, despite the early hour. The two ladies had taken breakfast not in the drawing-room itself, but on a little gravelled front terrace, raised a couple of feet, with a brick retaining wall, from which three steps led down to the garden; the awning above them was wound back so that their enjoyment of the fresh air would be in no way impeded, and both Effi and the Geheimrätin were absorbed in their needlework. Only occasionally did they exchange a few words.

'I don't understand,' said Effi, 'why I haven't had a letter for four days; he usually writes every day. Can Annie be ill? Or is he himself ill?'

The Geheimrätin smiled, 'He's fit as a fiddle, you'll see.'

Effi felt there was something unpleasant about the tone in which this was said, and was on the point of responding when the housemaid, who came from somewhere near Bonn and from her youth had formed the habit of assessing the most diverse phenomena by reference to Bonn students and Bonn hussars, came out of the drawing-room on to the terrace to clear away the breakfast things. She was called Afra.

'Afra,' said Effi, 'it must be nine by now. Hasn't the postman been yet?'

'No, my lady, not yet.'

'What can be the reason for that?'

'The postman, of course; he's from Siegen way, no gumption. I've already told him he's downright slack. And the way he has his hair, I don't think he's ever heard of a parting.'

'Afra, you're being a bit hard on him again. Just think what it's like to be a postman day in day out in this eternal heat…'

'Yes, my lady, you're right. But others manage; if you've got it in you, it can be done.' And as she said this, she balanced the tray skilfully on her finger-tips and went down the steps to take the shorter route to the kitchen through the garden.

'A pretty girl,' said Frau Zwicker. 'And so brisk and bright, one might say she has natural grace. Do you know, my dear Baroness, that this Afra – wonderful name by the way, isn't it, they tell me there was even a Saint Afra, not that I think ours is any relation –'

'There you go again, my dear Geheimrätin, off at a tangent, this time it's Afra, and quite forgetting what you really meant to say –'

'Not quite, my dear friend, I'm coming back to it. What I was about to say was that our Afra, for me, bears an uncommon resemblance to that impressive girl I've seen in your house…'

'Yes, you're right. There is a similarity. Except that our maid in Berlin is definitely prettier, her hair is much fuller and more beautiful. I've never seen hair as beautiful and flaxen as our Johanna's, absolutely never. You do see it of course, but never in such abundance.'

Frau Zwicker smiled, 'It's not often you hear a young wife lavishing praise on her housemaid's flaxen locks. And on their abundance too! You know I find that touching. For really, choosing maids is always a delicate matter. They have to be pretty, because every caller, or at least the men, are put off if a long beanpole with a pasty complexion and a grimy collar and cuffs comes to the door, truly it's a blessing that most lobbies are so dark. But pay too much attention to maintaining outward appearances and creating so-called first impressions, and maybe even give the pretty little thing one frilly apron after another, and you'll never have a moment's peace again, you'll constantly be asking yourself, unless you're *too* vain and *too* self-confident, whether you ought not to remedy the matter. "Remedy" was one of Zwicker's favourite expressions, he frequently used to bore me stiff with it; but of course every Geheimrat has his favourite expressions.'

Effi listened with very mixed feelings. If the Geheimrätin had been just a little different, it would all have been charming, but as it was, Effi felt there was something unpleasant here that in other circumstances would perhaps simply have amused her.

'You're right about Geheimrat's tick, my dear, Innstetten has it too, but he always laughs when I draw attention to it, and apologizes afterwards for using official jargon. Of course your husband had been in the service longer and was probably rather older…'

'Not very much,' was Frau Zwicker's tart rejoinder.

'But anyway, I can't really share the fears you express. The moral code, as it's called, still counts for something –'

'You think so?'

' – and least of all can I imagine that you of all people, my dear friend, could ever be exposed to these fears and anxieties. Forgive me for being so outspoken, but you have what men call "charm", you're good-humoured, fascinating, stimulating company, and if it's not indiscreet I would like to ask, with all these qualities of yours, whether what you have been saying is based on certain painful experiences in your own life?'

'Painful?' said Frau Zwicker. 'Oh my dear, dear lady, painful is putting it too strongly, even if one does chance to have been through a good deal. Pain is too strong a word, far too strong. In addition to which one has one's ways of coping, one's counter-strategies. You mustn't be too tragic about these things.'

'I can't really quite imagine what you're referring to. It's not as if I don't know what sin is. I do. But there's a difference between finding yourself inadvertently entertaining bad thoughts of whatever kind and actually letting that sort of thing become a part, or indeed a habitual part of your life. Not to speak of allowing it in your own home...'

'I'm not talking about that. That's not quite what I meant to say, although, to be candid, I do have misgivings about that too, or I should say I *had*. For it's all in the past now. But there are more discreet places. Do you know about country outings?'

'Of course. And I wish Innstetten showed more interest...'

'Do you realize what you're saying, my dear friend? Zwicker was always going out to Saatwinkel. I can tell you, I still only have to hear the name to feel a pang again. That goes for all those places people go to on the outskirts of our dear old Berlin! For I love Berlin in spite of everything. But the very names of all those places conjure up a world of worry and anxiety. You're smiling. But tell me my dear friend, what can you expect the state of morality to be in a city where just outside the gates (for there's hardly any difference between Berlin and Charlottenburg any more), huddled within half a mile of each other you have Pichelsberg, Pichelsdorf and Pichelswerder? Three places to get pickled in is just too much. Search the whole world, you won't find anything like it elsewhere.'

Effi nodded.

'And this,' Frau Zwicker continued, 'is all going on in the greenwood on the banks of the Havel. And that's only the west where at least you find culture and civilized behaviour. But go to the other side of the city my dear, up the Spree. I'm not talking about Treptow or Stralau, they're bagatelles, quite innocuous, but look at a local map, and alongside names that are to say the least strange-sounding like Kiekebusch or Wuhlheide... you should have heard Zwicker pronouncing that one... you'll find names with an unmistakably vulgar ring, names I won't offend your ears with. But, naturally, these are the preferred places. I hate these country outings, which in the popular imagination are patriotic charabanc parties with rousing choruses of "I am Prussian", whereas in fact they contain the seeds of social revolution. When I say "social revolution" I mean of course moral revolution, everything else is passé, and even Zwicker in his last days said to me, "Believe me Sophie, Saturn devours his children." And Zwicker, for all his faults and deficiencies, I have to give him his due here, was a thinking man and had a natural feeling for history... But I can see that my dear Frau von Innstetten, polite as she usually is, is only listening with half an ear. Of course! There's the postman over there, and so the heart flies out to anticipate the loving words in the letter... Well Böselager, what have you brought us?'

185

While she spoke, the postman had reached the table and was emptying his bag: several newspapers, two hairdresser's advertisements and lastly a large registered letter addressed: 'To Baroness von Innstetten, née von Briest.'

The recipient signed and the postman left again. Frau Zwicker ran her eye over the advertisements and laughed at the reduced price for a shampoo.

Effi was not listening; she turned the letter she had received over and over in her hands with an inexplicable reluctance to open it. Registered, sealed with two large seals in a stout envelope. What did that mean? Postmarked Hohen-Cremmen and addressed in her mother's handwriting. From Innstetten, it was five days now, not a word.

She took a pair of mother-of-pearl-handled embroidery scissors and slowly cut open the long side of the envelope. And now a fresh surprise awaited her. The sheet of notepaper was indeed covered with closely written lines from her mother, but folded up in it were banknotes with a broad paper band round them on which, in red in her father's hand, the amount of the enclosed sum was marked. She thrust the bundle of notes back into the envelope and began to read, leaning back in the rocking-chair. But she did not get far, the notepaper fell from her grasp and all the blood drained from her face. Then she bent down and picked up the letter again.

'What's wrong, my dear friend? Bad news?'

Effi nodded, but did not elaborate and merely asked for a glass of water. When she had taken a drink she said, 'It will pass, dear Geheimrätin, but I should like to go to my room for a moment... Could you send Afra to me?'

And with that she rose and went back into the drawing-room where she was visibly relieved at having something to hold on to, and to be able to feel her way along the jacarandawood piano. In this way she reached her room on the right, and when, fumbling and groping for the handle, she had opened the door and reached the bed against the wall opposite, she fainted.

31

Minutes went by. When Effi had recovered she sat on a chair standing by the window and looked out at the quiet street. If only there had been some noise, some altercation; but all that was on the paved roadway was sunshine, interspersed with the shadows cast by the railings and the trees. The feeling of being alone in the world descended on her with all its weight. An hour ago a happy woman, the darling of all who knew her, now an outcast. She had read only the beginning of the letter, but it was enough to bring her situa-

186

tion home to her quite clearly. Where to go? She had no answer to that, yet she was filled with a deep longing to get away from all that surrounded her here, away from the Geheimrätin, to whom it was all just an 'intriguing case', and whose sympathy, if she had any, would certainly be no match for her curiosity.

'Where to go?'

On the table in front of her lay the letter; but she did not have the courage to read any more of it. In the end she said, 'What is there to be afraid of now? What can they say that I haven't already told myself? The man for whose sake this all happened is dead, there's no going back home for me, in a few weeks the divorce will be granted and the child will be awarded to the father. Naturally. I'm the guilty party and a guilty woman can't bring up her child. And anyway, what with? For myself, I'll manage. Let's see what Mamma has to say about this, how she envisages my life.'

And with these words she took up the letter again to read it through to the end:

…And now to your future, my dear Effi. You are going to have to fend for yourself, and in that you can rely, as far as material things are concerned, on our support. You had best stay in Berlin (a big city is best for living down this kind of thing) and there you will be one of the many who have forfeited the open air and the light of the sun. You will live a lonely life, or if you don't want that you will probably have to move out of your own sphere. The world you have lived in will be closed to you. And the saddest thing of all for us and for you (yes, for you too, we think we know you well enough to say) is that your parental home will be closed to you. We cannot offer you a quiet corner at Hohen-Cremmen, there can be no refuge in our home, for that would mean closing this house to all the world, and that we are definitely not inclined to do. Not because we are so very attached to the world, or because saying goodbye to 'society', as it is called, seems absolutely unbearable, no, not for that reason. It's simply that we have to show what we stand for and show before the world, I'm afraid I have to say this, our condemnation of what you have done, of what our only child, whom we loved so dearly, has done…

Effi could read no further; her eyes filled with tears, and after struggling in vain with them, she finally succumbed to paroxysms of sobbing and weeping which relieved her heart.

Half an hour later there was a knock, and in response to Effi's 'Come in,' the Geheimrätin appeared.

'May I come in?'

'Of course my dear Geheimrätin,' said Effi, who was now lying on the sofa, covered with a light rug, her hands clasped. 'I'm exhausted. I've just made myself as comfortable as I could here, after a fashion. May I invite you to take a seat?'

The Geheimrätin sat down so that the table with its bowl of flowers stood between her and Effi. Effi showed no trace of embarrassment and made no adjustment to her posture, not even her clasped hands. All at once it was a matter of complete indifference to her what the woman thought; all she wanted was to get away.

'You have had sad news my dear, dear lady…'

'More than sad,' said Effi. 'At any rate sad enough to put a swift end to our being together here. I must leave here today.'

'I don't wish to pry, but is it something to do with Annie?'

'No, not with Annie. The news didn't come from Berlin, it was a few lines from my Mamma. She's worried about me, so I really feel I must dispel her worries somehow, or if I can't do that, at least be at home with her.'

'I understand only too well, much as I regret the prospect of spending these last few days here in Ems without you. May I put my services at your disposal?'

Before Effi could answer, Afra came in and announced that they were going in to lunch. All the guests were very excited, she said: the Kaiser was probably coming for three weeks, and at the end of his stay there were to be grand manoeuvres. The Bonn Hussars were supposed to be coming too.

Would it be worth staying on until then, Frau Zwicker instantly reflected, arriving at a definite 'yes' before leaving to offer Effi's apologies for her absence at lunch.

When Afra too made to leave, Effi said. 'Oh Afra, if you're free, come and help me with my packing for a quarter of an hour. I want to catch the seven o'clock train today.'

'Today, so soon? Oh my lady, that's a great pity, it really is. The fun's just beginning.'

Effi smiled.

Frau Zwicker, who still had hopes of hearing much more, had only been persuaded with difficulty not to see the 'dear Baroness' off. At the station, Effi had insisted, one was always so preoccupied, and only concerned about one's luggage and one's seat; and especially in the case of those one cared for it was best to take one's leave beforehand. Frau Zwicker concurred, though she sensed well enough that this was just a pretext; she had seen enough in her time to know at once what was genuine and what wasn't.

Afra accompanied Effi to the station and insisted on the Baroness promising faithfully to come back next summer; people who had been to Ems always kept coming back. There was nowhere to beat Ems, apart from Bonn.

Frau Zwicker had in the meantime sat down to write some letters, not at the rather shaky rococo secretaire in the drawing-room, but outside on the veranda, at the same table where she had taken breakfast with Effi not ten hours previously.

She was looking forward to writing the letter, which a Berlin lady of her acquaintance who was currently staying in Reichenhall was to have the benefit of. They had long been soul-mates and were united above all in viewing the entire male sex with deep-seated scepticism; they found that men consistently fell far short of anything that one might reasonably require, the so-called 'dashing' ones further than most. 'The ones who are so embarrassed they don't know where to look are the best for all that, after a short course of instruction, but the Don Juans are invariably a disappointment. And what else could you expect?' Such were the words of wisdom that passed between the two friends.

Frau Zwicker was already on her second sheet, expatiating on her highly rewarding topic – Effi – as follows:

All in all she was easy to get on with, she was well-mannered, seemed to be frank and open, without any trace of aristocratic snobbery (or else greatly skilled in concealing it) and she always listened with interest when she was told something interesting, which, as I don't have to tell you, I exploited to the full. I repeat, a charming young woman, twenty-five, or not much more. And yet I didn't trust that calm of hers, nor do I at this moment, indeed now less than ever. The business today with the letter – there's a real story behind that. I'm as good as certain. It would be the first time I've ever been mistaken in such a matter. The way she liked to talk about fashionable Berlin preachers, establishing the measure of each one's godliness, that and her occasional Gretchen look, as if butter wouldn't melt in her mouth – all these things together reinforced my conviction... But here is Afra, whom I've mentioned to you already, a pretty young girl, bringing a newspaper to my table, which she tells me the landlady has given her for me: there's something marked in blue. Excuse me while I read it...

P.S. The paper was most interesting and came right on cue. I shall cut out

189

the passage marked in blue and enclose it with this letter. You'll see from it that I was *not* wrong. Who can this Crampas be? It's not to be credited – first she writes notes and letters and then she goes and keeps *his* letters! What are fires and stoves for? That sort of thing should never be allowed to happen, at least not as long as this idiotic practice of duelling is still with us; in coming generations the passion for writing letters may perhaps be permitted (because then it will no longer be dangerous). But we are a long way off that time yet. For my part, I'm filled with pity for the young baroness, and the only consolation in all this for me, vain as one is, is that I was not wrong about her. And the case was not all that ordinary. A less acute diagnostician could have been taken in.

As ever,

Yours,

Sophie

32

Three years had passed and Effi had been living for almost as long in a little flat in Königgrätzerstrasse between Askanischer Platz and Hallesches Tor: two rooms, one front and one back, and a kitchen behind with a cubby-hole for the maid, all as plain and ordinary as one could imagine. And yet it was a pretty flat with a touch of style which made an agreeable impression on everyone who saw it, not least perhaps, on his occasional calls, old Geheim-rat Rummschüttel who had long since forgiven the poor young woman not only for the play-acting with rheumatism and neuralgia – that lay far in the past – but also for all that had occurred since, insofar as there was any need for forgiveness in his case. For Rummschüttel had seen far worse in his time. He was going on eighty, yet whenever Effi, who had latterly been given to frequent ailments, sent a letter asking him to visit her, he would be there next morning, brushing aside her apologies for living up so many stairs. 'Not a word of apology my dear lady, first because it's my job, secondly because I'm pleased, indeed rather proud to be able to climb three flights so easily. If I weren't afraid of inconveniencing you – after all I'm here as a doctor and not as a nature-lover and landscape enthusiast – I would probably come more often, just to see you and sit for a while at your back window. I don't think you quite appreciate the view.'

'Oh, I do, I do,' said Effi, but Rummschüttel would not be deterred and went on, 'Please, my dear lady, come over here just for a moment, or allow me to escort you to the window. Quite magnificent again today. Just look at all those different railway lines, three, no four of them, and look at the way trains constantly glide up and down them... and now that one over there is disappearing again behind a clump of trees. Really magnificent. And the way the sun is suffusing the white smoke! If St Matthew's churchyard wasn't directly behind it, it would be ideal.'

'I rather like churchyards.'

'Yes, you can say that. But for the likes of me! Inevitably the question for us is, couldn't one or two fewer have been laid to rest there? Anyway my dear lady, I'm quite pleased with you and my only regret is that you won't hear of Bad Ems; with these catarrhal infections of yours Ems would work...'

Effi said nothing.

'Ems would work wonders. But since you don't care for it (and I accept that) you can take the waters here. It's three minutes to Prince Albrecht's Gardens, and even if they don't have the music and elegant dresses and all the diversions of a proper spa promenade, there is the spring, which is the main thing after all.'

Effi expressed agreement and Rummschüttel took his hat and stick. But he went over to the window again. 'I hear the council is going to lay out terraces on the Kreuzberg, bless them, and once that bare patch at the back has more green... A charming flat. I almost envy you... And I've been meaning to say for some time dear lady, you always write me such delightful letters. Who could fail to enjoy them? But it must be such an effort each time – why don't you just send Roswitha over?'

Effi thanked him and on this note they parted.

'Why don't you just send Roswitha over...' Rummschüttel had said. So was Roswitha with Effi? Was she in Königgrätzerstrasse and not in Keithstrasse? Indeed she was, and had been for quite some time, for as long in fact as Effi herself had been in Königgrätzerstrasse. Three days before the move Roswitha had appeared at her dearly beloved mistress's lodgings and that had been such a great day for both of them that we must now go back and give it its due.

When her parents' letter came from Hohen-Cremmen casting Effi off and sending her from Ems back to Berlin on the evening train, she had not immediately taken a place of her own, but had found accommodation at a boarding-house by way of experiment, and it had proved tolerably successful. The two ladies who ran the boarding-house were educated and amply considerate, and had long since given up being curious. So many paths converged there that a desire to penetrate everyone's secrets would have caused altogether too many complications. That kind of thing could only be harmful to business. Effi, who still had Frau Zwicker's cross-questioning eyes fresh in her memory, was most agreeably touched by the landladies' restraint, but at the end of a fortnight had the distinct feeling that the prevailing atmosphere there, both moral and physical, was not one she could readily bear. There were mostly seven at table: besides Effi and one of the landladies (the other ran the kitchen behind the scenes), two English girls attending college, a titled lady from Saxony, a very pretty Jewish girl from Galicia – what she was there for no one knew – and a schoolmaster's daughter from Polzin in Pomerania who wanted to be a painter. It was an unfortunate combination and the round of supercilious backbiting in which the English girls did not, oddly enough, sweep all before them, but disputed the palm with the daughter of Polzin and her exalted sense of her artistic vocation, was dispiriting, yet Effi, who kept out of it all, could have coped with the strain this moral atmosphere imposed, had there not been the physical matter of the actual air in the boarding-house to compound her problems. Its exact composition was probably impossible to determine, but the fact was all too clear that, susceptible as Effi was, it caused her breathing difficulties, and it was this physical circumstance that very quickly forced her to look out for alternative accommodation, which she then managed to find quite close by. It was the flat already described in Königgrätzerstrasse. She had gathered together the essentials to move in at the beginning of the autumn quarter, and was counting away the hours in the last days of September before her merciful release from the boarding-house.

On one of those last days – she had withdrawn a quarter of an hour earlier from the dining-room and was preparing to take her ease on a sea-grass sofa upholstered in coarse wool with a large floral pattern – there was a quiet knock at the door.

'Come in.'

The sole maid, a sickly-looking creature in her mid-thirties who, as a result of constantly occupying the lobby, trailed about the pervasive fug of the boarding-house in every fold of her clothing, entered and said, 'Excuse me my lady, there's somebody to see you.'

'Who?'

'A woman.'

'Did she give her name?'

'Yes, Roswitha.'

And behold, Effi had hardly heard the name when she shook off her drowsiness, jumped to her feet and ran out into the lobby to take Roswitha by both hands and pull her into the room.

'Roswitha. It's you! What a pleasure. What's brought you here? Something good of course. A good old face like yours can only be bringing something good. Oh, I'm so happy I could give you a kiss. I would never have thought I could feel such pleasure again. Dear old heart, how are you? Remember what it was like in the old days, with that Chinaman haunting us? Those were happy times. I thought then they were unhappy, because I still had to learn how hard life is. I know now. Ghosts aren't the worst thing, not by a long chalk! Come here dear, good Roswitha, come and sit by me and tell me… Oh, I do so long to hear. How is Annie?'

Roswitha could scarcely speak and looked around the strange room whose grey and dusty-looking walls were framed by a narrow gold moulding. But at length she recovered herself and said that the Master was now back from Glatz; the old Kaiser had said that 'six weeks would be about enough in such a case', and all she had been waiting for was the day the Master came home, because of Annie. She had to have somebody to look after her. Johanna was of course neat and tidy enough, but she was still too pretty and too taken up with herself and goodness knows what she might have in mind. But now that the Master was there to keep an eye on things and see to it that everything was done properly, she had really felt she owed it to herself to come and see how her Mistress was getting on –

'That's quite right, Roswitha.'

– And she had wanted to see whether her ladyship needed anything, whether maybe she needed her, for if she did she would step in at once and stay and do everything and see to it that things began to go well for her ladyship again.

Effi had leant back into the corner of the sofa and closed her eyes. But suddenly she sat up and said, 'Yes Roswitha, that's a thought. It's a distinct possibility. For you see, I'm not staying here in this boarding-house, I've taken a flat. And I've had it furnished and I'm moving in in three days. And if you could be with me when I do, if I could just say, "No, not there Roswitha, the wardrobe goes there and the mirror there," yes, that would be something, I would certainly like that. And then, both of us tired after all the fetching and carrying, I'd say, "Now Roswitha, you can go across the road and fetch a jug of Spatenbräu, for a glass of beer goes down well after hard work, and while you're at it see if you can bring us something nice to eat from the Habsburger Hof. You can take the plates back later" – Yes Roswitha, just thinking about it makes my heart feel a great deal lighter. But I have to ask you. Have you given this enough thought? I don't mean Annie. You're very attached to her, she's almost like your own child – but Annie will be looked after, Johanna is attached to her too. So no more of that. But just remember how everything has changed before you decide to come back to me. I'm not who I was. Now I have a tiny flat, and the concierge won't have much time for you or me. We'll live very modestly, meals will always be what

193

we used to call Thursday fare, because that was cleaning day. Do you remember? And do you remember how dear old Gieshübler once called and had to sit down with us, and then said, "I've never tasted such a delicacy." Don't you remember how terribly polite he always was, even though he was the only person in the whole town who knew anything about good cooking. The rest of them thought everything was delicious.'

Roswitha rejoiced at every word and thought it was all going wonderfully until Effi again said, 'Have you given this enough thought? For you've – I have to say this even though it was my own household – you've been spoilt over the years. There was never any question of being careful, we didn't need to be thrifty. But now I do. Now I'm poor. All I have is what they send me, you know, from Hohen-Cremmen. My parents are very good to me. They do what they can, but they're not rich. So now tell me. What do you think?'

'I'll come and bring my trunk next Saturday. Not in the evenin' – first thing in the mornin', so I'll be there when you start movin' your things in. I'm a lot better at that sort of thing than your ladyship.'

'Don't say that Roswitha. I can do these things too. You can do anything when you have to.'

'My lady, just don't you worry about me. I'm not goin' to think, "That won't do for Roswitha." Anythin' Roswitha has to share with her mistress is fine, especially if it's somethin' sad. Yes, I'm really lookin' forward to it. I know a thing or two about that, you'll see. And if I don't, I'll learn, no bother. For I 'aven't forgotten that day my lady, you know, when I was sittin' in the churchyard without a friend in the world, thinkin' it'd be best all round if I was lyin' there with the rest of them in the row. An' who came along then? Who kept me among the livin' after all I've been through? That time my father came at me with the red-hot iron –'

'I know Roswitha –'

'Yes, that was bad enough. But sittin' in the churchyard that day with hardly any money an' nowhere to go was even worse. And then along you came, my lady. I'll never forget that, God rest my soul.'

And with that she stood up and went to the window. 'Look my lady, if you come over 'ere you can see 'im again.'

And now Effi approached the window too.

On the far side of the street sat Rollo, looking up at the boarding-house windows.

A few days later Effi, assisted by Roswitha, moved into her flat in the König-grätzerstrasse. She felt at ease there from the first. There was a lack of company of course, but there had been so little pleasure in her dealings with people in those days at the boarding-house that being alone was no hardship, at least not to begin with. Conversation with Roswitha on aesthetic matters wasn't possible, even a discussion of what was in the papers was beyond her, but when it came to basic human concerns and Effi began a sentence with 'Oh, Roswitha, I'm getting those fears again...' then the good soul always had the right answer, always a word of comfort and mostly sound advice too.

Until Christmas things went splendidly; but Christmas Eve was a sad affair, and as the new year approached, Effi began to be subject to severe melancholy. It was not cold, just grey and rainy, and if the days were short the evenings were that much longer. What to do? She read, she embroidered, she played patience, she played Chopin, but those nocturnes were not calculated to bring much light into her life, and when Roswitha came with the tea-tray, and on it, besides the tea things, were two small plates with an egg and a wiener schnitzel cut into little slices, which she put on the table, Effi closed the pianino and said, 'Draw up a chair Roswitha. Keep me company.'

And Roswitha did so. 'You've been playin' that piano too much again, my lady, I can see; it always makes you look like this, you come out in red patches. The Geheimrat said you weren't to do it.'

'Oh, Roswitha, it's easy enough for the Geheimrat to tell me what not to do, and it's easy for you to keep repeating it. But what am I supposed to do? I can't sit at the window all day looking out at the Christuskirche. On Sundays during the evening service, when the windows are lit up, I always look across at it; but it's no help, my heart just feels all the heavier.'

'Well then, my lady, you should go in one of these times. You did go over once.'

'Oh, more than once. But little good it did me. He's a good preacher and he's a very clever man, and I'd be happy to know a hundredth of what he knows. But it's all just like reading a book; then when he starts shouting and waving his arms and shaking those black curls, it puts an end to my devotions.'

'An end?'

Effi laughed. 'You mean I never began? There's probably something in that. But whose fault is that? Not mine. He's always talking about the Old Testament. And good as it may be, it's not edifying. I mean all this listening – it's not what I need. What I need is to have so much to do that I don't know which way to turn. That would be the thing for me. There are those societies where young girls learn to be housekeepers or sewing teachers or kindergarten nurses. Have you never heard of them?'

'Yes, I've 'eard of 'em. There was talk of Annie goin' to kindergarten.'

'There you are, you know more about it than I do. That's what I want. To join one of those societies where I could make myself useful. But there's no point in thinking about it. The ladies wouldn't take me on, and they couldn't anyway. And that's the most dreadful thing of all, that the world is so closed to me that I'm not even allowed to join in doing any kind of good. I can't even give coaching to poor children…'

'That wouldn't do for you neither my lady. Those children always 'ave such dirty boots, and in wet weather they steam and reek somethin' terrible, my lady couldn't stand it.'

Effi smiled, 'You're probably right Roswitha. But it's too bad that you're right. I can see there's still too much of the old me there, and I'm still having it too easy.'

Roswitha would have none of this. 'When somebody is as good as you are my lady, she can't 'ave it too easy. But you shouldn't keep playin' all them sad tunes. Anyway I've this feelin' sometimes that everythin's goin' to be all right again, somethin'll turn up.'

And something did turn up. Effi wanted to be a painter, in spite of the schoolmaster's daughter from Polzin and that artistic conceit of hers which still haunted her mind as something particularly dreadful. She laughed about it herself, for she knew she could never be any more than the most modest of amateurs, yet she plunged in with enthusiasm because she now had something to occupy her, and it was just right for her because she could do it in silence and noiselessly. She applied to a painting teacher who was quite elderly and well-versed in Brandenburg's aristocracy, and at the same time so religious that he seemed to take Effi to his heart from the beginning. Here, he probably thought to himself, was a soul to be saved, so he was very warmly disposed to her and treated her like a daughter. Effi was very happy at this, and the day of her first painting lesson betokened a change for the better for her. Her poor life wasn't so poor any more, and Roswitha was triumphant, that she had been right and that now something had turned up.

The months went by in this fashion. But contact with humanity again, though it brought her happiness, equally gave rise to a wish to renew and extend such contacts. Longing for Hohen-Cremmen sometimes gripped her with real passion, and she longed even more passionately to see Annie again. She was her child after all, and when her thoughts dwelt on her, she also remembered Miss Trippelli saying once, 'It's a small world, even in Central Africa you can be sure that you'll bump into an old acquaintance', and was justifiably astonished never to have met Annie. But that too was to change one day. She came out of her painting lesson close to the Zoological Garden, and near the terminus got into a horse-tram that was going all the way down Kurfürstenstrasse. It was very hot and the drawn curtains flapping in and out in the strong breeze refreshed her. She was leaning back in the corner facing the front platform and examining several blue sofas decorated with braid and tassels that were engraved in a pane of glass, when – the tram had slowed right down – she saw three schoolchildren with satchels on their backs and little pointed hats jump aboard, two of them blond and carefree, the third dark and serious. It was Annie. Effi shuddered violently, and the thought of the meeting with her child which had been her ardent wish for so long filled her now with truly mortal terror. What should she do? Taking a quick decision, she opened the door to the front platform where nobody stood but the driver, and asked him to let her off at the front at the next stop. 'Against regulations Miss,' said the driver, but she handed him a coin and gave him such an imploring look that the good-natured soul changed his mind and muttered, 'By rights I shouldn't; but it can't do no 'arm this once.' And when the tram stopped, he lifted the gate and Effi jumped down.

When she reached home Effi was still in a state of great agitation.

'Just imagine Roswitha, I saw Annie.' And she recounted the meeting on the horse-tram. Roswitha was not pleased that there had been no scene of reunion between mother and daughter, and it was hard to convince her that it would not have done in the presence of so many people. Then Effi had to tell her how Annie had looked, and when with maternal pride she had done that, Roswitha said, 'Yes, she's sort of 'alf and 'alf. She gets 'er prettiness, and, if I may say so, 'er strangeness from 'er mamma; but 'er seriousness, that's 'er papa all over. And when I come to think of it, there's more of the Master in 'er.'

'Thank goodness!' said Effi.

'Well now my lady, that's the question, isn't it? There'll be those who'll be more for 'er mamma.'

'Do you think so Roswitha? I don't.'

'Now, now, I'm not goin' to fall for any of that, and I think your ladyship knows quite well how things really are, and what men like best.'

'Oh, we mustn't talk about that.'

With that the conversation was broken off, and was never taken up again. But though Effi made a point of avoiding any mention of Annie to Roswitha, she could not in her heart get over the meeting and the thought that she had run away from her own child preyed on her mind. It plagued her and reduced her to shame, and the desire to meet Annie assumed pathological proportions. To write to Innstetten and ask for a meeting was not possible. She was amply aware of her guilt, indeed she nursed the feeling with something resembling passionate dedication; but for all this awareness she also felt a certain resentment towards Innstetten. She told herself over and over again that he was in the right, but when it really came down to it, he was wrong. Everything that had happened was so long ago, a new life had begun – he could have let it bleed away quietly, instead of which it was poor Crampas who had bled.

No, writing to Innstetten was out of the question; but she did want to see Annie and talk to her and press her to her heart, and after she had reflected on this for some days she knew how it might best be done.

The very next morning she dressed with care in discreet black and walked towards Unter den Linden to call on the Minister's wife. She sent in her card which bore only the words: 'Effi von Innstetten, née von Briest'. Everything else had been left off, including 'Baroness'. 'Her Excellency will see you' – Effi followed the servant into an anteroom where she sat down and, in spite of her agitation, examined the pictures decorating the walls, first Guido Reni's *Aurora*, then opposite a few English etchings, engravings after Benjamin West in the familiar style of aquatints, full of light and shade. One of them was of King Lear on the blasted heath.

Effi had barely finished her examination when the door of the adjoining room opened and a tall, slender lady with an expression that instantly won her petitioner over came towards her and held out her hand. 'My dearest lady,' she said, 'What a pleasure to see you again…'

And as she said this she walked towards the sofa, where she drew Effi down beside her.

Effi was moved by the kindness of heart that all this betokened. No trace of superciliousness nor of reproach, just the milk of human kindness. 'Now what can I do for you?' said the Minister's wife, once again taking the initiative.

There was a quiver at the corner of Effi's mouth. Finally she said, 'What brings me here is a request, one which might perhaps be fulfilled with your Excellency's help. I have a ten-year-old daughter whom I have not seen for three years, and I would like to see her again.'

The Minister's wife took Effi's hand and looked at her kindly.

'When I say I haven't seen her for three years, that's not strictly true. Three days ago I did see her again.' And then Effi gave a vivid account of her meeting with Annie. 'Running away from my own child. I know once one has made one's bed one must lie on it, and I'm not asking for my life to change. It is how it is and I can't expect it to be otherwise. But as for the child, that is too hard, and so I do wish to be allowed to see her now and then, not secretly and furtively, but with the knowledge and consent of all concerned.'

'With the knowledge and consent of all concerned,' the Minister's wife repeated Effi's words. 'So what you mean is with the consent of your husband. I can see that he has chosen to bring up the child out of reach of her mother, a procedure I don't propose to comment on. He may be right, if you'll pardon my saying so, my dear lady.'

Effi nodded.

'You accept your husband's attitude and all you ask is that a natural feeling, the finest of our feelings indeed (we women at least are agreed on that), should be given its due. Have I got that right?'

'Exactly.'

'So I am to seek agreement for occasional meetings at your house where you can try to win back your child's affection.'

Effi once again expressed her assent while the Minister's wife went on, 'I shall do what I can then, my dear lady. But it won't be easy. Your husband, you'll excuse me if I continue to call him that, is not a man of moods and whims, he's a man of principle, and to give up his principles, or even just relax them momentarily, will be hard for him. If that were not so, his behaviour and the way he is bringing up his daughter would have changed long ago. What is hard for your heart is what he considers to be right.'

'So perhaps your Excellency, you think it would be better to withdraw my request?'

'Not at all. I was merely seeking to explain your husband's actions, not to justify them. At the same time I was trying to indicate the problems which we are likely to encounter. But I think we'll manage it just the same. For we women, if we go about it cleverly, and don't overdo it, can achieve all sorts of things. In addition to which your husband is a particular admirer of mine, and is unlikely to refuse any request that comes to him through me. We're having a *cercle intime* tomorrow at which I shall see him, and the day after tomorrow you'll have a note from me in the morning to tell you whether I've gone about it cleverly, by which I mean successfully, or not. I think we shall win our cause and you will have the pleasure of seeing your child again. She's said to be a very pretty girl. Which is not surprising.'

33

Two days later, as promised, a note arrived, and Effi read:

I am pleased, my dear lady, to be able to give you good news. It all went as we wished; your husband is too much of a man of the world to be capable of refusing a lady's request; however – and this I must not conceal from you – I could see clearly his agreement did not correspond to what he considers wise and proper. But we mustn't quibble when we should be rejoicing. What we have arranged is that your Annie will come around midday, and may a propitious star smile on your reunion.

It was the second post that brought Effi this note, so presumably Annie would be arriving in less than two hours. A short time, but still too long, and Effi paced restlessly through the two rooms and then back into the kitchen, where she talked to Roswitha about anything and everything: the ivy across the road on the Christuskirche, and how by next year the windows would be completely overgrown, the concierge who once again had not turned off the gas tap properly (they would all be blown sky-high one of these days), how next time she should go back to the big lamp supplier on Unter den Linden for their paraffin instead of to Anhaltstrasse – she talked about everything and anything, but not about Annie, so as to suppress the fears that lurked in her heart in spite of the Minister's wife's note, or perhaps because of it.

Now it was midday. At last the doorbell rang timidly and Roswitha went to look through the spy-hole. Yes, it was Annie. Roswitha gave the child a kiss but said not a word, and very quietly, as if there were an invalid in the house, led her from the lobby into the back room and from there to the door into the front room.

'In you go Annie.' And with these words, not wishing to intrude, she left the child alone and went back to the kitchen.

Effi was standing at the other end of the room, her back to the pier-glass, when the child entered. 'Annie!' But Annie stopped at the door which was half-open, partly out of embarrassment, but partly intentionally too and so it was Effi who ran to the child and lifted her in the air and kissed her.

'Annie, my darling child, how happy I am. Come here and talk to me,' and she took Annie's hand and went over to the sofa to sit down. Annie, still looking timidly at her mother, just stood there and with her left hand reached for the corner of the tablecloth which was hanging down. 'Did you know, Annie, I saw you once?'

'Yes, I thought you did too.'

'Now you must have lots to tell me. My, how you've grown. And there's your scar; Roswitha told me about it. You always were so wild and heedless when you were playing. You get that from your mamma, she was like that too. And what's happening at school? I expect you're always top of the class, you look to me as if you are a model pupil and only ever bring home top marks. I've also heard that Fräulein von Wedelstädt has praised you. That's as it should be; I was ambitious too, but I didn't go to such a good school. Mythology was always my best subject. What are you best at?'

'I don't know.'

'Oh, you must know. Everyone knows that. What did you get the best marks in?'

'Religion.'

'There, you see, now I know. Yes, well, that's very good; I wasn't so good at that, but that was probably because of the teaching. We only had an ordinand.'

'We had an ordinand too.'

'And has he gone now?'

Annie nodded.

'Why did he go?'

'I don't know. Now we have the Minister again.'

'Whom you all like very much.'

'Yes. Two girls in the top class are going to convert.'

'Ah, I see. That's good. And what's Johanna doing?'

'Johanna brought me as far as the house…'

'And why didn't you bring her up with you?'

'She said she would rather stay downstairs and wait opposite, by the church.'

'And you are to meet her there.'

'Yes.'

'Well, I hope she won't get impatient. There's a little garden at the front, and the windows are half-overgrown with ivy, as if it was an old church.'

'I shouldn't like to keep her waiting though.'

'Oh, I see you're very considerate. I have to be pleased about that. So long as you have the right priorities… And now tell me, how's Rollo?'

'Rollo is very good. But Papa says he's getting so lazy. He lies in the sun all the time.'

'I can believe that. He was like that when you were quite little… And now Annie, tell me – for today we've just met for a short while – are you going to visit me often?'

'Yes, if I'm allowed.'

'We could go for a walk in Prince Albrecht's Gardens.'

'Yes, if I'm allowed.'

'Or we'll go to Schilling's and have an icecream, pineapple or vanilla – that was what I always used to like best.'

'Yes, if I'm allowed.'

And this third 'if I'm allowed' was the last straw; Effi jumped to her feet and a look burning with something approaching indignation fell upon the child. 'I think it's high time you were going Annie. Otherwise Johanna will be getting impatient.' And she pulled the bell. Roswitha, who was already waiting in the next room, came in at once. 'Roswitha, take Annie across to the church. Johanna is waiting there. I hope she hasn't caught cold. I'd be very sorry. My regards to Johanna.'

201

At that both left.

Scarcely had Roswitha closed the door when Effi, who was on the point of suffocation, tore open her dress and subsided into convulsive laughter. 'So that's what a reunion's like', and she dashed forward, opened the windows wide and looked for some source of comfort. And in her heart's hour of need she found something. For there beside the window was a bookshelf, a few volumes of Schiller and Körner, and on top of the volumes of poetry which were all the same size lay a Bible and hymnbook. She picked them up because she had to have something she could kneel and pray to, laid the Bible and hymnbook on the edge of the table, just where Annie had stood, and threw herself down in front of them with a violent jerk and said half out loud, 'God in heaven, forgive me for what I have done. I was a child... No, no I wasn't a child, I was old enough to know what I was doing. I *did* know, and I don't want to take away from my guilt... but *this* is too much. For what's happening here with the child, that's not *you*, God, punishing me, it's *him*, and him alone! I thought he had a noble heart and I always felt small beside him; but now I know *he's* the one who's small. And because he's small, he's cruel. All things small are cruel. *He's* taught it to the child, he was always a schoolmaster. Crampas called him that, making fun of him at the time, but he was right. "Oh yes, if I'm allowed." You don't *have* to be allowed. I don't want any of you any more, I hate you, even my own child. Too much is too much. A careerist, that's all he was, nothing else. – Honour, honour, honour... and then he went and shot the poor fellow whom I didn't even love and whom I'd forgotten because I didn't love him. It was just stupidity, and now it's blood and murder. And me to blame. And now he sends me the child because he can't say no to a Minister's wife, and before he sends the child, he trains her like a parrot, and the phrase he teaches her is "if I'm allowed". I'm disgusted at the thought of what I did; but I'm even more disgusted when I think of how virtuous you both are. Away with you. I have to live, but it won't be for ever.'

When Roswitha came back Effi was lying on the floor, her face turned away, as if lifeless.

34

Rummschüttel, when he was called, found that Effi's condition gave some cause for concern. The symptoms of hectic fever he had observed in her for some time seemed more pronounced than before, and what was worse, there were also the first signs of a nervous complaint. His calm and kindly manner however, into which he contrived to inject a dash of whimsy, did Effi good, and she was calm as long as Rummschüttel was with her. When he finally left, Roswitha accompanied the old gentleman out into the hall and said, 'Mary Mother of God, I'm so frightened, Herr Geheimrat; supposin' it 'appens again, which it could; Mary Mother of God – I'll never 'ave another moment's peace. But it did go too far, that business with the child. Poor mistress. And 'er so young. Others are just startin' at 'er age.'

'Now, now Roswitha. It's going to be all right. But she must get away. We'll have to see. A change of air, fresh faces.'

Two days later a letter arrived at Hohen-Cremmen.

My dear Madam,
My long-standing friendly association with the houses of Briest and Belling and not least the warm affection with which I regard your daughter will justify this letter. Things can't go on as they are. Unless something happens to take your daughter out of the loneliness and pain of the life she has been leading for some years, she will quickly decline. She always had a tendency to phthisis, which is why, years ago, I prescribed a cure at Ems; this old ailment has now been joined by a new one: her nerves are under severe strain. What is needed to arrest this deterioration is a change of air. But where? It would not be difficult to pick one of the Silesian spas, Salzbrunn would be good, and Reinerz, because of the nervous complication, even better. But the only possible place really is Hohen-Cremmen. For, my dear lady, what your daughter needs to get well is not air alone; she is wasting away because all she has is Roswitha. Loyal servants are good, but loving parents are better. Pardon an old man for meddling in matters that are outside his professional competence. Or perhaps not, for in the final estimate I'm speaking as her doctor in this too and making this demand, if you will pardon the word, out of duty... I've seen so much of life... but no more of this. Please remember me to your husband.

Your most respectful servant,
Dr Rummschüttel

Frau von Briest had read this letter to her husband; both were sitting on the shady flagged path with the garden room behind them and the roundel with its sundial in front of them. The Virginia creeper that climbed round the window was moving gently in what light breeze there was, and a few dragonflies hovered over the water in the bright sunshine.

Briest was silent, drumming his fingers on the tea-tray.

'Please, don't drum your fingers; say something instead.'

'Oh, Luise, what is there to say. My drumming my fingers says it all. You've known for a long time what I think about it. At the time, when Innstetten's letter came like a bolt from the blue, I agreed with you. But that's an eternity ago; am I to play the Grand Inquisitor till my dying day? I'm sick and tired of it I can tell you, have been for a long time…'

'No reproaches Briest, please; I love her just as much as you do, perhaps more. We all have our own ways. But we're not in this world just to be weak and affectionate and make allowances for every infringement of the law and the commandments and what people condemn, and – for the time being at least – rightly condemn.'

'Oh, come on. One thing's more important.'

'Of course one thing's more important, but what is it?'

'Parents' love for their children. And then if you only have the one…'

'Then you say goodbye to catechism and morality, and the claims of Society.'

'Oh, Luise, catechism if you like and as much as you like, but don't talk to me about "society".'

'It's difficult to get along without society.'

'Without a child too. And believe me Luise, "society" can turn a blind eye whenever it suits. This is how I see the matter: if the officers from Rathenow come over, that's fine by me, and if they don't, that's fine by me too. I'm just going to telegraph, "Come back Effi." Do you agree?'

She stood up and kissed him on the forehead. 'Of course I do. Only don't reproach me. It's not an easy step we're taking. The moment we do it, our life will change.'

'I can put up with that. The rape seed is doing well and I can go coursing in the autumn. And I can still enjoy my red wine. And once I have my child back in the house again, it'll taste even better… Now I'm going to send that telegram.'

Effi had been in Hohen-Cremmen for over six months now. She lived in the two rooms on the first floor that she used to have when she came to visit; the larger one was arranged for her personal use and Roswitha slept in the next room. The benefits that Rummschüttel had expected from her staying there, surrounded by kindness, had been realized, as far as they could be. Her cough subsided, the severe expression that had robbed her kindly face of much of its charm faded and there were days when she could laugh again. Kessin and all that was connected with the past there was seldom mentioned, with the sole exception of Frau von Padden, and of course Gieshübler, for whom old Briest had a great fondness. 'This Alonzo, this Spaniard out of

Preciosa who keeps a Mirambo under his roof and raises a Trippelli – he has to be a genius and nobody is going to tell me otherwise.' And then Effi had no choice but to do her Gieshübler impression, hat in hand, *toujours la politesse*, giving his endless little bows, all of which, with her talent for mimicry, she could pull off very well, though always with a certain reluctance because she felt she was doing the dear, good man an injustice. There was never any mention of Innstetten or Annie, although Annie was in their will and would inherit Hohen-Cremmen.

Yes, Effi was reviving, and her mother, who, being a woman, was not entirely averse to viewing the whole thing, painful though it was, as an interesting case, rivalled her husband in demonstrations of love and attentive concern.

'We haven't had a winter as good as this for a long time,' said Briest. At that Effi rose from her chair and brushed his thinning hair back from his forehead. But fine as all this looked as far as Effi's health was concerned, it was all merely on the surface and the truth of the matter was that the illness was still there and continued to eat away at her life unseen. When Effi – who was once again wearing a blue and white striped tunic-style dress with a loose belt as she had the day she became engaged to Innstetten – quickly came up to her parents with a spring in her step to say good morning, they looked at each other in pleasure and surprise; pleasure and surprise, but also sadness because they could not fail to notice that this was not the glow of youth, but a kind of transfiguration that gave the slender figure and shining eyes their peculiar expression. Everyone who observed her closely saw this, and Effi was alone in not seeing it, entirely immersed in the feeling of happiness that came from being back in a place so friendly towards her, so richly peaceful, living in reconciliation with those she had always loved and by whom she had always been loved, even in her years of misery and banishment.

She busied herself with all sorts of household tasks and saw to little improvements and embellishments about the house. Her aesthetic sense meant that she always got these things right. But her reading and above all her painting and drawing she had abandoned altogether. 'I've had so much of these things that I'm glad I can sit with my hands in my lap now.' They also no doubt reminded her too much of sad times. She developed the art of looking with quiet delight at nature instead, and when the leaves of the plane trees fell, when the rays of the sun glittered on the ice on the little pond or the first crocus flowered in the roundel when it was still half in winter's grip – all these things did her good and she could look at them for hours and forget what life had denied her, or perhaps more accurately, what she herself had thrown away.

They were not entirely without visitors; not everybody was against her; but her main contact was with the school-house and the parsonage.

That the daughters of the school-house had flown the nest did not matter much, it wouldn't have been the same, but her relationship with Jahnke himself – who regarded not only Swedish Pomerania but also the whole Kessin district as an outlying part of Scandinavia and was constantly asking questions about it – her relationship with this old friend was closer than ever. 'Yes Jahnke, we had a steamer, and as I believe I wrote to you, or perhaps have told you, I really once almost got across the sea to Visby. Imagine, almost as far as Visby. It's funny, but there are a lot of things in my life, actually, of which I can say "almost".'

'A pity, a pity,' said Jahnke.

'Yes, it is a pity of course. But I did drive round Rügen. That would have been something for you Jahnke. Imagine, Arkona with a big Wendish camp you can still see, or so they say, for I didn't get that far; but not too far away there's Lake Hertha with the white and yellow water-lilies. I thought a lot about your Hertha there…'

'Ah yes, Hertha… But you were going to say something about *Lake* Hertha…'

'Yes, I was… And what do you think Jahnke, close to the lake there were two big sacrificial stones, quite smooth, still with the grooves in them where the blood ran down in the olden days. I've disliked the Wends ever since.'

'Oh, forgive me my lady. But it wasn't the Wends at all. Those sacrificial stones at Lake Hertha go back much further, much earlier, long before Christ; to the Germanic tribes we're all descended from…'

'Of course,' laughed Effi, 'we're all descended from them, the Jahnkes certainly and possibly the Briests too.'

And then she dropped Rügen and Lake Hertha and asked him about his grandchildren, and which he liked better, Bertha's or Hertha's.

Yes, Effi got on well with Jahnke. But in spite of his intimate knowledge of Lake Hertha, Scandinavia and Visby, he was a simple man, so inevitably the isolated young woman much preferred her chats with Niemeyer. In the autumn, as long as they could walk in the park, these were many and often; but with the onset of winter came several months' break because she disliked visiting the parsonage; Pastor Niemeyer's wife had always been a very unpleasant woman and now she took a very high moral line, although in the view of the parish she herself was not entirely free from blemish.

So things went on the whole winter, much to Effi's distress. But then, at the beginning of April when the shrubs began to show green at the edges and the paths in the park quickly dried out, the walks with Niemeyer began again.

On one occasion they were taking such a walk. In the distance they heard a cuckoo and Effi counted the number of times it called. She had taken Niemeyer's arm and said, 'There's the cuckoo calling. I don't like to ask him his prediction though. Tell me, my dear friend, what do you think of life?'

'Oh, Effi my dear, you mustn't ask me questions like that, they're for the experts. You must consult a philosopher or offer a prize for an essay competition at some university. What do I think of life? A little and a lot. Sometimes a great deal, sometimes a very little.'

'That's right my friend, I like that; that's all I need to know.' And as she said that they came to the swing. She jumped up with all the agility of her much younger days, and before the old man watching her could recover from his momentary shock, she was crouching down between the two ropes, skilfully getting the swing going by bending her body and shooting up straight again. In a few seconds she was flying through the air holding on with one hand as she took a little silk square from her neck and chest and waved it with all the appearance of joy and high spirits. Then she let the swing slow down and jumped off and took Niemeyer's arm again.

'Effi, you're still just like you used to be.'

'No. I wish I was. But that's all *far* behind me, I just wanted to have a try again. Oh, how lovely it was, and what a power of good the air did me. I felt I was flying up to heaven. Will I get there? What do you think, my old friend, you ought to know. Please, please tell me…'

Niemeyer took her head in his two old hands and kissed her on the forehead and said, 'Yes Effi, you will.'

35

Effi spent all day in the park because she needed the fresh air; old Dr Wiesike from Friesack was in agreement with this but gave her altogether too much freedom to do as she pleased, so that she caught a heavy cold during the chilly days in May; she had a temperature, coughed a lot, and the doctor, who had been coming over every three days, now came daily and found it an awkward case to handle since Effi could not be given the sleeping tablets and cough mixtures she was asking for because of her temperature.

'Doctor,' said old Briest, 'How's this business going to end? You've known her since she was a child, brought her into the world. I don't like any of this; she's losing weight visibly, and those red patches and the glitter in her eyes when she suddenly looks at me questioningly. What do you think? What's happening? Is she going to die?'

Wiesike wagged his head slowly from side to side. 'I wouldn't say that Herr von Briest. I don't like this high temperature. But we'll get it down, and then she'll have to go to Switzerland or Menton. Pure air and a friendly atmosphere to make her forget the past...'

'Lethe, Lethe.'

'Yes, Lethe,' Wiesike smiled. 'Pity our old friends the Greeks just left us the word and not the spring itself while they were at it...'

'Or at least the prescription for it; they're making artificial mineral water now you know. Damn me Wiesike, wouldn't that be a winner, if we could build one of those sanatoriums here, Friesack as Amnesia Springs. Anyway, we'll give the Riviera a go for a start. Menton is on the Riviera isn't it? Corn prices are bad again at the moment, but if it has to be, it has to be. I'll speak to my wife about it.'

And so he did, meeting with his wife's instant assent. Indeed recently, probably as an effect of their reclusive life, she had developed a strong desire to see the south for a change, and this came to the aid of his suggestion. But Effi herself would hear nothing of it. 'You're so good to me. And I'm selfish enough to accept the sacrifice, if I thought it would do any good. But I'm quite certain it would only do me harm.'

'You're imagining that Effi.'

'No. I've become so irritable. Everything gets on my nerves. But not here with you. You spoil me and smooth the way ahead for me. But on a journey you can't do that, you can't just sweep the unpleasant bits out of the way; it starts with the ticket-collector and finishes up with the waiter. The very thought of their supercilious faces makes me go quite hot. No, no, let me stay here. I don't ever want to leave Hohen-Cremmen again. This is where I belong. I'd rather have the heliotrope round the sundial down there in the roundel than Menton any day.'

After this conversation the plan was dropped again, and Wiesike, for all he had expected of the Riviera, said, 'We have to respect this, this isn't just a whim; people who have this illness have a very acute sense, they know with remarkable certainty what will help and what won't. And what Frau Effi said about ticket-collectors and waiters is actually quite right, no air anywhere is beneficial enough to outweigh the annoyance of life in a hotel – if, that is, one really does find it annoying. So we shall let her stay here; it may not be the best thing, but it's certainly not the worst.'

And this proved to be the case. Effi recovered, put on a little weight (old Briest was a fanatical believer in weighing) and lost her irritability for the most part. All the while, however, her need for fresh air increased, and, especially when the wind was in the west and grey clouds moved across the sky, she would spend many hours in the open. On days like that she would even go into the fields and out into the Luch, often two miles away, and when she tired she would sit on a fence and look in a dream at the spearwort and the clumps of red sorrel waving in the wind.

'You're always out all on your own.' said Frau von Briest, 'You're safe enough with our people, but there are so many undesirables from other parts prowling about too.'

This made an impression on Effi, who had never given danger a thought, and when she was alone with Roswitha, she said, 'I can hardly take you along Roswitha; you're too fat and your legs aren't up to it any more.'

'It's not as bad as all that, my lady. I could still get married.'

'Of course,' Effi laughed. 'It's never too late for that. But you know Roswitha, if only I had a dog to keep me company. Papa's pointer pays no attention to me at all, pointers are so stupid, and he only stirs himself when the huntsman or the gardener takes the gun down. I keep thinking of Rollo.'

'Yes,' said Roswitha, 'there aren't no dogs like Rollo 'ere. Not that I'm sayin' anythin' against 'ere. 'ohen-Cremmen is just grand.'

Some three or four days after this conversation between Effi and Roswitha, Innstetten entered his study an hour earlier than usual. The morning sun, which was very bright, had wakened him, and probably because he felt he wasn't going to get back to sleep, he had got up to start on a piece of work that had been awaiting completion for some time.

Now it was a quarter past eight and he rang. Johanna brought the break-fast tray, on which, beside the *Kreuzzeitung* and the *Norddeutsche Allgemeine*, there were also two letters. He ran his eye over the addresses and saw from the handwriting that one was from the Minister. But who was the other from? The postmark was not completely legible, and 'The most excellent Baron, Herr von Innstetten,' bespoke a happy lack of familiarity with titular conventions. This was appropriately matched by handwriting of a very primitive character. But the address itself was remarkably exact: 1C Keith-strasse, 2 stairs up, Berlin W.

Innstetten was enough of a civil servant to break the seal of his Excellency the Minister's letter first. 'My dear Innstetten, I am pleased to inform you that His Majesty has graciously approved your appointment and I offer my sincere congratulations.' Innstetten was gratified at the Minister's kind note, more almost than at the appointment itself. For as far as climbing up the lad-der was concerned, since the morning in Kessin when Crampas had taken leave of him with that look which he still had in his mind's eye, he had become rather critical of such things. Since then he had measured things on a different scale, looked at everything differently. Distinctions, what did they amount to in the end? As the days flowed ever more dismally by, he had more than once involuntarily thought of a half-forgotten ministerial anecdote from the time of the elder Ladenberg who, on being awarded the Order of the Red Eagle after a long wait for it, threw it aside in rage, exclaiming, 'You can lie there till you turn *black*.' Probably it did go 'black' in time, but much too late and certainly without bringing the recipient any real satisfaction. Everything that is meant to give us pleasure is bound to time and circumstance, and what delights us today is worthless tomorrow. Innstetten was deeply conscious of this and, important as honours and distinctions coming from the highest level had once been to him, he was now convinced that there was nothing much to be got from the glittering prizes, and that what passed for 'happiness', if indeed it existed, was something other than this glitter. 'Happiness, if I'm right, consists of two things: the first is to be in the exact place where you belong (but what public servant can say that of himself?), and the second and best is the smooth running of the little things of life, such as sleeping well and having boots that don't pinch. If the seven hundred and twenty minutes of a twelve-hour day pass without particular annoyance, that may qualify as a happy day.' Innstetten was in the mood to dwell on such painful considerations again that day. He now picked up the second letter. When he had read it he brushed his hand across his brow, with a distinct and painful sensation that happiness *did* exist, that he had once known it, but that he no longer had it and could never have it again.

Johanna entered and announced: 'Geheimrat Wüllersdorf.'

He was already standing in the doorway. 'Congratulations Innstetten.'

'You mean it, I know. The others will be annoyed. Anyway...'

'Anyway? You're not going to pooh-pooh the whole thing now surely?'

'No. His Majesty's kindness puts me to shame; the Minister's good opinion and support, to which I owe all this – almost more so.'

'But...'

'But I've forgotten how to be glad about anything. If I said that to anyone other than you, it would just sound like a glib phrase. But you can follow my drift. Look at this place; look how empty and desolate it all is. Johanna's a treasure, as they say, but when she comes into the room, my heart sinks. That act she puts on' (Innstetten mimicked Johanna's pose), 'that shapely bosom, it's almost comical really, the way it seems to have some special claim, whether on me in particular or on humanity in general I'm not sure – I find it all so triste and dispiriting, enough to make you shoot yourself if it weren't so ludicrous.'

'Innstetten, my dear fellow, do you propose embarking on your appointment as Permanent Secretary to the Minister in this frame of mind?'

'Bah, is there any other way? Read this, I've just got this note.'

Wüllersdorf took the second letter with the illegible postmark, smiled at 'most excellent Baron' and moved over to the window to read it more easily.

Your Lordship,

You will likely be surprised at me writing to you, but it's about Rollo. Little Annie told us last year he was getting lazy, but that's all right here, he can be as lazy as he wants here, the lazier the better. The thing is her ladyship would like it such a lot. When she goes into the Luch or across the fields she always says, 'I'm frightened Roswitha, I feel so alone out there. But who's to come with me? Rollo would be fine, he bears me no grudge. That's what's good about animals, they don't mind about things so much.' These were her ladyship's very words, and I'll leave it at that, and just ask your lordship to give my best to dear little Annie for me. And Johanna too.

Your most humble servant,

Roswitha Gellenhagen

'Well,' said Wüllersdorf as he refolded the paper, 'she's a cut above us.'

'My thoughts exactly.'

'And that's what's made everything seem so questionable to you.'

'You've hit it. I've been thinking about it for a long time, and these plain words with their pointed accusation – which may well not be intended – have tipped me right over the edge again. It's been plaguing me for years now and I would like to get out of this whole business; nothing gives me satisfaction any more; the more distinctions they give me, the more I feel it all means nothing. I've made a mess of my life and I've been quietly thinking I ought to turn my back on all ambition and vanity, and put my schoolmasterly nature, which is probably the real me, to use as some sort of higher moral preceptor. There have been people like that. That way, if it came off, I could become some terribly well-known figure, like say Doctor Wichern at the Rough House in Hamburg – that miracle-worker who used to tame any criminal by the sheer force of his gaze and his exemplary piety...'

'What can I say. Why not if it works?'

'No, it won't work. Not even *that*. For me every way ahead is blocked. How could I get through to a murderer's soul? It takes somebody who's unflawed to do that. And if you aren't unflawed any more and your hands are stained, then at the very least you have to be able to play the raging penitent for the brothers you are bent on converting, and put on a show of unbounded remorse.'

Wüllersdorf nodded.

'There you are, you're nodding. But I can't do any of that any more. I just can't bring myself to slip into a hair shirt now, let alone play the dervish or fakir and dance myself to death in a frenzy of self-accusation. So what I've come up with, since none of that would work, is this: I have to get away from here, go somewhere where the natives are black as pitch and ignorant of culture and honour. Happy people! For that's what has done it, it's that whole nonsense that's responsible for all this. That kind of thing is not done out of passion, which at least might be excusable. It's all for an idea... an idea, that's all!... First the other man goes down, then you go down. Except in your own case it's worse.'

'Oh, come on Innstetten, these are just whims, sudden thoughts that enter your head. Into darkest Africa, what's that supposed to mean? That's for debt-ridden lieutenants. But a man like you. Do you want to preside over a palaver in a red fez or be blood brother to King Mtesa's son-in-law? Do you want to grope your way up the Congo in a solar topee with six airholes in it, until you come out in the Cameroons or some such place? Impossible!'

'Impossible? Why's that? And if it *is* impossible, what then?'

'Just stay here and resign yourself. Show me someone who isn't depressed. Someone who doesn't say to himself every day, "A very questionable business, when you think about it." You know I have my own small burden to bear, not exactly the same as yours, but not much lighter. All this about creeping around in the jungle and spending the night in giant anthills is idiocy; leave that to those who enjoy it, it's not for the likes of us. Stand in the breach and hold the line till you fall, that's the best thing. And before you go, get as much as possible out of the small things of life, the smallest of all. Don't miss the violets in bloom, or the flowers coming out round the Luise Monument, or the little girls in high-laced boots jumping over their skipping-ropes. Take a trip out to Potsdam to the Friedenskirche where Kaiser Friedrich is buried. They're just beginning to build a vault for him now. And while you're at it, have a think about *his* life, and if that doesn't set your mind at rest then you are beyond help indeed.'

'All very well. But the year is long, and there's every day... and then the evenings.'

'That's the easiest part. There's *Sardanapalus* or *Coppélia* with dell'Era, and after that's over there's Siechen's beer-restaurant. Not to be sneezed at. Three small beers always do the trick. There are plenty of people who see things just as we do, and one of them, who didn't have his troubles to seek, once said to me, "You know Wüllersdorf, you can't get through life without auxiliary structures". The man who said that was a master builder, so he should know. And he was right to put it like that. Not a day passes when I'm not reminded of those "auxiliary structures".'

Wüllersdorf, after this unburdening, took his hat and stick. Innstetten however, whom his friend's words might have reminded of his own previous ruminations on 'modest happiness', nodded half in agreement and smiled to himself.

'And where are you going now Wüllersdorf? It's too early for the Ministry.'

'I'm taking the day off. First I'm going to stroll along the canal for an hour as far as the Charlottenburg lock and back. Then I'm going to pop into Huth's on the Potsdamerstrasse, taking care up the little wooden steps. There's a flower shop at street level.'

'And that's what you enjoy? That's enough for you?'

'I wouldn't quite say that. But it helps. There'll be several regulars there, taking their morning tipple, would be indiscreet to say who. One will tell a story about the Duke of Ratibor, another about Prince Bishop Kopp and a third probably about Bismarck. You always pick up something. Three-quarters of it isn't true, but if it's witty, no grounds for complaint and you're grateful for something to listen to.'

And at that he left.

36

May was fine, June still finer, and Effi, after successfully overcoming an initial spasm of pain when Rollo arrived, was filled with joy at having the faithful animal at her side again. Roswitha was praised and Briest expatiated to his wife on the merits of Innstetten, quite the cavalier, not at all petty, always with his heart in the right place. 'Pity that stupid business had to happen. They really were an ideal couple.' The only one to keep calm at the reunion was Rollo himself, either because intervals of time meant nothing to him, or because he regarded the separation as an aberration which had now been put right. The fact that he was growing old probably had something to do with it too. He was economical with his affections, just as he had been economical with any show of pleasure at the reunion, but his faithfulness had increased if anything. He never strayed from his mistress's side. He accepted the pointer in good part, but as a creature of lesser status. At night he lay at Effi's door on the rush mat, in the morning, if they were breakfasting outside, he lay by the sundial, always quiet and somnolent, and only when Effi rose from the breakfast-table and walked towards the hall to take first her straw-hat and then her parasol from the hall-stand, was his youth restored, and without a thought for whether his strength was to be put to a big test or just a small one, he would bound up the village street and back and only calm down when they were between the first fields. Effi, to whom fresh air meant more than beautiful scenery, avoided the spinnies and kept mostly to the main road which was lined first with ancient elms and then, where the paved highway began, with poplars on either side all the way to the station, a good hour's walk in all. She took pleasure in everything, she rapturously breathed the fragrant air wafting over from the fields of rape and clover, she followed the larks' ascent, she counted the wells and troughs where the cattle were watered. As she did so a faint ringing noise drifted over to her. And at that she felt as if she must close her eyes and lapse into sweet oblivion. Near the station at the side of the highway was a road-roller. This was her daily resting place from which she could survey the activity on the railway line; trains came and went and sometimes she saw two plumes of smoke which overlapped for a moment and then went their separate ways to left and right again until they disappeared behind village and copse. Rollo would sit beside her, sharing her breakfast, and when he had caught the last morsel, presumably to show his gratitude he would race down some furrow like a mad thing, only stopping when a couple of sitting partridges he had disturbed flew up from a neighbouring furrow right beside him.

'What a fine summer! I wouldn't have believed a year ago that I could be so happy again, dear Mamma' – Effi said this every day as she strolled round the pond with her mother or picked an early apple and boldly bit into it. For she had the most beautiful teeth. Frau von Briest would then stroke her hand and say, 'Just get well again Effi, completely well; happiness will come, not the old happiness, but a new kind. There are, thank goodness, many kinds of happiness. And you'll see, we'll find one for you too.'

'You're both so good to me. When you think I've changed your lives and made old people of you before your time.'

'Oh, Effi my dear, don't talk about it. That's what I thought when it happened. Now I can see that our quiet life is better than all the noise and bustle there was before. And if you go on like this, we shall still be able to travel. When Wiesike suggested Menton, you were ill and irritable, and because you were ill you were quite right in what you said about ticket-collectors and waiters; but when your nerves are steadier again it will be all right and instead of being annoyed we'll laugh at their airs and graces and their crimped hair. And then the blue sea and the white sails and the rocks, all covered with red cactus – I haven't seen it yet but that's how I imagine it. And I would like to see it sometime.'

And so the summer passed and the late summer nights with their shooting stars already lay behind them. These were nights when Effi had sat at the window till well after midnight, unable to get enough of them. 'I was always a bad Christian; but I wonder if we really do come from up there and go back again to our heavenly home when it's all over here, back to the stars up there, or even beyond! I don't know, and I don't want to know, but I do long for it.'

Poor Effi, you gazed up at the wonders of the heavens for too long, thinking about them, and the upshot was that the night air and the mist rising from the pond put her back on her sick-bed, and when Wiesike was called and had seen her he took Briest aside and said, 'Nothing can be done; the end won't be long, prepare yourself.'

He had spoken only too truly, and a few days later, not yet late in the evening, just before ten, Roswitha came down and said to Frau von Briest, 'It's the mistress, my lady, things are lookin' bad upstairs; she keeps talkin' to herself ever so quietly, and some of the time she seems to be prayin' though she won't admit it, but I don't know, it could be all over any time, I think.'

'Does she want to speak to me?'

'She 'asn't said. But I think she would. You know what she's like, she doesn't want to be no trouble to you nor cause you no worry. But it wouldn't do any 'arm.'

'Very well Roswitha,' said Frau von Briest, 'I'll come.'

Before the clock started to strike Frau von Briest went upstairs and into Effi's room. The window was open and she was lying on a chaise-longue by the window.

Frau von Briest drew up a little black chair with three gold spars in the ebony back, took Effi's hand and said:

'How are you Effi? Roswitha says you have a fever.'

'Oh, Roswitha does worry so. I could see she was thinking I was dying. Well, I don't know. But she thinks we should all worry as much as she does.'

'You're quite calm about dying then, Effi dear?'

'Quite calm, Mamma.'

'You're sure you couldn't be wrong? Everybody clings to life, especially the young. And you're still so young, Effi dear.'

Effi was silent for a while. Then she said, 'You know I haven't read much. Innstetten used to wonder at that. He didn't like it.'

It was the first time she had mentioned Innstetten's name, which made a deep impression on her mother and showed her clearly that it was all over.

'I think,' said Frau von Briest, 'you were going to tell me something.'

'Yes, I was. It was because you said I was still so young. And of course I am still young. But it doesn't matter. In the good old days Innstetten used to read to me in the evenings; he had very good books, and one of them had a story about someone who had been called away from a festive dinner, and

215

the next day asked what had happened after he left. And the answer was, "Oh, all sorts of things, but really you didn't miss anything." You see Mamma, these words stuck in my mind – it doesn't matter much if you are called away from the table a little early.'

Frau von Briest was silent. Effi however raised herself a little and said, 'And since I've talked about the old times and about Innstetten, there's something else I want to tell you Mamma.'

'You'll excite yourself Effi.'

'No, no; getting something off my mind doesn't excite me. It makes me calm. So what I wanted to say was, I am dying reconciled with man and God, and reconciled with *him*.'

'Did you have such bitterness towards him in your soul? Because really, if you'll forgive me my dear Effi for saying this now, it was you who brought suffering on both of you.'

Effi nodded. 'Yes Mamma. And it's sad that it should be so. But when all those awful things happened, ending with that business with Annie, you know what I mean, well at that point, if I can use such a ludicrous expression, I decided to put the boot on the other foot and managed to convince myself in all seriousness it was his fault, for being cold and calculating and in the end cruel too. And I even cursed him aloud.'

'And that weighs on you now?'

'Yes. And I want to be sure he will know that it all became clear to me here during the days of my illness, which have been my most beautiful days of all almost; that it became clear that he was right. Everything he did was right. The business with poor Crampas – what else could he possibly have done? And then – that was what hurt me most – bringing my own child up to ward me off, hard as it is for me, and painful as it is, that was right too. Let him know that I died convinced of that. It will console him, strengthen him, perhaps reconcile him. There was a lot of good in his nature, and he was as noble as anyone can be who lacks the real capacity for love.'

Frau von Briest saw that Effi was exhausted and seemed to be sleeping or wanting to sleep. She rose quietly from her chair and went out. However, hardly had she gone when Effi rose too and sat by the open window to draw in the cool night air once more. The stars shimmered, not a leaf stirred in the park. But the longer she listened, the more clearly she could again hear something falling like a fine drizzle on the planes. A feeling of liberation came over her. 'Peace, peace.'

It was a month later and September was on the wane. The weather was fine but the leaves in the park were already showing many tints of red and yellow, and since the equinox which had brought three days of storms, leaves lay strewn everywhere. On the roundel a small alteration had taken place. The sundial had gone; the day before a white marble slab had been laid in its place with the simple inscription 'Effi Briest', and beneath it a cross. It had been Effi's last request: 'On my gravestone I would like my old name back; I didn't do the other one much honour.' And that had been promised her.

Yes, the previous day the marble slab had arrived and been laid, and Briest and his wife were now sitting facing the spot and looking at the heliotrope, which had been spared and now framed the stone. Rollo lay beside it, his head between his paws.

Wilke, whose gaiters got wider and wider, brought breakfast and the post and old Briest said, 'Wilke, have the small carriage brought out, Frau von Briest and I will take a turn in the country.'

Frau von Briest in the meantime had poured the coffee and was looking over at the roundel and its flower-bed. 'Look, Briest, Rollo is lying in front of the stone again. It's gone even deeper with him than with us. He's stopped eating too.'

'That's it Luise, dumb animals. It's what I'm always saying. We're not all we're cracked up to be. With them we always say it's just instinct, but when all's said and done, it can't be bettered.'

'Don't talk like that. When you start philosophizing – don't take this amiss Briest, it's really beyond you. Common sense you've got, but when it comes to questions like that –'

'I'm out of my depth.'

'And if it's a matter of questions, there are others demanding answers Briest, and I can tell you that not a day passes now that the poor child is lying there, without these questions coming into my head...'

'What questions?

'Whether perhaps it was *our* fault after all?'

'Nonsense Luise. What do you mean by that?'

'Whether we should perhaps have brought her up more strictly. Us that is. For Niemeyer is really useless, because he leaves everything open to doubt. And then Briest, I'm sorry to have to say this... there were your constant risqué remarks... and finally, and this is what I reproach myself with, for I don't want to seem blameless in the matter, I wonder if perhaps she wasn't too young.'

Rollo who wakened at these words shook his head slowly from side to side, and Briest said calmly, 'Ah Luise, that's enough... that's *too* vast a subject.

Notes

Page 5: *Elector Georg Wilhelm.* Margrave of Brandenburg (1595-1640), Elector of Brandenburg from 1620, father of *Friedrich Wilhelm* (1620-88), the 'Great Elector' who set the Hohenzollerns and Prussia on the road to greatness.

Page 6: *Rathenow.* Hussars' garrison thirty miles west of Berlin in the Prussian administrative District *(Bezirk)* of Potsdam. The prestigious 3rd Brandenburg Regiment of von Zieten's Hussars was stationed there. A Landrat von Briest came to the assistance of the Great Elector during the surprise attack on Rathenow in 1675. See note to page 46.

Page 7: *Fritz Reuter.* Humorous writer (1810-74). The twins *Mining and Lining* are characters from his most famous novel *Ut min Stromtid (Seed-time and harvest: or, During my apprenticeship),* written in *Plattdeutsch.* The names suggest middle-class respectability.

Page 7: *Landrat.* Prussian official, appointed by the crown. He was in charge of a *Kreis,* the smallest administrative district, so Innstetten was the biggest fish in a small pool. The *Bezirk* was a larger district centred on a more important town, such as Potsdam. See notes to pages 6 and 9. There were thirty-five *Bezirke* in Prussia. The largest units of administration were Provinces. Kessin would have been a *Kreis* in the Province of Pomerania.

Page 8: *Wedding Eve.* It is traditional in Germany to celebrate the *Polterabend,* the night before a wedding, with a festive meal, amateur theatricals, dancing and riotous merriment which may include breaking crockery, a custom originally intended to frighten away evil spirits.

Page 9: *Ritterschaftsrat.* Land-owning aristocrat with a seat in the Prussian provincial parliament.

Page 9: *war of 1870.* The Franco-Prussian war (1870/71) was the last of a series of victorious campaigns for Bismarck which brought about the unification of Germany and the declaration of the German Empire. The first German empire, the Holy Roman Empire, had ceased to exist in name in 1806 in the aftermath of Napoleon's victory at Austerlitz, and in fact it disintegrated much earlier.

Page 9: *Perlebergers.* Four squadrons of the 11th Regiment of Uhlans, Prussian lancers, were stationed in Perleberg in the District of Potsdam. The word 'Uhlan' is of Polish derivation and the uniforms incorporated features from Polish national dress, whereas the more prestigious Hussars were of Hungarian origin, a fact similarly reflected in their uniforms. The Hussars' most glorious days were as new crack cavalry regiments under Frederick the Great.

Page 16: *Hôtel du Nord.* From this high-class hotel on Unter den Linden Effi could go and order her furniture at *Spinn and Mencke* and her trousseau at *Goschenhofer,* both elegant shops on Leipzigerstrasse.

Page 16: *Alexander Regiment.* 1st Regiment of the Emperor Alexander's Grenadier Guards, named during the Napoleonic Wars after Tsar Alexander I of Russia. It is significant that Dagobert, the only representative of the younger generation of the Prussian military, is in a regiment associated with a period of Prussian military defeat and betrayal. Tsar Alexander made common cause with the Prussians against Napoleon in the war of 1806-07, which included Prussia's crushing defeat at Jena (1806), only to leave the Prussians in the lurch by entering into an alliance with Napoleon by the Treaty of Tilsit (1807). This is a further subtle suggestion that Prussia's glory and the legitimacy of the established order are transient and subject to change, relative and not absolute phenomena.

Page 16: *Fliegende Blätter.* Illustrated satirical weekly.

Page 16: *Kranzler's.* Famous restaurant and cake shop on the corner of Unter den Linden and Friedrichstrasse.

Page 16: *Café Bauer.* Café on Unter den Linden opposite Kranzler's, frequented by the demi-monde in the afternoon and evening, hence 'respectable' only before lunch.

Page 16: *The Isle of the Blessed.* Dagobert intends to refer to *Die Gefilde der Seligen (The Elysian Fields)* by Arnold Böcklin (1827-1901), which caused a furore when it was hung in the Berlin National Gallery in 1878. It showed a centaur surrounded by naked nymphs in an idyllic landscape in the centre of a lake. He confuses it with another Böcklin, *Die Insel der Seligen,* a more sombre and mysterious painting showing figures in a boat crossing the water to an island of cypresses, which suggests the passage from life to death.

Page 17: *Princess Friedrich Karl.* Maria Anna von Anhalt (1837-1906), wife of Prince Friedrich Karl of Prussia, who was Kaiser Wilhelm I's nephew and from 1870 Prussian Field Marshal.

Page 17: *Demuth's.* High-class supplier of leather and travel goods.

Page 18: *Luch.* A name used in north-east Germany for a low-lying, marshy area. Here the reference is to the Kremmen Luch, part of the Havelland Luch north-west of Berlin.

Page 18: *Das Käthchen von Heilbronn.* Romantic chivalric drama by Heinrich von Kleist (1777-1811). The heroine Käthchen falls asleep under an elder tree and in a dream declares her love to the knight Wetter vom Strahl.

Page 19: *Hohenzollern in disguise.* Allusion to the dramatist Ernst von Wildenbruch (1845-1909), grandson of Prince Louis Ferdinand of Prussia.

Page 19: *'Cinderella'. Aschenbrödel,* comedy by Roderich Benedix (1811-73).

Page 20: *Sedan Day.* September 2nd, anniversary of the capitulation of Napoleon

III in 1870 at Sedan. A national holiday in imperial Germany.

Page 23: *Prince Friedrich Karl.* See note to page 17.

Page 26: *Hövel's.* H. von Hövell, at 12/13 Unter den Linden, manufacturer of chocolates and sweets, supplier to the imperial court.

Page 26: *Kögel.* Rudolf Kögel (1829-96), conservatively inclined court chaplain from 1863.

Page 27: *Valhalla.* Temple of Honour at Donaustauf near Regensburg, opened in 1842 to house busts of famous Germans, named after the mythological resting place of Germanic warriors.

Page 29: *Pinakothek... the other gallery.* The Alte Pinakothek art gallery in Munich housing old master paintings; the other which Effi cannot spell is the Glyptothek, the sculpture gallery.

Page 29: *'Four Seasons'.* Still today one of the best hotels in Munich, a traditional staging point for upper-class honeymooners on the way to Italy.

Page 30: *'In Padua he lies buried'.* Goethe, *Faust* Part I, line 2925. Mephisto's wily words to Frau Marthe Schwerdtlein about her husband.

Page 31: *St Privat panorama.* This cylindrical panoramic painting by Emil Hünten of one of the decisive moments of the Franco-Prussian War, the storming of St Privat near Metz on August 18th, 1870, was displayed under the title *Nationalpanorama* in Herwarthstrasse from 1881. Sound and light effects and models in the foreground were added to give the spectator the impression of actually being present at the action.

Page 31: *ten miles.* The German *Meile* which Fontane uses was 7.5 kilometres, that is about 5 miles. All distances in the novel have been converted accordingly.

Page 32: *Varzin.* Village in the Prussian administrative District of Köslin (now Koszalin in Poland) where Bismarck had an estate. He frequently stayed there up to his dismissal in 1890 by the young Kaiser Wilhelm II.

Page 32: *starost.* 'Elder' (Polish). In Poland, a nobleman who had been given estates by the crown and generally had reponsibilty for judicial matters in the local community.

Page 34: Christian Julius *de Meza* (1792-1865), commander of the Danish troops in the German-Danish War of 1864. He was descended from Portuguese Jews fleeing persecution, who emigrated to Holland.

Page 37: *Small and narrow is my hut.* Allusion to Friedrich Schiller, *Die Braut von Messina (The Bride of Messina)*, 'There is space in the smallest hut / For a happy loving couple.'

Page 40: Friedrich Ernst Count von *Wrangel* (1784-1877), Prussian Field-Marshal from 1856, had a highly distinguished military career in all major Prussian campaigns from 1807 on and in later life was a popular figure in Berlin, known for his caustic wit.

Page 42: *black and white with a little red at best.* The Prussian colours (black and white) were preferred to the German national flag (black, white and red).

Page 44: *president of the high court. Gerichtspräsident,* senior judge at a higher court.

Page 45: *district judge. Amtsrichter,* judge in a small locality who sat at the *Amts-gericht,* the first judicial instance.

Page 46: *attack on Rathenow.* As a prelude to the Battle of Fehrbellin, General Doerfflinger liberated Rathenow from Swedish occupation on June 25th, 1675. See note to page 6.

Page 46: *Fehrbellin.* Famous victory won on June 28th, 1675 by the Great Elector over the Swedes. It was considered decisive in freeing Brandenburg from the territorial ambitions of Sweden. *Froben.* The master of horse Emanuel von Froben is credited with saving the Elector's life by exchanging his horse for the Elector's conspicuous white charger in the course of the battle. Froben was then killed.

Page 48: *conqueror of Saarbrücken.* On August 2nd, 1870 Saarbrücken was taken, temporarily, by the French in the first skirmish of the Franco-Prussian War.

Page 48: *Jewish banker.* Baron Alfons de Rothschild (1827-1905).

Page 48: Karl Eduard *Nobiling.* Anarchist whose unsuccessful assassination attempt on Kaiser Wilhelm I on June 2nd, 1878 served Bismarck as justification for his measures against the Socialists.

Page 51: *'White Lady'.* Ghostly apparition said to haunt various Hohenzollern castles, warning of imminent disaster. According to legend the widowed Countess Agnes of Orlamünde in the late thirteenth century murdered her children to be able to marry Albrecht von Nürnberg, an ancestor of the Hohenzollerns.

Page 67: *Orpheus, Kriemhild, Vestal Virgin.* Operatic roles for female voice, from Gluck's *Orpheus and Eurydice* (1762), Heinrich Ludwig Dorn's *Die Nibelungen* (1854) and Gasparo Spontini's *The Vestal Virgin* (1807). The discarded pieces are *Erl-King,* Schubert (or possibly Löwe's) setting of Goethe's poem; *Mill-stream...,* from Schubert's song cycle *Die schöne Müllerin,* setting poems by Wilhelm Müller; *The Bells of Speyer,* Löwe's setting of Maximilian von Oer's ballad. Miss Tripelli performs *Sir Olaf,* a poem by Heinrich Heine which Fontane has apparently confused with Löwe's setting of *Herr Oluf* from the folksong anthology *Des Knaben Wunderhorn;* and other dramatic pieces concluding with Friedrich Hebbel's ballad *Der Heideknabe (The Boy on the Heath)* in a setting by Schumann (1853) for declamation and piano.

Page 68: *business of the spirit writing.* In mid-nineteenth-century Germany the psychograph, an instrument used at séances for automatic writing of messages purporting to come from the spirit world, was an object of widespread interest.

Page 75: *Eugen Richter.* Liberal politician, opponent of Bismarck in the Reichstag (1838-1908).

Page 76: *Landwehr.* Territorial reserve commanded by either former or still active officers.

Page 76: *Wilms.* Robert Friedrich Wilms (1824-80), Berlin surgeon, personally known to Fontane.

Page 77:   *Count Gröben.* Prussian major-general in the Franco-Prussian War (1817-94).

Page 77:   *Swedish Pomerania.* The only part of Lower Pomerania to remain in Swedish hands after the Peace of Stockholm (1720); Prussian from 1815.

Page 77:   *Breitling.* The estuary of the Warnow. Fontane has combined elements from the Warnow at Warnemünde and the river mouth at Swinemünde in his descriptions of the scenery round the fictitious river Kessine.

Page 77:   *Registrar.* The lowest rank of the civil service.

Page 79:   *Biliner water.* Mineral water from the Bohemian spa Bilin.

Page 79:   *Visby.* Old Hanseatic town on the Swedish island of Gothland. It became Swedish in 1648.

Page 79:   Jürgen *Wullenweber* (1492-1537), mayor of Lübeck who tried unsuccessfully to defend the Hanseatic League and Protestantism against the Bishop of Bremen.

Page 79:   *Stockholm Bloodbath.* In 1520 King Christian II of Denmark ordered the execution of 600 Swedes who had taken part in an uprising against Danish rule.

Page 82:   *Eichsfeld.* Catholic enclave south-west of the Harz mountains.

Page 83:   '*Reeperbahn*'. North German: a long, sheltered area where rope was twisted.

Page 84:   *Königgrätz.* Decisive Prussian victory over the Austrians on July 3rd, 1866. Also referred to as the Battle of Sadowa in English.

Page 85:   *Assessor.* Higher civil service post.

Page 85:   *exact words from the Bible.* Revelation iii.16: 'So then because thou art lukewarm, and neither cold nor hot, I will spue thee out of my mouth.'

Page 85:   *Rock of St Peter ... Rocher de Bronze.* The Catholic Church, an allusion to Jesus's words in Matthew xvi.18 by reference to which the papal succession goes back to Peter. The 'bronze rock' of Prussia is Bismarck.

Page 85:   *Justizrat.* Title granted to a respected lawyer without a civil service post.

Page 91:   *Vionville.* Prussian victory over the French near Metz on August 16th, 1870.

Page 92:   '*War in Peace*', '*Monsieur Hercules*', *Wilbrandt's 'Young Love*' ... *Gensichen's 'Euphrosyne'. Krieg im Frieden* (1881), comedy by Gustav von Moser and Franz von Schöntan; *Monsieur Herkules* (1863), farce by Georg Friedrich Belly; *Jugendliebe* (1871), comedy by Adolf Wilbrandt; *Euphrosyne* (1877), play by Otto Franz Gensichen on the subject of Goethe's love for the actress Christiane Neumann-Becker who died young.

Page 92:   *Castalian Spring.* Spring on Mount Parnassus at Delphi to which powers of poetic inspiration have been attributed since the nymph Castalia, according to legend, threw herself into it to escape the pursuit of Apollo.

Page 95:   *opera.* Giacomo Meyerbeer's opera *The Prophet* (1849), whose hero is the Dutch Anabaptist Jan Bochold von Leyden (1509-36).

Page 97:   Johann Bernard *Basedow* (1723-90) and Johann Heinrich *Pestalozzi*

(1746-1827) were among the most famous educationists of their time.

Page 97:   *Schnepfenthal, Bunzlau.* Christian educational institutions in Thüringen and Silesia respectively, the latter referring to the pietistical Herrnhuter community at Gnadenfrei.

Page 97:   *cherub with the sword.* According to Genesis iii.24 God placed 'Cherubims, and a flaming sword' to guard the garden of Eden after the expulsion of Adam and Eve.

Page 100:   *Vineta.* According to legend the sunken town lies at the bottom of the sea off the Baltic island of Usedom.

Page 100:   *Heine's poem.* Heine based his poem *Seegespenst* (*Sea Spectre*, 1827), of which Crampas gives a slightly distorted account, on the Vineta legend.

Page 100:   *'You have diamonds', 'Fingers soft ...'.* First lines of poems from Heine's collection *Buch der Lieder* (1827). The word 'soft' has been added by Crampas.

Page 101:   *'The giver, not the gift ...'.* In the original Crampas's punning reply, literally translated, is: 'A basket lid is not a basket', which plays on the German idiom *jemandem einen Korb geben* ('to give someone a basket') meaning 'to turn someone down'.

Page 102:   *companion piece.* Heine's poem *Spanische Atriden* in the collection *Romanzero*, Book 2.

Page 102:   *Elizabeth's mother.* Anne Boleyn. Hulda is embarrassed because the name sounds like the German for 'mistress', *Buhle.*

Page 102:   *Order of the Black Eagle, Pour le Mérite.* Prestigious Prussian decorations, the first introduced by Friederich I on his coronation in 1701, the second by Frederick the Great on his accession to the throne in 1740.

Page 103:   *Josephine factory.* Glass factory near Schreiberhau in the Giant Mountains, Silesia.

Page 103:   *King of Ultima Thule.* In Goethe's ballad *Der König von Thule* the king is given a goblet by his 'mistress' *(Buhle = rhyming appendage)* as she dies.

Page 104:   *Friedrichsruh.* A property of Bismarck's near Hamburg, purchased with largesse from the Kaiser on the founding of the Empire in 1871.

Page 105:   *'Buhküken von Halberstadt'.* Nursery rhyme about the eleventh-century Bishop Burkhard II of Halberstadt, in the Harz region, who was kind to children.

Page 105:   *One False Step ... Arthur von Schmettwitz.* Arthur is the husband of the heroine Ella - Effi's role - in Ernst Wichert's romantic comedy *Ein Schritt vom Wege* (1872). In this piece about mistaken identity the young aristocratic couple face an awkward situation in a spa hotel when Arthur loses his money and papers and receives a bill for a champagne breakfast. Ella is disguised as 'Signora Carlina', a famous singer from Milan, and gives a concert to cover the cash-flow problem. Coincidentally the ruler of the pricipality is rumoured to be travelling incognito with an opera singer. Arthur is then mistaken for the prince and his wife for the lady of dubious respectability, while the real prince is suspected of highway robbery. The plot casts ironic light on social assumptions and the importance of appearances. This is another of Fontane's subtle strategies for presenting his characters in shifting constellations to explore hidden aspects of their lives and aspirations and reflect on the relativity and superficiality of social values. The dramatist Wichert held a high position in the judiciary.

Page 106: *Kammergerichtsrat ... Königsberg.* Ironic allusion to the fact that Wichert, writer of comic plays, was both highly placed in the Prussian judiciary and came from the home town of Immanuel Kant, who developed the idea of the 'categorical imperative' based on the concept of duty.

Page 106: *Seven beauties ... Hans Sachs.* Allusion to Boccaccio, via Hans Sachs's version. In Boccaccio's story *Ameto* there are seven beautiful nymphs symbolizing the Seven Virtues. By jumping into the water with the nymphs the simple youth Ameto acquires their virtues. Innstetten's remark reflects a curious combination of morality and eroticism.

Page 109: *Schleswig under Wrangel and Bonin.* The uprising of Schleswig-Holstein against the Danish threat of annexation in 1848 was supported by Prussia in a campaign led by Wrangel (see note to page 40) and General Eduard von Bonin.

Page 109: *the storming of the Danewerk.* The old Danish frontier wall was taken by a successful Prussian attack during the Battle of Schleswig on April 23rd, 1848.

Page 111: *Teutonic Knights in Marienburg.* The seat of the semi-religious order founded during the crusades was transferred in 1308 from Acre to Marienburg Castle in West Prussia (now Malbork in Poland). Its banqueting hall has a fine vaulted ceiling.

Page 111: *Oliva Abbey.* Cistercian Abbey near Danzig.

Page 111: Joachim *Nettelbeck* (1738-1824). Exemplary Prussian patriot; as mayor, together with Major Schill and the town commandant Neithard von Gneisenau, he led the successful defence of Kolberg against Napoleonic troops in 1807.

Page 112: *legendary king.* Sigurd Ring appears in *Frithiofs Saga,* a Swedish epic poem (1825) by Esaias Tegnér based on an old Norse saga.

Page 112: *Köslin.* Town in Eastern Pomerania near the Baltic coast (now Koszalin in Poland).

Page 113: '*three rings*'. Allusion to the parable of the rings in *Nathan der Weise* (*Nathan the Wise,* 1779), Lessing's play about religious tolerance. The rings stand for the Christian, Jewish and Muslim faiths.

Page 116: *Lake Gothen.* Lies between Gothen and Heringsdorf on the island of Usedom.

Page 120: *Radegast and Swantowit.* Slav deities: Radigast - god of reason and mental powers; Swatowit - the holy or bright conqueror.

Page 121: *Luther... Table Talk.* Johann Aurifaber's sixteenth-century edition of conversations recorded at Martin Luther's table by students and friends was regarded as edifying reading in Protestant households in Germany.

Page 131: *Dressel's.* Exclusive restaurant on Unter den Linden.

Page 132: *Ministerialrat.* Head of a section within a Prussian ministry department.

Page 135: *Friesack.* Town in the District of Potsdam where Fontane has located Hohen-Cremmen.

Page 140: *Tiergarten.* Extensive park from which the elegant district of Berlin just to the west of the centre takes its name.

Page 141: *Kladderadatsch.* Satirical Berlin weekly: two lieutenants, *Strudelwit and Prudelwit,* and *Charlie Miessnick,* a schoolboy, were recurrent characters in it. At first leftwing, it later supported Bismarck.

Page 142: *Wee Wippy from Bernau.* Character in the Berlin satirical paper *Berliner Wespen (Berlin Wasps).* Wippchen produced humorous reports of the Russo-Turkish War (1877/78) direct from Bernau on the outskirts of Berlin.

Page 142: *plovers' eggs.* A favourite dish of Bismarck's.

Page 143: *bad joke.* In the original, the answer, translated literally, to Dagobert's punning riddle is: 'No more sorrow shall befall you', and is taken from the Book of Job.

Page 143: *Geheimrat.* Privy Councillor, a purely honorary title.

Page 145: *Willibald Alexis.* Historical novelist (1798-1871). *Die Hosen des Herrn von Bredow (Baron Bredow's Breeches,* 1846) is his most popular work.

Page 145: *Rummschüttel.* The name is slightly comical and suggests 'to shake about'.

Page 149: *'A little lamb white as snow'.* Line from 'Das Lämmchen', a nursery rhyme by Friedrich Julius Bertuch (1747-1822).

Page 150: *Helm's ... Red Castle ... Hiller's.* Helm's and Hiller's were exclusive restaurants and the Red Castle was the nickname for commercial premises with an imposing redbrick façade on the Schlossplatz.

Page 150: *Chancellor's Palace.* Innstetten signs the book laid out for birthday congratulations to Bismarck on April 1st in the Imperial Chancellor's Palace on Wilhelmstrasse.

Page 151: *Charlottenburg Palace.* The Royal Palace a few miles to the west of the city centre was built in the eighteenth century as a summer residence for the Prussian King.

Page 151: *Belvedere.* Pavilion in Charlottenburg Palace park where the medium Johann Rudolf Bischoffswerder, a favourite of Friedrich Wilhelm II (1744-97), conducted séances.

Page 152: *Grosser Stern.* A large roundabout in the Tiergarten on the axis joining the Royal Palace to Charlottenburg Palace.

Page 152: *Rügen:* Island on the Baltic coast, a popular holiday destination.

Page 152: Major Ferdinand von *Schill* (1776-1809). Commander of a regiment of Prussian Hussars who led the struggle to liberate Prussia from Napoleon, and fell at Stralsund on the Baltic in the attempt.

Page 152: *Scheele.* Karl Wilhelm Scheele (1742-86).

Page 154: *goddess Hertha.* Nerthus or Hertha, goddess of the earth and fertility, worshipped by Germanic tribes round the Baltic and the North Sea. There is no evidence that the cult of Nerthus ever existed on Rügen.

Lake Hertha lies north of Sassnitz.

Page 159: *The Storming ... Heights of Lipa.* Scenes of Prussian victories. The storming of the Heights of Düppel north-east of Flensburg was decisive in the German-Danish War of 1864, when Schleswig-Holstein was in dispute. The other picture is a scene from the Battle of Königgrätz; see note to page 84.

Page 161: *Rat.* Literally 'Councillor', a person of some considerable social standing with the title *Rat,* which may be honorary as in the case of *Geheimrat,* or may designate professional status as in *Landgerichtsrat.*

Page 162: *Landgerichtsrat.* Judge at a regional court of law.

Page 163: *Almanach de Gotha.* Genealogical handbook of the German nobility.

Page 165: *Geheimrätin.* The wife, or as in this case widow, of a *Geheimrat.* See note to page 143. In Germany the male title is not only acquired in feminine form by the wife (e.g. *Frau Professor)* but can also be retained together with its prestige after the husband's death.

Page 165: *'on the appointed hour's stroke'.* Quotation from Schiller, *Piccolomini,* I, iv, line 528: 'the task upon the appointed hour's stroke.'

Page 169: *lead-water.* A dilute solution of acetic lead applied to relieve swellings, bruising and abrasions.

Page 180: *Fremdenblatt ... Kleines Journal.* Berlin newspapers. The latter specialized in society and court news.

Page 183: *Niemann's Tannhäuser.* Albert Niemann (1831-1917), heroic tenor, celebrated Wagnerian at the Berlin Opera from 1866.

Page 185: *Saatwinkel ... Pichelsberg ... Pichelsdorf ... Pichelswerder.* All popular places with Berlin daytrippers, lying to the north-west of the city by the river Havel. *Picheln* means 'to booze'.

Page 185: *Kiekebusch, Wuhlheide.* More of the same but to the south. Kiekebusch suggests 'peeking in the bushes'; Wuhlheide, 'rummaging and burrowing in the heath'. Places where upper-class men might take their mistresses on outings away from the public gaze. In Fontane's novel *Confusions, Delusions* (chapter 13) there is a celebrated description of such an excursion, to Hankels Ablage.

Page 189: *Gretchen look.* Ironic allusion to the innocence of Gretchen in *Faust* Part I.

Page 191: *Prince Albrecht's Gardens.* Popular park beside the palace of Prince Albrecht of Prussia (1837-1906) by the Askanischer Platz.

Page 191: *Kreuzberg.* A hill to the south of the city centre where a memorial to the dead of the Napoleonic Wars was erected in 1878. In 1888-94 the Viktoria Park was laid out with artificial rock formations and a waterfall.

Page 193: *Glatz* (now Kłodzko in Poland). Town with a fortress prison in the Prussian District of Breslau where Innstetten serves his sentence for killing his opponent in a duel. There was strong public feeling against the practice of duelling in Germany at this period; the punishment was three months to five years for taking part, and two to fifteen years' imprisonment in the event of a fatality. Innstetten's early release however

227

was typical for someone of his position. Kaiser Wilhelm I had Ardenne released after three weeks of his two-year sentence.

Page 193   *Habsburger Hof.* An inn on the Askanischer Platz, by the Anhalt Station, near Effi's apartment.

Page 201:   *Schilling's.* Cake shop on the corner of Friedrichstrasse and Kochstrasse.

Page 202:   Karl Theodor *Körner* (1791-1813). successful dramatist and poet in the style of Schiller, who wrote and fought for the cause of German freedom and was killed in action in the Napoleonic Wars.

Page 209:   *Kreuzzeitung ... Norddeutsche Allgemeine.* Conservative Berlin newspapers. The *Kreuzzeitung,* properly speaking the *Neue Preussische Zeitung,* called after the emblem of the Iron Cross on the front page, was read by the Mark Brandenburg nobility.

Page 210:   *Ladenberg ... Order of the Red Eagle.* Philipp von *Ladenberg* (1796-1847), Prussian Minister of State, 1837-42. The *Red Eagle,* introduced in 1705, was a middle-grade Prussian decoration, unlike the Black Eagle. See note to page 102.

Page 211:   *Doctor Wichern ... the Rough House.* Johann Hinrich Wichern (1808-81), Protestant theologian who founded das Rauhe Haus in Hamburg (1833), an innovative educational institution for criminals and under-privileged persons.

Page 212:   *King Mtesa.* Ruler of Uganda, 1841-84.

Page 212:   *Friedenskirche where Kaiser Friedrich is.* Friedrich III (1831-88), the son of Wilhelm I and father of Wilhelm II, ruled only for 99 days. He was buried in the so-called Church of Peace in the palace gardens of Sanssouci.

Page 212:   *Sardanapalus or Coppélia with dell'Era.* Antoinetta dell'Era-Santriri was prima ballerina at the Royal Opera House in Berlin in the 1880s, dancing in Paul Taglioni's ballet *Sardanapalus* and Delibes' *Coppélia* among others.

Page 212:   *Siechen's.* Berlin brewery and beer restaurant frequented by actors.

Page 213:   *Huth's.* Wine merchant's with a wine bar, later an exclusive restaurant, a few doors up from where Fontane lived at 134 Potsdamerstrasse.

Page 213:   *Duke of Ratibor.* Viktor, Duke of Ratibor and Prince of Corvey (1818-93), owner of extensive estates in Silesia, was president of the upper chamber of the Prussian state parliament from 1877.

Page 213:   *Prince Bishop Kopp.* Georg Kopp (1837-1914), Prince Bishop of Breslau from 1887, worked to restore relations between the Prussian government and the Catholic Church.

READ MORE IN PENGUIN

In every corner of the world, on every subject under the sun, Penguin represents quality and variety – the very best in publishing today.

For complete information about books available from Penguin – including Puffins, Penguin Classics and Arkana – and how to order them, write to us at the appropriate address below. Please note that for copyright reasons the selection of books varies from country to country.

In the United Kingdom: Please write to *Dept. EP, Penguin Books Ltd, Bath Road, Harmondsworth, West Drayton, Middlesex UB7 0DA*

In the United States: Please write to *Consumer Services, Penguin Putnam Inc., 405 Murray Hill Parkway, East Rutherford, New Jersey 07073-2136.* VISA and MasterCard holders call 1-800-631-8571 to order Penguin titles

In Canada: Please write to *Penguin Books Canada Ltd, 10 Alcorn Avenue, Suite 300, Toronto, Ontario M4V 3B2*

In Australia: Please write to *Penguin Books Australia Ltd, 487 Maroondah Highway, Ringwood, Victoria 3134*

In New Zealand: Please write to *Penguin Books (NZ) Ltd, Private Bag 102902, North Shore Mail Centre, Auckland 10*

In India: Please write to *Penguin Books India Pvt Ltd, 11 Community Centre, Panchsheel Park, New Delhi 110017*

In the Netherlands: Please write to *Penguin Books Netherlands bv, Postbus 3507, NL-1001 AH Amsterdam*

In Germany: Please write to *Penguin Books Deutschland GmbH, Metzlerstrasse 26, 60594 Frankfurt am Main*

In Spain: Please write to *Penguin Books S. A., Bravo Murillo 19, 1°B, 28015 Madrid*

In Italy: Please write to *Penguin Italia s.r.l., Via Vittorio Emanuele 45/a, 20094 Corsico, Milano*

In France: Please write to *Penguin France, 12, Rue Prosper Ferradou, 31700 Blagnac*

In Japan: Please write to *Penguin Books Japan Ltd, Iidabashi KM-Bldg, 2-23-9 Koraku, Bunkyo-Ku, Tokyo 112-0004*

In South Africa: Please write to *Penguin Books South Africa (Pty) Ltd, P.O. Box 751093, Gardenview, 2047 Johannesburg*

READ MORE IN PENGUIN

A CHOICE OF CLASSICS

A CHOICE OF CLASSICS

READ MORE IN PENGUIN

A CHOICE OF CLASSICS

La Fontaine	**Selected Fables**
Madame de Lafayette	**The Princesse de Clèves**
Lautréamont	**Maldoror and Poems**
Molière	**The Misanthrope/The Sicilian/Tartuffe/A Doctor in Spite of Himself/The Imaginary Invalid**
	The Miser/The Would-be Gentleman/That Scoundrel Scapin/Love's the Best Doctor/ Don Juan
Michel de Montaigne	**An Apology for Raymond Sebond**
	Complete Essays
Blaise Pascal	**Pensées**
Abbé Prevost	**Manon Lescaut**
Rabelais	**The Histories of Gargantua and Pantagruel**
Racine	**Andromache/Britannicus/Berenice Iphigenia/Phaedra/Athaliah**
Arthur Rimbaud	**Collected Poems**
Jean-Jacques Rousseau	**The Confessions**
	A Discourse on Inequality
	Emile
	The Social Contract
Madame de Sevigné	**Selected Letters**
Stendhal	**The Life of Henry Brulard**
	Love
	Scarlet and Black
	The Charterhouse of Parma
Voltaire	**Candide**
	Letters on England
	Philosophical Dictionary
Emile Zola	**Zadig/L'Ingénu**
	L'Assomoir
	La Bête humaine
	The Debacle
	The Earth
	Germinal
	Nana
	Thérèse Raquin